You Can't Blame the Flower

~ Ruthie Stevens ~

ISBN: 978-1-7377271-1-8

"Where flowers bloom, so does hope . . ."

- Lady Bird Johnson

Guest List

YOU ARE CORDIALLY INVITED
TO WHIMSER ...

Xenergy Corporation Employees:

Lilyanna Rivers	Commercial Attorney
Tessa Hernandez	Engineering and Construction Attorney
Ryan Six	Employment Attorney
Barret Florenstein	Environmental Attorney
Joe Gregorin	Associate General Counsel
Tristan Anderson	Senior Vice President
Jillian Pyke	Junior Vice President and Securities Attorney
Alyra Cole	Human Resources Director
Andrew Heatherton	Commercial Director
Rich Scott	Commercial Manager
Tyson Green	Commercial Representative

Other Guests:

Saharie Turner	Hair and Makeup Artist
Kyah Clark	Employment Attorney
Dylan Reiss	Dance Choreographer
Waya Lestari	Dance Choreographer

Staff:

Jarvis Bixton	Caretaker
Sylvie Thompson	Housekeeper
Nina Thompson	Housekeeper
Ms. Howard	Chef

Prologue

Mirrors are terrible liars. Lilyanna Rivers assessed her five-foot-five slender frame in the full-length mirror shakily hung on the wall of her student apartment. The mirror explicitly insisted that no matter how much makeup she applied, how many times she restyled her thin unruly blonde hair hanging down to her chest or which blouse she paired with her most professional black dress pants, she would still look like a child in her mother's clothes. Her prominent blue-grey eyes gave away too much of the inner workings behind them.

Orphaned at sixteen, Lilyanna moved from Dallas to attend college in Austin, Texas, when her older brother Luke moved to Washington, D.C., for his job in international development. She wanted to stay with Luke, but his frequent overseas travel made it impractical, and she refused to be a burden to him, despite his insistence otherwise. Besides, an introvert by nature, Lilyanna didn't mind being alone. Now in her senior year of college, she contented herself with completing her studies and serving in the coveted role of student assistant to the renowned writer and beloved professor, William Whimsergarden.

Succumbing to the mirror's critique, she scrubbed off her foundation with makeup remover in frustration and started over. The end result proved no more satisfactory than its predecessor, but Lilyanna had no more time to waste. She smoothed her hair one last time and turned her back on the mirror's reproach. He would be waiting . . .

***

William Whimsergarden leaned over the desk in his university office, taking out his frustration with his writer's block on Layne Meride, his forty-two-year-old brunette publicist spread-eagled on the desk facing him. He aimed each thrust at the seemingly impenetrable wall in his mind cock-blocking his advances to a jaw-dropping end to chapter twelve of his latest novel. Layne tilted her head back, her starched white blouse unbuttoned and navy slacks in a heap on the floor, and moaned airily, beating her distracted partner to the pinnacle of functionally acceptable performance. William followed suit in physical satisfaction, but his ultimate goal remained elusive.

While Layne buttoned her blouse and slipped back into her pants, William poured himself a glass of whiskey. "Drink?" he asked her.

"It's a bit early, don't you think?" she replied, finger-styling her sleek brown bob back into place.

"Not if you want me to finish chapter twelve before you hit retirement age."

"I'd like you to finish it by the deadline next week. So, I'll see you in two weeks after my book fair?"

"I'll be gone for the summer by then," he noted without regret.

"Oh, right, your summer retreat. What's it called again?"

"Whimser."

"Well, I could go there if you want. It must get lonely locked away in the Texas country with nothing but your own thoughts." She slipped on her neutral flats and hoisted her leather Theory satchel onto her shoulder.

"A disconcerting prospect indeed, but I don't entertain guests at Whimser. I'll be focused on work."

She did her best to conceal any personal offense. "Far be it for me to get in the way of your creative genius. Well, be in touch, and William, try not to drink yourself into an early grave before your submission deadline," she told him curtly before making her exit.

William returned to his desk with his whiskey. Still unable to convert his thoughts into written word worth reading, he turned to a pile of old student pieces in front of him. An hour passed when his secretary knocked on his door. "Professor Whimsergarden, Lilyanna is here."

"Send her in," he replied offhandedly without looking up. Lilyanna peeked into the office, and William waved her inside. "Good evening, Lily," he leaped from his chair and greeted her with a warm smile. "How about a drink? I got the Chablis you like," he offered, taking a bottle of white wine from his wine fridge.

"It looks like you started without me," she noted with a nod to his half-empty glass as she sat down in the chair on the other side of his desk.

"My mind was especially blocked today. Tried everything to get the thoughts flowing." He handed her a glass of wine and sat back down in his chair. "As such, I started poring over some old student works and came across this gem." He tossed a stapled packet titled *Cold-Blooded Sirens* across the desk to her.

Lilyanna grimaced, "Oh, no!" She cringed at the sight of her first short story as a student. "You should've destroyed it!" She took a deep drink of Chablis, reflecting on the countless nights in her college career spent in Professor Whimsergarden's office grading English papers for his lower-level classes, hashing out plot lines for his fiction novels, editing his manuscripts and bantering for hours.

Her mind flashed to the first day she met the acclaimed writer at her small but prestigious college near Austin, Texas. Not only brilliant and successful, he was also a six-foot replica of a Lifetime movie actor—in one of the higher budget films—in his early sixties with feather grey hair and turquoise eyes. Eager students clamored for his favor and recommendations. While a sophomore in Professor Whimsergarden's entry-level creative writing class, Lilyanna initially avoided the good professor out of sheer intimidation. She never knew why he gave her the time of day, other than the fact that she submitted twice as many writing samples as her peers for critique, and he read every one.

Gradually, he began inviting her to his office to talk through his reviews, which evolved, or degenerated, into discussions about her goals and personal life. Her shyness in his presence faded while her writing ability improved exponentially, giving her the companionship she'd missed since the loss of her family and the confidence to prepare for her goal of attending law school right after college. The day he chose her as his student assistant changed her life. She shook off the snide whispers and sneers from classmates jealous of her position; only Professor Whimsergarden mattered.

"I admit, the story lacked much merit," he chuckled.

"Oh, come on, it wasn't that bad for my first attempt." She brushed her long wavy hair from her shoulder and dabbed the tears of laughter from her slate eyes.

"You can't even say that with a straight face, Lily."

"But I made a point at least! It's more than just a naive woman attracted to a bad guy. It's about human nature, a particular type of person—attractive, luminous, charming people—who reach others on a deeper level than what is socially normal. These, social sirens, if you will, don't like you or need you. They just happen to have alluring personalities that draw you in, and it's so natural to them that they use it to their advantage without even having any malicious intent. People fall for them without understanding the sirens for what they are and then fall apart when their feelings aren't reciprocated. The point is to be wary of people like that, and don't let them lure you in."

"So, we should assume anyone who gives us positive attention must be a sociopath? Constructive."

"I didn't describe a stereotypical sociopath! Sociopaths don't have the capacity to care about other human beings and may even have negative intentions. Cold-blooded sirens are different. They're not necessarily unfeeling for other humans generally. They're just so captivating that the masses objectively desire them, and they can get whatever they want from whomever they want without reciprocity."

"And you needed two Irish gunmen to make that point?" William raised his eyes at Lilyanna over his scotch glass.

Lilyanna squeezed her eyes shut. "Okay, okay, it's terrible! Please get rid of it."

"Not a chance! It only goes to show how far you've come. You found your footing and became my star English student and editor. My last two books would still be a pile of unfinished manuscript excerpts if not for you."

"I learned from the best."

William gazed at her slender pale face in amusement. "One more question, and then I'll stop torturing you with your first-year short story assignments. Why were the gunmen in your story Irish?"

"Because you're Irish."

"You think I'm a villain, your captor?"

"Maybe," she replied with a sinister grin before taking another sip of wine.

He sighed. "Perhaps you're right. I'm not ready to release you, Lily."

"I'm not sure you have a choice. I'm graduating this month."

"I'm aware, but you have the summer before you start law school. Come with me to my estate for the summer."

Lilyanna lowered her chin and directed her no-bullshit gaze on him. "I really need to work this summer."

"Then work for me! There is plenty of editing to do and manuscripts to read and review. You're the only one I trust for the job. Plus, reading and writing is the best way to prepare for law school. You can work as much or as little as you want, and leisure activities abound at Whimser House in your free time."

She contemplated his offer. "I am interested to see the haven you write about so often, and the inspiration for your side hustle," she nodded at several impressionist-style landscape paintings gracing his office walls.

"Yes, my summer getaway is my real home where my mind is free to write and paint. You would fit perfectly there with me. There's nothing for you here. Come with me to Whimser."

CHAPTER ONE
Eve of Spring

(7 years later—March 16, 2020)

There are some people who are always running from a bear. That's what Jen, the pelvic floor therapist, told Lilyanna. Jen said that certain people with chronic anxiety exist in a default state of urgency, perceiving everything as an immediate matter of life and death. Such people struggle with relationships, intimacy and normal life tasks—because who can think about those things when a bear is about to pounce?

Lilyanna wasn't looking for a pelvic floor therapist when she met Jen; rather, she sought counseling after Williams's death that summer before she started law school, but she found no help. Lilyanna never made it past the first question in any therapist's office, the standard, "What brings you to see me?" or "How can I help you?" She had no idea how to explain what made her seek counseling, and how could she be expected to know how a doctor could potentially help her? She thought she was paying them to figure that out! It didn't matter, though, because Jen explained things better than any psychiatrist, bestowing on her a simple and logical explanation for her brand of stress—the love child of past trauma and a type A+ personality that over time conditioned the brain into a perpetual state of panic—as well as instructions for the most effective kegel exercises.

The bear of the day emerged as an artificial deadline on a steel supply contract for one of Lilyanna's internal commercial clients at Xenergy Corporation. Headquartered in Austin, Texas, Xenergy was the largest infrastructure contractor in the central United States, providing services to private energy companies and governmental entities. As the newest and youngest addition to Xenergy's legal department, Lilyanna had just begun her second year with the company and fourth year as an attorney.

She sat upright in her desk chair, hammering away furiously on the keys of her desktop computer to finish the contract she had been working on since the lunchtime she didn't take. *Just breathe, it's not the end of the world if this doesn't get done. There is no bear.* Before she could finish her self-coaching stress-management technique, Andrew Heatherton, a commercial director, bounded into her office.

"Hey, Lily, do you have a second?" North of six feet tall and fit with trim black hair and brown skin, his dark eyes widened with anticipation as he closed the door behind him without waiting for her response. Most of the male internal business clients Lilyanna supported kept the door open when meeting with her alone, but Andrew no longer bothered. Initially a relationship born of necessity, Andrew had no one to rely on but

Lilyanna for legal review of contracts for the most profitable department in the company, and Lilyanna went directly to Andrew when the underlings in his department fed her incomplete or incorrect information. Thus, over a relatively brief period of time, they settled into a routine of reasonably comfortable interactions, though Lilyanna still had to remind herself not to gaze too long at his handsome features.

"I need a favor," he said, leaning over her desk.

"I just love conversations that begin this way," she sighed, reluctantly looking up from her computer screen.

"I got a markup of the Master Services Agreement back from Leron Construction, and I want to send them a response ASAP. Do you think we could fast-track our review?"

She narrowed her gaze in annoyance. "You mean can *I* fast-track *my* review." As Lilyanna supported close to fifty internal clients, she usually rejected the frequent requests to prioritize one client's project over another. When Andrew made a special request, however, she knew it was for a good reason. "If I agree to have a draft to you tomorrow, you can't tell anyone. I can't officially have favorites."

"So, you would only do this for me, right?" he grinned.

"Are you asking me to tell you you're pretty?"

He chuckled and flashed his smile of straight white teeth as he backed toward her office door. "Not pressing my luck. Thanks, Lily! For the record, you're my favorite too."

"A real compliment considering there are no other attorneys that support your team."

"If there were, I would still come to you."

"Then I'm too nice to you. Easily rectified—out of my office so I can actually get some work done today!" she snapped.

Less than two hours later, Lilyanna stopped typing and looked up from her monitor. It wasn't the sirens echoing from the street twenty-six stories below or the routine barrage of more interesting thoughts than liability provisions that diverted her attention from her close-of-business deadline, but the lack of the normal hustle and bustle of the legal floor outside her office.

Cautiously, Lilyanna poked her head out of her office door. The only voice she heard echoed from the adjacent office of her best friend and fellow young attorney, Tessa Hernandez. Lilyanna followed the voice to the doorway of Tessa's office where she found Tessa resting her forehead in her hand next to the speaker of her desk phone, listening in annoyance to the sales pitch from the other end. "Miguel," she interjected, lifting her head. "Your 'family-owned' business structure is not a selling point for us. All I care about is a quality of work that won't get us sued at a price that enables us to make a profit. Those are my criteria for hiring subcontractors." Tessa proceeded to argue with the voice on the other end of the line in Spanish and then hung up the phone in exasperation and rolled her eyes at Lilyanna.

"I've worked with this sub for four years, and he still doesn't know his audience," Tessa vented. "Selling a family-owned business model to a single millennial makes me trust you even less than usual. Like, if you have a falling out with Daddy, are we not getting the services we paid for? Non-starter." Tessa massaged her temples. "So, what's up, Lily?"

"Nothing, literally. There's nobody around and no noise on our hall."

"Oh, right. Everyone's watching the governor's press conference." Tessa hopped out of her chair and nodded for Lilyanna to follow her out of her office. "Come on, there's a TV in the Board conference room." Lilyanna slowed her pace slightly as Tessa's long silky black ponytail swished past her. Lilyanna generally preferred to avoid the other side of the U-shaped twenty-sixth floor that the legal department shared with the officers of the company and stay confined to her comfort zone in the legal hall.

"I didn't get the memo to go to the conference room."

"That's because you don't bribe tech services with donuts once a month to keep you in the loop," Tessa replied. "Hurry up, we're already late!" Tessa grabbed Lilyanna's arm and pulled her along into the packed Board conference room.

"Where have you two been?" Ryan Six, an employment attorney in his early forties with dark hair and skin, slid over to make room for Lilyanna and Tessa.

"You missed the governor's announcement that he found the cure for COVID-19," their friend Barret Florenstein whispered. Shorter than Six and heavyset and pale with thin curly hair and round black-framed glasses, he served as the environmental attorney on Xenergy's legal team.

"I bet he's announcing he got COVID," Six retorted.

"I've got the cure in the bottom drawer of my desk, Six. It's an eighteen-year-old bottle of Chivas.

Good luck getting decent liquor once the borders close," Barret replied.

"Probably more effective than anything the governor will do," Lilyanna added as she stood on her toes trying to see the TV over the sea of bodies crammed in front of her. "Not that I will know if I can't see anything."

"Having trouble?" Tristan Anderson, the senior vice president of Xenergy in charge of finance, asked in his posh South London accent. "Here, let me help." He locked his sparkling blue eyes on Lilyanna and gestured for her to step in front of him. His wavy dark hair feathered softly over his forehead as though he'd been running his fingers through it in frustration all morning.

Only those who looked closely would notice the few faint grey streaks throughout his soft waves subtly advertising his vintage, and Lilyanna *had* looked closely. She noticed his quick-to-clench chiseled jawline, and his broad shoulders, and best of all, his naked ring finger. A divorcee in his mid-forties standing right at six feet tall with a built physique, he drew looks when he entered a room, even in the morally squeaky-clean office environment of Xenergy. Over her years with the company, she'd watched him alternate between his standard clean-shaven look and one with moderately controlled facial hair. She could never decide which she liked best—possibly the facial hair—but today she couldn't imagine him looking hotter than with his clean-shaven look.

"Oh, um, thanks." Hesitantly, she stepped in front of him, avoiding his eye. Conscious of his proximity, Lilyanna struggled to comprehend the governor's speech announcing the approaching state-wide lockdown to curb the spread of COVID-19.

The conference room remained silent for a moment after the governor completed his lackluster address and then erupted with chatter. Without thinking, Lilyanna turned to look at Tristan, but he had already moved to the front of the room and stood next to Xenergy's president, Harlyn Marks. On the other side of the white-haired stocky president stood junior vice president and securities attorney Jillian Pyke, a slender blonde woman in her mid-fifties, wearing a grey sheath dress and three-inch matching heels. Always chic and dignified, Jillian commanded a room more naturally than Marks. Jillian's mesmerizing charisma and general badassness had amazed Lilyanna the first time she met her, and the adoration only grew once Lilyanna witnessed firsthand Jillian's talent at her job.

Jillian whispered into Marks' ear before he addressed the room. Marks' aloof public speaking voice chilled the room of panicked mutterings. "Everyone, a moment, please." Silence again. "I know this is a shock, but there is no need to panic. As the leading infrastructure contractor in the country, we are in communication with the governor's office as well as federal agencies regarding operations during the COVID-19 pandemic. We are strategically positioned to maintain our business during this pandemic, and our new COVID-19 Response Committee is hard at work developing policies for the upcoming quarantine."

"Since when do we have a COVID-19 committee?" Barret whispered to Six.

"Since now." Six looked down at his phone and checked an unread email. "Looks like I'm the legal rep on the committee."

"Everyone, please return to your offices. Management will send out instructions for how to proceed by the end of this week," Marks concluded. He promptly left the room, whispering to Tristan and Jillian, who walked beside him.

Back in her office, Lilyanna aimlessly shifted papers on her desk, lacking the focus to actually read anything. Distracting her from her distractedness, her desk phone rang with a call from the administrative assistant, Carline.

"This is Lilyanna."

"Lily, Marks would like to see you in his office."

Lilyanna hesitated. "Marks? You mean Harlyn Marks, the president? Now?"

"Yes, President Marks, and now, but Joe said to stop by his office first. Good luck."

Panic seized Lilyanna as she tried to smooth her hair. She had never exchanged more than two words with the president, and then only when forced to while trapped on an elevator with him. There could only be one reason for the summons to President Marks' office—management started layoffs due to COVID-19, and, as the least experienced attorney in the legal department, she would be first on the chopping block.

Her stomach taking up residence in her pointed black flats, she left her office, perhaps for the last time as an employee, and trudged to the gallows. She stopped in the office of her boss and associate general counsel, Joe Gregorin. If anyone would have an interest in fighting for her continued employment, it would be Joe since the two of them served as the legal support for the largest commercial department of the company.

Lilyanna heard Joe on the phone as she reached his office doorway. He reclined in his office chair with his feet on his desk, his grey socks peeking out at the ankles just below the hem of his charcoal slacks, as he spoke into his desk phone. Joe waved her in when he saw her in the doorway and beckoned for her to shut the door without pausing his call.

Joe ran his index finger over his coarse copper mustache in thought. "Dwayne, there's no reason to get cold feet on the commitment term. Someone ate a bat, and now we all have to suffer. Uh-huh, that's why they're closing all the buffets. Yep, I was always suspicious of the one on Third Street. The Crock Pot, that's right!" Lilyanna grimaced as she turned to close the door behind her.

"Anyway, the price of gas will rebound, and then you'll be offering me a handy twice a week to put these terms back on the table." Joe rolled his eyes and lit a cigarette in response to whatever unsatisfactory monologue he received in response from the voice on the other end of the line. "Look, there's no shame in accepting a good deal as is! You don't have to negotiate a sentence in the contract just to make it look like you showed up to work today."

Joe swung his chair around to face his computer monitor and took a long drag from his cigarette. "Alright, for the sake of my time, your dignity and the utility of this conversation, all of which are descending dangerously close to the sphincter of rock fucking bottom, here's what's going to happen. I'm going to take one year off your company's product commitment, and starting in the fifth year of the contract term we're raising your rate an additional 2.5% percent on top of the annual escalations, and you're going to have this contract signed today. If you say no, or I have to listen to any more excuses in that dime-store southern choir boy accent of yours, I might just have to dig out my pictures from last year's Corporate Counsel Conference. I'm sure your wife would love to see time-stamped photos showing the inordinate amount of time you spent in the men's room with the college-aged DJ named Stan after the farewell reception. So, spare us both the shit dive and help me close this deal today. Then I can go back to real work and you can go back to whacking off under your desk to pictures of '90s boy bands. Everybody wins!"

A cloud of smoke seeped from behind Joe's chair and surrounded his cropped copper hair. "Right, electronic signatures by three o'clock works for us. Say hello to Kathy for me. Talk soon, Dwayne." He hung up the phone and swung his chair back around to face Lilyanna, his worn loafers thudding the floor.

"Sorry about that, Lil. He sets me wrong every time. Do as I say in your business relationships, not as I do," he instructed, pointing at her with his cigarette.

"No worries there, boss," she assured him, making no effort to hide her disgust. "I thought you quit smoking in the office?"

"I did, for the second half of last week during the biannual inspection of our fire alarms. My predecessor, may he rest in peace, left me this gem when he retired." Joe reached into his center desk drawer and pulled out a thick distorted paper clip bent into a crooked line with a hook on the end. "The clever bastard used it to dismantle the smoke detector in the hall so he could smoke in this office without setting off the alarm. Before every inspection, I turn the alarm on and then turn it off again right after."

"Wow, clever indeed," Lilyanna nodded slowly.

"It's beyond me why poisoning my lungs makes everything else feel so much better. Oh well, let's go see what Daddy Marks wants."

Marks occupied the largest corner office in the officers' suite, with a wall of floor-to-ceiling windows, an L-shaped black cherry teakwood desk and a round conference table. A deep breath later, Lilyanna followed Joe through the open doorway. Marks and Justin Mercier, Xenergy's general counsel and Joe's boss, waited for her at the conference table. Tristan also occupied a seat at the table and rose when she entered the room.

"Ah, Miss Rivers, please join us," Justin greeted her on behalf of the firing squad.

Tristan approached her, his eyes locked on her but his expression blank, and then brushed past her to close the door. "Please take a seat, Miss Rivers. You too, Joe," Justin instructed.

This wasn't the first time a group of middle-aged White men presumed to decide her fate. She had attended college and law school in Texas, where supposedly everything was bigger, including White male dominance.

Lilyanna sat down next to Joe at the conference table for the longest and most grueling twenty seconds of awkward silence she had experienced to date. "I'm sure this seems unusual, Miss Rivers, since we don't all usually meet," Justin began.

Meaning the corporate officers and general counsel would never deign to involve someone of her level in their regular discussions, Lilyanna interpreted.

"But everything that is happening is unusual right now, so we must act accordingly," Marks interceded, wasting no time on small talk. "COVID-19 cases are quickly rising in the country, and other businesses are already starting to close offices, temporarily. It's only a matter of time before we have to do the same. The state is days away from implementing a mandatory quarantine."

Here it comes. Just tell me if there will be a severance package!

"We provide critical infrastructure to this country," Marks continued. "Therefore, it is imperative that our business survive if this country is to have any chance of recovering from the pandemic. Our field employees will continue to work under new health and safety guidelines, but all office workers will have to work remotely from their homes. Leaving our key office employees to their own devices during this uncertain time presents a major control problem for us. We are not so worried about surviving financially; we are worried about having a competent workforce left to run the company should the worst occur." Lilyanna fought the confusion creeping into her expression. "We have an idea as to how to protect a select few of our office employees and ensure they are able to keep working during the lockdown, but it will require your cooperation."

"In what way?" she asked, looking Marks in the eye.

"Well, to start, I am currently having my country cabin in South Texas prepared to host several key employees for at least a month, perhaps longer. Justin, two commercial directors, several managers and I will be quarantining there."

Lilyanna considered his words. "But, what about their families?" Nearly every employee at Xenergy was married with children, except Lilyanna, Tessa and Barret.

"We are hoping that the chosen employees will be willing to make sacrifices to ensure this company's future," Marks replied nonchalantly.

"You're requiring employees to leave their families during a pandemic? I hope you did not call me in here to ask for my legal opinion on this!"

"I told you she speaks her mind," Joe smiled at his pet pony's trick.

Marks continued unfazed, "No opinion is necessary. We cannot, as you noted, require employees to participate. Rather, we are strongly encouraging it and hoping they will see this as a means to job security. It is in all of our best interests to keep this company running, for the country and our own employment."

Lilyanna nodded, tight-lipped. Then she spoke as calmly as she could. "To my original question, how does this involve me?"

Marks nodded at Tristan. Tristan sighed, "Lilyanna, uh, Miss Rivers," he corrected himself, "Marks' summer house can only accommodate eight employees or so, and second properties owned by other employees are out of state. We know that you own a sizeable property a couple of hours outside the city."

Lilyanna's eyes widened. "How do you know that?"

Tristan ran his fingers through his wavy hair and looked away from her. "It's not difficult information to find. Please don't be offended."

Lilyanna looked down at the table, wishing she could melt into it. "You want to use the house to sequester more employees."

"Yes."

"The company would cover all costs for food and resources, and we can have a contractor out there within a couple of days to make any renovations and wire the house for increased internet and phone usage," Justin added like he was making a grocery list.

"I don't visit the place often," Lilyanna replied quietly.

"What better time? It looks quite nice on Google Earth. What's it called?"

"Whimser," Lilyanna whispered, digging her fingernails into her wrist.

"Lovely! Did you inherit it from a family member?"

"Not exactly."

"There's a lake and plenty of outdoor space and nature-ish things," Justin offered as if reading from a camp pamphlet. "It would provide ample space and a closed circuit."

"There must be a more practical option," she insisted.

"There's not, Lilyanna. Please, work with us on this. We must prepare for the worst," Tristan pressed, staring her down.

She met his gaze for a moment and then looked away. His accent alone could've sold her on worse. "Alright, but I make no guarantees of results. I won't have any liability if this is a disaster in the making."

"Spoken like an attorney on my team!" Justin approved. "We're all in agreement."

"Thank you, Miss Rivers. This company is grateful for your dedication. Tristan will take care of all your concerns," Marks added.

Lilyanna looked up at him in surprise, "I'm sorry, what?"

"This is all the time we have. Tristan will follow up on the details, and I believe the COVID-19 Response Committee will be in touch as well."

"Uh, that committee doesn't actually exist yet," Justin corrected him.

"Then form it immediately and backdate its inception for the press release," Marks boomed.

***

Tristan passed a stack of documents and manila folders to Lilyanna across the conference room table. "Here's the information for each employee who will be staying at your house."

Alyra Cole, the director of HR, and Jillian sat on either side of Tristan, each peering over his shoulder at the documents. Lilyanna scanned a master list of employee names and began perusing the file names. In addition to files for herself, Tristan, Joe, Jillian, Alyra, Tessa, Barret, Six and Andrew, she found files for Rich Scott, a commercial manager under Andrew, and Rich's direct report and youngest of the bunch, Tyson Green. She hesitated when she came across a spreadsheet with a breakdown of each employee showing his or her gender, ethnicity, age and marital status. "What's this?" she asked Tristan.

"Oh, just basic employee information for internal purposes," he quickly snatched back the spreadsheet.

"You mean personal information about employees that should not be circulated without HR approval," Alyra corrected him indignantly. "I'll take that," she held out her hand for the document.

Tristan reluctantly handed her the document and continued explaining the plan. "The list of employees is subject to change if someone tests positive for COVID-19. Everyone will be tested three days before moving into your house."

"We're sure these tests are accurate? I've read there is a significant margin for error with some of the available tests," Lilyanna noted.

"Well, there is always a chance for error." Tristan took the list of employees from her. "The tests are, like, 99.9% effective."

"Isn't that the effective rate for Clorox wipes?" Lilyanna raised her eyebrows at him.

"It's all in the same, err, category of effective rate, to our knowledge at this time."

"Lily, there's staff at the house, right?" Alyra interjected, studying her iPad.

"Yes, Bix, Jarvis Bixton. He lives in a cottage on the grounds and takes care of the property. I'll move in this weekend and help with last-minute prep before everyone arrives Monday," Lilyanna replied.

"Nobody is expecting you to provide a five-star resort experience, Lily," Alyra assured her.

"Good—because it won't be. Let's see, we have seven twin-sized beds coming to supplement the existing beds, new bedding sets, an extra washer and dryer, extra kitchen supplies and enough cleaning products to last at least two months. I'll also hire a housekeeper or two."

"And grocery deliveries will start the same day as the new chef," Alyra checked off her list. "Who else will be staying in the house?"

"I promised two of my guy friends they could stay in the guesthouse for a couple of weeks. They're dance choreographers and need a place to stay. Two of my lady friends are coming from Dallas to stay as well. They will all be tested in advance."

"All of that's fine. Just let us know your final cost estimate," Jillian replied.

All guests on the Whimser quarantine list joined them in the conference room for debriefing. As the others sat at the rectangular conference table, Tessa drew floor plans of Whimser on the whiteboard. Lilyanna stood next to her, internally battling her nerves at the thought of discussing Whimser with her colleagues. Jillian gave a brief welcome address and then yielded the floor to Lilyanna.

With shaking hands and legs the consistency of Jell-O, Lilyanna stepped up to the whiteboard, begging the marker in her hand to magically transfigure into a shot of vodka. "Okay, so, I'm going to go over the layout of the property and room assignments. The estate is called Whimser, and it consists of a house, guesthouse, cottage for the caretaker, and about five and a half acres of land leading down to the edge of Lake Whimser. Tessa has drawn a basic layout of the house on the board so you can see what space to expect." Tessa accurately drew and labeled each room on the two floors, though the graphic could not capture a legitimate first impression of Whimser's grandeur.

Lilyanna did her best to generally describe the layout of the house and casually threw in that everyone would be expected to help the staff with chores. "As for bedrooms, there is a hallway off the main entry hall on the first floor, which we'll call the men's hall. The front bedroom will have three twin beds for Andrew, Rich and Tyson. The three of you will share Bathroom 1 labeled here." Lilyanna wrote each employee's initials in the room and bathroom assigned to them. "The next bedroom will be Tristan and Joe's. You will share Bathroom 2 with Barret and Six, who have the bedroom across the hall. Finally, there is a bedroom behind the front stairs in the hall with two full-sized beds for Jillian and Alyra, and you have your own Bathroom 3.

"Now, for the upstairs," Lilyanna continued. "Right now, there is a master bedroom, small guest room and large game room. We have contractors onsite making a few adjustments. Once finished, the upstairs will have one large bedroom with a king-sized bed and two twin beds for four women total—myself, Tessa and two of my friends from Dallas who will be staying in the house with us. The extra room will be reserved in case anyone gets sick. There are two bathrooms upstairs, one master and one smaller bathroom, to be shared among everyone staying upstairs.

"Outside the house there are trails and woodlands leading down to the lake, and we have full use of the lake. Several tenants rent their properties around the lake from us, from me, I mean, but they won't be near the house. There is also a guesthouse that two of my friends will be occupying, and a cottage for Jarvis Bixton, or Bix, the property caretaker. Any questions about, um, anything?"

Silence. The commercial reps exchanged glances, and so did Six and Barret. Joe whispered something in Jillian's ear. Tyson voiced everyone's thought. "Wait a minute, are we sure about this?" All eyes focused on him. "'Group quarantine' is not a thing. The point of quarantining is being alone. How do we know we won't all get COVID-19?"

"We don't," Alyra answered. "This is a risk you choose to assume."

"Legal is working on a liability disclaimer," Six added. "Of course, the company can wipe its ass with it if Texas state courts find it unlawful."

"Which is why it is voluntary," Jillian continued. "If you choose to participate, it's at your own risk, like Alyra said."

"When do we leave?" Andrew asked.

"Monday. The company will provide transportation. Nobody will be allowed to have a vehicle on the property except Lilyanna," Tristan explained. "Once quarantined on the property, there will be no leaving and returning."

"That's not creepy," Barret muttered under his breath.

Lilyanna spoke up, "The roads leading up to the house can be difficult to navigate. It's best that nobody who is unfamiliar with the area drive."

"Now, hold on. Samuel L. Jackson said to stay the fuck at home. I believe him," Tyson pointed out.

"So did the governor, and the mayor," Andrew lowered his eyes at Tyson.

Inwardly, Lilyanna beamed at the courage of the youngest millennial in the room, unafraid to speak up in front of his professional superiors. But outwardly, she performed her duty to promote the plan. She swallowed her smile, and nerves, and took a deep breath. "Look, nobody is forcing you. There is no guarantee this won't be an absolute disaster. One or more of us could get COVID-19 from being locked up together, or worse.

"Everyone in this room is capable of weighing the potential risks and benefits and making a decision accordingly, or else you would not be here. You would also not be here if you didn't have concern for this company surviving. Nobody knows how bad things will get during this pandemic, and it's in all of our interests to stay employed. If anyone prefers to stay at home, there's the door, and maybe there will be a job for you if and when this is over, maybe not. There's no judgment. I just need an accurate head count for planning purposes. Please leave now if that's your choice."

Nobody moved.

CHAPTER TWO
Whimser

Lilyanna knew one day she would return to Whimser. It was a part of her life she didn't want to relive but also a past from which she'd never moved on. The single-lane dirt road to Whimser wound through an overgrown forest, up and up into the hills above the lake. The ravine beckoned to unwary travelers who dared to venture too close to the sharp drop-off from the cliff side. Lilyanna hunched over the steering wheel of her Honda Accord, bearing seven years' worth of apprehension.

Equally tense, Tessa clung to the center console with one hand and the door of the passenger seat with the other. "I understand what you meant about the roads now! This drive is treacherous."

Lilyanna didn't take her eyes off the road. "I had guardrails installed several years ago. Cars can't go off the ravine as easily anymore."

"Anymore? Is that supposed to make me feel safer and convince me to pull my nails out of your dash?"

"Those were my intentions."

"The same ones that paved this road to hell."

Lilyanna's thoughts drifted to her first ride on the perilous road to Whimser.

She gazed out the passenger window of William's Land Rover at the ravine below. "You didn't see a need for guardrails when building your fantasy land?"

William smiled slightly, keeping his eyes on the road. "When I purchased this property in the '80s, there was no lake here at all, just hills and woods. We had to carve out a lot of the slope for the lake and to prevent too much erosion. I would have liked to clear more trees for a proper two-lane road, but it was impractical with the sharp incline of the hills and the depth and mass of the tree roots."

The terrain had given way reluctantly to William, and the roadway followed suit half-heartedly, but the surrounding woods refused to be tamed to fit his development scheme. "Not to worry, my lady, these hills haven't succeeded in shaking me off yet."

After a twenty-minute ascent, the narrow road ceased its scare tactics, yielding to a more amenable plateau. "Ah, straight ahead is our gate. If you go left of our gate, there is a gate leading to the Acadis' property, the only residents out here I would actually select as neighbors if given the choice."

"What's wrong with the others?"

"They're just difficult."

Lilyanna didn't press him further. She focused on the trees that whisked by in the window, perhaps waving at her in welcome, or rustling their leaves in annoyance at the presence of another human mechanist trespassing on their domain.

When the thicket cleared, a sprawling two-story manor house of ivory stone and grey shutters proudly held its ground against the encroaching woods. Unlike the traditional southwestern-style houses common in Austin, Whimser was a hybrid of a sprawling English country estate and a Newport mansion. William beamed at the sight of his architectural achievement, and, to his credit, Whimser pleased the eyes. But, to Lilyanna, the size and grandeur of the house only made it more out of place—a pseudo-modern castle in the middle-of-nowhere, Texas.

Whimser kept the woods at bay seven years later. After so many years, the beauty of Whimser still induced a respectable dopamine rush. Lilyanna turned the car off the dirt road and onto a side drive that wound behind the house to the garage.

Lilyanna inadvertently left Tessa behind in the driveway, muttering about her ruined manicure, and walked cautiously to the mansion. An ivory terrace graced the front of the house, overlooking the expansive yard that led to the woods beyond. She felt relieved to see that her orders to maintain the property and grounds had been followed in her absence. The specks of afternoon sunlight filtering through the puffy cirrus clouds cast the spotlight on Whimser as it basked in the glory of its return to the stage after years in the shadows. A designer ball gown at a barbeque, Whimser deserved admiration, and its due compliments would've been paid in full in a different setting.

Lilyanna's feet carried her up to the front door without her consent. Hesitantly, she grasped the knocker and tapped on the front door. Whimser was technically her house, to which she held a key, but not her home. In fact, she felt more at home at certain hotels than at

Whimser. When nobody answered, Lilyanna unlocked the door to let herself in, peering into the silent front hall. The light breeze from outside blew through the house to awaken it from its slumber, whirling dust through the hall and into the adjoining rooms.

Entering the front hall of Whimser for the first time, Lilyanna stepped through a doorway to a past she never lived. The hall led to a white marble spiral staircase in the center with a formal parlor on the front right side and an intricate web of corridors and single rooms spanning out in all directions. The walls proudly displayed several landscape paintings, many impressionistic, of enchanting bucolic scenes.

"Did you paint all of these?" Lilyanna asked William.

"Not all of them, no. I painted the ones on these two walls of the rose bouquets. Maybe I'll be so fortunate as to paint a lily while you're here. Come, the parlor is over here." A pale green Victorian sofa and matching armchair posed on either side of a round tea table in the parlor.

"Ah, Mr. Whimsergarden, so glad you have returned," a short balding man nearing his early sixties in brown slacks and matching jacket shuffled into the hall, followed by a gangly teenage boy and an attractive brunette woman in a simple grey dress with an apron over it.

"Thank you, Bix. Allow me to introduce my guest for the summer, Miss Lilyanna Rivers. Lily, this is our butler and caretaker, Jarvis Bixton. We call him Bix."

"It's nice to meet you, Bix. Thank you for having me." Lilyanna smiled politely and extended a hand to greet him.

Bix glowered at her open hand as though it contained a touch-activated poison. The house obliged to allow any guests its owner invited, but Jarvis Bixton shared no such attitude of tacit acceptance. Instead of shaking her hand, he nodded curtly, "Welcome, Mistress Rivers."

"Oh, please call me Lilyanna or—"

"All of the rooms have been prepared for your arrival," Bix told William, cutting her off.

Failing to notice, William turned to the teenage boy. "Excellent. Tom, please take our luggage upstairs. Miss Rivers will be staying in the second-floor guest room."

"At once, sir."

"And I'll take your car keys, Mr. Whimsergarden," Bix added.

"Ah, yes, please." William handed him the keys and went to speak with the housekeeper.

"Mistress Rivers, please note I always hide the keys in the center drawer in the kitchen so that Mr. Whimsergarden will not drive if he has had anything to drink. He tends to enjoy an evening drive, but also an evening bottle," Bix whispered to her.

"I see. Thank you for letting me know."

"Oh, and Lily, this is Sylvie Thompson, our housekeeper," William called to her. Lilyanna nodded at Bix and went to meet Sylvie.

"If there is anything I can do for you, miss, please just ask," Sylvie nodded coolly. Her long light brown curls swished down to her chest when she moved, framing her pale heart-shaped face.

"Oh, thank you. I appreciate it." Lilyanna guessed Sylvie to be nearly the same age as her.

"Welcome to Whimser, My Flower." William took Lilyanna's arm and led her up the spiral staircase.

Lilyanna's footsteps echoed on the marble footsteps of the vacant hall. The only other sound was the breeze sweeping in around her. "Come in, My Flower," the wind whispered to her in William's voice. He beckoned her inside, surely from the parlor, where he sat waiting for her with a pot of tea. She followed the voice, past the familiar landscape paintings and dusty floors. He would be pleased to see her . . .

But no one was waiting for her. No welcome committee appeared, and there was certainly no tea in the parlor, just dust and tarped furniture. The only light came from the floor-to-ceiling windows on either side of the door. *At least Bix had bothered to open the curtains.* As Bix knew the day of her expected arrival, she took it as a straight-up middle finger to her personally that Bix disregarded his duty of caring for the front of the house.

Lilyanna's eyes fixated on a large oil panting hanging in the spot of honor on the wall of the parlor. It depicted a young blonde woman in a white dress lying on the grass by the house amidst a garden of pink, blue and yellow roses, tulips and lilies. William's signature was scrawled across the bottom right corner.

Shaking slightly from a chill, Lilyanna turned away from the painting. "Hello, Bix? Is anyone here?" Lilyanna called, not wanting to be alone in the parlor.

Bix made his fashionably late entrance, wearing his signature brown suit with a hunter green shirt and tie underneath. "Mistress Rivers, how nice to see you after all these years," he lied in his superficial

upper-middle-class-hybrid-American-English-that-
didn't-actually-exist accent.

"Call me Lilyanna or Lily, please, Bix. Let's get
down to business. The house looks a bit, unkempt,
and we have people arriving in two days."

Bix regarded her in contempt, "I assure you,
Mistress Rivers, I make every effort to maintain the
house, but it is not feasible for one person to maintain
all rooms of the house at all times. With the staff cuts
you implemented, standards have rightfully slipped."

"You don't need a full-time chef and housekeeping team
for a house nobody lives in!" Lilyanna hissed. "I cut the
budget when necessary to ensure Whimser's sustainability.
If you want it to be sold, just say the word!"

"Lily, am I interrupting?" Tessa stepped into the
hall, pulling a large hardcover suitcase in one hand
and a weekender tote in the other.

Lilyanna sighed and ran her fingers through her
messy hair. "Of course not, come in. Tessa, this is
Bix; Bix, Tessa."

"A pleasure, ma'am," Bix inclined his head.

"Look, we have two days to get this place ready.
It will take all of us to have a chance at pulling off
that miracle. Did you at least talk to Sylvie about
working full time again?"

"I expect her to arrive within the hour. She has
also requested to bring her sister Nina."

"Great, we'll need the extra help. In the meantime,
let's start with a walk-through of the bedrooms. At
least the house hasn't been pillaged in my absence."

"All of the new furniture has arrived and been set
up, though I have not gotten around to making up

the beds," Bix called from the bottom of the staircase as Lilyanna hauled her luggage upstairs.

Of course you haven't; that would require work! To her surprise, she found the upstairs better tended than the ground floor. The construction work on the master bedroom had been completed, and Bix, or some contractor with a hint of mercy in his or her soul, had cleaned up all the debris. The new layout also allowed for a modest den space between the master bedroom and the extra bedroom.

"Do I get to choose my bed?" Tessa asked, surveying the new bedroom.

"Yep, I figured you and I would take the twins, and Kyah and Saharie can share the king."

"Yeah, I'll take my own bed, no matter how small," Tessa agreed.

Sylvie and her younger sister Nina arrived later that afternoon, along with the chef Ms. Howard, stout in both physique and demeanor. Ms. Howard had scarcely been in the house half an hour before banning everyone from "her kitchen" until she deemed it in order. The rest of the motley crew set to work on prepping the interior of the house for the approaching corporate invasion.

After thoroughly cleaning the downstairs bedrooms and bathrooms, Lilyanna helped Sylvie put new linens on the upstairs beds. "I'm sorry we haven't had a chance to catch up," Lilyanna started awkwardly as Sylvie tossed her half of a fitted sheet for the king bed. "I suppose it's strange for you to be back here after all these years."

Sylvie kept her eyes on her work. "No stranger than it is for you, I'm sure. But, with everything going on, I'm grateful to be here with my sister," she replied.

"We are grateful that you could both be here as well. I feel like I'm asking too much of you to keep this house in order with so many people. Please know that everyone will help out, and you and your sister are not expected to do all the work or cater to anyone."

"I don't mind the extra work, ma'am." Sylvie grabbed the top sheet and crammed the bottom corners under the mattress.

"But you were in school, right? I don't want you to feel obligated to put your life on hold while you're here. And please don't call me ma'am. I think we know each other well enough to be on a first-name basis."

Sylvie's face showed no emotion. "I actually finished my bachelor's degree in Biology two years ago . . . Lily. I've been working at a health clinic to save up for nursing school, but the clinic is being closed temporarily and all of the medical professionals diverted to hospitals and larger facilities due to COVID-19. I'm supposed to start nursing school this fall, but who knows what will happen now."

"I see. Congratulations on getting your degree! I hope the pandemic doesn't delay your plans."

"Thank you. Well, this room is done. I should go and give the den a once over." Sylvie flashed a brief plastic smile on her way out of the room. Sylvie's coolness didn't surprise Lilyanna. Despite Lilyanna's best efforts, a distance always separated the two women, and their relationship never evolved beyond mere cordiality. However, Lilyanna hoped this would change, as she needed Sylvie as an ally in the house.

That evening, Lilyanna, Tessa, Sylvie and Nina ate dinner together in the dining room. Bix refused to join them and ate in his cottage. "I have to say, I never thought I would eat in the dining room of a house I work in," Nina confessed in between bites of stir fry.

"This is your home now too," Lilyanna reminded her.

"At least we can be confident in Ms. Howard's cooking. I got nervous when she barred us from the kitchen indefinitely, but she obviously knows her stuff."

"Agreed. I don't want to know what beasts were lurking in the kitchen before she got here," Lilyanna added.

"Probably Bix's pet ogre," Sylvie suggested.

Lilyanna smirked, "I thought Bix *was* the pet ogre."

"This house is definitely haunted, though, Lily," Tessa insisted. "Beautiful, but haunted. You're a little young to be the hostess of a haunted mansion."

"I think that makes me a ghostess, actually."

Lilyanna's first night sleeping at Whimser in many years triggered dreams of William. Together they strolled through the woods on a partly cloudy afternoon in late May. The few rays of sunlight peeking through the canopy gleamed off the silver in his hair as he led her through the thicket. "This is the quickest path down to the water's edge." Countless oak and elm trees towered over them, while varieties of shrubbery and wild brush blanketed their feet, but Lilyanna failed to spot a single flower.

"Why are there no flowers with all this greenery? Shouldn't you at least plant a garden closer to the house?" Lilyanna asked.

"Believe me, I tried for years. Flowers don't grow here. The soil has too much clay, and we don't get consistent rain."

Lilyanna paused her stroll. "You live in a place without flowers?"

He turned and looped his arm through hers and continued walking at her pace. "Not anymore. Now I have a Lily."

Lilyanna woke to the unwelcome ringing of the alarm on her phone. Disoriented, she sat up and groggily assessed her surroundings, realizing she was waking up in a mansion in the countryside and not her one-bedroom apartment in Austin. Tessa likewise began stirring in the adjacent twin bed. The dream left Lilyanna drowsy and even less eager to wake up and function than any non-morning person generally at seven o'clock.

"Well, we might as well enjoy our only morning of each having a bathroom to ourselves for the foreseeable future," Tessa yawned as she sat up in bed.

"Damn, you're right," Lilyanna sighed, stretching her arms.

"What will we do if our co-workers see us without makeup?" Tessa thought aloud.

"We can just keep makeup on right up until we go to bed."

"But my skin needs rest some days!"

"Skin heals, dignity does not."

After a quick breakfast of oatmeal and fruit in the kitchen, which Ms. Howard finally opened to the residents under her watchful eye, the group set to work again. Sylvie and Nina swept and vacuumed while Lilyanna and Tessa conducted a survey of all the new furniture, appliances and supplies delivered to the house.

Tessa changed her mind at least three times on where the living room furniture should go before acquiescing to an acceptable arrangement. The high-ceilinged living room sported thin ivory carpet and a floor-to-ceiling window with blue-grey embroidered curtains. A light grey sectional, matching three-seat sofa and loveseat and four armchairs were aligned opposite a brick fireplace large enough to heat the whole lower floor, or burn it down. "Please tell me the furniture in the den is already set up," Lilyanna stated out of breath.

"I'll have a look," Tessa replied. Lilyanna and Nina exchanged annoyed glances.

"Mistress Rivers, your phone is ringing continuously in the parlor," Bix called from the doorway into the hall.

"Yes, alright, coming." She grabbed her phone just in time to accept the FaceTime call from her older brother Luke.

"Dear sister, how are you?" The same blue eyes and beige blonde hair greeted her on the phone screen.

"I'm better now. What's happening in DC?"

"We've gone into lockdown here. Our COVID-19 cases are already getting out of control. Are you at your Versailles knock-off?"

"I am," she sighed.

"Interesting. You've always avoided that place like the plague."

"Well, now that I'm actually faced with the plague, it seemed like the better alternative."

"You should've just come here and stayed with me! I've been trying to get you to move here for years."

"My work is here, Luke, and it's too late to change any plans now. I have a legion of Texas corporate infrastructure employees moving into the house. I'm sure they'll make Whimser great again."

CHAPTER THREE
Alone Together

"We are officially lost! We've been in this van for three hours, and Lily's house is only two hours from the city. Tristan, we need to pull over and ask for directions. We lost cell service an hour ago and can't access Google Maps or call Lily," Jillian insisted from the front row of seats in the ten-passenger van transporting the remaining company employees to Whimser. She sat between Alyra and Joe, while Six and Barret sat in the middle row, and Andrew, Rich and Tyson crammed in the back.

"Do you know where we are?" Tristan asked the driver from the front seat.

"I apologize, sir, but no more than you do with the GPS not working," the driver replied. "But I believe there's an old Irish town up ahead. We can stop there."

"An Irish town in the Texas countryside?" Andrew asked.

"Yes, sir, I've driven through it before. There's an Irish festival there every year."

After driving another two miles, a ramshackle brown brick building appeared on the side of the road ahead. "What's that? Can we stop there?" Six asked.

"That looks like a pub, sir. I can pull over if you wish," the driver answered.

"Wait, what does the sign say?" Jillian asked, squinting out the window. A small marquee stood in the parking lot with black letters stating "PUB IC HOUSE."

"Pubic house," Joe confirmed flatly.

"As inviting as that looks, maybe we should wait for a better option," Barret suggested.

"By the state of this area, I don't think it's going to get better the farther we go. Can we please stop the van so I can piss?" Rich called.

"I'm not going to the restroom in there!" Tyson snorted.

"Then stop the van so I can smoke," Joe ordered.

Alyra agreed, "Yeah, I need to get out of this thing, now, Tristan."

"I'll take the pubic house over this van," Andrew confirmed.

"Legally, I advise against this," Six added.

"Yeah, I'm with Six. They might have COVID-19, and my masks are in my suitcase in the back!" Tyson cried.

"The CDC said not to wear a mask," Alyra noted.

The tormented passengers piled out of the van and into a gravel lot surrounded by trees and a dirt path leading to the front door of the pub. "I'll go in and ask for directions," Tristan said, motioning for the driver to follow him.

"What if they won't help us?" Tyson asked.

"I wouldn't help us," Joe replied, lighting a cigarette and leaning against the side of the van. "We look like a knock-off retired version of *The Breakfast Club* riding in a white van with tinted windows through Podunk Ville."

"I wouldn't stand so close to a white van with that mustache," Barret quipped.

"Lily should've warned us. She didn't mention her house would be this hard to find," Jillian muttered.

"She didn't mention we were moving to Schitt's Creek either," Joe huffed as he smoked.

"I feel like I'm in a B class horror movie, stuck in this hell hole, riding in a cheap-ass van all day to escape a global virus just to wind up at some bar in the middle of nowhere," Alyra complained as she swatted at a mosquito.

Tyson laughed, "I've never heard you curse, Alyra."

"You've worked for Xenergy, what, four months? Don't even start," Alyra dismissed him with an annoyed wave. "I'm going in there to pee and probably not coming out again. Come on, Jill." She stomped up to the door with Jillian and went inside.

"I'm not going in there. I'll pee outside," Rich said.

"Yeah, I'm good with that," Andrew followed him, along with Tyson, into the woods next to the gravel lot.

"We'll guard the van," Six offered, standing next to Barret and surveying the lot.

"Since it's at such high risk of theft and all," Tyson snickered.

Barret agreed, "I'll just get a bladder infection—that's curable. COVID-19, and whatever else is on the menu at this establishment, may not be."

"I have a bad feeling about this place," Six told Barret in a hushed tone. "I don't think they want Black people out here. This looks like the town in *Get Out*. If I see one MAGA hat, I'm getting the fuck out!"

Tristan and the driver emerged from the pub about the same time as Andrew, Rich and Tie returned to the lot. A short man in a green sweater and Donegal cap followed Tristan and the driver to the edge of the road near the parked van.

"Like I told you, you go back the other way a wee bit and keep going for twenty miles or so," the man explained in a thick Irish accent while pointing in the direction from which they had just traveled.

"But where do we turn off the main road?" the driver asked.

"You should turn right on the side road and stay on it for ten miles, and then you will pass signs for some smaller towns. The first is Dikbang, and you keep going past Dikbang until you reach Cunnyslit. That's where you turn to take the road through the woods." Silence followed.

"He's jerkin' us off, right?" Joe whispered to Tristan. "Now, is that north or south of Butt Fuck, Egypt?" Joe asked the short man in exasperation. "Sir, we don't have time for games."

The man's face contorted in confusion. "Now, I'm telling you where to go like you asked."

"And we appreciate it, sir, thank you," Tristan cut in.

Joe threw his cigarette butt to the ground and stamped it out. "Alright, fine, did you boys get all that, Dikbang to Cunnyslit?"

"Hang on, I'm putting it in my phone," Tyson replied. "How do you spell Dikbang? Is that Celtic?"

Joe took a deep breath and coughed slightly, "Quit fuckin' around and get back in the van." He opened the door to the van and motioned for everyone to get in.

"Did we get directions?" Alyra asked as she and Jillian rejoined the group.

"I'm not entirely sure. Just get in," Tristan ordered in annoyance.

***

"They should have been here an hour ago!" Lilyanna blustered around the living room, re-straightening throw pillows and lamenting every flaw, real or imagined.

"Lily, the house looks great. Just calm down," Tessa tried to soothe her.

"I am calm!" Lilyanna bellowed. "You know I hate it when people tell me to calm down! The response you're always going to get is me telling you how calm I am in an even less calm voice than I was speaking in before you gave me that absolutely useless directive!"

"We could rearrange the furniture again. Would that make you feel better?"

"No! This is a terrible idea! I should never have agreed to this." Lilyanna plopped onto the sofa next to Tessa. "I mean, I'm a private person. I live alone, and I don't even do that many social things. I, like, go to your apartment on Friday nights and watch *Game of Thrones* reruns."

"I'm the same way, Lily. I get it. I don't know how to live with other people either. We'll just have to figure out a way to make our own space when we need it. And we can still watch *GOT*, up to the last half of season eight when everyone forgot the storyline of the last decade. Oh, come on, you'll be the perfect ghostess with the mostest."

Lilyanna nodded slowly. Maybe she could get through it since Tessa and her other friends would be there. "This is going to be the longest and weirdest sleepover ever." They laughed softly in spite of their anxiety.

The van pulled up to Whimser by mid-afternoon. Lilyanna, Tessa, Bix, Sylvie and Nina hurried outside to help the guests with their luggage. "You made it! Welcome," Lilyanna greeted the group with a nervous smile.

"Yeah, no thanks to you!" Tyson yelled.

"What happened?"

"Couldn't find the cunny slit," Joe rasped, throwing a duffle bag over his shoulder and heading for the front door.

"What?" Lilyanna puzzled, hurrying after him. "Bix, please show the guys to their rooms. Tessa, can you show Jillian and Alyra to the first-floor master? Does anyone need help with luggage?"

Andrew pulled suitcases out of the back of the van for their owners to collect. "Nah, we've got it, Lily. This is crazy! I never would have guessed a huge house was here. I thought we were lost in the woods on another road to nowhere."

"Yeah, it's quite well hidden. Does it make you feel better or worse to know the slim chances of anyone finding us out here?" she asked as she grabbed a rolling suitcase and walked with Andrew into the house.

"Ask me in a week."

"Will do, if we survive that long."

Xenergy employees milled around the front hall trying to claim their belongings while Sylvie and Nina directed them to their rooms. Whimser had never witnessed so much action. Even when William summered at the house, he never invited enough guests to fill all of the rooms.

Tristan entered the house last. Cool and composed amidst the surrounding chaos, his chiseled jawline never faltered and not a wrinkle creased his white dress shirt. He breezed into the hall with his sleeves rolled up, revealing a leather-banded designer watch, and a black leather travel bag draped over one shoulder, his wavy hair cascading softly over his forehead.

Lilyanna could feel the blood rushing to her face at the sight of him. She wanted to dash up the stairs and take sanctuary in her room, but, not only did she no longer have a room to herself, she was responsible for Whimser—its hostess and owner. William would've wanted his house well represented. *You cannot run! You cannot be weak!*

Doing her best to appear at ease, Lilyanna approached Tristan. "Need help finding your room?"

"Please," he nodded, waving her in front of him. He followed Lilyanna to the men's hall and into the last bedroom on the left.

"This is your room and Joe's. It's the only room on this hall with two full-sized beds, in case you need more space."

Tristan stared at her with a hint of humor shining through his blue eyes, but he said nothing.

"I mean, not that you would need more space . . ." she awkwardly corrected herself.

"I got it, Lily, thank you," he interrupted her without altering his gaze. Her flight response failing to kick in, she remained in her place, but managed to keep her eyes fixed on his.

"Heyyy, Lily! Where are you?" a shrill voice called from the front hall.

"Excuse me for a minute," Lilyanna smiled awkwardly at Tristan and headed for the entryway.

Kyah Clark, Lilyanna's friend from Dallas with shoulder-length blonde hair and a curvy figure, entered the hall, followed by their mutual friend Saharie Turner, who stood a couple of inches taller than Lilyanna and Kyah with a dark afro.

"Hi, ladies!" Lilyanna rushed to the front hall and greeted her friends. Tessa beat her to the hall and hugged Kyah and Saharie.

"Missed you, loves!" Kyah embraced Lilyanna with one arm and pulled an extra-large Samsonite suitcase with a tote on top in the other. "The fab four is back together again!"

"Lily, why are we just now seeing the summer house?" Saharie asked, pushing her oversized sunglasses onto her head and surveying the hall.

"Oh, I, just don't come up here much. Besides, wouldn't you rather travel to exciting international destinations with me for our vacations?"

"Uh, obviously, but that might be off the table for a while, babe."

"Don't say that! Our summer Croatia trip hasn't been canceled yet! Don't get me worked up about that right now—I have enough to deal with."

"Speaking of which, a jeep pulled up behind our Uber in front of the house," Kyah noted.

"Oh, that's my friends staying in the guesthouse. Tessa, can you show Kyah and Saharie to our room upstairs?"

Kyah and Saharie followed Tessa up the main staircase and into the new shared master bedroom. "So, are our new housemates hot, Tessa? When do we get to meet them?" Kyah gushed.

"Um, no, they're not hot. They're my co-workers, and you're married, Kyah!"

"Okay, chill, I was just curious. Anyway, you, Saharie and Lilyanna are single! My husband is quarantined in Boston, so I'm totally going to live vicariously through you while you have forbidden secret hookups with your colleagues."

"That is not happening! Besides, I'm still kinda seeing Alec."

"Tessa, you've been on and off with him more times than Kyah with her birth control. I think you should move on," Saharie advised.

"Birth control made me gain ten pounds and lose my libido!" Kyah cried.

Tessa smirked, "Then you should definitely take it while in this house, for all our sakes."

"Which bed is mine?" Kyah asked, ignoring her.

"You two are sharing the king bed, and Lily and I are taking the twins."

"Get ready to cuddle, Saharie!"

"Bitch, take your birth control."

Downstairs, Lilyanna hurried outside to greet her final two guests Dylan Reiss and his fiancée Waya Lestari. The Uber driver backed the jeep away from the house as soon as Dylan and Waya stepped out and headed toward Lilyanna.

"Hey, gorgeous!" Dylan picked Lilyanna up off the ground and swung her into a full-body hug. He had soft sandy brown hair, hazel eyes and an endearing smile.

"Oh my gosh, hi!" she giggled.

"Air kisses, cause pandemic and all," he said, setting her back on the ground.

"Hey, Waya, good to see you," she hugged the leaner man with short black hair.

"You too, Lily! Thanks for letting us crash your company sleepover."

"Believe me, I'm glad to have real friends here. I'll show you the guesthouse where you'll be staying, and you're welcome to come up to the main house anytime."

Lilyanna led Dylan and Waya to a small one-bed, one-bath apartment across the yard from the main house. The guesthouse matched the main house in color and roof material with two rectangular windows. Inside, the front door opened to an entryway leading to a kitchenette with a few basic appliances and an adjoining, minimally furnished bedroom with a chestnut king-sized bed and matching chest of drawers.

"It's quaint, but you'll have more privacy than in the main house."

"It has toilet paper and allows us to safely go outside for fresh air. That's a huge improvement over big cities right now," Dylan assured her.

That evening, all of the house guests and staff gathered in the living room at Tristan's request for a group meeting. Dylan and Waya sat laughing with Kaya and Saharie on the floor in front of the occupied sectional, while Bix, Sylvie, Nina and Ms. Howard sat in chairs carried in from the dining room. Lilyanna sat between Andrew and Tristan on a couch nearest the front of the room.

Once everyone settled, Tristan stood up to address the group. "I thought it would be best for us all to get together to go over a few house rules and make sure everyone is reasonably comfortable with the living arrangements. Most of us know each other, but would those of you who don't work for Xenergy care to introduce yourselves, and then we'll go around and let everyone else give their names?"

"Sure, I'll start," Kyah offered. "I'm Lily's friend Kyah. I'm an employment law attorney at a firm in Dallas. I'll be working remotely while I'm here. My husband is stuck in Boston for work, and Lily invited me to stay here so I wouldn't be home alone." She turned and nodded to Saharie.

"Hi, I'm Saharie, also Lily's friend. I am a hair and makeup artist. I obviously can't do events right now, so I'll be blogging and doing videos for my Instagram and Youtube while I'm here."

"And, I'm Dylan, and this is my fiancée Waya."

"Hi, everybody," Waya gave a slight wave.

"We're dance choreographers, and we're staying in the guesthouse."

Nobody responded for several seconds. "Okay, uh, good, thanks," Tristan broke the silence. The rest of the group introduced themselves, followed by the staff. Tristan rounded out the introductions and then explained that everyone would be expected to help the staff with routine cleaning and laundry and how meals would be provided by Ms. Howard.

"Alright, let's see, a few more housekeeping items. Lily, people can receive packages, right?"

"Yes, Amazon and the other carriers deliver here. I set up a shelf in the kitchen where we can put any packages and mail."

"Great, thank you," Tristan continued. "I think that pretty much covers the basics. If you have any questions about the house or resources, you can ask Lily. Otherwise, the general chain of command in the house will be me, followed by Jillian, Alyra and Joe and then Lily and Andrew. Lily, is there anything you'd like to say about the house?"

Reluctantly, Lilyanna found her feet and stood next to Tristan. "I don't have much to add other than welcome, and I hope you all will be comfortable here. Obviously, nobody should be leaving the grounds, which is the reason my car is the only one on the property. I keep the keys in the center drawer of the kitchen island, but for emergencies only. If you need anything or can't find something, please let me know."

"Thanks, Lily. I know this may be a bit awkward, but we're all adults. As long as we all remain professional and respectful of one another, we should have no trouble doing our jobs in a shared space."

Yeah, except doing the job isn't the concern; it's living with a house full of co-workers during the rapid spread of a highly contagious illness! Lilyanna thought. "For the sake of transparency, I'm sure you've all noticed we can't constantly follow CDC Guidelines here," she noted. "There's no way to social distance properly at all times, so it's up to all of us to take what precautions we can—sanitizing, and, most importantly, not leaving the grounds. There's no safety in numbers in a pandemic."

CHAPTER FOUR
After Dark

The guests deluded themselves into thinking life was normal while doing routine tasks like eating dinner the first night at Whimser. Ms. Howard prepared a simple yet delicious meal of roasted chicken with vegetables and mashed potatoes, with a vegetarian alternative for Jillian and Rich. Lilyanna sat at a table in the kitchen with Saharie, Kyah, Tessa, Six, Barret, Tyson, Dylan and Waya, while the others ate in the dining room.

"Is this the kids' table?" Tyson asked.

"Only if you continue to sit here, Tie," Barret quipped. Lilyanna actually preferred the separation from the senior employees. She considered the people at her table friends, and eating a meal with them was nothing unusual. The free-flowing wine didn't hurt either. Lilyanna had made sure to direct Ms. Howard and Bix to maintain regular wine deliveries to the house.

"Where are all the groceries coming from?" Six asked.

"Yeah, my mom said they can't even get toilet paper at HEB or Walmart in Austin," Tie added.

"I really don't understand the toilet paper hoarding. Like, people think the world's ending and toilet paper will save them?" Saharie shook her head.

"Maybe it will become the new currency," Lilyanna joked.

"The real question is how the largest deforester in the world has a paper goods shortage," Tessa sighed.

"But how are we getting supplies here, like Six said?" Barret pressed.

"Well," Lilyanna began, taking a sip of wine, "since the office closed, management diverted some of our office supply deliveries here and some to Marks' house. In addition to that, Whimser has had a supply contract for years with the supermarket about half an hour away. I just increased the regular orders. We'll likely have more competition than usual for the store's inventory since more people may start shopping at stores outside the city right now, but hopefully we'll get most of what we order."

"If supply chains completely crash, we'll ration the guys' toilet paper first," Tessa assured him.

"How did you get this house, Lily?" Tie asked her from across the table.

Lilyanna paused, hoping someone would interrupt and change the subject. She had not yet concocted an abridged version of the story of how her late college professor and boss devised his beloved estate to her that sounded reasonably believable and at least partially true. "Ummm, it belonged to a close friend. He had no living family."

"Who's the friend?" Kyah asked. "You never mentioned him."

"Just a family friend," she lied. "He passed away before I went to law school."

"Sorry to hear that," Saharie added.

Lilyanna shook her head and forced a fake smile, "Thanks, but it's been a long time."

"Anyhoo, let's get to the fun stuff—who are the single Pringles in the house, besides Lily?" Dylan interrupted to Lilyanna's relief. The others silently exchanged glances before Saharie spoke up.

"I am," she shrugged.

Tie stared at her in surprise, "Me too."

"Let's see," Tessa began, "Kyah is married. I'm sort of seeing someone. Ummm, Barret is single, and Six is married with, how many kids?"

"I have a daughter and a son," he replied.

"Okay, and Andrew is married with a daughter. Jillian was divorced but is remarried with a grown son and stepson. Alyra is married with two kids. Rich is married, but I don't think he has any kids. And Tristan is divorced with two sons," Tessa continued. "Lily, is Joe married?"

"He's divorced and has a daughter in college."

"Let's take bets on who hooks up first! There are some hotties in the house," Dylan proposed through gulps of wine.

"Absolutely not!" Lilyanna cried. "Most of us work together."

"That's even hotter! A bunch of frustrated professionals locked up together. I should be filming this."

"Don't even think about it," Lilyanna warned.

"I feel like I'm at some, like, adult summer camp," Kyah mused between bites.

"I never went to summer camp," Saharie replied.

"I never went to summer camp either," Tie agreed, never taking his eyes off Saharie as he took a sip from his wine glass. Saharie looked at him indifferently. "So, you do hair and makeup?" he asked her.

"Yep, sure do."

"You have really pretty hair." The table got quiet as eyes bounced from Tie to Saharie.

"Oh, um, thanks," she answered coolly. "I was actually thinking I could give haircuts while we're here."

"Yes!" Lilyanna and Tessa exclaimed in unison.

"Cool, I brought a ton of styling products. I'll show you what I brought in my bag of tricks tonight."

Tie took another sip of his wine, "Can't wait to see."

"I think she was talking to the ladies. You guys are staying downstairs!" Tessa clarified.

"Okay, Mom, whatever you say," Tie held up his hands.

"Waya and I are allowed in the women's suite, right?" Dylan asked.

"Of course," Lilyanna assured him.

Tie tapped his glass on the table, "That's discrimination!"

Lilyanna raised her eyebrows, "Straight White men don't get to make that claim."

"Seriously, nobody will ever pity a straight successful White guy," Kyah agreed.

"I'm Native American actually—Chickasaw," Tie protested to the deaf ears around him.

Lilyanna wished dinner would last all night so she could avoid the awkwardness of the first bedtime in the house. As much as she would've liked to immediately retreat to the sanctuary of the women's suite upstairs after dinner, she couldn't shirk her duty to make sure everyone in the house got settled.

At half-past eight, her desire to be a proper hostess pushed her from her comfort zone at the kitchen table with her friends to turn her attention to the other guests. The senior employees meandered into the kitchen and, to Lilyanna's relief, took turns washing their dishes before loading them in the dishwasher. Lilyanna had worried the guests would rely on the housekeepers too much, and she would have to tell grown-ass adults to do their own dishes.

Lilyanna opened another bottle of wine for the guests as they congregated awkwardly as if at a never-ending house party. She thought of a quote from one of her favorite stories, *The Great Gatsby*, "I like large parties. They're so intimate. At small parties there isn't any privacy." She would have no privacy from then on. There were too many guests for personal space and not enough to allow for periodic unnoticed escapes.

"Well, is this where we all fight over the one TV downstairs?" Tie asked, stacking his dishes in the kitchen sink.

"If your balls haven't dropped yet, or you're under thirty, not sure which comes first, you don't get a say in what we watch on TV," Joe told him. He left the room to go outside on the front porch to smoke without waiting for a response.

"Hey, man, you don't get to talk to me like that! I'm close enough to thirty, and Lily is under thirty and it's her TV."

Lilyanna set the wine bottle she was holding on the counter with an audible thud, "Don't bring me into this. First of all, I'm twenty-nine—I have one toe left in my twenties—and secondly, you all make complex decisions every day, so I think you can work out a schedule for the downstairs TV among yourselves."

"Well said, Lily," Jillian nodded in approval as she washed her dishes in the sink.

"I have an HR complaint day one!" Tie insisted.

"I am HR!" Alyra snapped. "And I don't listen to whining. Unless someone starts stroking your undescended boy parts without your consent during business hours, you don't have an HR complaint." She grabbed an opened bottle of Cabernet Sauvignon from the counter on her way out of the kitchen. "We're watching the news. I want to hear the CDC's update. Apparently, we're supposed to start wearing masks in public now."

"Do as you will. I'll say good night," Tristan stated coolly and headed toward the bedroom he shared with Joe without a glance at anyone.

"So, does anyone care if I take the first shower?" Rich asked. Nobody responded at first, instead exchanging awkward glances. Lilyanna never thought there would be a day when she thought about her colleagues' shower schedules. All bets really were off in 2020.

Andrew leaned against the kitchen counter and shook his head while looking at his phone. "It's all you, man."

When Tessa, Kyah and Saharie went upstairs for the night and Dylan and Waya departed for the guesthouse, Lilyanna stayed behind to find Sylvie in the laundry room beside the back stairs. "Hey, Sylvie, do you need help with anything before people start going to their rooms for the night?"

"No, thank you, Nina and I are about to knock off," Sylvie assured her while pulling a bundle of towels out of one of the washers.

"Okay, great. Just let me know if you change your mind or if anything gets crazy down here. I'm going upstairs, but I'll come down before I go to bed to check on everything and lock up."

Once upstairs, the women unpacked their belongings, which consisted of spreading clothes, cosmetics and accessories over every surface of the master bedroom, including the floor. Saharie commandeered the ivory vanity table for all of her makeup and hair products, while Tessa and Lilyanna divided up the four drawers in the matching chest of drawers.

"Saharie, where did you get all this makeup?" Tessa asked as Saharie pulled out cosmetic bags full of makeup and hair products.

"Advertisers send me tons of samples to use in my videos and for my clients."

"Hell yeah! We can do some damage with these goodies," Kyah mused, testing a coral lipstick on the back of her hand. "So, now that it's just us ladies, Lily or Tessa, please tell me who you want to bang?"

"OMG Kyah, not happening!" Tessa insisted as she folded her t-shirts into a stack on her bed.

"Oh, come on, you know some of these guys are gorgeous. That Andrew guy, and Six—"

"Are married," Lilyanna finished for her.

"And Tristan looks like an Armani model," Kyah continued down the list. "I bet he's amazing in bed."

"Don't go there, Kyah," Lilyanna stopped her as she folded her intimates into a drawer.

"Why not?" Kyah grabbed Lilyanna's black lace thong from the opened dresser drawer and tossed it to her. "Here, just slip into this and go down to his room, ya know, to make sure he 'has everything he needs for the night.' I guarantee we won't see you again til morning."

"Will you stop?" Lilyanna stuffed her underwear back into the drawer and slammed it shut. "I would never do that! I don't even want to think about it."

"Ohhh, you like him, don't you? You always get prude and standoffish when you're actually attracted to someone," Kyah teased.

"No, I don't! And I'm not into him, like that."

"It's okay, Lily, he's divorced, right? That makes him totally available. What's the problem?" Saharie asked, lounging on her bed next to Kyah.

"He's the vice president of my company! Even if getting involved with him were acceptable, which it's not, he has no interest in me. I'm not, I mean, he would not, think of me in that way."

Kyah smirked, "He's a man! He thinks of you the same way all straight men think of pretty young women."

"Yeah, with one body part in particular doing the thinking," Saharie mumbled.

"Exactly! Lily, you're young and pretty, and you can't possibly think you're not good enough for him, if that's what you're getting at. You're a successful attorney! Not to mention, you have huge tits for someone your size. Here, just take this off and wear a low-cut cami." Kyah jerked Lilyanna's quarter-length sleeve blouse over her head. A light blue silk camisole underneath revealed Lilyanna's perky C-cup cleavage.

"Hey, my shirt!"

"You look fantastic!" Kyah assured her.

"Well, thanks, that's sweet, but it's just not a good time for me to be thinking about . . . intimacy."

"You've been saying that since we were in law school."

"Kyah has a point, Lily. The timing is never going to be perfect. You need to start putting yourself out there. We all finished our Brazilian laser hair removal treatments, so you should be good to go!" Saharie encouraged her.

Kyah laughed, "That's right! My vagina is silky and smooth. Come on, we didn't go through all that torture and spend the money not to show off the results."

Lilyanna laughed. Girl talk gets anatomical quickly. If it doesn't, you're not really friends. "Maybe you should take your own advice, Saharie. Tie flooded his basement for you."

"He's, like, way younger than me!"

"You're twenty-nine, and he's twenty-eight—that's nothing," Kyah insisted. "You both need to relax and have a little fun. It's only a matter of time before these guys start going nuts locked up under the same roof with plenty of eye candy and no significant others. How else do you ladies normally relieve stress?"

"I get drunk and watch *Lady Bird*," Tessa admitted.

"That's a good one," Lilyanna agreed.

"Oh my gosh, you're both crushing my soul," Kyah winced. "You need to seize this opportunity cause there's not going to be any love for single people as long as this pandemic continues. People who don't live together have to socially distance!"

"Yeah, I mean, unless the guy has a six-foot dick, I don't see how singles will be hooking up for a long time," Saharie added.

"I'm honestly just glad we can reasonably trust these guys not to assault us," Tessa replied. "I've worked with them long enough to feel safe on that front."

Lilyanna nodded, "Yeah, I'd be freaking out if we were locked up with men I don't know. I think safe is the most we can ask for at this point."

A little after ten-thirty, Lilyanna threw on a pair of lounge shorts and quietly descended the back staircase to make sure the doors were locked for the night. The lights were already out in the living room and dining room. Seeing nobody around, she stepped into the den to turn the lights off when a noise from the kitchen caught her attention. Cautiously, she crept across the hall and toward the kitchen where a dark figure suddenly blocked the doorway.

"Geez, Bix, why are you in the kitchen this late? I thought everyone had gone to bed!" she hissed, stepping back from him. "You scared me to death!"

If only, his eyes screamed at her. "My apologies, Mistress Rivers. I merely sought a cup of hot tea before retiring to my cottage," he explained, holding up a steaming mug. "Is there anything I can do for you this evening?"

"No, just quit lurking in the shadows! Good night." She followed him to the hall and closed the front door behind him. Eyeing the deadbolt, she briefly analyzed which would be riskier, leaving the door unlocked and the house open to intruders, or locking up a house full of clashing personalities overnight. *It might actually be more dangerous to keep out the unknown evil at the expense of keeping in the known.* Her fingers hesitant as her mind grappled with the dilemma, she slid the deadbolt into place and leaned against the door, taking a deep breath. There was no way out now.

She closed her eyes for a moment and rested her head against the wall, absorbing the sounds of Whimser that could only be heard when undisturbed by residents. No human noises pervaded the hall, but neither did silence. Walls creaked, echoing off the marble floors, and the exterior braced against the early spring winds, a melody of rhythmic palpitations with no audience to hear but her.

A sudden chill pulled Lilyanna away from the front door. With the door closed, there was no obvious source of cold air, yet a soft breeze swept around her as she meandered through the hall. The closer she moved to the parlor, the louder the breeze whispered to her.

"Is someone there?" she called softly.

"I'm always here, My Flower," the breeze whispered back.

Lilyanna froze, chill bumps forming on her arms and her heart pounding to the beat of the settling noises of the house. "William? Is that you?"

"My Flower, My Flower," the wind sang again. Her feet dragged her forward into the parlor. It remained vacant, with only the breeze swirling around the furniture and dissipating as quickly as it formed. Confused and panicked, Lilyanna turned and dashed back into the hall where she ran headlong into a half-naked Andrew.

"Wooo, hey!" Andrew held up his hands to block her and nearly knocked her over in the process. He was shirtless with wet hair and a towel tied around his waist.

"Oh my gosh, I'm so sorry!" Lilyanna cried, trying to steady herself and avoid touching his chest at the same time.

"It's okay, it's okay! Are you alright?" he firmly grabbed her shoulders to steady her on her feet.

"I'm fine," she nodded, trying to catch her breath and stepping back from him. "I'm sorry, I didn't see you!"

Simultaneously, Tristan rushed into the hall behind Andrew, also shirtless and clad in only a towel around his waist. "What's going on?" He glanced from Andrew to Lilyanna, his brow furrowed in confusion.

"Oh, wow, ummm, nothing," Lilyanna stammered, putting her hand over her face and turning away from the men. "I just came downstairs to lock the doors and turn the lights off, and I crashed into Andrew. I'm so sorry! Wait, what were you two doing?"

Her reaction reminded the men they were mostly undressed in front of their colleague. "Well, I, he, ummm . . ." Andrew started. "We were just in the shower."

Lilyanna stared, tilting her head slightly. "Together?"

"No, no!" They cried in unison.

"I was in one shower, and he was in another shower . . . at the same time, I presume," Tristan tried to explain.

"Yeah, I was in a very different shower!" Andrew confirmed. "And then I got out of the shower, that different shower, and I realized one of my bags got mixed up with Tristan's. I was going to his room to swap bags."

Lilyanna fought the urge to let her eyes linger on their bodies, but a couple of inadvertent glances were enough to tell her they were stunning. Andrew, slimmer and a couple of inches taller than Tristan, had a trim build with dark chest hair. His abs were

CHAPTER FOUR: After Dark

defined, but not fully chiseled into a six-pack, which actually gave his frame a more natural and inviting appearance. Tristan, on the other hand, sported broad shoulders and muscly pecs with a thinner dusting of black chest hair and a more filled-out midsection.

"Right, and I finished my shower and realized my case was missing as well and went to search for it. We were not in the shower together," Tristan confirmed, a damp wave of his dark hair draping over his forehead. His eyes drifted to Lilyanna's chest for a split second before he caught himself and looked away.

"Well, I mean, I offered, but Tristan said no, so I just took a shower by myself," Andrew joked, trying to alleviate the tension.

Lilyanna and Tristan laughed awkwardly. "I apologize, Lily. We should have dressed first." His British accent combined with his half-toweled appearance tested even Lilyanna's willpower.

She felt a deep blush rising in her face and fought it with a forced smile and looked each of them in the eye. "Don't apologize! This is technically your home now, not the office, and for the record, it takes a lot more than this to make me uncomfortable. Well, good night," she nodded with as much confidence as she could muster.

"Good night," Tristan replied as he watched her leave for the back stairs.

"Night," Andrew echoed. He and Tristan exchanged mutterings and a few soft laughs on the way to their rooms.

Lilyanna tossed and turned in her bed that night, visions of William and Tristan alternating in her head. She couldn't have really heard William's voice. It must have been a mind-fucking combination of stress and exhaustion, which only worsened as her anxiety increased, knowing the exhaustion wouldn't end if she didn't sleep. She imagined lying next to Tristan, his strong arms around her pulling her against him. She wanted that, to touch him, intentionally, and unapologetically. She mentally rested her head against his firm chest as he caressed her into a dreamless sleep.

CHAPTER FIVE
The New Abnormal

L ilyanna had been so preoccupied with getting through the first night with all of the guests in the house that she forgot to worry about the logistics of the first morning. Her phone alarm went off at six-thirty, drawing moans from Kyah and Saharie. Barely able to force her eyes open enough to see the clock on her phone, Lilyanna snoozed her alarm for another fifteen minutes of dozing.

She wanted to chuck her phone out the window when the alarm went off again. "Lily, turn it off!" Kyah groaned, throwing her pillow at the foot of Lilyanna's bed and turning on her side. Though Lilyanna despised waking up early, the thought of her colleagues seeing her sleep through her get-ready time forced her dutifully from her bed and into the master bathroom.

The mirror pointed out the dark circles under her eyes and the stress-induced stringiness of her hair. She craved her morning coffee but couldn't risk being seen downstairs. Everything is easier after a strong cup of coffee or tea.

Lilyanna opted for face makeup and only mascara on her eyes—the goal being to avoid letting her co-workers see her without makeup while not looking like she was trying too hard. Tessa joined her in the bathroom about fifteen minutes later to get ready for the day. "What are you wearing? Like, we don't have to wear business clothes, right?" Tessa asked, running a straightener through her silky dark locks.

"Good question. Uhhh, I don't think so. That would be weird. I'm just going with Athleta pants and a striped shirt."

"And shoes?"

The women looked at each other with uncertainty. "I don't know," Lilyanna admitted. It was too complex a question for early in the morning during a pandemic.

Barret, Six and Tie were already seated at the kitchen table eating breakfast when Lilyanna and Tessa made their way downstairs. Andrew, Rich, Joe and Alyra stood around the center island chatting and drinking coffee, while Jillian spooned oatmeal into a bowl from a pot on the counter. Lilyanna relaxed a little when she saw her wardrobe choice matched the styling of the group, though slightly more casual than the men's jeans and button-down shirts. The women all wore some type of athleisure pants with casual blouses. Jillian looked like a high-end clothing model in cream linen ankle pants and a rose silk blouse.

"Good morning," Lilyanna greeted them shyly. "Is everyone, um, doing okay?"

"Well, we're still a group of adults sharing rooms in a house in the middle of nowhere who may or may not be infected with a deadly virus that's ravaging the world, but, on the other hand, nobody got murdered, assaulted or humiliated to the point of running away—on the first night that is," Joe explained, his morning voice even deeper than usual.

Crickets chirped in response.

"Just to clarify, should we be expecting someone to get murdered, assaulted or humiliated to the point of running away on subsequent nights?" Barret asked, pointing his spoon in Joe's direction.

"That sounds like a question for our employment attorney," Rich nodded at Six.

"Legal advises against setting expectations during a pandemic," Six replied matter-of-factly. Barret chuckled nervously but stopped when nobody joined.

Kyah and Saharie appeared just in time to break up the tension. "Good morning, dear housemates," Kyah cooed. Still wearing pajama shorts and a sports bra with a sheer tank top, she had not bothered to dress or do her hair or makeup. Saharie at least wore yoga pants and a long-sleeve t-shirt.

"Good morning!" Tie greeted Saharie. He slid his chair away from Barret's and pulled up another chair in between them. "There's an empty chair here if you want to sit down."

"Did everybody sleep well, all cozied up together?" Kyah asked in a high-pitched tone.

Another awkward silence followed. "I think that's my cue to get to work," Joe sighed.

"There's workspace in the library for you and Tristan," Lilyanna reminded him.

"Like sleeping in the same room with him doesn't give us enough quality time together. Where the hell's the library in this maze?"

"I'll show you, Joe," Jillian offered, following him out of the kitchen. "I'm using the library, too." Alyra left as well, to work in the den.

"I don't know how Tristan got any sleep. I could hear Joe snoring from our room," Tie said.

"That was probably Barret you heard," Six smirked.

"I have a deviated septum!" Barret cried.

"Maybe you guys should switch rooms, then," Saharie suggested to Six. "Put the snorers together and then you room with Tristan."

"Nah, Barret's my boy," Six insisted, balling up his hand for a fist bump with Barret.

A few seconds later, Tristan sauntered into the kitchen, wearing fitted jeans and a cream-colored half-zip sweater. Despite how quietly he moved or how casually he dressed, his captivating presence dashed any hope of subtlety for his entrance. Lilyanna knew she shouldn't look at him, especially after last night's embarrassing moment, but she couldn't look away either. She didn't think he could look more handsome than he did last night shirtless and wrapped in a towel, but the sweater and jeans were a close call. He looked composed as usual, not a bit sleep-deprived.

"Good morning," he said coolly, perching next to Andrew at the kitchen island.

"Morning. Can I get you some coffee?" Lilyanna asked with a shy smile. *Please don't blush!* she begged herself. *You have to coexist with this man without blushing every time you speak to him.*

"Yes, thank you."

She poured the last of the coffee from the coffee pot into a mug and set it on the island in front of him. "Do you like it sweet?"

"What?" he asked, his eyes flicking up to hers.

"Do you want sweetener for your coffee?"

"No, black is fine. Thanks."

"You didn't offer me coffee," Kyah complained with a wicked grin.

"I have to make some more," Lilyanna muttered. She grabbed the coffee pot to refill it with water for another round.

"There's a Keurig for people who prefer stale coffee over dirty filter coffee—pick your poison," Barret pointed out, nodding to the appliance and rack of k-cups. "I'm a coffee traditionalist, myself," he continued when nobody took up the slack to prevent an awkward silence.

"Oh my gosh, everyone is going to have to loosen up if we're going to live together!" Kyah bellowed, her outburst drawing the attention of the room. She strutted over to Lilyanna and put her arms around Lilyanna's waist while she reset the coffee maker. "Everyone is sooo tense."

"That's not making me any less tense, Ky," Lilyanna sighed. Aware of her audience, Kyah gave her a soft love bite on her neck.

"Ouch, Kyah! You better not have drawn blood," Lilyanna pushed her off and massaged her neck with a slight laugh in spite of herself. She could feel the men staring at her in shock, all except Tristan, whose eyes gave nothing away. Maybe Kyah had a point— she couldn't be a robotic professional all the time. She could walk on eggshells in high heels at work without a crack, but living on eggshells day and night would not be sustainable. While the group quarantine blurred the line between public and private life for the new residents of Whimser, so too must the norms exclusive to each domain yield to practicality.

After breakfast, Lilyanna set up her laptop and stack of open files in the dining room, with Andrew, Rich and Tie each sitting several chairs apart at the table. Tessa and Barret shared the living room, Six worked with Alyra in the den and only Kyah ended up with her own workspace in the upstairs den, as Saharie chose to stay in the bedroom. Ms. Howard insisted everyone stay out of her kitchen until lunchtime so she could finish inventory, so Sylvie and Nina set up a coffee and tea station in the parlor for those in need of a caffeine break throughout the day. Anyone needing to make a private call could use one of the bedrooms or go outside.

A snapshot in time of the residents during working hours would reveal proper social distancing. Limiting the capacity of each of the main rooms to only a few people and strategically planting hand sanitizer throughout the ground floor, combined with Sylvie and Nina cleaning around everyone, enabled the following of CDC guidelines during most of the day on weekdays. Until the fourteen-day mark of captivity, the risk of anyone transmitting COVID-19 remained a threat, especially during mealtimes and non-working hours when social distancing became impracticable. Of course, Lilyanna knew that if anyone arrived at the house infected, it would be only a matter of time before they were all hosed.

The shared workspace arrangement worked on paper. In practice, however, forcing employees who were accustomed to private offices into a single room with several co-workers proved challenging.

"Okay, first project of the day," Tie began reading from his laptop. He sat on one side of the rectangular dining room table across from Rich, while Lilyanna and Andrew sat at either head of the table. "I'm going to reach out to HSC Corp about a new agreement for pipe maintenance at Fort Worth." The others at the table stared at him.

"Are you going to dictate every task you work on?" Rich asked from behind his own laptop screen.

"Well, normally, I would pick up my desk phone and call you to tell you what I'm working on, but now that we're in the same room . . ." he shrugged. "I can call your cell phone if you prefer."

Rich rolled his eyes. "That would disturb everyone else in the room. We're working on different projects at different times."

"Ummm, so, Lily, if I need you to draft a services agreement for a new customer in Texas, should I tell you that or email you?" Andrew interjected.

"You just told me," Lilyanna stated flatly.

"Yeah, right, but I didn't know if I should email you from across the table."

"Rich is emailing me from the side of the table," she replied.

"I was trying not to interrupt everyone!" Rich cried.

Tie sighed and shook his head, "We are, like, not being efficient."

"Your perceptiveness overwhelms me, as always. Andrew, I think he's ready for a promotion!" Rich smirked.

"Okay, enough, let's just calm down," Andrew ordered.

Lilyanna gave her default response to the unwelcome mandate—screeching in a tone anything but calm, "I am calm!"

"Yeah, we're calm," Tie nodded. "But seriously would you mind not typing so loudly?" he asked Rich.

***

The overall edgy mood at dinner that night suggested the other work groups had not fared much better. Lilyanna stood at the kitchen island helping Ms. Howard set out plates and silverware when Alyra stomped into the kitchen with Six on her heels. "I'm just saying, you don't have to answer every single phone call and have a full conversation each time."

"What is your problem, Alyra? My conversations are only as long as they need to be!"

She stopped in the middle of the kitchen and turned to face him. "When a telemarketer or someone with the wrong number calls you, you don't have to answer the call! If it's an out-of-state number, or shows up as 'spam risk,' you don't answer, and if by chance you do answer, you don't then explain to the caller how they have the wrong number or why you're not interested in what they're advertising. You just hang up!"

"I can't help it if I have to talk to do my job!" he thundered. "What do you want me to do? Go work in the bathroom?"

"Great idea, or maybe I will! It's the only place I can get any privacy around here!"

"How about some wine?" Lilyanna offered in a falsely cheerful tone.

"I'll take a glass," Tristan sighed, appearing for the first time in the kitchen doorway. His dark wavy hair looked more ruffled than usual. Lilyanna poured him the first glass of Beaujolais.

"May I have a word with you in private?" he whispered when she set the glass in front of him on the counter. The nerve endings in her body tingled at the sound of his voice and closeness of his body.

"Of course," she inclined her head toward the hall and led him out of the kitchen.

"Look," he started in a low voice to Lilyanna, "we need to talk about the office arrangements. I respect Joe, I do. I just don't think we're well suited to spending all day and night together."

"Okaayyy, well, none of us are well suited to spending all day and night together, and we're a bit short on office space," Lilyanna reminded him. "Is there a reason in particular it's not working?"

"I know, and I'm terribly sorry to complain, but he smokes like a chimney in the library all day. I feel like I'm in a cheap casino, except I'm not free to leave. If he would just go out of doors . . ."

Lilyanna sighed and looked away, "You know he's my boss, right? I can't tell him what to do, or what not to do."

He ran his hand through his hair only to have his stubborn wavy locks feather back down over his forehead. It was almost too much for Lilyanna to stand there and watch without touching him. She wanted to ruffle his hair and tuck it away from his icy blue eyes for him. "Bollocks. You're right, I shouldn't put you in an uncomfortable position."

Thank God he didn't say that in front of Kyah.
"COVID beat you to that," she retorted. "Ummm, okay, let me think. It would not be well-received if I tell him, or if you do since you're his roommate. I'll ask Alyra to speak to him. She can tell him not to smoke in the house, and we need to rearrange some of the workspace assignments anyway. My group is also struggling, with four people in the dining room."

"Ah, I'm sorry," he sighed. "I would never want to make things more difficult for you." He cocked his head slightly, tightened his jaw muscle in a remorseful look and gently grabbed her upper arm, running his thumb back and forth over her skin.

His touch sent delightful warm fuzzies through her body. She focused all of her energy on stopping the blush rising in her cheeks, but it was no use. He probably thought of her as some pathetic schoolgirl with a crush, and he would be right. She didn't even have the confidence to reach up and reciprocate his touch.

"Mistress Rivers," the least welcome voice interrupted. Bix regarded them coolly as Tristan released her arm and turned away.

The warm tingling sensation in her body ceased instantly, exasperation taking its place. Nobody could kill the mood quicker than Bix. "For the millionth time, please stop calling me Mistress Rivers! Call me Lily or Lilyanna, or pretty much anything else! Now, what is it, Bix?"

"As you wish, madam. I have left today's mail on the designated shelf in the kitchen, but there were no package deliveries today. I shall check again tomorrow."

"Fine, thank you." She resented the bullshit interruption the rest of the evening. The daily mail delivery would not normally warrant Bix speaking to her. She felt certain he had seen her having a moment with a man and contrived an excuse to ruin it. *Antagonistic bastard!*

After everyone finished dinner, Tie suggested a walk down to the lake. All of the guests joined except for Alyra, Jillian and Joe, who opted to stay inside to call their kids. Lilyanna put on her charcoal grey trench coat and faux leather black boots that hit just below her knees. She led the group down to the edge of the front yard in the chilly evening air where Dylan and Waya joined the group.

With the temperature still well below sixty degrees near dark, the remnants of winter tightened their grip on the twilight. "It's supposed to be spring!" Saharie groaned, wrapping her black sweater around her.

Tie pushed past Barret and Tessa and rushed to Saharie's side. Barret gave a high-pitched moan at being shoved. "Allow me." Tie draped his arm around Saharie and pulled her close. Kyah and Tessa exchanged wide-eyed glances when Saharie did not resist.

Lilyanna walked ahead between Six and Andrew, pointing out the various paths through the woods. "The quickest way to Lake Whimser is this path to the right. The woods opens to sand dunes before you get to the beach."

"My dog would love the woods," Six remarked.

"It's a decent amount of open space," Lily replied, but it was William's voice she heard.

"This is our kingdom by the sea," William extended his arm, displaying the foliage leading to the sand dunes above the shore of the lake. Lilyanna stood next to him, surveying the beach and the water beyond. Hardly a sea, but the lake was indeed vast enough so she had to squint just to barely make out the opposite bank.

"*Our* kingdom?" she raised her eyebrows.

"Of course. What's mine is yours, My Flower." William took her hand and laced his fingers through hers. "I designed Whimser to my specifications for perfection, but it was missing something. With you here, my vision is complete."

"Lily, are there always so many trees?" Dylan called from the back of the group, swatting at a stray tree branch. "Lily!" he called again when she did not answer.

"What?" she answered, leaving William standing on the beach in time.

"Are we almost there? There's just, like, twelve too many trees for me."

"Yeah, the lake is just up ahead. The trees were here long before us and will be here after us." *This is their woods. We are just visitors.*

"Quite the poet," Tristan remarked with a glimmer in his eyes, walking up next to her.

She smiled softly at him, "I think Whitman would disagree with you."

The last sliver of the setting sun lingered over the lake when they arrived at the sand dunes above the water's edge. Reeds fanned out among the dunes as though they were growing through the sand. "All this sand actually looks like Hilton Head," Tessa noted.

"William, the man who built Whimser, his family immigrated from Ireland to South Carolina. That's where he grew up," Lilyanna explained numbly.

"So, he thought he'd bring it with him?" Barret retorted, stomping through the sand.

"I think I might have COVID-19. I can't smell the sea," Rich noted.

Lilyanna inclined her head and lifted her eyebrows. He was right in that the briny, salty scent of the sea was missing. "You don't have COVID. The lake doesn't smell like the ocean or sea."

"But that's one of the most important features," Tessa pointed out. "It should smell salty and delightfully damp, like yummy pirates."

Saharie laughed, "How many pirates have you seen that are yummy? I wouldn't even put the Disney ones in that category."

Indeed, Lake Whimser left wanting the olfactory gratification of a seaside village. In William's quest to construct his paradise, he failed to replicate every sensation induced by the natural wonders. A convincing knock-off, Whimser offered a deceptive delusion of a private coastal haven primed to serve as the setting of an Agatha Christie novel, but it didn't take Detective Hercule Poirot to spot the flaws.

Whimser's imperfections, however, did not detract from its beauty. The dark blue water at the shoreline faded to a light orange at the horizon in the distance. For that moment at least, nobody complained about anything. Even the end-of-winter wind stopped biting.

"So romantic," Waya said to Dylan. They shared a peck on the lips. Saharie broke away from Tie and went with the other women to feel the water.

"It's freezing!" Tessa confirmed after stopping to skim the surface with one hand.

"Yeah, it'll be a few weeks before it warms up," Lilyanna told them.

"I don't think that will matter much for me," Barret told Rich as they walked off on their own. "I can't swim."

"Really? Have you actually tried?" Rich slowed his pace to match Barret's lumber.

"Uh, I mean, in water that was over my head, not exactly."

"Well, I can teach you, if you want."

"Wow, that's really nice of you, but I wouldn't want to put you out."

"I don't mind. I was on the swim team in college."

"You must be really athletic, like an outdoorsman." Barret gazed at Rich in awe.

The other guys congregated several yards down the shore and discussed how they would adapt their workout routines with the lake and woods as a substitute for a gym. "Cardio starts tomorrow, then?" Tie asked Six, Andrew and Tristan.

Andrew groaned and threw a rock into the water, "Anything to distract me from the exercise I normally get at home and won't be getting here."

"Like what?" Tie asked in a knowing tone.

"Ummm . . ." Andrew started, and then genuinely laughed.

Six and Tristan chuckled as well. "Man, don't even bring that up. I haven't been away from my wife for more than a few days," Six replied.

"I hear ya," Andrew agreed. "I, like, have to look both ways down the hall before I dash to the bathroom in the morning. I'm afraid one of the ladies will see me and think I'm a complete perv."

Six and Tie burst out laughing. "So, you won't feel like a perv if one of us sees you with a massive boner?" Tie asked.

Andrew laughed slightly, "Well, you got the massive thing right."

"None of us will judge you when we're doing the same thing," Six said. "We need hand signals or something to say when it's safe to run down the hall."

"Not me!" Tie snorted. "I'm single, and there's a gorgeous woman in the house who is also single. Saharie is a goddess!"

"What about Lilyanna?" Six asked.

The other men hesitated. "What about her?" Tristan asked with indifference.

"Come on, you can't pretend the lady of the house isn't a looker. She's got a nice body, and she's smart too. So is Tessa," Tie added.

"Lily is young, and our co-worker," Andrew insisted.

Tie narrowed his eyes, "Tessa is nearly the same age, and also our co-worker."

"They're both off-limits for discussion, then," Andrew insisted.

"I don't think age matters. Lily clearly likes older men," Tie said.

"What are you talking about?" Andrew asked, brushing rocks with the heel of his boot.

"The guy she inherited this place from was old. I think he was, like, over sixty when he died," Tie explained.

"What guy?" Tristan asked.

"Did you guys really not look it up? I read online that the house and land belonged to a guy named

William Whimsergarden. He was a college professor and a writer. He died in a car wreck like seven years ago, and Lily got everything."

Andrew's eyes widened in surprise. "Wait, what? How did she know him?"

"I don't know. I just know Lily went to the college where he was a professor." The men didn't speak for several seconds.

"Uh, well, not touching that one," Six stated.

"Age is just a number, dude. Saharie is a little older than me, and that doesn't matter," Tie insisted.

"It might matter to her," Andrew noted. "I wouldn't get too cocky."

"For real, you have to actually convince Saharie to get with you," Six pointed out.

"Yeah, see ya in the hallway in the morning," Andrew laughed.

"If you get somewhere with her, my bet is it'll take a few weeks at least, just in time for the quarantine to end," Six taunted him.

"You don't know that the quarantine will end within a few weeks. We could be here for a long time, months even. And I'll be hooking up with her while you guys jack each other off when you pass in the hallway. *My* bet is, you won't be laughing then." Tristan, Andrew and Six exchanged glances in silence as the last rays of daylight faded beneath the horizon.

CHAPTER SIX
Pandemania

When the downstairs lights went off for the night and the guests settled into their rooms, Lilyanna finally relaxed on her bed upstairs. It was the only time of day she didn't feel she had to be 'on,' trying to play the proper hostess and stressing about how she and the house appeared to her co-workers. She looked forward to the couple of nighttime hours she could spend alone with her best friends.

"Saharie, will you curl my hair?" Tessa asked, sitting at the vanity table and brushing her hair.

"Sure, plug in my curling iron."

Kyah stretched out on her bed, scrolling through her Instagram feed. "So, Saharie, you seemed cozy with Tie tonight."

"Yeah, what was that about?" Tessa asked.

Saharie shrugged, grabbed the hairbrush from Tessa and began sectioning off her hair. "I mean, he's kinda sweet."

"And he's a babe—tall and cute," Kyah added. "I'm so happy you're into him! Go for it!"

"Hold up, I'm not, like, dating the guy. He's young, and I don't know him yet. We'll see."

"Please just bang him and relieve the sexual frustration in this house!" Kyah begged.

"I think that's just you," Tessa laughed.

Kyah ignored her. "And Lily, why are you not all over Tristan? I was looking at him tonight, and he is head-to-toe gorgeous. He's muscly but not too built, and you can't tell me you haven't noticed his ass! It's, like, full and plush."

"I don't look at him that way," Lily lied casually, glad that she had kept secret the shirtless encounter. She'd never hear the end of it.

"Youth and beauty are wasted on the prude," Kyah huffed.

"You are young and beautiful, and you're married!" Tessa reminded her.

"Marriage doesn't automatically render a person blind or asexual," Kyah replied.

"Kyah, you're the only one of us in the exclusive wives' club," Lilyanna pointed out. "I don't know why you'd want to live through us."

"Seriously!" Tessa agreed. "There's something special about married women. Like, their desirability persuaded a guy to do something so contrary to his nature—go out of his way to buy a ring and make a legal commitment to one woman."

Kyah shook her head, "Giving men that much power is the reason your relationships fail. Hubs persuaded me to relinquish my single status. You have to quit surrendering that much power to the male ego."

"Lily, I worry about that for you with Tristan," Saharie interjected, rolling a strand of Tessa's hair around the curling rod. "He seems a bit egotistical. I could see him being one of those guys who never bought his wife flowers. Like he thinks 'I'm hot and rich, so you should be grateful to be with me without me putting in any effort.'"

"I don't think so," Tessa replied. "Guys like that are actually insecure, and Tristan is definitely not."

"Everybody is insecure, men and women," Kyah corrected her.

"He's also a big guy," Saharie continued, "maybe too big for you."

Kyah sat up and tossed a pillow at Saharie. "Don't say that! You'll make her question herself."

"Too late for that," Lilyanna sighed. "It was self-doubt at first sight."

Kyah burst out laughing, "No, no! He's exactly your type, Lily, physically and otherwise. You would be a beautiful couple! And you've always had a thing for British guys."

"I just think there's a chance he might break you in half," Saharie warned.

"Yes, please!" Kyah insisted.

"Uh, I don't see how that's a good thing, Ky! I never understood that saying anyway. Like, who says, 'Oh, I hope I get broken in half tonight'?"

Kyah replied, "You don't know what you're missing. Now, I'll be in the upstairs den having Zoom sex with Hubs. Do not disturb!" She grabbed her laptop and jetted off.

"What is Zoom sex?" Tessa asked.

"The future for singles," Saharie remarked in dismay.

The women were all in REM sleep at two a.m. when a clamor echoed from downstairs, waking them all. Lilyanna sat up with a start at the sound of several consecutive banging noises. Before she could collect her thoughts, a voice called from the bedroom doorway.

"Lily! Lily, it's Sylvie. Someone or something is trying to get into the house from the front door. People are waking up downstairs."

"Whyyyyyy?" Saharie groaned in a low, half-awake tone.

"I'm coming, Sylvie. Thanks for waking me." Lilyanna jumped out of bed and put on the first bra she could find in the dark with her powder blue silk mini robe over it. She tied her robe closed as she hurried down the front staircase without waiting for the others.

Andrew, Rich and Tie were gathered in the front hall, wearing gym shorts and t-shirts and shouting at each other in confusion. Tristan joined the group just as Lilyanna reached the ground floor, and Jillian and Alyra peeked around from behind the stairs. Joe, Six and Barret were the last to arrive. Joe wore a brown cotton bathrobe, while Barret wore green and black flannel pajamas.

"Nice jammies, Barret," Tie smirked.

"What the hell is going on?" Lilyanna cried, rushing to the front door, suddenly conscious of her lack of makeup.

Tristan stepped briskly up next to her, shirtless and wearing black gym shorts. "There's someone at the door." He stopped at the sight of Lilyanna in nothing but a short satin robe. Andrew also gazed at her in surprise before tearing his eyes away. Self-consciously, she tied her gown more tightly around her and pulled as much hair as possible in front of her natural face. The banging on the door continued more aggressively.

"Who is it?" Andrew called. No response.

"You won't be able to hear if someone answers. The door was designed to limit outside noise."

"Then why were we woken up to the sound of someone banging it down?" Joe asked, lighting a cigarette.

"Lily, what's happening?" Tessa called from the top of the staircase. "Should we come down?"

"No, just stay up there!" Lilyanna replied, turning to Andrew and Tristan, who were closest to the door. "We need to open it. It could be a neighbor or someone needing help."

"Uh, it could also be a robber or a murderer, or the zombie apocalypse," Tie pointed out.

"Hello, or COVID-19!" Barret exclaimed.

"Let's invite it in for a drink," Joe said, taking a slow drag from his cigarette.

"You're not at all concerned?" Barret asked.

"Sure I am. I'm a smoker in the midst of the spread of a highly contagious virus that destroys people's lungs." Joe exhaled a puff of smoke.

"You're not supposed to smoke in the house, Joe!" Alyra called through the hall.

"Everybody shut up!" Lilyanna cried. "I'm opening the door." She attempted to brush past Andrew to reach the lock on the front door, but Tristan stepped in front of her to block her way.

"Absolutely not! Go back upstairs and let us handle this," he demanded in his irresistible British accent.

"Since you've clearly got it under control? Fuck no! I'm responsible for this house!" she hissed.

Tristan exhaled and narrowed his eyes in frustration at Lilyanna. Despite the intensity of his stare, she held her ground and maintained eye contact.

"Alright, fine, I'll answer the door," Andrew offered. "Everyone get back."

"Put on a mask, Andrew!" Alyra yelled. "The CDC said to start wearing masks when you're around people you don't live with."

"That's not what the World Health Organization said," Joe stated flatly.

"Go with the CDC!" Jillian affirmed.

Six sighed, "The CDC changed course."

"We don't have any masks anyway," Barret shouted.

"I saw a Youtube video where people made masks out of underwear," Tie added.

Sylvie ran in from the laundry room carrying a hand towel. "Here, use this." She tossed the towel to Andrew.

"Thank you." He tied the towel around his nose and mouth and stepped up to the front door. "Stay behind the door," he told Tristan. "Rich and Six, be ready on the other side of the hall."

"We got your back, man," Rich assured him. They stood to the left of the door where a potential intruder couldn't see them. Tie stood at the base of the stairs as if standing guard, while Barret shuffled behind the stairs.

"Do we have a baseball bat or something?" Kyah shouted from upstairs.

"I'm getting the curling iron," Saharie replied.

Tristan grabbed Lilyanna's arm and pulled her next to the front wall, behind where the door would open. "Get behind the door."

Her heart pounded in her chest as he pressed her into the space between the wall and himself. *What if she was wrong to open the door? Was she endangering the whole house?*

"Here we go," Andrew said with a deep breath. Lilyanna automatically grabbed Tristan's arm. In response, he put his arm around her waist and pulled her close against his side. Resting against the side of his bare chest, every nerve in her body pulsed as vigorously as her pounding heart.

With a turn of the dead bolt, Andrew partially inched the door open. "Who's there?" his deep voice boomed through his makeshift mask.

"It's us!" Dylan's voice shook. "Or what's left of us after freezing our balls off out here!"

"What?" Andrew opened the door the rest of way, and Dylan and Waya pushed into the house. Tristan pulled Lilyanna out from behind the door.

"Are you shittin' me with this?" Joe grumbled. Andrew yanked the towel off his face and threw it on the floor. Barret emerged from behind the stairs, and Rich and Six relaxed their ready-to-pounce stances.

"What are you doing?" Lilyanna shouted at them. "You woke up the whole house!"

"I'm sorry! But the Wi-Fi went out in the guesthouse, and we can't get cell service out there without Wi-Fi for Wi-Fi calling. I couldn't call or text you!"

"You almost gave us all heart attacks because of Wi-Fi? We thought someone was trying to break in!"

"Who breaks into an occupied mansion by banging on the front door?" Waya retorted. "If anyone was at risk, it was us! No cell service out there alone, and then waiting on the porch in the cold for an eternity because you wouldn't open the door!"

Tristan sighed and held up his hands, "Alright, steady on, let's all call it a night."

Lilyanna nodded, "I understand not wanting to

sleep out there without cell service, so just stay here in the house tonight until we can fix the issue tomorrow. There's a second bedroom upstairs that I had reserved in case anyone gets sick. You can sleep in there tonight."

"Perfect, lead the way," Dylan held out his hand for Lilyanna to pass. "Oh, I like this." He tugged on the sleeve of her robe. "I'm sleeping in your bed," he teased.

"Everyone go back to bed," Tristan ordered sharply.

Tie led the way down the corridor to the men's bedrooms. "Samuel L. Jackson said 'Go the fuck to sleep.'"

Lilyanna showed Dylan and Waya to the extra upstairs bedroom with one queen-sized bed, and then went back to her own bed, her heart still pounding and her mind on Tristan.

The next morning, Lilyanna inspected the router and wiring in the guesthouse with Andrew, Barret and Bix. "We can't reset the main router in the house a third time. It kicks everyone off the Wi-Fi, and people are trying to work," Lilyanna said as she held a flashlight over the router box for Barret and Andrew.

"That won't do any good anyway. I think AT&T installed the wrong router," Andrew concluded, replugging the connecting wire into the secondary router box on the wall of the kitchenette.

"There's a shocker," Barret retorted.

"Bix, when can AT&T send someone to fix this?" Lilyanna asked.

Bix stood in the entryway with a cordless phone to his ear, tapping his foot on the hardwood floor. "Agent, representative. No, I do not speak Spanish!

Are you a person? Agent, immediately!" he growled into the phone. "I'm still on hold, Mistress Rivers."

"Of course you are. Dealing with cable companies is on par with airline disputes on my annoyance scale. They can't even use COVID as an excuse since their service was just as bad before." After another twenty minutes of waiting on hold followed by useless troubleshooting techniques, the group returned to the main house in defeat.

"What's the verdict?" Joe asked as he poured coffee into his mug in the kitchen. The other guests crowded around the kitchen island and table, finishing breakfast.

"AT&T doesn't want to send someone out because of COVID. They're going to try some troubleshooting techniques on their end that could take a full day to work," Lilyanna replied.

"In the meantime, I think we'll be staying in the extra room upstairs," Dylan confirmed.

"I'll move into the guesthouse!" Tie offered. "My phone gets service without Wi-Fi."

Joe almost spit out his coffee. "Like hell! Did you already forget our conversation about your place in the hierarchy? You're the last person on the list for the guesthouse."

"Then how about two of us share it?" Andrew suggested. "Tristan and I can move out there, and then, Joe, you'll have your own room."

"Are you going to share the one bed in the guesthouse?" Lilyanna replied coolly.

Andrew paused, "Oh. Never mind."

"You seemed open to sharing a shower, so I wasn't sure," Lilyanna whispered loudly enough for only Tristan and Andrew to hear and then reached around

Tristan to grab a coffee cup from the kitchen island. Tristan laughed softly and nodded in tacit acceptance. "Nobody is moving into the guesthouse right now," she announced. "I want to keep a space open in case someone gets sick and needs a place to quarantine."

"We defer to the lady of the house," Joe lifted his coffee mug in her direction.

***

By the end of the workday on Friday, the guests sprawled out on every lounge surface and the floor of the den to watch the evening news. "COVID-19 cases continue to rise nationwide," the reporter announced. "Hospitals are nearing capacity in many Texas cities. The president continues to insist the virus is under control."

"I think his teleprompter is broken. He said the same thing the past five days," Tie sighed.

"Is it possible to be bored, stressed and exhausted at the same time?" Saharie asked from one of the sofas, her head on a pillow on Tessa's lap.

"It's pandemic fatigue, dear," Jillian explained.

"It's pandemania," Barret clarified.

"We've got the best drug for that right here!" Dylan smiled, strutting into the den followed by Waya, their arms filled with unopened bottles of Grey Goose vodka, whiskey and champagne. "Come on, bitches, it's Friday night, and we have a ton of alcohol! We survived our first week of playing house together, and the world could be ending any day now. Let's rage!"

Within minutes, drinks were flowing all around. Sylvie, Nina and even Ms. Howard joined the party, carrying in flutes and vodka glasses from the kitchen. Waya switched off the TV and connected his iPhone to the living room TV. *Blinding Lights* by The Weeknd blared throughout the ground floor as Dylan popped a bottle of champagne.

"Woo, the first good idea I've heard in lockdown!" Kyah grabbed a champagne bottle and began filling more glasses. Andrew, Rich, Joe and Six went for the whiskey, and Tristan found a bottle of scotch in the kitchen.

"Fuck COVID-19!" Dylan toasted once everyone had a drink. They all raised their glasses and clinked them together.

As the group downed glass number one of the evening, Dylan pulled out a plastic bag full of marijuana from his pocket. "Anyone up for some other party favors?"

"You smuggled that in here?" Tessa asked incredulously.

"No, I just put it my bag. I wasn't getting on a plane, so I didn't think I had to shove it up my ass."

"Dylan, you can't have weed here!" Lilyanna cried. "I draw the line at illegal drugs."

"She means you can't have weed here unless you share!" Kyah corrected her.

"Yeah, dude, you've been holding out on us," Barret chided him, grabbing the bag from his hand.

"I'm sure it's medicinal, Lily. It'll be legal soon anyway. Roll the herbal remedies!" Alyra ordered.

"The great and powerful HR has spoken!" Six boomed. "Lily, you need this more than anyone."

"What? No, I'm fine."

"No, like, really, he's right. You need to chilll," Kyah told her.

The bottles emptied steadily, and a dense cloud of marijuana smoke formed over the ground floor as joints circulated. Lilyanna sat on a sofa in the den with Andrew, Tessa, Rich and Barret. Andrew took two hits of a joint and then passed it to Lilyanna.

"I don't smoke."

"Neither do I," he replied. Reluctantly, she accepted the joint and took a hit.

The 'herbal remedies' worked quickly on Lilyanna. Ever the lightweight, two drinks and a few puffs later, the room melted into one of William's impressionistic paintings. Lilyanna left her spot on the sofa and meandered around the adjacent rooms in her substance-induced fog. She passed Alyra, Joe, Six and Jillian laughing hysterically on the corner of the sectional in the living room. In the dining room, Kyah, Saharie, Sylvie, Nina and Tie played a game of beer pong.

The absence of one guest in particular drew Lilyanna to the front hall, where the front door stood open. She found Tristan casually hunched over the edge of the terrace sipping from a glass of dark liquor. He was back in his fitted jeans and a navy sweater. Lilyanna recalled Kyah's comments about his perfectly rounded ass. She wasn't wrong. "You're missing the party," she said as she stepped onto the front porch a few feet away from him.

"Am I?" He turned his head toward her in amusement. "Appears you are enjoying the evening. Did it take two whole drinks to make you tipsy?" he teased.

"Ummm, I'm not tipsy. I'm just fine, and I was at least on my third drink. I just don't know where I set it down." She realized she no longer had a glass in her hand.

He laughed lightly and slid closer to her. "Here, try this." He handed her his half-empty glass.

With conviction, she looked straight into his shining blue eyes and took the glass. One deep sip later, she scrunched up her face while trying not to choke. "Wow, that's strong," she coughed.

He took the glass with a smirk. "It's scotch."

"I know," she lowered her gaze at him.

"So, now that you have shared a drink with me, I assume you're comfortable with being closer than six feet?" he asked.

"I was already comfortable with that. We've been living in the same house for a week."

"True, just didn't want to be presumptuous." He closed the remaining gap between them, and they both gazed at the woods in the distance. "Since we're so close now, are you ready to tell me the real story of how you came to own this place?"

She rolled her eyes and sighed, "It's not a secret. I inherited the property from a man named William Whimsergarden."

"And how did you know him?" He offered her the scotch glass again.

"I think you already know the answer to that." She took another drink, more gracefully this time. "It's either in my personnel file, or you looked it up, or heard from someone else who looked it up."

"I'd much rather hear it from you." He reached for the glass, but she pulled it away from his grasp.

"Fine," she sipped his scotch. "He was a writer and my professor in college. That's how we met. I became his student assistant and helped him with editing his novels and reviewing other authors' work. William had no living family. He passed away the summer after I graduated from college and left the estate to me."

"He thought of you as family, then?"

She hesitated, "I don't know what he thought. But he was the closest thing to family I had nearby. My parents died when I was a teenager, and my only brother lives in DC."

"I'm sorry about your family, and him."

Lilyanna shrugged, "That's life I guess, or death, actually."

"How did he die?"

"Car accident. He was driving on the winding road down from Whimser during a storm, and the car went over the ravine. There were no guardrails at the time."

"Did you ever consider selling the property and putting the proceeds toward a home in Austin?"

"Of course I did. But I couldn't do it. William loved this house and would've wanted me to protect Whimser." Lilyanna never used any of the money in William's estate to fund her own living expenses. She maintained a simple yet comfortable lifestyle to afford the cost of living in Austin and paid back her law school debt in the first few years of her law practice with her associate attorney salary. She was tempted to tap into the estate's funds a few times during her education, but she didn't want to risk casting Whimser into financial hardship.

"Maybe he intended for you to sell it and start over."

"I don't think so. William had no trouble expressing himself, in writing or otherwise. He wrote down everything, and he wore his emotions on his sleeves. If he had been concerned for me, he would have left a note or instructions, or something. He knew his age and the consequences of having no familial heirs. He went to the trouble of changing his estate plan and setting everything up with his attorney to name me as his beneficiary, but he made no effort to even write me a letter. He provided only for the handling of the property he created, per the terms of a trust. I think William thought himself immortal, and there would never come a time where he couldn't have the last word."

"It's yours now."

"No, Whimser is not mine. It will always belong to someone else." High-pitched laughter echoed from inside the den. "Speaking of, I should make sure it's not being destroyed from within."

Tristan nodded, "Allow me to accompany you."

Lilyanna's throat burned from the scotch. Neither her brain nor her liver welcomed the additional doses of alcohol in their already inebriated state. She paused in the front hall to steady her balance.

"Are you alright?" Tristan asked, sliding his arm around her waist. She nodded in embarrassment as he guided her through the hazy scene. The beer pong game in the dining room had broken up, and Saharie sat on Tie's lap, making out with him.

In the living room, Jillian and Six sat on a sofa engrossed in conversation in low voices while Joe sprawled across the sectional in his undershirt and a cowboy hat with a cigarette hanging from his mouth.

Tristan and Lilyanna sat down on a sofa with the remaining group in the den. "There you are, man," Andrew greeted Tristan. He held out a lit joint to Tristan. To Lilyanna's surprise, Tristan took it. With a cool smile in his eyes, he raised it to his lips and inhaled.

Help us all if he ever gets hired to advertise for a tobacco company. Viewers would be sprinting to the nearest convenience store for a pack of cigarettes after watching him light up.

"Hello, lovelies!" a high-pitched voice interrupted her thoughts. Waya model-walked into the den next to Dylan, wearing six-inch platform heels with his t-shirt and shorts and sporting a platinum blonde wig. Saharie, Tie and Kyah followed behind them clapping and cheering for Waya's performance. He gave a high kick and slid down into a right split.

"Work, bitch!" Dylan yelled.

"I'm not watching this," Rich huffed. "I'm going to bed." He got up from the sofa and stomped out of the room.

Couples began partnering up and dancing to the hip-hop playlist booming from the TV speakers. Saharie and Tie danced next to Waya and Dylan, while Andrew and Tessa partnered up, as did Six and Kyah.

"How about it?" Barret asked Lilyanna.

"Thought you'd never ask!" Knowing Tristan wouldn't show any initiative, she grabbed Barret's hand without looking at Tristan. Maybe it was the alcohol and weed, but for the first time since quarantine started, all of Lilyanna's self-consciousness disappeared. Barret twirled her around and always caught her right before debilitating dizziness knocked her over.

"Thanks for keeping me on my feet," she shouted to him over the music.

"That's what friends do."

"My turn with Lily!" Dylan cut in. Waya twirled into Lilyanna's place to dance next to Barret.

"You're so gorge!" Dylan grabbed her waist and grinded up next to her.

She laughed and flung her untamed hair out of her face, suddenly feeling younger and unburdened. Thus far, Dylan had been right about the cure for pandemania—you could drink it away, smoke it away, or party it away. You could probably fuck away some of the stress, but the latter remedy remained untested to date. Nobody could judge her when they were equally intoxicated. Well, almost nobody. Out of the corner of her eye, she spotted Bix peering in from the doorway of the den, his expression full of disdain.

Lilyanna stopped dancing and strode to the doorway to confront him for lurking around. But when she reached the doorway, he was gone. The hall was empty as well, reverberating the noise from the adjacent rooms but producing none of its own. Despite the vacant hall, she could not shake the feeling of watchful eyes upon her. *Bix knows Whimser better than anyone. He's probably watching from some hidden nook.* She almost hoped it was Bix watching because the alternative was far more troublesome. If it wasn't Bix watching, there was only one other person with a pathological obsession with the goings-on at Whimser—the master architect himself, William Whimsergarden.

William cannot be here. He is dead and buried. The only ghost at Whimser is Jarvis Bixton, and living ghosts are to be pitied, not feared. Resenting herself for falling for Bix's ruse, Lilyanna returned to the party.

The dancing had continued in her absence, though a few people took a break. Six, Barret and Kyah gathered in the kitchen to snack on chips and cookies. Meanwhile, Andrew lay on his stomach on the sectional with his shirt pulled up while Tessa knelt beside him on the floor, drawing a monarch butterfly on his lower back with Saharie's waterproof eyeliner.

The debauchery lasted until sometime in the early morning hours when the guests gradually stumbled to their beds. However, not everyone made it to his or her own rooms. Andrew and Barret passed out on either side of the sectional in the living room, and Dylan and Waya slept in the den. Her eyes barely open, Lilyanna ambled to the front door to make sure it was locked before making her way to the front staircase to go to bed.

"Finally retiring for the night, Mistress Rivers?" Goose bumps formed on Lilyanna's skin at the sound of Bix's slow, chilling elocution. He stood between her and the staircase.

"I thought you had gone to your cottage for the night," she replied stiffly.

"I thought it my duty to make sure the house, and guests, remain intact, given this evening's soiree."

"The house is fine. Everyone is fine. I'm going to bed, excuse me."

But he continued his patronizing monologue without moving out of her way. "I would have expected you to refrain from excessive alcohol consumption in the house, but I suppose I shouldn't expect so much from—"

"What is that supposed to mean?" she rounded on him.

"Only that there are consequences to over-indulgence," he replied nonchalantly.

"How dare you!" she asserted fiercely, pushing past him and pausing on the first step of the staircase. "I'm not responsible for William driving that night!"

Her mind flashed to a rainy summer evening at Whimser seven years ago. She and William drained the last few drops of Sauvignon Blanc from their wine glasses while sitting at a table on the terrace, eating raspberry macarons and laughing about a manuscript they had both just reviewed.

"What was that ending?" he cried. "No resolution, no drama, the heroine just left, an aloof French exit with no closure!"

"So what?" she burst out. "There doesn't have to be a dramatic finale! People don't always get closure—that's life! Endings are not natural anyway."

"You're acquiescent!"

"You're drunk! I'm going to lie down, and you should do the same. We need to sleep it off." She stood up with both their wine glasses in hand and carried them inside.

He staggered behind her toward the front door, "Fine, I'll be up in a minute."

Bix's accusatory tone snapped her back to real time. "Precisely, Mistress Rivers, you didn't do anything when Mr. Whimsergarden drove during a storm after drinking wine with you all evening. You of all people know what can happen when residents of Whimser don't have their wits about them."

"Is that a threat?" She stepped back down off the staircase and glared up at Bix.

"Not at all, merely a reminder that what you sow today, you reap tomorrow."

CHAPTER SEVEN
Socially Distant

Joe groggily rummaged through his suitcase, where he still kept the majority of his clothing, until he found a metal pocket-sized container. He sat on the edge of his bed and opened his prized box full of white powder. With shaky hands, he carefully spooned cocaine into each nostril and returned the box to his suitcase. He stood up, inhaled deeply and stretched his arms over his head, ready to begin his day with a surge of artificial energy.

***

"Where's the aspirin?" Barret asked, lumbering around the kitchen and opening cabinets and drawers a little after ten o'clock in the morning.

"Here, pass this around," Tessa handed him a bottle of generic painkiller from a cupboard above the stove.

"Remind me to order more," Lilyanna instructed while she trudged around the kitchen tossing empty bottles into a trash bag with help from Dylan and Waya.

"Can everyone please lower your voices? My brain is rattling inside my skull," Saharie droned. She sat at the kitchen table next to Tie, her legs propped up on Tie's lap.

"Have we made sure everyone's alive? Where's Kyah?" Tie asked.

"Still sleeping," Saharie yawned.

"How do you know if it's a hangover or the start of COVID-19? COVID symptoms can be minor at first and then turn fatal," Barret pointed out.

"If one of us stops breathing, we'll know," Six replied. The residents exchanged nervous glances, knowing the insidious disease could be right there in the room with them, poised to claim more victims.

After cleaning up the kitchen, Lilyanna headed for the front staircase, where a desperate voice intercepted her. "Lily! Psst Lily, please come here!" Andrew called to her in a hushed whisper from the doorway to the men's hall. He was once again shirtless and wearing a pair of navy gym shorts.

Perplexed, she looked around to make sure she was alone and then hurried down the men's hall. "What is it?"

"Come in here!" He grabbed her arm and pulled her into one of the bathrooms behind him and shut the door.

"What are you doing?" she hissed, keeping her eyes on his and not his half-naked body.

"Lily, you have to help me! I can't get this thing off! I've showered twice, and it won't come off." He turned around to display the perfectly intact image of a monarch butterfly on his lower back, its wings outlined in thick black and bedazzled with glittery blue and violet eyeliner.

Her self-consciousness fading, she fought back laughter. "Nice tramp stamp. I hear morning-after regrets are common with tattoos. Make sure not to gain too much weight, or it will stretch." She turned toward the door and reached for the handle, but he pulled her back.

"No, no, please, don't go! Help me take it off! What if my wife were to see it on a Zoom call?"

"Do you usually put your back to the camera on a Zoom call?"

He put his hand over his forehead and squeezed his eyes shut. "Please, Lily."

"Okay, okay, relax. You just need some heavy makeup remover. We have that upstairs. Ummm, okay, give me a minute's head start and then come up the back stairs after me. Nobody is up there except Kyah, and she's asleep."

"Good, great, thank you!" he nodded, trying to calm down.

Minutes later, Lilyanna locked the door of the upstairs master bathroom behind Andrew. "This stuff is essentially paint thinner that is safe for skin." She poured a generous amount of makeup remover onto a facial cloth. "Can you just, uh, lean forward a little, please?" She gently pressed on his lower back, internally begging her face not to blush.

He leaned forward over the bathroom countertop. "Is that better?"

"Yeah, thanks. Tessa is quite the artist. I almost hate to defile her work." Lilyanna firmly rubbed his lower back with the cloth, trying not to think about the fact she was toweling off the commercial director, who also happened to be her most important internal client, and a tall, fit, absurdly handsome guy.

"I think I was the one defiled!" Andrew huffed.

"You seemed willing enough last night."

"God, Lily, don't remind me. I acted like a frat boy, and I'm sorry."

"Don't be sorry. We all got carried away." She soaked the cloth with more makeup remover and continued scrubbing. "It's almost off."

"I'm sure the guy who left you this house would be thrilled to see what we are doing to it."

She stopped scrubbing and looked up at Andrew's face in the mirror. "Why would you say that?"

His brow lines creased in sudden concern. "Oh, I just meant that I felt guilty for being careless last night. I didn't mean anything negative."

She shook her head and resumed her project. "Of course not, sorry."

"So, who was he? The guy who left you the property."

"William Whimsergarden."

"Was he, like, your boyfriend?"

"What? No! He was a professor and fiction writer, and I assisted with some of his editing, that's all." Lilyanna ran the cloth under hot water in the sink and then rubbed down Andrew's lower back again.

"Sorry, I didn't mean to pry. I was just curious."

"Okay, it's off. Take a look."

Andrew turned away from the mirror and looked over his shoulder at the reflection of his bare lower back. "Yesss! Thank you so much, Lily. You never disappoint." Without any hesitation, he rested his hand on her shoulder.

She didn't want to like his touch, but it was unavoidable. There was something so reassuring in the way he moved and the way he spoke, so confident, leaving no margin for doubting him. "My pleasure," she nodded awkwardly. "You should go downstairs before you draw questions." She pulled away from him and left the bathroom.

***

The guests succumbed to lethargy through mid-day. Lilyanna lounged at the end of her bed reading a guidebook on Dubrovnik, Croatia. "Saharie, look at this. The second restaurant listed on page twelve is where I made dinner reservations for our second night in Dubrovnik," Lilyanna said, holding out the guide.

Saharie didn't take the book. Instead, she continued applying her eyeliner in the vanity mirror. "Lily," she sighed, "I think you need to start preparing yourself for the fact that our trip is going to be canceled."

Lilyanna threw the book on the floor in frustration. "You don't know that! The airline hasn't canceled our flight." Saharie didn't flinch as the book sailed to her feet.

"I think she's right, Lily," Tessa agreed, sitting cross-legged on the edge of her bed in front of her laptop screen. "Europe is in a complete lockdown. Even if restrictions ease by this summer, I doubt they will welcome foreigners that soon, except celebrities of course."

"Let me guess, you chose Dubrovnik because you want to do the *Game of Thrones* tour," Dylan said without looking up from his phone as he sprawled out on the king-sized bed next to Kyah.

"That is definitely one factor, but not the whole reason. Dubrovnik looks like my dream vacation

CHAPTER SEVEN: Socially Distant

spot—European beaches, medieval old town, and, yes, the official *Game of Thrones* tour," she explained.

"I'm just saying your dream vacation may be delayed," Tessa clarified.

"Don't go there! Travel is the highlight of my year." Lilyanna lived for trips to Europe every year. She constantly craved the eudaimonia that only a vacation overseas could provide. Without a family, her lifestyle depended on mobility. She had no husband or children, but the trade-off was that she could pick up and go anywhere she wanted to the extent of her PTO days. COVID-19 now threatened that lifestyle, like everything else.

"Mine too, but it's out of our hands," Saharie sighed.

"Anyhoo," Tessa changed the subject. "Lily, do you want a pair of these Athleta pants? I get free shipping if I order two pairs." Tessa handed Lilyanna her laptop.

"Oh yes, these joggers are cute. They look like they come with a built-in quarantine hug in all the right places without the threat of fatal illness. I'll take the black ones and Venmo you, thanks." She handed the laptop back to Tessa.

Saharie smirked, "You should do their marketing, Lily."

"You all need to quit ordering leggings and order something sexy for the man candy downstairs," Dylan interjected.

"Okay, I'm on it." Waya smiled from his pallet on the floor.

"Uh, have you seen what retailers are putting out right now?" Lilyanna asked. "Their idea of adapting to the pandemic is offering some hybrid of athleisure wear and extremely casual business casual clothes as work-from-home wardrobing. There's nothing sexy about the WFH outfits they're marketing. Like, are they trying to encourage social distancing by making people look ugly AF so nobody comes near them?"

Dylan and Waya laughed. "If you see something that says 'comfortable,' don't buy it!" Dylan instructed. "Lily and Tessa, you're both hot and single, why are you not going for it? Just put on some short shorts and go walk around downstairs. And maybe never wear that shirt again, Tessa."

"This is sustainable!" Tessa cried defensively, looking down at her coral-colored crewneck t-shirt.

Dylan scrunched up his face. "Why would you want to sustain it?"

"By the way, I'm single too!" Saharie exclaimed.

"And I'm seeing someone, sort of, sometimes," Tessa huffed.

"Nah, that Tyson guy is so hard for you, Saharie, I don't know how he can move. And you two are super cute together, so I have to refuse to let you be on the market," Waya explained. "Tessa, I don't know what guy you are seeing sometimes, but it's not that serious if you haven't mentioned him until now. He's a douche if he hasn't locked you down."

"I've been saying the same thing to Lily and Tessa since day one! Seriously, what is wrong with you two?" Kyah added.

"What do you expect from us?" Tessa exploded, snapping her laptop closed. "Most of the guys are married, and the ones that are single are not exactly chasing after us. You know Lily and I are not forward. We both internalized the He's-Just-Not-That-Into-You mantra when we were teenagers. If a guy wants you, he will come to you. Aside from Dylan and Waya, no guys are beating down the door of our bedroom."

"Touché!" Lilyanna approved. "We're not the kind of women guys want."

"Exactly," Tessa nodded.

"What is it you think straight men want that you're not?" Dylan asked.

"Like, free spirits, for one," Lilyanna mused.

"What do you consider 'free spirits?'" Dylan asked.

"I think they shop at Urban Outfitters," Saharie noted.

Everyone burst out laughing. "Then be glad you're not a free spirit!" Dylan smirked.

Lilyanna inhaled deeply, "I just think guys like women who are carefree and spontaneous. I've never been those things."

"Yeah, we're too uptight and type A, and we have stressful jobs. We're not wifey or mistress material," Tessa agreed. "You need not apply if your mouth is bigger than your tits, at least in this part of the country."

Kyah rolled her eyes. "Quit feeling sorry for yourselves. Do you know how many women would kill to be thin and have pretty faces like yours? You'd make a fortune on OnlyFans."

"Yass, one of you please do OnlyFans!" Waya clapped.

"Just put on some sexy lingerie, I'll take the pictures and promote your accounts, and we'll share the profits. Come on, it'll be our quarantine side hustle, and we'll all get rich!" Kyah pressed.

"Yeah okay, sure," Lilyanna replied flatly.

"I'm serious! You'd make money, Lily. It's all about looks. They won't know about your mental state."

Lilyanna's eyes widened at the dig, "Wow, thanks for clarifying that."

"Just focus on the part where she said you're pretty," Dylan suggested.

But Lilyanna didn't feel pretty. She could count on a couple of fingers the times in her life she'd genuinely felt pretty, and not one of those times occurred since she started her career. She appreciated the compliment from her friends. A woman should be pretty to her best friends, even if the mirror doesn't share their affectionate bias. Mirrors only display the reviews of the harshest critic.

***

Sunday afternoon, all of the guests gathered in the living room on Alyra's orders. "Self-defense!" she began. "A topic we've neglected but that is worthy of our time and attention, according to upper management."

"Are we preparing for the zombie apocalypse?" Barret asked.

She ignored him. "Given the, uh, break-in scare the other night, and concerns about looting in the event conditions deteriorate further during lockdown, upper management has decided we need a company-wide initiative on basic self-defense."

"We all need to take this seriously," Jillian agreed. "If there is ever a real break-in, we need to be prepared."

"Are we going to have safe words or something?" Tie asked from his spot on the floor in front of one of the sofas. The room fell silent.

"What does a safe word have to do with anything?" Kyah asked.

"Like if one of us is knocking on the door, they have to say the safe word that only the people in the house know so we'll know it's really them and open the door," Tie explained.

"You mean a code word?" Rich said slowly.

"Yeah, a safe word."

"A safe word and a code word are two different things," Dylan told him. "A safe word is like when Waya and I are—"

"Okay, I think we can move on," Lilyanna cut him off.

"Perhaps Sarah-hee can show him the difference," Joe drawled.

"Her name is Sa-*har*-ie," Lilyanna enunciated each syllable.

Barret sighed, "Alyra, it's still the weekend. Can't we just have the day off?"

"You, sir, just volunteered for our first demonstration. You think I like spending my Sunday showing you how to not get your ass kicked? I have orders from President Marks, so you have orders from me! Get up here and learn something so I can go binge-watch a TV show that makes me forget I'm here."

Reluctantly, Barret pushed himself off the sofa and ambled over to Alyra. "Ah, fine." He cracked his neck to one side and rolled his shoulder back. "Who am I body slamming?"

"Actually, Tessa is a red belt in taekwondo and has agreed to teach us some moves. Tessa, you have the floor." Alyra sat down in an armchair next to Joe as Tessa joined Barret in the center of the room.

"Wow, I didn't know that, Tessa," Andrew remarked, impressed.

"Woo, go Tessa!" Kyah cheered.

"Maybe Barret should choose a safe word," Lilyanna smirked. Tristan and Andrew stifled a laugh on either side of her.

Tessa ignored them. "To start, Barret will be the assailant. Come at me, Barret." She faced him and beckoned for him to approach her.

"Okay, so just, like, try to grab you?" Hesitantly, he stepped toward her and reached for her arm. Before he could make contact, Tessa stepped to the side, shoved his arms down and then gave his hip a forceful nudge with her foot. Barret went tumbling to the ground on his side.

"Oh, shit!" Six covered his mouth.

"Now, when your assailant starts to get up from the ground," Tessa continued, reaching down and grabbing Barret's shirt.

"Wait, no, no! I didn't attack you!" Barret cried. But Tessa paid no heed to his pleas. Despite being twice her weight, Barret was no match for Tessa's technique and body control. He never remained on his feet for more than a few seconds before Tessa pitched him off balance.

"She's a *beast!*" Tie roared. "Someone get her a chair."

"No, don't do that!" Barret cried as he went sprawling across the floor again. "Okay, okay, I tap out," he wheezed.

"Great job, Tessa!" Alyra clapped and stood up next to her. Barret still lay on the ground trying to catch his breath. "Now, I think we should all break into pairs or small groups to practice. Ladies, I suggest you practice with a guy."

Tessa reached down and helped Barret off the ground while everyone else glanced around the room awkwardly, except Dylan and Waya, who stood up immediately. "We'll go next!"

"Great, are you the assailant?" Tessa asked Waya.

"Well, I'm a bottom." *Silence.*

"Okayyyy, everyone spread out throughout the house with your partners," Alyra instructed. "Tessa will come around to observe and give tips. I'll work with partners in a room with a TV."

Lilyanna looked around and unintentionally met Tristan's eye. "Shall we?" he raised his eyebrows.

"Sure," she nodded, trying to sound calm. The group slowly broke up and dispersed around the house, except for Joe, who went out on the front terrace to smoke.

Lilyanna remained with Tristan, Alyra and Tessa in the living room. "So, to state the obvious, I'm a big guy," Tristan began.

That you are. He wore a navy t-shirt that made his eyes look even bluer, and slate grey athletic shorts. Lilyanna wore a teal V-neck workout top and black jogging ankle pants.

"Yeah, Lily, you're pretty petite. Maybe she just needs to work on her running speed," Alyra suggested to Tessa.

"Size doesn't always matter!" Tessa exclaimed in exasperation. Alyra lowered her gaze at Tessa. Lilyanna avoided Tristan's piercing eyes at all costs and focused on not dying of embarrassment.

"Lily, you just need to be quick and throw one good solid punch to buy you time. Then be able to run away really fast," Tessa explained.

"Yeah, Lily, girl, you gotta come in hot!" Alyra agreed.

Tessa stood in front of Lilyanna and grabbed her right hand. "Here, strike upward with the palm of your hand. Since your fist is so small, you'll do more damage to your attacker and less to yourself if you use your palm and go for the face."

"Well, I'm not going to punch Tristan in the face."

"You think you can hurt me?" he smirked.

"I would leave my mark," she replied, her tone more confident than she felt.

"That's the spirit. Let's try," Alyra said.

"Give it a go," Tristan nodded.

"What? I can't just punch you in the face!"

"Just walk through it slowly," Tessa told her.

Lilyanna hesitated. If she had known she would be punching someone, she would've partnered with Bix.

"Come on, we don't have all day," Alyra urged.

"Just do it!" Tessa shouted.

"Will you all shut up!" Lilyanna yelled.

"Ah, for fuck's suck!" Tristan rushed toward Lilyanna to grab her hand. Caught off guard by his advance, Lilyanna whirled around to face him and subconsciously thrust her palm at Tristan's left temple. She made solid contact, sending him staggering backward.

"Oh my gosh, I'm so sorry!" Lilyanna clapped her hand over her mouth and stepped toward Tristan. He held up his hand to stop her and massaged his temple. "I swear I didn't mean to hit you! Are you okay?"

"Oh, wow, I didn't think you were actually going to hit him," Tessa said. "But that was really good technique!"

"Well, I think you've got the gist of it," Alyra nodded. "I'm just going to go check on the other groups."

Tessa followed her. "You two keep working."

"Tristan, I . . ." Lilyanna started.

"It's alright. You said you'd leave your mark. I won't underestimate you again," he said, a slight gleam returning to his eyes.

"I'm seriously so sorry! Can I, um, help you?" she stepped toward him again and slowly reached up to touch the side of his face.

He caught her hand in mid-air and gripped it tightly. "No, we're not finished." He looped his other arm around her waist and lifted her off her feet.

"Hey! What are you doing?" Shocked by the blitz, she struggled against him and tried to hit him again with her free hand, but he restrained her arms and lowered her to the floor.

"I told you I wouldn't underestimate you again," he stated softly.

"Tristan, what the hell?" She pushed against his chest, but she would've had more success moving a boulder up the side of a mountain. Tessa had been right—she only had one quick blow to the face. After that, she couldn't overcome a man's physical strength.

"If this is the best you've got, we need to work on your ground game," he quipped as he pinned her to the floor on her back and hovered over her. She tried to knee him, but he blocked that as well. "Good try, but not a chance." He straddled her, with one knee on each side of her hips, and kept just enough weight on her to keep her lower body from moving. He then lifted both her wrists and pinned them on either side of her head. She made soft incoherent moaning noises while struggling under his weight, trying to free herself from his hold.

"Now, how are you going to get out of this?" he asked, his eyes touting the easy victory of the rest of his two hundred-pound physique.

"I could scream."

He directed his most penetrating sultry stare into her eyes. "You could." He lowered his face to within an inch of hers.

Her heart beat so intensely she was sure he could hear it. *What is he doing? Is he about to kiss me?* Unable to move, she was his captive audience at the mercy of his undeclared intentions.

His tempting lips hovered over hers momentarily. She closed her eyes and lifted her head slightly, but he lowered his mouth just in time and just barely brushed the tip of his upper lip over her chin. "But you won't." He proceeded to lightly brush his cheek against hers and then the side of her neck a couple of inches below her ear. The tingle of his subtle facial stubble against her neck and the contrast of his soft cool skin over his chiseled jawbone sent a euphoric shudder through her body. Her back arched as much as it could in the limited space between the floor and Tristan's body, pressing her body against his.

"I think I finally found a weak spot." Gradually, he slid his hands up from her wrists and interlaced his fingers with hers, still keeping her arms by her head. She willingly ran her fingers through his and locked them tightly. In response, he let his lips rest against the same spot on her neck and then slowly dragged them toward her prominent collarbone. Closing her eyes, she pressed the side of her face against his. She wanted to wrap her arms around him, but she couldn't move.

The pandemic relegated physical touch to a taboo, a dangerous venture, stigmatized even. Signs went up in public establishments requiring that patrons maintain six feet of distance, violations of which rules received contempt, at best, and civil or criminal penalties, at worst. The unintended consequence of restricting a natural human tendency, however, is breathing new life into its demand. Tell people they can't physically connect, and it's suddenly what they desire most. Closeness is so much more enticing when touch is at a premium.

Tristan's face rested against hers a moment longer. Suddenly, he lifted his face away and gazed down on her. She opened her eyes at the change of pace. His sapphire eyes cooled, his mind seeming to grapple with how to proceed at the intersection of diverging courses of action.

"That was for the slap," he stated matter-of-factly. He unlaced his fingers from hers and swiftly climbed off her and onto his feet. "You should keep practicing," he called without looking at her on his way out of the room. Stunned, Lilyanna remained frozen on the living room floor, staring at the ceiling but seeing nothing.

***

That evening, Whimser glimmered in the setting sun, reflecting the final rays of daylight off its grey shutters. The flawless façade concealed the chaos within. Downstairs, the men fumbled around trying to sort their laundry for the start of the workweek the next day, with Sylvie and Nina going room to room to right any mix-ups.

Six burst into the bedroom occupied by Andrew, Rich and Tie. "Do any of y'all have my drawers?"

"Uh, no, man, sorry," Andrew replied, folding a pile of shirts on his bed.

"Not me either," Rich confirmed. He lay on his side on the bed reading from his phone.

"Where's Tie?"

"Right here, man. What's up?" Tie entered the room with Joe on his heels.

"Did either of you grab my Calvin Klein drawers? I'm missing three pairs."

"Nope, sorry, but I'm missing my white undershirts."

"Unless you're missing tighty whities, I wouldn't ask Tie," Joe retorted. "Andrew, I think these are yours." Joe tossed him a pair of folded black dress pants.

"Yes, thank you! I looked everywhere for these. Honestly, I have no idea how to do laundry."

"Yeah, my wife usually does this," Rich muttered.

"This is a clusterfuck," Joe complained. "We need a better system. Where's the girl who does the cleaning?"

From the kitchen, Lilyanna heard Joe and Sylvie bickering near the laundry room. She stood ready to come to Sylvie's aid, but Sylvie held her own, insisting that the men properly label their belongings or take a more active role in the laundry. Good for her, and good for Lilyanna, who had no desire to take any chances of running into Tristan. She grabbed two bottles of wine and several glasses from the kitchen and headed for the back stairs when the mail shelf caught her eye. Upon closer examination, she saw several packages addressed to Saharie. She crammed them into her arms with the wine bottles and glasses and hurried upstairs to her sanctuary.

Lilyanna found Dylan and Waya joining the women in the upstairs master bedroom. Waya sat on the floor with his hair wrapped in a towel while Dylan knelt behind him and massaged his back. "Saharie, these are for you." Lilyanna set the packages on Saharie's bed and began filling wine glasses.

"What did you order?" Tessa asked.

Saharie scooted to the edge of her bed and ripped open the packages. "I didn't order anything." Each package contained two thin beige boxes, with each lid bearing a single emblem in gold script m~V~p. "Ohhh, I know what these are. They're vibrators from this company I'm supposed to collaborate with on a video for women's wellness during the pandemic."

"Let me see." Kyah grabbed one of the boxes. "The MVP of vibrators, huh? I don't know, I'm attached to the one I have."

"Well, we each get one since they sent me four." Saharie handed out the samples.

"I'll take one. It's the most action any of us will get for a long time, I think," Tessa sighed.

"Are you and Alec fighting again?" Saharie asked.

"Aren't we always? He's a douche."

Curious, Lilyanna opened her box and took out a pearl-colored curved wand with several buttons on the end. Given the day she had, the device looked tempting. If she had a room to herself, she might have considered trying it out. As it was, she had no privacy, no way to assuage her sexual frustration that rivaled a caged lioness in heat, and no way to resolve the confusion in her head about Tristan's intentions, and her own insecurities. But what she did have was an unlimited supply of wine. She filled her glass to the brim.

"Ooh, let me see," Dylan snatched the vibrator and turned it in his hand. "Fancy! You can have O's all night with these babies."

"Do you think that's what the guys are doing downstairs?" Tessa asked as she checked the batteries in her new toy.

"Whack off circle for sure," Kyah said, sipping a glass of wine.

"Here, I'll put on some Cardi B to get you in the mood," Waya offered. He started blasting a Cardi B playlist from his phone and grabbed the vibrator from Dylan to use as a microphone.

Kyah and Saharie burst out laughing. "OMG yes!" Kyah jumped off her bed and onto the floor next to Waya. "Cardi B is my cardio!" Lilyanna chugged her wine and poured a second glass, trying to forget her predicament.

Meanwhile, downstairs, Tristan and Six stood in Andrew, Rich and Tie's room having a beer. "What do you think the ladies are doing upstairs?" Tie asked.

"That's a dangerous question, man," Six shook his head.

"You don't think they're, like, having pillow fights, naked?"

Six laughed, "You're such a kid!"

"Saharie would be so good at that," Tie mused.

A sudden thud on the ceiling stopped the laughter. "What the hell was that?" Rich asked, looking up from his phone.

In response, another small series of thuds and a buzzing sound echoed from the ceiling. "Maybe someone should go up there and make sure everything is okay," Andrew suggested.

"Go on, then," Tristan said.

"I wasn't volunteering! Why don't you go?"

Another thud from above answered him. "Fuck it," Tristan sighed and left the room for the front stairs.

In the master bedroom, Dylan threw the vibrator in his hand onto Lilyanna's bed. "Hang on, guys, I gotta pee." Upon entering the hallway, Dylan spotted Tristan coming up the front staircase. "Ahhh, I knew it was only a matter of time before a fox found his way to the hen house. You're either lost, or incredibly hor—"

"Would you please ask Lilyanna to come out?" Tristan cut him off, glaring in annoyance.

"My pleasure," Dylan replied. He bowed to Tristan and went back to the master bedroom.

"Lily, you have a visitor in the hall." He then continued on his way to the bathroom.

"It's probably Sylvie." Wine glass in hand, Lilyanna closed the door to the bedroom behind her. To her surprise, she found Tristan at the top of the stairs in the hall glancing around awkwardly.

"Can I help you?"

He raised his eyes to hers and narrowed them into a weary no-bullshit gaze. "Lily," he stated quickly in a low, unamused tone.

He's so cute when he's grumpy.

"We heard noises downstairs."

"Noises, huh? Can you describe these noises?" She made eye contact without giving away any emotion and gently swirled her wine glass.

He dropped his chin and widened his eyes, "Are you drunk?"

"Not yet." From the bedroom, Cardi B lyrics blared, "My pussy glitter as gold."

"'The fuck is that?"

She took a sip of her wine. "You've never heard Cardi B?"

"Not quite so candidly." He stepped forward away from the stair railing.

"Ya know, I used to be kind of awkward about using the word 'pussy' but now, thanks to Cardi B, I can't get enough of it."

The creases around his eyes relaxed, and he couldn't fight off a burst of soft laughter. He looked away from her and shook his head. "How liberating."

"You should stay for the chorus, gets wild." She took another deep drink.

He pushed his wavy hair out of his face, and the stubborn waves fell right back into their original place over his forehead. "Look, I'm sorry about earlier. I went too far, and I apologize." His smile faded, the weariness returning.

Lilyanna cocked her head and narrowed her eyes, pointing her index finger of the hand in which she

CHAPTER SEVEN: Socially Distant

clutched her wine glass. "So, that's what you're sorry for? That you went too far?"

"Yes? That's what I should be sorry for."

"I didn't ask how you should feel. I asked how you do feel."

He considered her for a moment. "What is it you need from me that you're not getting, Lily?"

"I don't *need* anything from you. What I *want*, is not to be a joke to you and for you to realize I'm bending over backwards to make this whole thing work, so don't play games with me." She wondered whether this guy was some sort of sociopath, mind-fucking her as foreplay—trying to make her think he's interested in her one minute and that she's misunderstanding the next.

He sighed and took a step closer. "I know you've sacrificed for this arrangement."

"No, you don't! That's just it. You think it's easy for me to be back in this house, and it's not. I am here only because you asked me to be."

Her words struck him. "Specifically, because it was me who asked?"

"Now it sounds like it's you who needs something from me," she noted, raising her wine glass.

"God, Lily." He looked away from her for a second. Focusing his eyes on her again, he took a deep breath. "You could never be a joke to me."

"Unless I rap Cardi B lyrics to you, right?"

"I think that would be torture, not a joke. Truce?" he held out his hand toward her.

She hesitated a moment and then shook his hand tightly. "Fine, truce." She let go and stepped

123

backward. "We'll try to keep the noise down." She turned her back on him to go back to the bedroom.

"Good night," he called.

She turned her head and looked at him one last time before he went back downstairs. "Sweet dreams."

Dylan stopped her in the hall before she reached the bedroom door. "What did he want?"

"Apparently, we're being too loud."

"What did he really want?" he asked again.

"That remains to be seen."

"Lily, I, um, you may not want my advice, but you're getting it anyway. I've known you a long time, and I think you have a tendency to, hold back, at times."

"Please don't start! I'm not going after this guy."

"And I think that's partly the problem."

"What do you mean?"

"I'm just saying that I can tell you like him, but you're expecting him to make all the moves and *persuade* you to be with him. I understand you want to be pursued, and you should be, but this situation is not conducive to that model."

Lilyanna thought for a moment. In all the years she'd known Dylan, he was not only the consummate life of the party but also the person she could stay up with all night for deep conversations. Insightful and knowledgeable about people, when he chose to impart his wisdom, it was usually worth listening to. "Go on."

"I'm just saying, you're not in circumstances where he can make his intentions clear by asking you to dinner or something. Not only are you in a house full of your co-workers, but he's in charge of all of them. You've said that he's your colleague and in a superior position, but I think that's actually more of an issue for him than it is for you. I'm sure he's concerned about being seen as the VP who hits on a young female employee. He doesn't want to lose his job, or worse."

"You think he's worried I would make a complaint about him or something?"

"I'm sure it's crossed his mind."

"But he should know the difference between what is consensual and what is forced. There's no excuse for ignorance on that. I have no patience for men who are scared of being assertive because of #metoo."

"Oh, I completely agree, but let's give him the benefit of the doubt and assume he's at least woke enough not to shake in his boots over #metoo. Assuming that's not too generous, his main concern is probably an appearance of impropriety, and maybe the possibility that if things went south between you, and I don't mean in a good way, you would say he came on to you or something."

"I would never do that!"

"I know that, and you know that, but he doesn't know you that well, yet. He doesn't know that you tend to be a little closed off when it comes to intimacy, and you need the right person to assertively work through that with you. It's normal for a guy to perceive your shyness as disinterest." He held up his hand when she started to object. "Also, given his age and that he's been divorced, he may have been burned before. Part of his brain is always in ass-covering mode."

"He doesn't trust me not to turn on him any more than I trust him not to lead me on and screw me over."

"Exactly. So, my advice—next time he flirts with you, flirt back. Give him an indication that you're interested. You don't have to throw yourself at him, just meet him part way."

"But what if he doesn't actually like me, and I just look like an idiot?"

"That's the risk you take. He's taking a risk too. That's how it works!"

"Damn, I'm really bad at this."

"You're both really bad at this. I'm so glad I'm gay!"

Lilyanna laughed. "Waya is a lucky guy."

Dylan reached out and drew her into a hug, and she rested her head on his chest. "There's always room for you, Lily."

Downstairs, a buzzing sound from the ceiling echoed through the dark in the bedroom shared by Andrew, Rich and Tie. Rich pulled a pillow over his head to block out the noise and fell back asleep.

CHAPTER EIGHT
Remotely Learning

A ndrew's morning began with stolen alone time in the bathroom, naked and jerking off into a towel. He kept the sink turned on to drown out the inadvertent expressions of his efforts. Panting, he leaned over the sink, clutching the marble edge with one hand, the other doing its damnedest to replicate physically the gratification of the unfulfillable fantasies in his mind. The subject of those fantasies? Perhaps past scenes with his wife of six years, or maybe someone closer and more available at present, like the single women dressing a floor above him. With a final turbulent convulsion, his fastidious imaginings culminated in the desired effect as he soaked the towel with a low moan.

"Hey, man, you almost done in there?" Tie tapped on the bathroom door.

Andrew inhaled deeply, trying to steady his voice. "Yeah, be out in a sec." Quickly, he cleaned himself up and checked his reflection in the mirror. He smoothed down his black hair growing longer than he usually allowed and wrapped a clean towel around his waist before gathering his used linens and leaving the solace of the only private space in the house.

***

The employees gradually settled into their new routine on workdays. Lilyanna and Alyra reshuffled the workspace assignments to provide for more privacy and less irritable tempers. Under the new arrangements, Tristan and Jillian shared the library, with Joe working primarily on the front terrace on days when the weather cooperated, and in his bedroom the other days. Lilyanna and Andrew moved into the living room with Barret and Tessa, with a room divider splitting the room in half. Rich and Tie remained in the dining room.

Per the fewer complaints, Lilyanna assumed the new arrangements were working. The productivity level-shaming mass email from Justin Mercier reminding all employees of their duty to continue working diligently even though away from the office might also have contributed to the work drive. It was one of those emails poorly disguised as semi-motivational where the sender clearly meant to make all recipients feel insecure.

Lilyanna, for one, became more productive and less annoyed, not due to the email, but because she worked just with Andrew. If she had to co-office with someone, Andrew was by far the best choice. They could work independently on different deals without interrupting each other and then quickly coordinate on deals they were working on together. He even figured out that she preferred coffee in the morning and tea in the afternoon and diligently brought her timely beverages. When he decided she was concentrating too hard, he occasionally threw wadded up pieces of paper at her, and at Tessa and Barret around the room divider. Under the new arrangements, Lilyanna also got more fresh air during working hours since she had to go out to the terrace to discuss projects with Joe.

On Tuesday morning of that week, Lilyanna worked on her laptop in the living room as usual with Andrew on the opposite side of the sectional. "Lily, can you approve this final version of the Settlement Agreement for that company out of Houston? It's the one where we were overcharging for routine maintenance services." Andrew tossed a document to her side of the sectional.

"Yeah, I'll review it. I'm glad you decided to settle that one." Andrew was decisive in ways that the directors of other departments were not. Once he had the available information, he did not hesitate to make a decision. He did his job. If he feared repercussions or doubted himself, he did so privately. "Then I'll have to get Joe to sign off on it."

After making sure the other party did not make any unauthorized changes to the Settlement Agreement, she took a copy out to Joe on the terrace. He sat at a patio table in front of his laptop, talking into his phone in one hand and holding a cigarette in the other that he puffed between dialogue, cool as a spring rain, with a pungent scent of tobacco.

"You're telling me the billing department hasn't billed the customer for the past five years? Isn't that the sole function of the billing department?" He paused to take a drag. "Alright, I'll see what I can do." He nodded to no one and ended the call, tossing his phone on the table.

Lilyanna stepped into the sunlight on the terrace, taking in the Vitamin D. "I think you have the nicest office here."

"HR always gets it right in the end," Joe replied. He took a long drag from his cigarette and looked up at Lilyanna. "Make sure you weigh *all* the pros and cons when taking up a potentially fatal vice. Sometimes, the thought of quitting smoking actually worms its way into my mind, but then my phone rings with the next impossible request, and a smoke is always there to answer. It's the second devil wife I chained myself to after the first one almost killed me."

"More accounting mistakes?" she surmised.

"As usual. These people fuck up the one task they're hired to perform, and we get the job of un-fucking it."

"I hate to add insult to injury, but I have another one for you. Can you sign off on this Settlement Agreement for maintenance overcharges? I've approved all the changes. I can walk you through what the other party changed."

Joe held up the document and skimmed it. "No need. If you approve, I approve." He initialed the signature page of the document and slid it to the other side of the table. "Your work speaks for itself. Enjoy the sun, Lily. It always shines again, sometimes I think just to mock us, but you never know when."

***

"Haircuts! If anybody wants one, you can sign up for a time tomorrow. I'll put the schedule here in the kitchen." Saharie taped a sign-up sheet to the fridge.

"Bless you!" Barret exclaimed, grabbing a strand of his ashy brown hair. "I'm starting to get scruffy."

"This is good timing," Andrew agreed. "We have a Zoom meeting Friday morning with President Marks."

"Who's we? I didn't know anything about a Zoom meeting," Tessa said, pouring a cup of coffee.

"Oh, it's just a status call for upper management," he replied casually.

"Right, we want to make sure upper management's concerns about captivity get addressed," Tessa retorted.

"I'll need you ladies to take turns pitching in with the hair appointments," Saharie redirected the subject. "One of you can be shampooing while I cut and style."

"Count me out. I have a brief due by close of business Friday," Kyah replied. "I'm loving WFH over being in the office, and I want to show I can still meet all my deadlines so this can continue. I have no desire to be back at my office."

"I'll take a break from work to help when I can," Lilyanna agreed.

"Me too," Tessa nodded.

The next morning, Sylvie and Nina helped Lilyanna, Saharie and Tessa turn the laundry room and adjoining half bathroom into a makeshift hair salon. Saharie set a kitchen bar stool in the bathroom for cutting and styling. Two low sinks in the laundry room would be used for washing.

Tessa took the morning shift assisting Saharie, and then Lilyanna reluctantly relieved her in the afternoon. She felt guilty taking a break from work. Maybe it was the added stress that was making her irritable. "Okay, Lily, while I'm cutting and styling in the bathroom you can be shampooing the next one in here. There's men's shampoo and deep conditioner by the sink."

"Yeah, yeah, got it," she groaned.

"What's wrong?"

"Sorry, I'm just in a mood. I don't know why."

"Okay, well, don't take it out on the clients' hair. I have a reputation to uphold."

Six and Barret had the first afternoon appointments. They waited outside the door of the laundry room.

"Wo, these scissors are hella sharp. You're doing all the cutting, right?" Lilyanna asked, holding up Saharie's salon-grade shears.

"For sure, snip, snip!"

Six and Barret exchanged worried glances. "What does she mean, 'snip, snip'? What's she snipping? Just our hair, right?" Barret whispered to Six.

Six nodded slowly, "Yeah, yeah, I'm sure that's it, but why don't you go first just to make sure."

"Next victims!" Saharie called into the hall.

"Do you want to hold hands?" Barret asked. Six shot him an exasperated look and marched bravely into the makeshift salon. Saharie washed Barret's hair and then took him into the bathroom for cutting while Lilyanna washed Six's hair. Lilyanna made quick work of scrubbing Six's cropped dark hair and sent him into the bathroom.

They had a coordinated rhythm down by the last couple of appointments. Tie and Tristan were the last on the schedule. "I'll take care of Tie," Saharie volunteered nonchalantly.

"I'm sure you will," Lilyanna smiled.

Saharie directed Tie to sit in a chair in front of one of the sinks in the laundry room and began rubbing shampoo into his hair. Lilyanna quickly scrubbed out the other sink to prepare for the next person. Saharie was flirting with Tie and massaging his head over the sink when Tristan peeked into the laundry room and knocked on the side of the door frame. "Hello, should I come in?"

"Yes, please," Lilyanna smiled politely. "Have a seat." She gestured for him to sit in the chair in front of the unoccupied sink. His hair had grown a good two inches longer than his norm, and he had a healthy growth of facial stubble.

Tristan glanced at Tie and Saharie giggling at each other as Saharie leaned over him, her impeccable D-cup cleavage spilling over the top of her black camisole right above Tie's face. Lilyanna gave Tristan an apologetic look.

"Lily, wash his hair while I finish up with Tie in the bathroom," Saharie instructed, oblivious to the implications of her words. She guided Tie out of the laundry room and into the bathroom, leaving Lilyanna and Tristan alone.

"Hope you're not in a hurry," she commented to Tristan. He laughed softly. "Okay, will you lean your head back, please?" She reached for the bottle of shampoo above the sink, but Tristan caught her arm.

"Do you know what you're doing?" he asked, his voice laced with concern.

"Well, it's hardly open-heart surgery."

"What are you putting in my hair?"

"It's just shampoo! It's not going to, like, turn your hair blue or something." Her response did not calm him.

"Look, I know things between us got a bit tense the other day, but we agreed to a truce."

"I'm aware, and I have every intention of honoring said truce. I'm not going to mess up your hair. Quit being a pussy!"

His lips curved into a partial smile, and he loosened his grip on her arm for a moment but then tightened it again. "I just, like my hair the way it is."

"I like your hair the way it is too." She could feel the blush creeping into her face. She forced herself to stare deliberately into his eyes. They looked almost teal today. Sensing him relax a little, but not all the way, she slowly lifted her free hand and touched his wrist that blocked her other arm. Gently, she pulled his hand away to release her arm and lowered his hand down to his side. He didn't try to stop her. "Just relax." She softened her voice and softly took hold of either side of his neck, tilting his head into the sink.

His dark wavy locks draped over his forehead as usual. Finally, she had the chance to run her fingers through those stubborn black waves that had been taunting her since the first day she saw Tristan. Knowing it might be her only opportunity to touch his hair, she took her time. She carefully brushed the waves back from his forehead, one strand at a time. Tristan closed his eyes without her asking. She turned on the water and soaked his hair thoroughly before applying a modest amount of shampoo. His hair slid through her fingers as she gently scrubbed his scalp with her nails.

"That feels incredible," he sighed softly.

"Shhh, just keep relaxing." She poured a teaspoon of conditioner into her palm and then ran it through his hair, continuing to massage his head and the sides of his neck while the conditioner worked. She shut off the water. Tristan opened his eyes slightly and looked up at her. Instinctively, her face drew closer to his, his eyes a magnet pulling her towards them. He didn't reach up and touch her. He didn't have to. She was caught in some sort of trance stronger than her misgivings.

"Are you two about done?" Saharie called from the bathroom.

Instantly, Lilyanna jerked her head back, and Tristan looked away from her. "Yeah, one second," Lilyanna called back. She turned the water back on and quickly rinsed the conditioner out of Tristan's hair. When she finished, she dried his hair with a hand towel and looped it over his shoulders.

"Saharie will trim your hair now in the bathroom."

"Right, great. Do you think I should shave, like completely?" he rubbed the stubble on his chin.

She didn't even try to conceal her blush. "Uh, no, I don't think so. I think it looks, good, you know, as it is."

"Okay, good, um, thanks for that."

"No problem," she nodded. As soon as he left the laundry room, Lilyanna sank into the chair he had been sitting in and leaned over her knees, her head in her hands. All of the endorphins drained from her, resulting in a surge of frustration and a deluge of tears threatening to pour. For a moment, she didn't understand why her mood had plummeted. She was getting used to Tristan's teasing and temperamental persona, so it shouldn't upset her more than usual. It was then she remembered she had taken the last pill in her pack of birth control for this cycle, her period threatening to start any moment.

Lilyanna felt certain there were some women out there who did not struggle with their menstrual cycles, but she was not one of them. She took birth control for the sole purpose of only having a period every other month to delay the debilitating brain fog, fatigue, anxiety and depression that Mother Nature saw fit to bestow upon her each cycle. The hormonal disruption exacerbated her existing stress and negative thoughts. When her hormones worked against her, every nightmare intensified, every negative thought darkened. Everything worsened during her period.

Lilyanna ran to the kitchen to find Sylvie sweeping the floors and Tessa grabbing a bottle of water from the fridge. "Sylvie, I think we should add some womanly products to the delivery list for this week. I have enough for me, for now, but we may need more for everyone."

"We're all done," Saharie announced, entering the kitchen with Tristan behind her. Saharie had done as requested and given him a minor trim, just enough off the top for his high-end, clean-cut look, but with facial hair.

"Thanks for the haircut, ladies," he nodded and breezed past them into the hall.

"God, my back is killing me," Saharie groaned, clutching her side and leaning backward. "I just started my period."

Lilyanna swore. "Great, we're all synced up. We were just talking about that. Sylvie, please add several boxes of tampons to this week's grocery order."

"I'm still a few weeks away, I think," Tessa said.

"We're so happy for you," Saharie retorted.

"I'll take care of it, Lily," Sylvie assured her.

Before dinner, Lilyanna freshened up her makeup in the upstairs bathroom, trying to pull herself together and cover up her skin's cyclical hormonal tantrum. Her lower abdomen began cramping severely while she applied her mascara. Sure enough, Mother Nature kicked her in the ovaries.

A plethora of foundation to cover her skin breakout and a couple of ibuprofen later, she sat between Andrew and Six at the kitchen table eating a dinner of grilled salmon and vegetables. A deviation from the normal age division, Joe, Jillian, Alyra, Tristan and Kyah sat at the table as well, while the others ate in the dining room.

"If the pandemic closes a lot of businesses, I guess I'll have to quit doing employment law and switch to family law," Kyah said.

"We might all end up doing family law if domestic disputes are the only source of legal work post-lockdown," Jillian agreed.

"Not me, I'm not touching family law again," Six replied. "I did family law at a national firm for a year after law school. It's just a bunch of rich White people refusing to recognize contentment even when it's sitting on their laps stroking their . . . egos."

Jillian laughed, "I think I saw that one on Netflix."

"So, Lily, what do we have to look forward to when millennials run the world?" Joe asked.

Not in the mood for philosophical conversations, or even social contact at all, Lilyanna drained her glass of Chablis. "There will be free candy," she replied flatly.

He laughed. "Throw in cigarettes, and you have my support," Joe raised his glass of whiskey.

"We haven't even gotten to healthcare yet," Kyah noted.

"Candy and cigarettes first. Create the problem and then follow up with a solution," Lilyanna explained.

"Like the Democrats are doing with COVID," Joe coughed. Tristan laughed, but everyone else got quiet.

"Come on, man," Six replied, shaking his head. "Are you one of those people that thinks COVID will just disappear when Biden wins the 2020 election?"

"No, cause I don't think Biden will win the 2020 election."

"I do!" Kyah disagreed. "If Americans are self-destructive enough to make the same mistake a second time, then there's no hope for us, and that's irrational thinking."

"I wouldn't bank on the majority of Americans being rational after what we've seen so far this year," Jillian stated coolly.

"Even if Biden wins, he's not going to fix everything overnight." Six reasoned. "People are dying. That won't just stop when the election is called."

"Don't get me wrong, I wish it would," Joe added. "Let Biden pass around government-funded, federally-mandated, individually-wrapped containers of combination vaccine and unity blue juice, just ignore the Chinese labeling." Jillian shook her head and drank from her wine glass.

While the group cleaned up the kitchen after dinner, Saharie rushed in and thrust her phone in Lilyanna's face. "Lily, the airline just canceled our flight to Croatia this summer, look!"

"What?" Lilyanna snatched the phone and scrolled through the email. "Maybe it was a glitch. Let me see if I got the same email." She pulled her phone from her pocket and checked her email account. Sure enough, the first email in her inbox contained a standard cancelation message from the airline, with no explanation or helpful information. "Yep, it's canceled. You've got to be kidding me."

"Sorry, Lil," Andrew refilled her wine glass.

"Well, at least it's just a trip," Jillian shrugged. "I need to go call my son. He's in his residency at a hospital in Manhattan." She got up from the table and went to her room.

If looks could kill, Lilyanna's eyes would've stabbed in her in the back as she walked away. She could feel her chest constricting and the frustrated, anxious, disappointed tears forming behind her eyes. "I'll call the airlines," Lilyanna told Saharie. She tossed her plate in the sink and bounded out the front door for the woods.

It took yelling "Agent, Representative" ten times to the robot operator and another thirty minutes of waiting on hold to get to a human receptionist only for the airline to confirm the cancelation of their flight. "Are there any other flights available for the same dates?"

"I'm sorry, ma'am, all flights to and from Europe are canceled through the end of June. At this time, we do not know when international flights will resume." That was it, then. The airlines had no more intel than anyone else. Lilyanna asked the agent to issue refunds and ended the call in dismay.

Dragging her feet along the tree-lined path, she took deep breaths to try to calm down. It was not 'just a trip' to her. Annual Eurotrips were her escape—an escape from thoughts of her parents, and William, and stress. When she went to Europe with her friends, she felt free. Bears couldn't find her there. Her head pounded as she made her way to a clearing in the woods.

Whimser had a hold on her now. It curled its vines around her like a hundred manacles, not in an embrace, but a straitjacket from which she couldn't escape. She fell to her knees on the grass in submission. It hadn't felt constraining when she was there with William. It was different then . . .

The sun glinted off Lilyanna's white V-neck midi dress as she lay on her side on the grass, her face resting on her hand. "Perfect, just keep looking straight ahead," William called to her. He stood in front of an easel bearing a 36 x 24-inch canvas that he meticulously stroked with his paintbrush.

"Don't you want to come join me?" she teased him with a smile.

"I'm enjoying the view," he smiled back.

William finished the painting within three weeks, record time for him. The finished product showed Lilyanna lying on the grass in her white dress surrounded by various flowers in bloom with Whimser in the background. He hung the painting above the fireplace in the parlor. "Now, Whimser has a garden," he beamed with pride.

After sunset, Lilyanna forced herself to return to the house. To her relief, she found the kitchen empty and the dishes cleaned up. She opened the fridge and searched for the least healthy snack option. A single-layer six-inch chocolate cake sat on the top shelf, tempting her. *What could that be for?* It wasn't large enough to serve the whole house, and to her knowledge, nobody had requested a cake for a special occasion. Her ovaries wanted that cake; they *needed* that cake. She owned the house, and therefore the cake inside the house. Ms. Howard would have to get over it. She took the cake out of the fridge and grabbed a fork.

As she perched on the bar stool polishing off her fourth bite of chocolate therapy, Tristan sauntered into the kitchen. "What's going on here?"

"Nothing meant for your eyes." She was too down to fake perkiness. Instead, she dug her fork deeper into the side of the cake.

"I disagree." He got a fork from the kitchen drawer and pulled up a bar stool next to Lilyanna. "I can't let you do this alone."

"Good, you can share Ms. Howard's wrath."

"You are smashing this! I have to say I'm impressed," he remarked before eating a forkful of cake.

"I'm an expert at smashing desserts," she assured him.

"So am I, but I have a few pounds on you. You're petite."

"My appetite is not."

He lifted his eyebrows and nodded between bites. "This is really good."

"It's *so* good!" she agreed. She smiled because he was smiling.

"I'm sorry to hear about your trip."

"Thanks. I feel guilty complaining about it. I know people have way worse problems right now."

"By all means, complain away. Nobody gets out of this unscathed in one way or another."

"What about you? How are you holding up?" she asked.

"Better now, to be honest. I was, err, on the phone with my sons, and they're struggling with distance learning since the schools closed."

"How old are they?"

"Fifteen and fourteen—high school."

"Wow, it must be difficult for you to be away from them."

"It is, but I need to be here right now."

"I'm glad you're here. Thanks for not letting me do this alone."

"I'm not sure if you're referring to the cake or quarantine, but, either way, I'm happy to oblige."

She stopped eating and gazed up at him. Saharie did solid work on his hair, just a minor trim of the edges. His stubborn waves were left untamed, just how Lilyanna liked them. "Your hair came out good." Gently, she reached up and brushed a wave off his forehead. It fell right back into place. She laughed, for no reason, and so did he.

* * *

Before going to bed, Lilyanna went downstairs to lock up and make sure all lights had been turned off. Instead of Whimer's usual nightly melody of creaks, she heard Ms. Howard and Bix shouting in the kitchen and hurried to investigate. Upon entering the kitchen, she found Ms. Howard pointing at Bix with a spatula as she berated him. "I set it right inside the fridge, and now it's gone!"

Bix stepped back from her to reclaim his personal space. "Get that thing out of my face! You must have misplaced it."

"It's a cake! You can't misplace it. Someone stole it! It's your job to make sure that doesn't happen."

"I'm not the kitchen security guard! It's your job to manage your inventory. How dare you accuse me of misfeasance!"

She stepped towards him with the spatula. "I'm accusing you of being a pompous, lazy—"

"Then you're fired!" he stormed, holding his ground.

"You can't fire me! I already quit!" she shouted, tossing the spatula onto the counter.

"What is going on?" Lilyanna cried.

"I fired Ms. Howard for insubordination!" Bix thundered.

"You can't fire her, Bix, you're not her employer. Ms. Howard, please don't quit! I'll fix whatever is wrong," Lilyanna begged.

"This mongrel allowed the theft of a cake I spent all afternoon making and then blamed me for losing it!"

Lilyanna's eyes widened. "A cake? You mean the chocolate cake that was in the fridge?" She braced for Ms. Howard's reaction.

Ms. Howard eyed her suspiciously, "Yes, that one. You stole it, didn't you?"

Lilyanna held up her hands and softened her voice. "I wouldn't exactly say I stole it."

"Then do you plan to give it back?" Ms. Howard retorted. "That cake was a surprise for Sylvie and Nina, who do all the work in this house!"

Lilyanna dropped her head towards the floor and sighed. "I'm so sorry, I didn't know. I should have asked you first. This is completely my fault." Bix's scowl curved into an ugly grin as Lilyanna replaced him in the line of fire.

"It's both of your faults!" Ms. Howard insisted, shifting her chastising glare from Lilyanna to Bix.

Bix started to protest, but Lilyanna stopped him. "Please, Ms. Howard, I'll pay for the cake and overtime for you to make another one."

"You're taking her side?" Bix cried incredulously. "You reward her insolence with a pay raise? She should be fired immediately!"

Lilyanna narrowed her eyes at him and cocked her head in frustration. "We need a skilled chef to feed a house full of people. A disagreeable caretaker skulking around not actually taking care of anything, on the other hand . . ." She brushed past Bix and left Ms. Howard to glower at him, still sulking, but vindicated in regards to Bix.

***

Lilyanna tossed and turned in her bed that night. She dreamed that Whimser was crashing down around her—the walls shaking and then tumbling down, stone by stone, brick by brick. Desperately, she ran through the hall yelling at everyone to get out of the house. Tristan stood at the front door, unruffled by the chaos. She ran to him and grabbed his rock-solid arms.

"Tristan, we have to save the house, now!"

"I can't help you. I'm sorry."

"What?" she gasped. "I need your help, Tristan, please! You can't leave me!" She dropped to her knees in front of him in supplication.

"Lilyanna," his deep voice cut through her like a blade of ice. "My commitment is not to you. I cannot help you." He pulled his arms from her grasp and turned his back on her and Whimser. The roof began caving in through the center of the hall.

"Tristan, Tristan!" She called in vain after him. She whirled around in time to see the painting of herself hanging crooked on the wall before it slid to the marble floor. A barrage of roof tiles crashed down on top of it.

Lilyanna woke with a start, icy sweat droplets forming on her forehead. Quietly, she slid out of bed and made her way in the dark to the bathroom and closed the door behind her. Taking a deep breath, she turned on the light and waited for her eyes to adjust. The mirror showed no mercy. Lilyanna stared at the creases under her eyes and her extra pale, tired skin— another dreaded premenstrual symptom.

Unable to shake the nightmare, she splashed cool water on her face. She couldn't understand how she went from having the most natural encounter with Tristan yet to a nightmare of him leaving her as Whimser collapsed. The worst part was she *begged* for his help! That would not do. Straightening her posture, she made eye contact with her haggard reflection. The mirror her witness, she declared aloud, "I will never beg a man for anything!"

CHAPTER NINE
Nature's Dalliance

L ater in the week, Lilyanna sat at the kitchen table with Saharie, guzzling coffee in an attempt to clear her lingering brain fog.

"Make it stop," Saharie groaned.

"One more day, and I can start my next pack of birth control pills and get my hormones under control," Lilyanna replied.

"Lily, Ms. Howard asked me to give you the, um, items you ordered," Sylvie interjected.

"The what?"

"The feminine items you asked me to order. I had Ms. Howard add them to her grocery delivery list." Sylvie handed her a plastic bag full of several cardboard boxes.

"Oh, right, thanks." Lilyanna took the bag and pulled out the boxes. "What the hell?" All of the boxes were labeled as multi-packs of pregnancy tests. "Sylvie, I thought you were ordering tampons?"

Sylvie squinted over Lilyanna's shoulder. "I asked Ms. Howard to order tampons! She must have been confused."

"Confused on the difference between a tampon and pregnancy test?" Saharie asked, reading the back of one of the boxes. "What are we supposed to do with all of these?"

"Well, she is quite a bit older," Tessa reasoned.

"Sylvie, please hide these in the upstairs master bathroom," Lilyanna sighed, massaging her temples.

"Anybody up for a morning run with me?" Tessa asked. Lilyanna, Saharie and Sylvie glared at her. Again, if looks could kill . . . "I'll just be outside," Tessa took the hint along with her water bottle and jogged into the hall.

Andrew caught her by the front door. "I'll run with you, if you're up for it," he offered.

"Absolutely, if you can keep up." She smiled and dashed out the front door ahead of him.

"The morning news is on, want to watch?" Barret asked, peeking his head into the kitchen.

"My pointiest boots are on, want a kick in the nuts?" Saharie retorted.

"Damn, sorry I asked!" Barret stomped back down the hall toward the den. "All the women are on their periods," he whined to the others watching the TV in the den. Joe, Jillian, Alyra, and Six didn't even look at him. They stared at the World News reporter giving the morning update on European conditions during the pandemic.

"The Venice Canal is the cleanest it has been in decades, with the return of swans and dolphins being reported due to the sharp decline in tourism. Likewise, air quality readings from the world's most polluted cities show a drastic improvement."

"Well, at least there's an upside for someone," Joe remarked.

***

CHAPTER NINE: Nature's Dalliance

Friday morning, Lilyanna, Tessa, Saharie and Tie cleared the dining room table to set up for a Zoom call with upper management. As a mere associate-level attorney, she did not make the attendee list. Only Tristan, Jillian, Andrew, Alyra and Joe would be participating.

"Great, we do all the bitch work and are not deemed important enough to join the meeting," Tessa huffed. "I guess it doesn't matter. Nothing actually gets accomplished in those meetings anyway. Upper management will just compare sizes via Zoom since they can't do it in person now."

Tie chuckled, "I bet Alyra is the biggest."

"Yass, big dick energy for sure," Saharie agreed.

"I never understood that term," Tessa shook her head.

"If you have to ask, you don't have it," Saharie teased.

"But a guy is either big or not, and for a woman it doesn't make sense at all," Tessa reasoned.

"I think it's a lot more impactful when used in reference to a woman," Lilyanna mused as she straightened the dining chairs around the table. "It's just, a subtle confidence a person exudes, like badass vibes. It's not about actual size."

"So, are they comparing sizes or just energies?" Tessa asked, folding up the tablecloth.

"I think you're overthinking this," Saharie replied.

Joe and Andrew arrived early for the meeting, wearing suits and ties for the first time since quarantine began. Tristan joined them a few minutes later, likewise trading in his jeans for a navy suit and matching tie with silver stripes. All trimmed with controlled facial hair, except for the mustachioed Joe, an outsider would think quarantine agreed with them. Jillian and Alyra followed, dressed in neatly pressed pantsuits.

"You all look dashing," Lilyanna approved.

Andrew fidgeted with his tie. "Are you sure? Could you just?" he held his sky blue tie out to Lilyanna, and she tightened and straightened it up.

"There, it's perfect."

He grinned sheepishly, "Thanks, my wife usually does that."

Tessa watched Lilyanna and Andrew from behind the dining table. The ease of their interactions discomforted her.

Tristan turned to Jillian and asked her to straighten his tie. "You almost had it," she told him. "Just a minor tweak."

Lilyanna looked up in time to see Jillian and Tristan smiling at each other as she adjusted his tie. Feeling out of place and resentful, Lilyanna turned away and headed back to the kitchen.

"Thank you," Tristan nodded at Jillian and then took his seat next to her at the dining table. Tessa closed the door to the exclusive management war room.

In the kitchen, Dylan poured coffee for himself and Waya. "What's with all the sausage in suits?" he asked.

"Zoom meeting with upper management. They'll be in there most of the morning," Tessa replied.

"They are looking fine. Saharie, you should've taken a group pic of them for your Instagram to show off your quarantine work," Dylan told her.

"Damn, you're right! I'll have to wait til they get scruffy again and then do a before and after shoot."

"I was thinking, none of your co-workers call each other 'sir' or 'ma'am', or Mr. or Ms. so and so," Waya commented, blowing gently on his coffee. "Is your whole company like that?"

Lilyanna thought for a moment. "I mean, I guess. We have a relatively informal culture."

"Thank God," Tessa added. "I would feel super weird calling any of those guys 'sir'. Like, I don't think I could do it."

"I don't think I could either," Lilyanna agreed. "I would feel so awkward."

"Why?" Waya asked.

Lilyanna and Tessa looked at each other quizzically. "I honestly don't know," Tessa said.

"The word just sticks in the throat for some reason," Lilyanna shrugged.

"Too 'Mr. Grey will see you now'?" Dylan offered.

"Exactly!" Lilyanna and Tessa exclaimed in unison.

"Oh my gosh that's terrible, but it's true," Lilyanna cringed.

Kyah laughed. "Corporate culture is not immune to pop culture."

"But what if a guy says it? I feel like that's different," Tessa posited. "Like, if Tie were to call Joe or Tristan 'sir' it wouldn't be that weird."

"That sounds right," Lilyanna agreed. "So, it's really only cringeworthy for a woman to say it to an older or more senior man. I should totally write about this experience. I could be the next E.L. James, but without the whips and chains."

"Or with," Kyah added. "You could, ya know, keep those."

"Fifty Shades of COVID up in here," Dylan raised his coffee cup.

Waya smirked, "Well, there's no love in the time of COVID in this house, except for Dylan and me, so I guess that's as close as you guys can get."

***

By dinnertime, the winds kicked up outside, and a steady rain pelted Whimser. The group ate quickly before Ms. Howard shooed them from the kitchen. "I want to get everything cleaned up before we all get blown away," she insisted.

Everyone gathered in the den to watch the weather report. "We're expecting wind gusts up to seventy miles per hour, golf ball-sized hail and heavy rains throughout the night. We advise not to drive unless absolutely necessary, and, if you do, stay alert for flash flooding," the meteorologist instructed.

"2020 just keeps on giving," Joe huffed. As if in response, the lights flickered three times and then went out, plunging Whimser into darkness. "Ah, fuck."

"I can't see!" Waya cried.

"Somebody's stepping on my foot!" Tie yelled.

Tessa reached out and began stroking the arm of the person next to her. "Kyah, is this you?"

"No, that's me!" Rich shouted.

"Oh, shit."

"Everyone, stay calm!" Lilyanna shouted as they all pulled out their phones as a light source. "Sylvie, where are you?"

"Right here, Lily," Sylvie touched her arm.

"Help me find all the flashlights and candles in the house. I know there are some in the kitchen."

"We'll all help, Lily." Andrew stepped beside her and followed her to the kitchen.

In the kitchen, Lilyanna, Tessa, Andrew and Tristan pulled out every drawer and opened every cabinet, finding five flashlights and twelve candles of various brands and scents. They passed them out to the others to distribute throughout the main rooms on the ground floor.

Tristan bent down to feel around in the back of a bottom cabinet. "Are we sure there's no backup generator? Perhaps in the gairidge?"

Tessa blinked at him. "What is a gairidge?"

"The gairidge. The place where you park a car."

"Oh, a garage, sorry, couldn't understand the accent."

"No, there's nothing helpful in the garage," Lilyanna sighed.

"I don't think you're saying it right either, Lily," Tessa pointed out. "You're adding like a French 'j' sound. It's not 'garaj' it's 'ga-rage'.

"Garage, with a 'dg' sound," Andrew confirmed.

"I don't care how you pronounce it!" Lilyanna exploded. "There's no generator in the gairidge, or the garaj, or the garage!"

Tristan gave her a wide-eyed glance and then stifled a laugh.

"Okay, okay, sorry, I guess it was a bad time," Tessa apologized.

Bix entered the kitchen carrying a vintage oil lantern that cast a dim yellow light just bright enough to reveal his olive raincoat and a brown wide-brimmed hat. Clearly not making it to the main house before the rain started, he resembled a secondhand, half-drowned Paddington Bear. Lilyanna had to admit, Bix did show up when peril threatened Whimser. Joe, Barret and Alyra followed behind him. Barret held his cell phone up to the ceiling, trying to get service.

"Mistress Rivers, here are two more flashlights and all the spare batteries we have." He set two wide-beam flashlights on the kitchen island with a plastic sack full of unopened battery packs.

"Where did he get a lantern?" Tessa whispered. "Is this like a 'one, if by land, and two, if by sea,' thing?"

"What does that mean?" Tristan asked.

"You know, Paul Revere's Ride—the Revolutionary War."

"The British are already here," Joe quipped.

"We didn't spend much time on that one where I went to school in England."

"Ha, I bet not," Joe snickered, lighting a cigarette.

"You can't smoke in the house, Joe!" Alyra chided.

"Well, I can't exactly go outside during a hurricane!"

"Will everyone shut the fuck up? I'm trying to get my phone to work, and I can't think with all the bickering," Barret shouted.

"That was rude," Tessa stated.

"Sorry, *please* shut the fuck up," he repeated, holding his phone up in the air again.

"Bix, are any of the landlines working?" Lilyanna asked.

"The desk phone in the library is working for the moment."

"Good, please call the Acadis on the other side of the lake and see if they have power."

The group set to distributing candles among the kitchen, dining room and living room, with the flashlights consolidated mostly in the living room, and a couple reserved for bathrooms and the hall. Dylan and Waya stockpiled snacks and board games and decks of cards in the living room, and everyone except Lilyanna followed.

"Obviously, you have game night when the power goes out," Dylan explained. "What should we play first?"

"Let's play Who Am I?" Waya suggested. "Everybody write a name on a piece of paper, and then we'll draw. It can be a character or a famous person. You hold up your paper to your forehead so everyone but you can see, and then you have to ask questions and try to guess who you are."

Lilyanna slipped into the dining room and pulled back the curtains of the floor-to-ceiling window and watched helplessly as the storm wreaked havoc on the terrace. Hail clamored down on the ivory stone, and the wind tossed brush across the front lawn. Creaking but not breaking, Whimser stood vigilant against the assault.

As Lilyanna mentally prepared a remediation plan for the morning, Tristan appeared next to her. He slid his arm around her shoulders, and she let him pull her against him, wrapping her arm around his lower back. Without hesitation, she rested her head against the side of his chest, and together they watched nature's showdown. His body felt warm and firm against hers, the rock she had been craving to keep her upright. He smelled of clean men's body wash and musk, with just a hint of lingering designer cologne—a combination more enticing than any bottled fragrance on the market. She wanted to throw her arms around his neck and leap into his arms. Instead, she curled her body into his side, her other hand on his chest below her face.

"It will be alright," he told her softly. Gently, he rested his lips on her forehead, not to tease her this time, but as a comfort. In that moment, she didn't think she could resist kissing him any longer. The touch of his lush lips, the lure of his intoxicating scent and the magnetic pull of his solid physique all at the same time was too tempting.

"Mistress Rivers, I've spoken with Dr. Acadi," Bix interrupted without an apology. "They too are without power. Dr. Acadi said the power company is aware of the outage and estimates it will last at least until morning."

Annoyed, she lifted her head from Tristan's chest. "Just great. Thanks, Bix. We can sort out a place for you to sleep in the house tonight. You can't go outside in this."

Bix smirked, "Save your concern, Mistress Rivers. Nature has been trying to consume Whimser for decades, and yet here she stands, and I with her. It will take something more destructive than that to bring us down." He turned to leave the room.

"Or *someone*," she replied. Bix paused in his tracks for a moment before continuing on his way.

"That bloke's a piece of work," Tristan sighed.

"Don't get me started."

"Who are the Acadis?"

"Neighbors across the lake. They are the only other residents up here that actually own land. Dr. Acadi is a vet, and her husband is a plant biologist. The others are tenants, renting from William, or me, I guess."

"I see. That's a lot to manage."

"The attorney for the estate takes care of most of it. I just make sure the property expenses are covered."

He slid his hand down to her waist and angled her body facing in front of him. "You do so much for someone so young."

"I don't feel young," she stated flatly, looking up at him. "I never have."

"But you are." He dropped his eyes and then slowly raised them up to hers and swept her blonde locks off her shoulder.

"Am I Dr. Fauci?" Rich's voice rang out from the living room.

"No. Am I J.Lo?" Waya asked.

Lilyanna looked up at Tristan, and they both laughed.

"This game sucks. Let's play Spoons. Lily, where are you? Come play Spoons!" Dylan called.

Tristan released Lilyanna, and she slid her hand into his. "Come on, let's go play Spoons," she told him.

"What's Spoons?"

"You'll see."

"Am I the big spoon?"

Lilyanna laughed and pulled him out of the dining room. "It's not that kind of spoons."

They found everyone except Bix and Ms. Howard sitting in a circle on the floor of the living room. Lilyanna took a seat next to Andrew, who was chatting with Tessa, and Tristan sat on the other side of her.

"There you are," Andrew greeted her.

"I was just watching the yard get blown to pieces."

"We'll put it back together tomorrow," he assured her. Tessa stared at them both skeptically.

Suddenly, a thunderclap boomed down above Whimser like a shot from a cannon, sending the room into a stunned silence. "That is, unless we get blown to pieces first," Andrew corrected himself.

"I'm more concerned about freezing. It's going to get really cold in here tonight without heat, and we don't have any space heaters."

"Does the fireplace work?" Tristan asked.

"It should, but we don't have any wood chopped, except what is in there now. I didn't think we would need it since we don't usually get storms here."

"Well, if the power doesn't come back on soon, we'll try the fireplace," Andrew agreed.

"Okay, got the spoons you asked for," Sylvie said, handing Dylan a pile of spoons from the kitchen.

"Thanks. We'll put the spoons in the middle of the circle and use two decks of cards. Each person starts with four cards, and you can only hold four cards at a time. The idea is to get four of a kind. I'll draw one from the deck, and either keep it and discard one of my others, or discard the one I draw, and pass it face down to the next person, and they do the same thing. You have to move fast so the cards get passed around the circle. The first person to get four of a kind should discreetly grab a spoon. You have to watch the spoons and your cards at the same time because whoever doesn't get a spoon is out."

"I haven't played this since I was, like, twelve," Tessa remarked.

"I've never even heard of this game," Tristan replied.

"They didn't teach you this at British school either?" Tessa teased.

"K, here we go." Dylan dealt the cards and then quickly began drawing and passing cards around the circle. Within a few minutes, the sound of two spoons clanking together between Barret and Six caught everyone's attention. Dylan reached out and grabbed a spoon, and then Lilyanna did the same. Tristan immediately followed her lead. The only person without a spoon was Barret. "Who had four of a kind?" Dylan asked. Everyone looked at each other in confusion.

"I thought you did," Saharie said. "You grabbed a spoon first."

"I heard someone else grab a spoon in this general area," he swished his hand in the direction of Barret and Six. "So how do you not have a spoon?" he asked Barret.

"I didn't grab a spoon! I was just reaching for the Pringles, and I think I hit the spoons by accident," Barret explained.

"Are you kidding me?" Dylan narrowed his eyes in annoyance. "None of you have four of a kind?"

"Do you not have it?" Tristan asked Lilyanna, peering over her shoulder to see her cards. "I grabbed a spoon because you did."

"I grabbed one because Dylan did! Dylan, you started the mix-up!"

"I only grabbed a spoon because he did!" he pointed at Barret.

"I just wanted some Pringles!" Barret cried.

"Here's your fucking Pringles!" Dylan chucked a can of original Pringle chips at him. "Now put the spoons back and keep going," he ordered. Everyone burst out laughing. Lilyanna covered her face, nearly in tears.

The game continued for almost an hour until Tessa finally won. Lilyanna had never seen Tristan laugh so much. He looked younger and lighter, his inner boyishness visible for the first time.

"Damn millennials," Joe scoffed under his breath. "I'm callin' it a night."

"But the power's still off," Tie noted.

"Aren't you astute. I'm one of those rare people who sleeps with the lights off." Jillian and Alyra also went to their room for the night.

"What other games do we have?" Rich asked.

"Oh, we have Clue," Tessa proposed, looking through the stack of board games.

"I do love Clue!" Lilyanna admitted.

"We have too many people for Clue," Dylan said. "Unless we want to split up. We have a couple of chess boards and Scrabble."

"Let's play a different card game, like rummy," Saharie suggested as she popped a Frito into Tie's mouth.

"Mmmm, thanks, babe."

"Anyone want to play me at chess?" Tessa asked.

"I'll play chess," Lilyanna agreed. Andrew, Rich and Barret volunteered to play chess, and the others chose rummy.

"Should we make it interesting?" Dylan asked.

"How so?" Lilyanna hesitated.

"If you lose whatever game you're playing, you take off an article of clothing."

"Absolutely not!"

"Absolutely yes!" Kyah contradicted her.

"Ah come on, Lily, your boss went to bed. We'll just go down to underwear. We've already seen you in that blue mini robe of yours," Dylan replied.

"Okaayyy, this conversation is over."

"I'm up for it," Andrew shrugged.

"Good, socks are the buy in. Everyone take them off," Dylan said.

"But there's no heat in here without electricity!" Lilyanna reminded him.

"I'll light a fire," Tristan offered, getting up off the floor. Lilyanna glared at him. He grinned innocently back at her. "Are you doubting your skills?"

"No!"

"Then there's nothing to worry about." Sylvie retrieved some matches for him, and he, Andrew and Rich got a respectable fire blazing in the fireplace. If they hadn't been enabling the debauchery against her will, Lilyanna would've been grateful to have the guys helping around the house. She had been so used to living alone that she forgot what it was like to have someone help with routine tasks like lighting a fire. It reminded her of spending the summer with William, her only frame of reference. He knew how to do everything, or he at least knew whom to call to get things done when he didn't.

"Now we're officially at summer camp," Tie remarked.

Lilyanna played Rich at chess first, and Tessa played Barret. Both women won within twenty minutes of the first move. "Well, that was pathetic," Rich sighed, tugging off his black hoodie.

"Have you guys actually played chess before?" Tessa asked.

"Apparently not as often as you," Rich admitted with a sheepish grin.

Lilyanna then played Andrew and beat him just as easily. "Guess I should have thrown a jacket on," Andrew laughed. "Oh, well." He boldly pulled his white t-shirt over his head. If Lilyanna hadn't seen his body already, she might have been as awestruck as the others.

Dylan gawked at him. "Damn, so that's what you have under there? I would never wear clothes if I looked like that."

The ever-unruffled Andrew didn't even blush. "Okay, then you two play the loser's bracket," he told Rich and Barret.

"And you play me," Tessa smiled sweetly at Andrew. "Game on!"

"Do you prefer to play white? It has an advantage."

"No shocker there," Saharie remarked under her breath.

Tristan and Six each excused themselves to go call their children, while Lilyanna played a quick game of rummy with the others and lost to Kyah. Hesitantly, she unzipped her grey fleece jacket, leaving her shivering slightly in a teal camisole. Kyah scooted over and threw her arms around Lilyanna as they watched Andrew and Tessa's game. "Lily, you wouldn't be so cold if you'd gain a little weight."

Lilyanna hugged her back. "Go get me a cheeseburger, then."

***

Six paused on the way to his room when he saw Jillian enter the main hall from the kitchen. Jillian heard footsteps behind her and turned around, raising her candle to eye level. "Who's there?"

"It's me, Jill," Six replied.

She lowered the candle and glided over to him, casting a willowy shadow on the wall. "Off to bed?" she asked softly.

"I was just going to—"

"Call Drea?" she finished for him.

"Yes. Did you call your husband?"

"I did." She stepped closer to him. "Do you know what this night reminds me of? That night in Miami when it rained for hours and the air conditioning went out in the hotel hosting the CLE conference. Do you remember?"

"I remember," he lowered his voice, not moving as she stepped even closer to him.

"It was so hot that all the hotel guests went outside in the middle of the night," she continued, whispering into his ear.

"Everyone except us." He nuzzled her cheek and grabbed her waist. Breathing deeply, she rested her chest against his and traced her fingers along his neck.

"We can't, Jill. You know we can't. Not now that we're both with other people."

Jillian's grey eyes glowed in the candlelight as she looked up at him. With one final caress, she stepped back and blew out the candle, leaving Six standing alone in the dark hall.

***

Tessa moved her black rook in front of Andrew's king. "Do you guys think Andrew wears boxers or briefs? We're about to find out. Checkmate!"

"Ah, are you serious?" He ran his fingers through his short dark hair. "Fuuuuck." With a sigh, he hopped to his feet and unbuttoned his jeans to the tune of spontaneous catcalls. Under his jeans, he wore a pair of navy boxers.

Tie pulled out his wallet and took out a few dollar bills that he tossed in Andrew's direction. "Lookin' good, boss!"

"Is that all I'm worth to you, man?" Andrew kicked the dollar bills back toward Tie.

In the corner of the room, Rich and Barret's game continued, neither one taking a clear lead. "I'm as bad at this as I am sports," Barret sighed.

"You're no worse at this than me." Rich moved his white pawn forward two spaces.

"You can't do that. You can only move a pawn two spaces the first time you move it."

"Oh, see? Point made. And as for sports, are you still up for swimming lessons once the weather dies down?"

Barret toyed with his knight. "I mean, I suppose. If you are."

"Yeah, for sure. Come for a jog with me in the morning. It will help if you start getting in shape."

"I'm not really a runner."

"Then we'll walk first."

Barret looked up at Rich, who grinned back at him.

Tristan stopped in his tracks next to the sofa, stuffing his cell phone into his pocket. "What happened to you?" he pointed at Andrew.

"Made a wrong move."

"No shit." Tristan's face turned slightly rosy as he laughed at Andrew. "Alright then, play me," he nodded at Lilyanna and sat down on one side of the chess board.

"You sure?" she asked, sitting opposite him.

"Dude, don't play chess! Go with poker or something," Andrew warned him.

"Have some dignity!" Lilyanna chided him, setting up her board.

"That's hard to do when you're almost naked!"

"Double or nothing," Tristan proposed. "If I win, he gets to put his clothes back on, and you take off something."

"And if I win?" she raised her eyebrows at him.

"Then I get my kit off with him," he inclined his head toward Andrew.

She suppressed a laugh. "Fine. You can play white. Your move."

To his credit, he played with more skill than his predecessor. Tristan managed to hold his own through the middle of the game, capturing only two fewer pieces than Lilyanna. But his end game proved to be worthless. When he played in the past, which could not have been often, he must have been used to winning quickly and never planned for the long haul. Lilyanna captured his white queen and advanced her knight and rook on his open king.

"Bollocks," he huffed, intently studying the board.

"You're in check."

"I noticed, thank you," he glared at her.

"I'll give you one move," she offered.

"I think I've got it." He reached for his king, but Lilyanna reached out and caught his hand and steered it slowly to his remaining bishop.

"Stop moving your king so much. You should've castled when you had the chance, but you can't now that you're in check. Let your defenders help you. Block with your bishop." She rested her hand on his for a second, and he looked up into her eyes. Taking her advice, he moved his bishop to cover his king. He recovered briefly, making a few more reasonable moves but lacking a cohesive strategy. It was mate within a few moves.

"Yes! Good job, babe!" Dylan cheered. Sitting on the sofa, Andrew hung his head and groaned.

"Have I already said double or nothing?" Tristan asked, scrunching up his face.

"Yes, and you lost, but I'd be willing to give you another shot." As much as Lilyanna would have enjoyed seeing him take off his clothes, she wanted to preserve a teaspoon of his dignity in front of the others. "What do you think you can beat me at?"

"Arm wrestling," he proposed without hesitation.

She laughed, "Can I use both arms?"

"Sure, do you think that will make a difference?" he rolled up his sleeves.

"No, can I use my whole body?"

"I'm quite confident I can pick you up with one arm." He held up his arm, bent at the elbow, and she stood up and pushed with all her weight against it. Smoothly, he slid his arm under her ribs and stood up, picking her body up off the floor with him.

She gave a soft high-pitched cry of surprise that quickly faded to laughter. "That's game. Andrew, put your trousers back on, mate." He set her back on her feet.

Dylan yawned. "Well, if we're done bingeing on man candy, I'm going to bed and hopefully waking up to electricity instead of further proof that we're living in a third-world country."

The group splintered off to go to their bedrooms, except for Lilyanna, who insisted on sleeping on the couch in case the storm caused any more damage to the house. The chill of the heatless house setting in and realizing one of the women must have taken her jacket, she made up the half of the sectional closest to the blazing fire to sleep.

Just as she prepared to lie down, Tristan returned carrying his pillow and blanket. He had changed into black gym shorts and a rugby team hoodie. "I thought you went to bed," she said in surprise.

"No, I just went for a pee." He tossed his pillow and blanket on the other half of the sectional with his pillow right below Lilyanna's. "Guess I'll take this half."

She stared at him quizzically. "What are you doing?"

"Well, there's a monsoon going on, no electricity and a fire we have to allow to burn all night in a mansion full of sleeping people. I think it's best I stay out here to make sure there are no catastrophes."

"But that's why I'm sleeping out here."

"Good, then double the chances of someone waking up before the house falls apart." Seeing the uncertainty in her eyes, he jested, "Ah, come on, you've done my hair, I've heard you say 'pussy' and seen you high; we're practically best friends."

She cringed in embarrassment. "Remind me to require a piece of your dignity to hold as collateral next time I interact with you while I'm intoxicated."

He laughed, "Well, you've seen me half naked."

"That doesn't count."

"Why not?"

"Because you look good like that." She instantly regretted her candor and avoided his eye.

Surprised, he paused for a moment and regarded her thoughtfully. Then his face softened into amusement. "Errr, thanks for that. You look good in that dressing gown of yours."

"Uh, thanks," she blushed, paying unnecessary attention to straightening her blankets.

"You look cold." He pulled his hoodie over his head and handed it to her, leaving a white t-shirt underneath. "Here, take this."

"Oh, wow, thanks. That's sweet of you." Trying not to smile too much, she pulled on the hoodie. It smelled like him—that delightfully natural guy-ish scent, with a hint of Boss, or was it Dolce? She doubted he intended anything other than courtesy with his gesture, yet it felt undeniably intimate. Wrapped up in something that had been hugging his body—a small taste of how it would feel to be wrapped up in him.

"No worries." He settled into his couch bed with his head next to Lilyanna's pillow and his body stretching out in the opposite direction from her sleeping space. She hesitantly shifted her blanket around and then climbed onto her part of the couch, resting her head next to his and facing the opposite direction.

She wasn't sure how long they talked as the rain poured and the wind howled outside. "So, you're from South London originally?"

"Kensington. I grew up there and then went to boarding school, and then university. I worked for a company in London for several years before moving to the U.S. to take another job."

"Wait, you went to boarding school? Like Harry Potter style?"

He chuckled. "I did. It wasn't Hogwarts, but yeah."

"What was that like?"

"Overall, it was honestly quite positive. I got a great education. My brothers went there as well, and we're fairly close in age. And there were sports."

"Did you play football, or soccer, I guess, in England?"

"I did play some European football, but mostly rugby. Loved rugby."

"I'm sure you did. Man, you would've crushed it at American football."

"I do like American football. Really like watching the games."

"Did you get married in the States?"

"Yes, I was working in finance at a company in Boston at the time. We were married for five years before we moved to Austin, and then another six years after that, and had our sons. Divorced about four years ago."

"What happened? If you don't mind me asking?"

"No, it's fine. It's nothing scandalous or dramatic. We just married young and grew apart, wanted different things. I was working a lot and couldn't always be as available as my ex-wife preferred. She remarried a couple of years ago, to a high school teacher. What about you? Did you ever come close to getting married?"

She smirked, "No, never. I've pretty much always lived alone since living with my brother for a year before going to college. I went straight to law school after that."

"How did your parents die?"

"My dad, he died of a rare heart condition, and my mom was in a car accident."

"They weren't together?"

"Nope, separate incidents. They divorced when I was young. Crazy, I know."

"Damn. And then in college you met the guy who built this place?"

"Yes, William. He was the only other person I lived with after my brother, and it was just the one summer I spent here."

"You're smart not to marry young."

"I'm not young anymore."

He laughed, "Yes, you are. When you get to be my age—"

"Don't start! You're only in your forties."

"How can I be young if you just said you're not young?"

"Man years differ from woman years. Men get better with age, like fine wine. Women do not."

Tristan twisted his neck to look back at her face. "What imbecile told you that?"

She turned on her stomach to face him. "It's common knowledge."

"No, it's not." He narrowed his gaze at her.

"Well, I wouldn't expect you to admit it."

He likewise turned his body to face her. Exhaling and pursing his lips, he studied her narrow face and softly brushed a strand of hair off her shoulder. "You have nothing to fear from age. Years don't count for the timeless."

Lilyanna stared at him, captivated even more by his words than his piercing eyes. No scintillating thought penetrated her mind; no clever retort contorted her lips. But it wasn't words he wanted anyway. He rolled onto his side with his head back down on his pillow. Extending one arm in front of his head, he softly tugged Lilyanna's wrist toward him. She shifted into the same position, their forearms loosely interlocked as she gently stroked his arm with her fingertips.

CHAPTER TEN
Will of the Weed

The morning sun highlighted the fallout from the previous night's tempest. Power service to the house returned by dawn as Whimser shook off the debris from the last twelve hours. Lilyanna and Joe surveyed the damage from the terrace. The lawn looked like the woods had vomited up a concoction of tree branches, leaves and shrubs. Other than a few paint scratches on the terrace, however, the house remained unscathed.

Joe leaned over the railing of the terrace and smoked a cigarette. "Well, this'll be a fun cleanup project." Lilyanna stood next to him, staring resignedly at the lawn. Joe handed her a cigarette. She took it without a word, and he lit for her.

Bix stomped around the yard, kicking brush into a pile and yelling into his cell phone. "Your schedule is unacceptable! I need someone out here tomorrow to clean up this mess!"

Lilyanna exhaled a cloud of smoke, her lungs burning from the carcinogenic attack, and rested her hands on the railing. She couldn't understand how Joe could chain smoke all day every day and still breathe on his own.

Andrew opened the front door and joined them on the terrace a moment later. "Lovely view this morning," he noted sarcastically and sauntered over to Lilyanna, whose eyes remained fixed on the woods. Casually, he slid his hand over hers and gripped the cigarette between his index and middle fingers, pulling it from her grasp. Standing next to her, he inhaled a couple of slow puffs.

Bix climbed the front steps to the terrace, cursing under his breath. "The blasted contractor can't come out this week."

"We'll do what we can in the meantime," Lilyanna assured him groggily.

Everyone participated in the cleanup effort the rest of the day, which Alyra took it upon herself to direct from her chair on the terrace. "Last night was a drill! Come on, people! We need to be prepared in case a real emergency happens. We need a couple of brooms out here, and everyone else in the yard," she called.

Kyah, Saharie, Sylvie and Nina set to sweeping the terrace, including under Alyra's feet, while Dylan and Waya bagged up leaves. Joe, Tristan and Jillian piled up branches and large debris on the east side of the terrace, while Rich and Barret did the same on the other side. Wearing white ankle pants and a sun hat, Jillian looked more like a vacationer on a mega yacht on the Mediterranean than a member of the cleanup crew.

"See, this is how you get in swimming shape," Rich jested as Barret struggled next to him, dragging an armful of branches to the edge of the woods.

"I'm not cut out for this," Barret heaved.

Lilyanna and Tessa walked the grounds taking pictures of the damage in case Lilyanna had to file an insurance claim. "It could be worse," Tessa commented as they trudged through the yard.

"Please don't tempt nature any further. My mental health and insurance premiums can't take much more."

When they returned to the front of the house, Kyah beckoned them inside. "Lily, Tess, come here. You gotta see this." They followed Kyah into the house and to the back door at the end of the main hall. Saharie had pulled back the drapes of the window next to the back door, and the other three women poked their heads out on either side of her. Tristan, Andrew, Six and Tie were shirtless and gathered around a stack of logs, each taking turns chopping them in half with an axe.

"Holy hell. Well, firewood shouldn't be an issue anymore," Tessa remarked, her eyes honing in on Andrew. She watched the way his sleek, toned back flexed with each swing of the axe, and his shorts hugged the 'v' at his hips.

"Nope, I think the hard wood is covered," Kyah quipped. She pulled back the curtain further as Andrew handed Tristan the axe. "Look at that ass. It's a peach!" The top of his heather grey briefs peeked out above his black gym shorts as he slammed the axe down, splitting the log in half.

Lilyanna turned away, her emotions bound up in frustration with herself. "Where did they get an axe anyway?"

"Probably the gairidge," Tessa snickered.

Kyah followed Lilyanna out of the hall and into the den where they could talk alone. "What's wrong, Lily?" They sat down together on the sofa, keeping their voices low. Lilyanna told Kyah about her night with Tristan.

"That's all good! He's clearly into you, so why the hesitation?"

"Even if he has some level of interest, which I'm not sure about, I don't think I can follow through."

"What do you mean?"

"It's like I have a mental block or something on sex!" she spoke with her hands and then dropped her head and stared at the floor. "It's been so long, and I think I would be absolutely terrible at being with someone if I tried. That just makes me even more nervous, and I can't get in the mood when I'm that nervous."

Kyah laughed, "Lily, the first time with a new person is usually pretty bad anyway, so it doesn't matter. Everyone's nervous when they get with someone new, but that's also part of the lure—it's novel and exciting."

"It's easy for you to say, you're good at intimacy! A lot of women are, and it comes naturally to them. He'll be expecting me to be like that, and I'm not."

"If you keep focusing on his expectations, the nerves will continue controlling you instead of you taking control of them. Forget his expectations, which are likely much lower than you think, to the extent he even has any. Focus on what feels right to you. You want to be with him, and the only way you're going to get past this so-called 'mental block' of yours is to practice. It's time to get over this, Lily. Aren't you ready to try again?"

Lilyanna lifted her head and nodded earnestly.

***

Monday morning, Lilyanna woke up half an hour early for a little extra get-ready time. Though still by no means a morning person, her phone alarm didn't incite its usual level of dread. In the place of her morning default setting of foggy exhaustion, peevishness and slight nausea, she found a rush of happy hormones and excitement, though still with a bit of nausea. Romantic intrigue is a powerful force, and Lilyanna knew she had fallen under its influence. As long as she didn't think of it as feelings of 'love'—which was for people who didn't know better—she could enjoy the high without cynicism toward the drug.

A little extra eyeliner and highlighter went a long way in brightening up her face. After donning slim grey jeans and a slate blue silk blouse that matched her eyes, Lilyanna studied her reflection in the bathroom mirror. To her delight, the mirror cast fewer insults than usual. She looked more awake, with clear, rejuvenated skin. Her hair could've done with more styling, but at least her long waves were relatively tamed. Overall, she'd achieved an attractive smart casual style.

The mood in the house also improved across the board, as the group reached the fourteen-day mark of being in the house with no COVID-19 infections. "Mimosas all around?" Dylan suggested in the kitchen as the group ate a special breakfast of French toast, courtesy of Ms. Howard.

"Nah, man, it's a workday," Six reminded him between mouthfuls of French toast.

"Essentially, this changes absolutely nothing, then," Dylan sighed.

"Guess you'll have to cancel the celebratory orgy," Joe stated matter-of-factly, sipping from his coffee mug in the corner of the kitchen.

Jillian shrugged, "Well, when we continue to fail to socially distance, we'll worry about it even less than before."

The last to come downstairs as usual, Kyah saw Tessa and Andrew entering the main hall through the front door after a morning run, covered in sweat. Tessa wore yoga pants and a sports bra, and Andrew was in gym shorts and a grey dry-fit shirt.

Andrew struggled to catch his breath. "I have way longer legs than you, and you still kick my ass."

Tessa smiled and grabbed his arm playfully. "I don't know how you could even see me in the fog this morning."

"Ah, is this what I miss by sleeping in every morning?" Kyah gushed, descending the staircase. "I'll have to start waking up earlier for this view." Andrew laughed awkwardly and excused himself to eat breakfast. Kyah gave Tessa a knowing look.

"It's not like that," Tessa started.

Kyah rolled her eyes, "M'hmm, it never is."

After breakfast, Lilyanna went out to the front terrace. The temperature had warmed up considerably into the seventies, and a dense fog enveloped the lawn, hiding the woods from view. With the humidity nearing ninety percent, Lilyanna tried to control her frizzing hair.

Andrew joined her a moment later with coffee mug in hand, followed by Tristan. "With the fog so thick, you can't really see the damage from the storm," he said.

"Well, if you can't see it, it must not exist," Lilyanna retorted. "In which case we might as well quit hiding from COVID."

"Couldn't agree more," Tristan replied.

Six opened the front door and called behind him, "She's out here." He stepped out onto the terrace. "Lily, Bix is looking for you."

Bix stepped out the front door carrying his phone. "Mistress Rivers, I spoke with a contractor who can come out to touch up the paint on the terrace, if you approve. He will not come inside the house."

"Yes, good, I approve."

"Very well, I'll make the arrangements. It's the same contractor who did the work to restructure your and Mr. Whimsergarden's master bedroom before the quarantine, so the quality of work is reliable." She froze, his words pouring like ice water over her thin blouse. Their implication was not lost on Tristan, Andrew or Six either. Now they all knew she had been sharing a bed with William.

Lilyanna stepped in front of Bix and glared at the glimmer of triumph in his eyes. Without a word, she brushed past him into the house and dashed straight out the back door behind the hall. Once she and Bix departed, the three men exchanged fuck-me glances.

"Now we know where the 'Mistress' title comes from. They were in a relationship, and not a familial one," Andrew stated the obvious.

"Damn, he shouldn't have called her out like that," Six shook his head. "She clearly didn't want people to know."

Tristan leaned against the railing and clenched his jaw muscle. "Let's not make it into something it's not. We suspected it anyway. It doesn't change anything."

Andrew slammed his coffee mug down on the outdoor table. "It does for her."

Lilyanna wandered aimlessly into the mist in the backyard through a doorway to her past. She sat with her legs draped over William's lap on the canvas seat of William's motor launch as they drifted on Lake Whimser one evening. He wore an ivory sweater and khaki shorts, his full grey hair billowing in the light breeze on the lake. She gave him a sultry smile as he pulled her body closer to him until his lips could reach hers.

Neither of them even noticed when the sun went down. William had to dock the boat in the dark and then carry Lilyanna the last half of the way up to the house because her shoes were flooded with lake water and mud. He carried her over the threshold of the front door, and then all the way up to his bedroom, laying her down on the bed.

That was the first night she'd spent in William's bed, and the last night her belongings remained in the guest room. From then on, they lived as a couple at Whimser. Boating, hiking, writing, reading and painting during the day, and sleeping together at night, she spent all of her time with William.

Lilyanna could hear William walking through the mist toward her even now. Eagerly, she hurried through the yard to meet him, unable to see more than a couple of inches in front of her. "Lily," he called softly to her at first, and then more urgently, "Lily!" She sped up, pushing her way through the foamy fog.

"Lily! There you are." Andrew emerged from the fog in the middle of the yard and grabbed her arm.

"Andrew? What . . . ?" she turned and looked around her. Nobody was in the yard but the two of them.

"Didn't you hear me calling you? Come inside, this fog's too thick." He led her back to the cramped porch outside the back door of the house. Dazed, Lilyanna tried to refocus her thoughts on her current surroundings.

"What do you want?" she asked in irritation.

"I just wanted to make sure you're okay. Look, we don't care what the douche bag butler said. Nobody thinks any differently of you."

"Of course they do!"

"No, no, I swear they don't! I don't! Making love with an older guy is nothing to be ashamed of."

She tensed up her face as if she had just been slapped. "Please don't call it that! It makes me cringe."

He paused for a moment. "What? 'Making love'?"

"Yes, I don't like that phrase. That's not what it was."

"Okayyy, sorry, I'm just trying to follow along here. What term do you prefer?"

"Having sex, or hooking up, or anything else would be more accurate. 'Making love' is not a thing." Hearing it made her queasy.

"Uh, well, I have to disagree there. That's what I call it."

"Why would you call it that? The chances are slim to none that two people having sex are actually in love with each other in those moments."

He stared at her perplexed and then narrowed his eyes. "Wait, you've never actually done it, have you?"

"Done what?"

"Made love. You've never had sex with someone you loved, who you knew loved you back."

"I haven't done it because that doesn't happen. Men sticking it wherever they want has nothing to do with love."

"Wow," he leaned his head back and squeezed the bridge of his nose. "Are you saying you don't believe in love?"

"Excuse me while I choke on this soap opera therapy session. But since you asked, I will say I don't believe in the concept of unconditional romantic love. Love is the most conditional thing there is. It's conditioned on timing, logistics, physical features, all of which are dynamic variables."

"Okay, I'm processing."

She ignored him. "And anyway, I'm *not* ashamed of my relationship with William! It's just that, I've never talked about it with other people, especially not my co-workers. You guys would have no idea about my private affairs if we were still at the office, like normal."

"Uh-huh, yes, I get the latter part. Your private life is on display here in a way it wouldn't be otherwise, but that's true for all of us. The people we work with wouldn't have seen me almost naked in your living room the other night if not for the pandemic."

She laughed in spite of herself. "True."

He placed his hands on her shoulders and turned her to face him. "I will not say anything to anyone. You have my word. But since I do know the status of your prior relationship, and your, um, sex position, no, not that! Sorry," he looked at the ground and squeezed his eyes close. "I mean your views on, um, intimacy, I think you should consider some alternative viewpoints."

"Why do you care about my views on private matters?"

"Because I like you! I think you are an incredible human with so much to offer people, but you're mentally stuck under all the heavy shit you've been through. I want you to get out of that and see that you can have something, something more."

"But we work together, and you're married!"

"All the more reason. I'm a safe space—no pressure, no judgment and no disclosure to anyone."

"I'm not sure your girl talk skills are up to par," she jested. He put his arm around her and walked her back inside.

"Probably not, but I think you've been trapped in your own head too long on the negative spin cycle. My perspective can't do more harm than your own on repeat."

***

Lilyanna went out of her way to avoid Tristan and Six. She succeeded for the most part until she walked in on Tristan and Jillian doing dishes in the kitchen.

"I've got the dishes," Jillian assured him. He ignored her and grabbed a towel. She looked at him in surprise.

"What, you think I don't know how to do dishes? I live as a single man, Jill, and I have kids to look after."

"Okay, I concede, you are quite good at this, so good in fact that you don't need my help," she teased with a light splash of dishwater.

His face broke into a smile, "Oh, I see how it is now." He sent a splash her direction in return, and she laughed on her way out of the kitchen.

Lilyanna's face fell watching them, the last drop of the tingly excitement she woke up with dissipating. "What is it?" Tristan asked when he looked up and saw her.

"Nothing, I didn't say anything," she said defensively.

"No, you didn't. You didn't say anything last night when you had the chance, either. You could've told me about your former lover the other night."

"No, I couldn't." she insisted. "And please don't call him that!"

He grabbed her arm and turned her to face him. "It's *okay*, I swear. It doesn't matter!"

Before she could respond, Sylvie burst into the room. "Lily, it's Joe! I think he has COVID-19!"

Lilyanna glanced at Tristan in horror, and they both darted from the kitchen on Sylvie's heels. They stopped at the doorway to Joe and Tristan's room to find Joe lying in his bed, coughing into a towel, his face flushed and blotchy.

"I don't understand. He was fine this morning," Lilyanna told Tristan.

Gradually, the others started gathering in the hallway behind Lilyanna and Tristan to determine the source of the commotion. "Okay, does anyone have any unused masks?" Lilyanna asked.

"I have like, four, I think," Tie offered.

"Please go get them. Everyone else should stay away from this room."

"But how could he have COVID? We've been here over fourteen days!" Barret cried.

"We won't figure that out by crowding around the infected room," Alyra said, shooing away everyone except Jillian, Lilyanna, Sylvie and Tristan.

Lilyanna turned to Sylvie. "Please bring me a thermometer and then go order enough masks so everyone in the house has at least two. If you can find disposable ones, then order a bulk supply."

Tie sprinted down the men's hall with the cloth masks a few seconds later. "Thanks, I'll replace them." Lilyanna gave one to Tristan and took one for herself, saving the others for Jillian and Sylvie. "You need to get your stuff out of this room," she told Tristan. "We'll find another room for you."

"I'll be fine without this," he handed her back the mask.

"Uh, no, you won't. Do you really want to risk getting sick and infecting the rest of the house?" she held the mask up to him again. "It won't bite!"

Grudgingly, he took the mask and put it over his face as she did the same. Together, they crept into the room. Tristan quickly gathered his clothes from the closet and chest of drawers and threw them into his suitcase.

Sylvie returned with a thermometer and helped Lilyanna and Jillian assess Joe's condition. "Joe, can you describe your symptoms?" Lilyanna asked.

He tried to respond but ended up choking and coughing violently into a tissue. "Throat burns, feel cold, dizzy," he rasped.

"Are you having trouble breathing, though?" Jillian asked.

"No," he croaked, succumbing to another coughing bout.

"Sylvie, you worked at a health clinic, right?" Lilyanna asked. "Did you help with treating any COVID patients?"

"We had a few of the less severe cases before our clinic closed. In the cases I saw, the patients usually got worse after the first few days of symptom onset but then plateaued for a time and slowly improved. He'll have to be watched closely."

"101," Lilyanna reported, holding up the thermometer to Joe's forehead. "That's not terrible. We need to try to keep it below 103."

"Should we take him to a hospital?" Jillian asked.

"Not if his symptoms are manageable," Sylvie advised. "He could get worse in a hospital if he's exposed to sicker people, and they won't give him drugs that will make a difference anyway if he's not in critical condition. The best we can do is give him fluids and vitamins and let him rest in isolation."

"I'll watch him," Jillian offered.

"We can take turns," Lilyanna said. Nina left a bottle of water and a glass of orange juice at the door, and Lilyanna handed the juice to Jillian.

"Joe, you need to drink this," Jillian coaxed, handing him the juice.

"Is it whiskey?" he asked groggily.

"No, it's juice! It's time you put something healthy in your body for a change." Joe chugged the juice without arguing and then dropped his head back down on his pillow. They stared at Joe as his eyes closed and he drifted off to sleep. "He's breathing okay for now, so let him sleep." The women left the room and pulled the door closed as soon as Tristan finished carrying his belongings into the hall.

"Everyone in the living room for a team meeting, now!" Alyra called. "With a sense of urgency, please! *This is not a drill!*"

Lilyanna, Tristan and Jillian were the last to join the group seated around the living room. Alyra stood in front of the fireplace. "You'll have to move into the guesthouse," Lilyanna told Tristan. "There's nowhere else open. And Barret and Six, start using the other bathroom on the men's hall and the half bath by the laundry room so Joe can have his own for the time being."

"Does it even matter what precautions we take at this point?" Rich asked. "Haven't we already been exposed?"

"For real, I sat by Joe this morning in the kitchen. What the fuck do I do?" Six cried from the corner of the room.

"Stay the fuck over there!" Barret insisted.

"I peed while he was in the shower," Tie stated flatly. The others looked at him in confusion.

Six broke the silence. "Wha, what are you talking about?"

"Well, yesterday morning, someone was in the bathroom I'm assigned to, and I really had to pee. Joe was in the shower, so I asked him if I could pee while he was in there. He didn't care."

"Okay," Alyra boomed, "I get it, we've all been in contact with Joe at some point, but that doesn't mean we stop being cautious. Everyone needs to stay away from Joe's room, unless you are authorized to be in there."

Barret raised his finger, "But how did he get COVID? We have to answer that if we want to make sure nobody else gets it."

Nobody replied at first. "There has to be an explanation," Andrew started. "It's been over fourteen days since we got here, and we haven't had any visitors."

Tessa took a deep breath. "There's only one explanation, then. One of us has been leaving the house and got infected and gave it to Joe."

Her insidious words twisted their way through the room like poison ivy. "That can't be," Jillian said dismissively. "We all work with at least one other person during the day and share a room at night. There's no way someone could leave and take the car unnoticed."

"Someone could've left in the middle of the night after everyone else fell asleep," Kyah suggested.

"Yeah, like maybe someone with only one roommate who wouldn't wake up," Tie added.

Six turned to Tristan, "You're Joe's roommate, man, and we know Joe snores. He wouldn't have heard you leave."

Tristan tightened his jaw muscle and sat up straight. "You're accusing me? How dare you!"

"But you said Barret snores too, and he's your only roommate," Tie reminded Six.

"Maybe it's not a Xenergy employee," Rich interjected.

"So you're saying it's me or Waya?" Dylan snapped.

"I mean, nobody really knows what you two do. And one of you would give an alibi for the other."

Dylan tilted his head. "I don't mind telling you exactly what we do, even though it's none of your business. We have nothing to hide. We've been open and honest from the jump." Rich looked away and fell silent.

"That's the same for Kyah and Saharie," Barret said.

"Excuse me?" Kyah cried.

"Come on, you would all cover up for each other if it's one of you," Barret insisted.

"Hey, man, chill out on them," Tie ordered.

"You guys would all cover up for each other too!" Kyah shot back. "I've been trying to keep it *Downton Abbey* over here, but it's about to get *Bad Girls Club*."

"Everyone stop bickering! Accusing each other is not solving anything," Lilyanna insisted, her voice rising.

"Why, are you afraid of being accused?" Rich asked.

Lilyanna paused, "What? No! It's not me!"

"It's your house and your car. You know this place better than anyone," Barret pointed out.

"You need to calm down, mate," Tristan warned.

"You're right, it is my house and my car, so if I wanted to leave I would walk out the door in broad daylight with everyone watching!" Lilyanna snapped. "Look, I'll show you. The car keys are in the center drawer in the kitchen island, where I left them when we got here." She got up and headed toward the doorway.

"Follow her to make sure she doesn't move them!" Rich shouted. The group jumped up from their seats, crashing into one another and clamoring to keep up with Lilyanna. Six was the first on her heels as she stalked into the kitchen, the others filing in behind them.

Her hands shaking slightly, she pulled open the center drawer. No keys. Panicked, she fished around in the drawer, finding only a list of neighbors' phone numbers and a few household supplies. "The keys are gone!"

"What? Lily, quit fuckin' around. Where are the keys?" Dylan pressed.

"I swear, this is where I left them the day I arrived. This is where the car keys always go!"

"Then why aren't they there?" Tessa bellowed.

"I don't know! I didn't move them. I told you all at our first house meeting where the keys were, so any of you could have taken them."

"Don't you have a spare key?" Andrew asked.

Lilyanna paused, fighting to suppress her rising panic. "I do . . . in my apartment in Austin." *Cue groans of despair.*

"That's it, cut the bullshit! I want to know who took the keys!" Alyra demanded.

"Maybe it was a ghost," Tie suggested. "This place is definitely haunted."

Lilyanna shuddered at his suggestion. If there was a ghost in the house, she knew his name.

"It would have to be a poltergeist, then, not a ghost," Tessa clarified. "Poltergeists can touch things, ghosts can't. I'm a Ravenclaw. I know these things."

"You seem to have a lot of theories, Tessa. Maybe it's you," Rich suggested.

"Why, because I have ideas? You're saying there's something sinister about a woman with a brain?"

"No, I didn't say that!"

"There's someone else who knows the property well and has no roommate, cough, cough, Mr. Bixton," Andrew spoke up.

"Yeah, you could move around the house without attracting attention. And you're the butler! It's always the butler who did it." Tie stood up and pointed at Bix in triumph.

"Respectfully, you will need to alter your deductive reasoning because I do not have a driver's license and am not able to drive a vehicle," Bix stated in a cool, steady tone.

"He's telling the truth—he doesn't drive," Lilyanna sighed.

Barret massaged his right temple. "Let me get this straight, we're stuck in the middle of nowhere with no keys to the only vehicle on the property, and a COVID patient in the back bedroom, and we don't know which one of us is responsible?"

Dylan smirked, "I guess we're playing Clue after all."

CHAPTER ELEVEN
Vigilant Thorns

T he stock of privacy in the house rose faster than that of household cleaning supplies and leading pharmaceutical companies. Any attempt to go anywhere or do anything alone received immediate suspicion and borderline stalking. The group had searched the whole house, guesthouse and Bix's cottage for the missing car keys to no avail. Lilyanna fervently encouraged the guests to come forward with the keys if anyone found them in their belongings and insisted that the person wouldn't be blamed since whoever took the keys would likely try to frame someone else. *The culprit wouldn't hide the keys in his or her own things, or would he or she?*

It didn't matter what she said, though, as it became clear to her that she was the prime suspect. She heard the catty whispers cease when she entered a room. She felt the accusatory glares stabbing her in the back no matter which direction she turned. Only her roommates and Andrew and Tristan seemed to believe her. When one of the guys made a snide remark, her roommates counterattacked, gender dividing the house for the most part. Andrew would swoop in with a half-assed we're-all-in-this-together monologue about as palatable as the unity sing-a-longs from celebrities quarantined alone in their mansions and beach houses, followed by an I'm-sorry-I-wet-the-carpet-again sad puppy look at Lilyanna. Tristan mostly stayed out of it, working in the library during the day and then retreating to the guesthouse in the evening.

The speed at which Six and Barret turned on her made her head spin. Lilyanna, Tessa, Barret and Six had been close companions since she'd arrived at Xenergy. Their sudden betrayal struck her as not only disloyal but also illogical, two qualities she would never have associated with her colleagues. As if she had time to sneak off the property! In addition to managing the house and her normal workload, she had also inherited Joe's priority work while he remained out of commission. Bears in every direction! She only managed to keep most of the plates spinning due to extra remote help from the company's administrative assistant, Carline, who had sufficient skill to triage the incoming projects.

Even her care for Joe elicited contempt. When she delivered food to his room, or took his temperature, or sat with him to monitor his condition, she sensed the others assumed she was acting out of guilt. Really, she took extra Joe-watch shifts because his room was the one place nobody dared follow her. Only Lilyanna, Jillian and Sylvie were allowed in Joe's room, and they all took turns playing nurse. Since Joe slept most of the time, she could actually have some alone time in his room, a coveted resource unavailable to the rest of the house.

Unfortunately, the seclusion offered little peace, as she usually ended up spending her alone time agonizing over the worst-case scenario. *What if Joe died?* COVID was killing people all over the world. Why would it spare a middle-aged chronic smoker? *If he died, would they all be next, one by one?*

When not in Joe's room or forced to work in the living room, she sought refuge upstairs with her friends. She even took to eating her lunch up there most days. The other women joined her in solidarity sometimes that week and ate lunch upstairs as well. "Tessa, you're wrong for letting Lily take the heat for this when you're the one with a track record of getting people sick," Kyah called her out through mouthfuls of a club sandwich.

"What are you talking about?" Tessa asked indignantly.

"Um, that time we all went to Hilton Head, and you got the flu. The three of us got it a few days later."

"It wasn't my fault I got the flu! Like, I didn't think you could even get the flu in April. Besides, I'm sure I caught it from that couple from Georgia sneezing in the elevator. I knew they were up to no good."

"Are you sure it wasn't the Italian cabana boy you were sucking face with all weekend?"

"He was not a cabana boy! He was a hospitality representative."

Kyah choked on her sandwich. "Very hospitable indeed. We got free paddleboat and kayak rentals every day."

"I thought those came with our resort package?" Saharie interjected.

"Nope, those were courtesy of Tessa's gratified cabana boy."

"Hospitality representative!"

The fastidious monitoring of each other's movements and shared workspace took care of accountability issues during the day but left wanting a method to ensure no jail breaks occurred at night. The group gathered in the living room that evening at Alyra's direction to discuss options. "I'm done with all the blaming and shaming in this house. We don't know how Joe got infected, and until we do, we're going to take reasonable actions instead of pointing fingers."

"What actions?" Andrew asked.

"How should I know? I am HR, not the security department. It's up to ya'll to come up with a solution."

"What if we have this all wrong? Maybe it was Joe sneaking out," Tessa thought out loud. Silence replied to her theory.

Andrew nodded, "Yeah, I mean, he's the only one that is sick. That makes sense."

Tessa beamed. "Then no further action is needed."

Barret shook his head. "Without proof, I'm not convinced."

"Well, since we can be fairly confident nobody is leaving during the day, we just need someone to keep watch at night," Tie proposed.

"But that person would be up alone at night and could easily sneak out," Six noted.

"Then partners will keep watch," Jillian concluded. "A different pair will stay up each night. We can draw names, and no two roommates are allowed to be partners."

"If we support the theory that Joe is the culprit, do we still have to participate?" Dylan asked.

"Yes, this is not voluntary," Alyra clarified.

"Welcome to the Night's Watch," Lilyanna said with a satisfied gleam in her eyes. The guys were already deprived of sex and personal space. Now they could add sleep to the wish list. *This is what they get for falsely accusing me.*

Alyra held out a bowl, and the guys each drew a name. The pairings consisted of: Andrew and Lilyanna, Tessa and Tristan, Six and Kyah, Dylan and Barret, Rich and Saharie, Tie and Jillian, and Alyra and Waya. The household staff members were exempt from watch obligations. One member of each pair then drew a number to determine the order of watch assignments. Lilyanna felt relieved to be paired with Andrew, who hadn't turned against her.

"Please don't draw a one. I'm so tired," Lilyanna whispered to Andrew. He raised two crossed fingers in reply. Instead, he drew a two, putting them on watch tomorrow night. Dylan and Barret drew the first watch.

"Good, so that we're all clear on the rules," Alyria continued, "the pair on watch should remain downstairs, awake, all night, making sure nobody leaves the house, including the other half of the pair. And no drinking, or other distractions, while on watch!"

***

Dylan and Waya sat on the floor in the upstairs master bedroom that night before Dylan's first night of watch duty. "What am I supposed to do all night?" Dylan groaned.

"Just talk to Barret, he's a sweetheart," Tessa advised, lying on her bed and scrolling on her phone.

"He used to be sweet," Lilyanna clarified as she sat at the vanity and brushed her hair. "He's been a dick to me lately."

Tessa nodded slowly, "I admit he was quick to jump on the bandwagon of baseless accusations, but he'll come around. Everyone is just paranoid right now."

"Easy for you to say," Lilyanna huffed.

Kyah sat on the edge of her bed and towel-dried her hair. "All I know is this shit better get figured out before my turn. I'm too old to stay up all night."

"Here, Dylan, I'll send you the link to this Harry Potter thirst quiz. You and Barret can do this," Saharie offered, reading from her phone.

"What's a thirst quiz?" Lilyanna asked.

"Ya know, like a quiz to see which Harry Potter character you think is the hottest. They have female characters on here too, so Barret can play."

"I already know I pick Sirius Black," Dylan replied.

"I actually prefer Gary Oldman not as Sirius Black," Tessa mused.

"Same, Tessa," Lilyanna agreed. "I think it was the wardrobing that threw me."

"Don't even pretend like Jude Law as young Dumbledore isn't everyone's top pick, no matter what house you're in," Waya stated.

"Truth!" Saharie exclaimed.

"You have to tell us who Barret gets," Tessa told Dylan.

"I hope he gets Voldemort," Lilyanna muttered under her breath.

***

Lilyanna ate breakfast in the kitchen that morning, seeing no further need for reclusion. The nighttime watches would soon clear her of any suspicion. Already relishing her forthcoming triumph, she nibbled on an English muffin and read the morning issue of the Skimm on her phone. "It looks like Boris Johnson caught COVID too, so Joe is in good company."

"Old BJ got the COVID? Now the UK will be taking it seriously, I bet," Alyra predicted.

Barret emerged as everyone finished eating, still in his flannel pajamas, sporting puffy eyes and uncombed hair. "Aren't you looking sexy?" Six quipped.

"Where's the coffee?"

"Where it always is," Lilyanna retorted without looking up from her phone. He trudged over to the coffee pot to find it empty.

"There's no more coffee."

"Then make some more. You might have to get another bag out of the storage closet under the back stairs." Barret glared at her and then turned to leave the kitchen.

"Someone should go with him to make sure he doesn't slip out the back door," Saharie half kidded.

He whirled around to face the group seated at the kitchen table. "Do not even think of following me out of this room! I've been up all night like some unpaid mall cop, and now I have to be up to work so that I don't lose my real job! I'm tired, I'm sober, and there will be hell to pay if I don't get some space! You know what?" He stomped over to the kitchen island and grabbed a notepad and pen and began to scribble furiously.

"What are you doing? Are we really getting a written confession after only one night of sleep deprivation?" Kyah asked in a mocking tone.

"If it's an apology, I prefer flowers or chocolates. But since there are no flowers out here, I'll go with the chocolates," Lilyanna gloated.

Barret held up a yellow post-it note with garbled handwriting that read, *Barret's Shelf.* "I have earned some personal space in this house, so this is mine!" He slammed the note down on an empty shelf on the credenza below the mail shelf. "This shelf right here is *my* shelf!" He flourished his hand as if displaying a grand prize. "All of you can fuck all the way off from my space!" Heated, he traipsed out of the room, flipping off everyone over his shoulder.

The room erupted with laughter. Lilyanna later heard a rumor that by lunchtime the *Barret's Shelf* note had been unceremoniously moved to the toilet lid in the shared men's bathroom. She suspected Tie of the antics but never found proof.

***

To prepare for her long night of guard duty, Lilyanna made a pot of tea after dinner in the kitchen. She could only hope the extra caffeine and a pinch of adrenaline combined with Andrew's stimulating company would be an effective recipe for pulling an all-nighter.

Just as her Twinings Afternoon Tea blend finished steeping, Tristan casually trod into the kitchen, wearing grey slacks and a white button-down shirt with the sleeves rolled up just below the elbow.

Her endorphins revived in anticipation. She couldn't imagine ever being able to relax around this man. His mere presence sent her mind and body into a flurry of excited nerves.

"Oh, uh, hi. I haven't seen you much the last couple of days," she greeted him, aware of the complete lack of grace in her speech.

"Yes, I apologize for making myself scarce. I should have been more available during the, err, inquest."

"No worries. I just assumed you thought me the source of plague, like everyone else."

He took a seat on a bar stool at the kitchen island. "Hardly." He put his hand over hers on the counter briefly and gave her a small smile. Lilyanna was fairly certain she had quit breathing, but it wasn't oxygen her body craved in that moment. Self-consciously, he released her hand and looked away from her.

"How about a cup of tea?" she offered in an effort to prevent an awkward silence.

"Tea? I have not met many Americans who fancy tea."

"I'm not surprised. I think the Boston Tea Party eliminated most interest, except in iced tea, which I cannot abide," she stated in her attempt at a British accent.

His smile reached his eyes as he chuckled. "Not bad, but you need to work on the British 'r'. It's always the giveaway for a Brit trying to speak in an American accent and vice-versa."

"Noted. I'll add that to my to-do list." She filled an ivory ceramic teacup for each of them.

"Nobody has made me tea in a long time," he said.

"Glad I could break your dry spell," she quipped. He nearly choked on his sip of tea. "Anyway," she continued, pouring more tea into his teacup, "the inquest, as you say, should be at an end soon, once people realize I'm not sneaking off to some COVID hot spot at night."

"Ah, but once the mob clears you, they'll just move on to the next suspect, which I'm sure will be me. They'll claim I can leave the guesthouse at night without anyone noticing."

"So, my guilt means your innocence?" she concluded, taking a sip from her cup.

"And your innocence means the noose for me."

"Maybe we can buy a little more time before judgment day," she suggested, giving him a shy but smoldering glance. "I do hear time is steeply discounted during the pandemic."

"And what would we do with that time?" he asked with a knowing smile.

"If you don't already know the answer to that question, you shouldn't have asked." She smiled internally at her boldness. Dylan and Kyah would be proud.

***

Andrew joined Lilyanna in the living room as the rest of the house quieted down for the night. His face drawn, he looked like he had already gone without sleep. "Are you alright, Mr. Heatherton?" Lilyanna asked as he sat down next to her on the sofa.

"Yeah, fine," he sighed, resting his head against the back of the sofa. "I was just on the phone with my wife and daughter." Though worry lines creased his forehead, he looked younger than thirty-six.

"I'm guessing your absence is taking a toll?"

"You could say that. My wife is miserable being locked up alone. I feel terrible that I'm not there, but what choice do I have? We're dependent on my career, and the best way to ensure I keep it is to be here right now."

Lilyanna put her hand on his shoulder, desperately wanting to hug him. Seeing Andrew so downtrodden crushed her. She longed to throw her arms around him and console him, to tell him he was doing everything right when everything in the world was going wrong. "I'm sure she knows that. She just misses you. She's probably dealing with the loneliness and anxiety symptoms of the pandemic like most of the locked-down world. We're at least immune to the loneliness here since we're practically living on top of each other. Hold that thought for a moment," she told him. She got up from the sofa and returned quickly with a glass of scotch for him. "Don't tell Alyra."

"You're an angel!" He took a long drink of scotch. "I just feel so guilty." He rested his forearms on his knees and stared at the floor.

"That's normal. But this will end. Everything does—the bad, and the good. And when it does, you'll still have your career and your family."

"Thank you, Lily, really." He gave her a resigned smile. "But what will *you* have when this ends?"

Her stomach dropped. In all honesty with herself, she had been so focused on the day-to-day drama of holding the pandemic version of court at Whimser that, unlike most of the world, she wasn't thinking about what would happen when the pandemic ended. But she knew the answer. Once the COVID clock struck midnight, all would be as it was before in terms of her relationships. Her colleagues would return to their families and their separate lives. Dylan, Waya, Kyah and Saharie would go back to Dallas, and she wouldn't see them as often. At work, her colleagues would turn back into politically correct corporate employee pumpkins, overworked and lacking in self-care, faking a smile and a cordial head nod at one another in the hallway or the break room. She would lock up Whimser and go home to her apartment. In short, she would be alone in her head again.

"I guess I'll have my career, too," she shrugged.

"That's not enough."

"Why does that matter?"

"Because you can have more, Lily, if you would just be open to it."

"And what is more, Andrew? You think because I'm not married or in some romantic relationship I'm missing out on something great. Maybe you view your marriage as something to be missed, but I would bet my net worth that isn't the norm. The pandemic is highlighting the work-life imbalance of households. Couples come home exhausted to have missionary sex, or just pass out and have no contact at all except for irritable disagreements at the end of the day."

"Maybe, but that's not why I think you're missing something important. I think you're missing out because it's something you actually want—someone to love you and be your partner and family. You just don't think it's possible."

"I thought it was possible once."

"How did William Whimsergarden die?"

"I need a drink too if we're going down that road," she sighed.

"Here, finish this." He handed her his glass, and she drained the remaining liquor. "Now just tell me."

She took a deep breath. "I was spending the summer here with William before starting law school. One evening, it was raining, and we were drinking wine on the terrace, a lot of wine. I went upstairs to lie down, and I thought William would follow. When I woke up an hour later, I couldn't find him. It turns out, he had gone out in the storm and drove off the ravine on the road to Whimser. We never figured out where he was going, or how he even got his car keys. Bix always kept the keys in the kitchen drawer, and William wouldn't go looking for them as long as they were out of sight."

"You didn't cause his death, Lily. You can't blame yourself."

Lilyanna remained silent. "I don't blame myself for him trying to leave the house. I have no idea where he was going or why. There's a lot I didn't know about William before I got to Whimser."

"Like what?"

"Well, I wasn't the first young woman William brought to Whimser, but I was the last. There was a parade of them after his wife died of cancer." Her thoughts shifted to a prior argument with Bix.

"What's all this?" she cried, flipping through papers and photographs Bix tossed at her.

"Did you honestly think you were the only one?" Bix snarled. "And I thought you were one of the smarter ones." Her hands shook as she looked at photographs of William with at least ten other women. Most of them looked to be in their twenties, some blonde, some brunette, some curvy, some petite. There were even a couple of letters addressed to William from various suitoresses. "None of you could hold a candle to Mrs. Whimsergarden—the rose in a garden of weeds."

Lilyanna involuntarily shivered at the memory.

"But he left his most valuable possession to you, not the others," Andrew said, sensing her discomfort.

"Right, but I don't know why. I had no idea he'd named me in his will until after he died. I don't know if he changed his estate plan with every new piece of ass he brought home, or if he felt confident I would become a lawyer and would therefore have a better handle of the estate management, or—"

"He actually loved you and wanted to give you all he had," Andrew interrupted. It was Andrew's voice speaking, but William's face Lilyanna saw in her mind.

She shook off the mind fuckery. "I doubt that. If so, he would've explained, left a letter or something. William was suave and charming but not a man of mystery. He was loquacious and comfortable articulating his feelings."

"Maybe he just wanted you to move on to a better life, and he left you the means to do it." William's face flashed in Lilyanna's mind again as Andrew presumed to speak for the silenced voice beyond the grave.

"No, William loved this place more than anything. I think that's why he left it to me. He knew I would protect what he cared about most."

"Maybe he left it to you because he cared about *you* most." Lilyanna saw in her mind William looking at her with a soft earnest smile as Andrew spoke.

She shook her head again in disbelief. "That wasn't William's way, and he always got his way, until the end."

"But you don't know for sure his reason," Andrew pressed.

"No, I don't. I don't know where he was going that night. I don't know why he concealed so much from me, and I don't know why he then chose me as his beneficiary."

"You don't have to be alone until you figure it out."

"There are worse things than being alone, and I happen to be quite suited to it."

"You're able to endure being alone because you're strong. That doesn't mean you're suited to it."

"If we say that's true, for argument's sake, I will continue to endure it if and until someone shows me there's something better. I have yet to see this 'more' you speak of."

"Then that's my goal for you." He took the empty scotch glass from her and raised it.

"Goals are canceled for 2020," she remarked flatly.

"Pandemic generalizations don't apply out here. The upside down of the pandemic is turned on its head in our situation."

"So, we're right side up?"

"Maybe so. Maybe we've all been living upside down for too long, and now we're finally setting it right."

The pair talked late into the night. Andrew told Lilyanna more about his wife, a real estate agent, and their six-year-old daughter. He showed no reservation in candor and spoke openly of his relationships and role as a husband and father, and his related perceived shortcomings. Lilyanna continued to be amazed by his security and openness. Any weakness he might have had he wore like a designer coat, turning it into an attribute, or even a commodity.

Whenever Lilyanna spoke to married people with a child, it always sounded so normal and doable, expected even, like they always knew they would be married and have children. Lilyanna could not relate to any such expectation. To her, it all seemed an insurmountable obstacle. There were many aspects of her life she knew with relative certainty would happen, becoming an attorney, for example. She'd seen herself going to law school and working as an attorney as early as her high school years. She had also foreseen herself traveling abroad frequently. Those visions were nearly twenty-twenty. Marriage, though, and a family—she couldn't see at all. The space those should have occupied in her mind's eye remained blank, not merely blurry in the sense they were present but with undefined identities, but non-existent altogether.

She didn't recall falling asleep. She strolled through the sand dunes above the beach of Lake Whimser as a light breeze blew around her, not strong enough to disturb even the top layer of sediment beneath her bare feet. She could just make out the surface of the water ahead. A cloaked figure stood several yards ahead of her, waiting, as the sand carried William's voice. "My Flower, come with me." Slowly she drifted toward him, the sand gently pulling her along, a telepathic magic carpet. He was close now. She could almost reach his outstretched hand. All she had to do was take it. But another voice blocked the magic carpet from its promenade through the dunes.

"Lily, Lily!" the voice called to her in an urgent whisper. She ignored it and pressed onward through the dunes, desperate to reach William, but the voice persisted. "Lily, wake up!"

Lilyanna opened her eyes as William's face in the distance faded into Andrew's a few inches in front of her. "No, I can't, Will—"

"Lily, hush!" Andrew covered her mouth as he knelt on the floor beside the couch.

She pulled away from him in stunned confusion. "Why? What is it?"

"Someone's in the kitchen. Come on!" he whispered. She rubbed her eyes and tried to force her tangled hair out of her face before pushing herself up from the couch. Andrew took the lead as they tiptoed to the kitchen and ducked just behind the door.

They watched a shadow on the kitchen wall near the pantry. With short hair and on the stocky side, it had to be a man. "Who is it?" she mouthed to Andrew. He shrugged and shook his head. A second later, Bix revealed himself as the source of the shadow, carrying a flashlight and rifling through the pantry. Lilyanna glanced at Andrew in bewilderment. Together, they hid behind the door until Bix left the room and Lilyanna heard the back door close.

"What was that about?" Andrew hissed. Instead of replying, Lilyanna sprinted into the kitchen and immediately pulled out the center drawer of the island. "What are you doing?"

To her surprise, the drawer remained empty except for a few odds and ends. Annoyed and confused, she slammed the drawer shut. "I thought he was putting the car keys back. I was wrong, there's nothing there."

"Then what was he doing?"

"Who knows? Probably just restocking his cottage. Damn! I thought we had him." Andrew put his arm around her and exhaled deeply as she leaned against him.

"Well, he's the only person we've witnessed up at night. We know he gets around."

"Yeah, but let's keep it to ourselves until we know what he's up to."

***

In the morning, Lilyanna forced herself off the couch to check on Joe. Andrew lay snoozing on the other side of the sectional. She didn't want to wake him, but she also didn't want her watch partner to get caught sleeping. Reluctantly, she knelt beside him and gently shook him. "Andrew, I need you to wake up," she called softly. He didn't move at first. She massaged his shoulder and applied a little more pressure. "Andrew!" His eyes fluttered open and eventually focused on Lilyanna. "Hey, hi. It's morning, and we need to show we're awake. I'm going to check on Joe. Just look like you're awake, okay?"

"Wait, just stay here," he yawned, reaching for her arm.

"I have to check on Joe," she insisted. "I'll bring you some coffee when I get back."

Joe was awake in his bed when Lilyanna entered his room. His voice held steady, with no signs of congestion, and even his cough had subsided, though his words were nonsensical and mostly unintelligible. Occasionally, she could make out the name 'Laurlynna,' the name of his ex-wife. She dabbed at the beads of sweat on his forehead with a cool washcloth. The symptoms puzzled Lilyanna—delusions, and sweat, with clear breathing—not traditional COVID-19 symptoms. Curious, Lilyanna switched on the top light and set to examining Joe.

"Joe, I need to take a closer look at you. Please don't freak out." She checked his arms and raised his shirt but saw nothing out of the ordinary. Frustrated, she brushed her hair from her face and stared at him. *What was she missing?* Then, she saw it, a small nodule on the side of his neck. Carefully, she pulled back the collar of Joe's t-shirt to find a massive red mound with a white spot in the center. "Sylvie!" she called. "Sylvie, come in here please!"

Sylvie appeared in the doorway a few seconds later. "What is it?"

"Please get Dr. Acadi on the phone immediately! Joe doesn't have COVID-19."

CHAPTER TWELVE
Uncharted Waters

Lilyanna clung to a ray of hope as she, Sylvie and Jillian crowded around Lilyanna's iPad screen in Joe's room for a Zoom call with Dr. Acadi. The veterinarian with curly black hair and rectangular brown-framed glasses streamed live in front of bay windows in her dining room.

"Lily, will you please hold the screen up closer to his neck?" Dr. Acadi requested, leaning in closer to her laptop camera. Lilyanna obliged, pulling down Joe's collar to show the lump on his neck.

Joe groaned, "It ain't pretty, is it?"

"Oh, yep, that's a tick bite if I ever saw one, and I've seen a lot of them. You see the white area in the center that looks like a bullseye? Classic tick bite, and his symptoms are consistent with a tick-borne illness."

"How do we treat it? How do we know which tick-borne illness it is?" Jillian asked.

"A whopping dose of Doxycycline is the first line of defense," Dr. Acadi explained. "If that does the trick, he won't need to go to the hospital. Can he use Teladoc to get a mail-order prescription?"

"Yes, our company health plan includes Teladoc. I'll help him make the call," Jillian agreed.

"Good, then call me every day to give me an update."

"I'm getting medical help from a vet—I really am up Schitt's Creek," Joe groaned.

Lilyanna pulled the iPad away from Joe. "I'd trust someone who holds animals in higher esteem than humans over the opposite any day. Thank you, Dr. Acadi, we're very grateful for your help!"

"Can't argue with that."

Joe's antibiotics arrived within twenty-four hours, and Lilyanna hoped his new diagnosis would disperse the toxic cloud of suspicion in the house. Alyra, however, insisted on continuing the watch for a couple of nights since the car key mystery remained unsolved, to the dismay of Tristan and Tessa and Six and Kyah, the next pairs in line for watch duty.

Over the next few days, the night watches failed to yield any clues as to the missing keys, but Joe progressed each day on his antibiotic regimen. By the end of the week, he started leaving his room and venturing outside for a cigarette, against Jillian's and Lilyanna's explicit warnings. Alyra promptly disbanded the Night's Watch before her turn, citing Joe's recovery as proof nobody left Whimser.

"What about the missing car keys?" Barret asked at dinner.

"Well, the stakeouts aren't producing any results," Alyra insisted.

"Worst case, I'm sure there are plenty more white vans available for rent to get us out of here," Tie snickered.

"What if there's an emergency?" Barret pressed.

"It's not like we'd all fit in Lily's car anyway," Tessa pointed out.

"Yeah, man, what makes you think you'd get dibs on a seat in the car?" Tie smirked.

Barret gritted his teeth as he spoke, "Then why did we only allow one car on the property?"

Nobody responded at first. "That might've been my bad," Lilyanna admitted flatly. "Sorry, mistake number 224(a)."

"I better broaden the liability waiver," Six noted under his breath.

***

"Well, at least we all get to sleep tonight," Tessa sighed as she sat on the end of her bed taking off her shoes.

"Seriously, I could sleep for a week," Kyah yawned.

"How was your watch, Tessa?" Lilyanna asked, trying to keep her tone casual.

"Fine, I guess. Tristan's actually chill when you get to know him. He talked about his kids and stuff, pretty down-to-earth guy."

Lilyanna's chest ached with jealousy. *Had he told Tessa things he hadn't told her? Maybe he actually preferred spending time with Tessa.*

"How was your watch with Andrew?" Tessa asked.

"Same as yours, I suppose. Nothing eventful."

"Really, cause it seems like you two are close, like closer than you should be with a married man," Tessa replied, not bothering to disguise her resentment.

Lilyanna paused and looked at her in surprise. "Uh, no, it's def not like that. We just have a good rapport. I think you know me better than that, Tessa."

"Wow, Tess, really?" Saharie interjected.

"What? Do you expect me to subtly dance around a flirtation with a married client?"

"Nobody could accuse you of subtlety," Lilyanna murmured.

Tessa ignored her. "It just seems odd that he suddenly started paying attention to you when he found out you own a mansion and got half a head nod from upper management."

"So, does it bother you more that I'm the one running this house, or that Andrew notices what I do?"

Tessa started to retort, but Kyah cut her off. "It sounds to me like you're both tired and need to chill. I understand you're frustrated with yourselves for missing a golden opportunity with your watch buddies, but let's not take it out on each other," Kyah advised, fluffing her pillow.

"Whatever, I'm going to bed." Lilyanna climbed into her bed and realized her pillow was missing. "Where the hell's my pillow?"

"Right here." Tessa tossed a pillow into the middle of the floor where Lilyanna couldn't reach it. Scowling, Lilyanna jumped off her bed, snatched up the pillow and got back into bed with her comforter pulled over her head.

The ceiling thudded in the largest bedroom on the men's hall. "What is going on up there?" Rich wondered aloud.

"We'll never know cause you guys pissed off the ladies," Tie sulked, reading from his phone in bed.

"I didn't!" Andrew replied indignantly.

"The rest of you did! I'm just saying, don't get butt hurt when half the house turns against you after you attacked their friend. Amateurs," Tie shook his head. Andrew and Rich exchanged chastised glances.

***

With Joe's recovery came Texas early summer weather. In true Texas fashion, the seasons jumped from winter straight into summer, with barely a nod to spring. Warm muggy days brought chirping birds back to the woods, and the lake finally started to reach a tolerable temperature in the afternoons.

On Friday afternoon, Rich took Barret for his first swimming lesson in the lake. "The water's still too cold. We should get out," Barret suggested.

"No, the water's fine! Just take a deep breath like we practiced and kick your legs. You can do it!"

Reluctantly, Barret submerged his head and floated for a few seconds, extending his arms and kicking his legs. He made it a few feet before poking his head up above the surface. Water rivulets rolled down his face as he stood up and sucked in air.

"Good job, man! You're swimming. We just need to work on your stamina."

"How did you know I wouldn't drown?" Barret asked, catching his breath.

Rich treaded water a few feet away and then swam back to the shallows next to Barret. "I wouldn't let you drown."

Barret breathed deeply, aware of his soaked t-shirt clinging to his untoned belly. Rich swam closer, ducking his head underwater and then emerging a couple of inches from Barret's face. Barret stared at him in silence for a second or two before hesitantly grabbing Rich's shoulder. Rich didn't flinch or pull away, he just stared back. Unsure, but determined, Barret leaned closer to Rich, their lips only an inch apart. When Rich still didn't adjust to reclaim his personal space, Barret pressed his lips against Rich's as the waves broke softly around them.

***

Most of the household gathered in the den for the morning news on Saturday. "COVID cases continue to surge in all counties as the struggle to flatten the curve wages on. Hospital capacity is threatening to exceed not only the number of available beds but also the staff available to service those beds. Until such time as the infection rate falls to the point where we can flatten the curve, the Stay-At-Home Order will remain in effect."

"So many people are dying," Saharie lamented.

"So many . . ." Jillian echoed.

"I need some air," Rich sighed, turning to leave the room.

"It's warm outside now if you want to go for a swim," Lilyanna offered.

Startled, Rich stopped and faced her. "What? Why would you say that?"

"Because the weather cleared up. It's warm outside now. I mean, it's cloudy today, and we might get some rain, but otherwise we're on the road to summer." She shot him a quizzical glance before leaving the den.

"Stimulus checks should be deposited into bank accounts this week," the reporter continued.

"Sweet, Dylan and I will get one of those. We're not able to teach the same amount of routines with in-person dance practices canceled," Waya said.

"I get one too!" Saharie exclaimed. "I had four weddings cancel this summer."

"I get one cause you guys don't pay me enough," Tie added flatly. Andrew and Rich exchanged awkward glances.

"Those checks should be paid every month while the pandemic is peaking, not just one time," Alyra sulked. "Families aren't going to survive on one check."

"You think the president cares?" Barret retorted.

"I don't think anyone in government cares."

***

Outside on the terrace, nimbus clouds began to form in the sky, compressing the humidity below the tree line. Lilyanna stood gazing out over the lawn when Tristan hurried out the front door and stopped on the steps leading to the yard. "Good morning. I'm going down to the lake in a few minutes. Care to join me?"

Stunned, Lilyanna wanted to respond gracefully, but eloquence eluded her. "Um, sure, yeah."

"Good, see you down there." He nodded and headed off toward the path down to the dunes. She stood there for a few minutes in disbelief. *Did he just invite her for a beach walk?* She futilely tried to smooth her hair down against the humidity. Her stomach in knots and legs wobbly, she slowly, yet determinedly, set off through the woods to the dunes.

Unsure where Tristan would be waiting, she did her best to appear composed, though she knew it likely did no good. Her hair styling proved no match for the dense morning humidity and the comforting sounds of nature no remedy for her nerves. Normally, she would've meandered through the dunes at her leisure, allowing them to sweep her back to another time, but today, someone was waiting for her—someone here, now, in this time. This morning, her intrigue tempted her mind to stay in the present, and she glided through the sand with purpose.

As she emerged from the dunes onto the beach, she slowed her pace at the sight of a trail of clothing leading to the water's edge. She stepped gracefully around a man's white t-shirt, followed by a pair of black gym shorts, and, closest to the lake, a towel. Tristan floated in the water up to his chest, his naked back to her. He turned toward her in the water. "Well? Are you coming in?" Trim black hair covered his pecs and down through his broad torso.

Stiffly, she shuffled her feet and glanced at the water's edge and then at him. "It looks cold," she noted with concern.

"It is," he nodded with a partial smile.

"I'm not wearing a swimsuit."

"Neither am I." His eyes gleamed mischievously. When she didn't respond immediately, he turned back around toward the horizon. "I won't look."

Lilyanna's flight and fight responses came to blows as she tried to decide what to do.

"Are you in yet?" he called.

"Almost," she replied, quickly pulling off her cami and white shorts and tossing them next to Tristan's clothes. Down to a navy bra and lace hip-hugger panties, she took her first steps into the chilly lake. Despite the iciness biting her ankles and up to her calves, she waded further into the depths. "Oh, it's really cold!" she cried as the shallow waves crept up to her waist.

Tristan turned around and swam toward her. "Here, come here." He reached out and grabbed her waist with both hands, gently guiding her toward him and further into the water. She shook slightly in the cold but didn't resist. "It's okay," he said softly, trying to soothe her. Gently, he pulled her chest against his, wrapping his muscular arms around her lower back. "Is that better?"

The sting of the frigid water faded with his touch. She felt only the warmth of his chest and firmness of his arms, so secure and alive. She nodded twice without saying anything. His facial hair had grown thicker than he usually allowed for work, giving him a delightfully rugged look that suited him even better than his clean-shaven style.

Trembling, she grabbed his shoulders and gradually slid her arms up around his neck. Their blue eyes locked on each other, and he raised his lips next to hers, leaving it up to her to close the remaining distance. She closed her eyes an instant before parting his lips with her own.

She had longed to feel those lush lips against hers, and they exceeded her lustiest fantasies—plush, smooth and replete with long-suppressed desire. She wanted more of them. Despite the gap in age, skill and life experience, he could not overwhelm her. She wanted him, needed him, to lead, and he did, but her touch, the artful curve of her lips and tongue danced the choreography as well as his. In that moment, they were equals—an exquisite *pas de deux*. His hands dropped to her hips, and he pulled her more tightly against him as she caressed his bottom lip between hers.

Suddenly, thunder rumbled over the lake, followed by a lightning strike off in the horizon. Lilyanna pulled her head back, and they both gazed up at the clouds. With an alluring smile, she pressed her forehead against Tristan's for a second, and they turned and waded quickly through the waves toward the shore. Thick rain droplets cascaded down just as they reached the beach. Tristan dashed ahead of Lilyanna to their pile of clothes, his soaked black briefs clinging to his thighs.

"You take the towel," he told Lilyanna as he tossed it to her. She put it over her head in an effort to keep her hair dry and threw on her white shorts, for all the good they would do in a rainstorm. Tristan slipped his shorts on and grabbed his shirt. "Come to the guesthouse, and I'll lend you some dry clothes." She nodded, and they sprinted through the dunes and the woods as fast as they could.

Running through the woods in the rain in her bra and bare feet, she might have been in a lucid dream. It wasn't the first time something deemed wholly unacceptable in mainstream society could be reveled in at Whimser.

Upon entering the guesthouse, Tristan ran to get more towels from the bathroom. "I'm soaked," Lilyanna told him, glancing at the made bed. *This is where he sleeps.*

"Me too," he smiled, handing her an extra towel. He went into the bathroom to put on dry shorts while Lilyanna took off her drenched shorts and underwear and wrapped a towel around her hips. She kept her bra on and used the other towel to dry off, facing away from the bathroom door. Thankfully, most of her hair had stayed dry under the towel.

Tristan emerged from the bathroom a minute later, still shirtless but wearing a different pair of shorts. He carried yet another pair of black shorts and a grey t-shirt in his hand for Lilyanna. Seeing her in front of him, drenched and half naked, he paused.

"Did you get clothes for me to borrow so I can get up to the house?" She kept her back to him and continued to towel off the ends of her wavy hair.

"I should be able to get in through the back door unseen. Nobody will look for me for at least an hour or so." When he didn't respond, she turned around and saw him staring at her, his blue eyes shining.

He cocked his head, "An hour, you say?" He tossed the shorts and shirt he'd been holding onto the floor by his feet and stepped away from them toward Lilyanna.

Lilyanna started to speak, "What . . . ?" as Tristan closed the distance between them. She stopped when he stood in front of her and grabbed her hips, pulling her towards him. He raised his glowing eyes to hers and pursed his lips slightly in a knowing look. He ran his thumbs over her hip bones just above where the towel hit.

Her body tingled in response, and she almost fell against him. He felt her shudder and pulled her closer, pleased at her willing *Oh*. Then she knew what he wanted. She wanted it too, but apprehension wedged between them. She put her hand against his chest to stop him from going any further.

"Tristan, I . . ." she started, looking at the floor.

"What's wrong?" he asked quietly in concern.

"It's just, ummm . . ." she struggled to find the words. She felt ridiculous for even needing words at such a time. Any available straight woman with an ounce of sense would've taken her clothes off for him the instant he showed interest, but she didn't have the confidence. The anxiety and self-doubt bears threatened to overtake her as she tried to articulate her worries without putting him off.

"Tell me," he urged patiently. He released her and took a step back to sit on the edge of the bed.

Regret surged along with her nerves. She didn't want him to let go or retreat. "It's nothing," she sighed, stepping toward him between his knees. She rested her hand on his shoulder and continued to stare at the floor. "It's just, it's been a while for me. I haven't been with anyone in a long time."

His concern faded to amusement. "So that's the hesitation—you're nervous."

"No, I just thought you should know, in case that's a problem." She stepped back from him, uncertain of how he would react.

He gazed at her thoughtfully. "Lily, that's not a problem for me. Do you want to stop? It's okay if you do. There's no pressure."

"No! No, that's not what I'm saying." The frustration rose in her voice. *Please don't cry!* she begged herself. "I don't want to stop," she stated with more composure.

He smiled and stood up. "Good. Neither do I." He stepped in front of her and took hold of her hips again, drawing her into a passionate kiss. She held her towel in place with one hand and gripped his forearm with the other. Still sensing her apprehension, he stopped and looked her in the eye. "We'll go slowly," he assured her. She nodded, relaxing her grip on his arm.

Keeping one hand on her hip, he unwound the towel behind her with his other hand, leaving her completely exposed from the back. He then took her hand that held the towel over the front of her waist and lifted it out of the way. The towel slid to the floor. Her skin prickled from the sudden chill of the air on her damp skin, but only for a second, as Tristan immediately pulled her against him, wrapping her up in the warmth of his body heat. His signature scent mixed with petrichor from the rain and lake water intoxicated her as she nuzzled his neck and chest.

His arms hugged her narrow waist and lifted her off the ground, setting her down on the bed as she giggled softly at the change in gravity. He climbed over her, and she quickly pulled off his gym shorts. Craving his touch, she pulled him on top of her. His kissing became more aggressive, yet still skillful, his tongue charming hers with each flourish. She moaned slightly as he rolled onto his side and took her with him, her leg gracefully winding across his hip. "You have a gorgeous body," she told him.

He pulled his lips away and gave her a slight smile. "You have long legs."

She nodded, "So I've heard."

He ran his fingers down her thigh and back up to her ass. "I must say, I quite fancy them."

"I can tell," she quipped, thrusting her pelvis against his playfully. Even through his briefs, she could feel his enthusiasm growing.

He laughed and pressed his lips against hers again before removing her bra and tossing it on the floor. Aware that she was now completely naked but he was not, she reached down and tugged on his briefs, but he caught her hands to stop her. "Lily," he started in a serious yet soft tone.

"What?" she propped herself up on her elbow.

"Are you on birth control?"

"Oh, yeah, I am."

He nodded in relief. "Good."

"But we should be careful anyway," she insisted.

"Yes, I agree." He slid away from her and reached for his wallet on the nightstand, returning a moment later with a condom packet that he set next to him on the bed. Not missing a beat, he pulled her leg back over him, kissing her even more intensely than before. This time, he let her pull off his briefs, leaving no barriers between them. The self-doubt returned when she saw exactly what she was getting into, but she tried not to show her apprehension.

Tristan's proficiency alleviated some of her worry. Unlike too many of his sex, he actually possessed an admirable understanding of how women's bodies generally work, which parts do what for a woman and therefore warrant focus. And he did focus, patiently, consistently and skillfully. Her neck, her breasts, and gradually, almost painfully slowly, down to her thighs, his tongue and masterful fingers played their aria. The savory tickle of his facial hair accentuated each note.

She moaned slightly, and then loudly, as his lips found hers again and his hand continued its crescendo between her legs. "Tristan," she whispered to him, her breathing shallow. But he kept going. Her thighs quivered and her face contorted in an exuberant release as she curled her face into his shoulder and squeezed his arm. She sighed deeply as he watched her in amused satisfaction.

He moved quickly after that, pressing her down on her back and kissing her neck. She massaged his back, barely noticing when he slipped on the condom. Kneeling over her, he pecked her on the lips and then looked in her eyes. "Squeeze my arm," he told her. She did as he said, gripping his upper arm with one hand and holding his side with the other. She had to remind herself to breathe, slowly and deeply.

"Just relax," he whispered, kissing her again on the neck.

What did Jen the pelvic floor therapist say about relaxing? She tightened her grip on his arm while he pushed inside of her. As she anticipated, it was a rough beginning. Her body had long forgotten the feeling of a man inside her, and the pains of being an uptight woman voiced their resent. But all of it waned when she focused on the deepness of his eyes and face, and his firm body pressed against hers. Not comfortable by any means initially, but tolerable—she would take tolerable as a win after all this time.

He set a slow but steady rhythm, and now the pleasured moans and shallow breathing were his. Together, they moved as one as the rain poured down outside the guesthouse. She kissed his neck and lightly bit his chest, relaxing her grip on his arm and massaging his back. Impulsively, she slid her hands down to his irresistible ass and gave it an overdue satisfying squeeze. Tristan came a minute later with a deep sigh and an O-face to make even the most desirable models jealous. Lilyanna got turned on again just seeing that face, with his eyes closed, lips parted slightly, and his jaw muscles clenching in pleasure rather than stress.

They lay next to each other, breathing deeply. Lilyanna turned on her side and rested her chin on his torso with a bashful smile. "What is it?" he asked, his eyes also smiling.

"I'm, well, surprised, that I had such a, um, positive reaction so quickly."

"Ah, well, I wouldn't have it any other way."

"You're very good at that," she told him.

"If you get to be my age and you don't know what you're doing, then you're either a complete idiot, or you just don't care to learn. Either way, men like that don't deserve your affection."

Wow, I don't think he realizes how many undeserving men are out there. But she changed the subject. She didn't want to consider that she could ever have to think of any other man when this titan of physical perfection lay naked next to her. "And you have an amazing ass," she noted, rubbing his side down to his hip. "Though I'm sure you hear that all the time."

He laughed in surprise, "Err no, that's a new one, but thanks."

"Wait, are you serious? Nobody has ever told you that?"

"No, I would definitely remember."

"Oh my gosh, that hurts my soul! You have the best ass I've ever seen. Someone should be telling you that every single day."

He laughed again and turned on his side to face her, draping his arm over her hip. "Well, feel free to show your admiration any time you like." She laughed too and kissed him on the lips several times.

"I should get back to the house." She didn't want to seem clingy or overstay her welcome. Reluctantly, she started to roll out of the bed.

"Wait," he pulled her hip back toward him. "Stay, please." With a smile, she rolled back toward him on the bed and kissed him deeply. "We'll just take this back." He draped her leg back over his hip and kissed her again, his lips pulling her back into their world alone together from which she never wanted to leave.

***

The grounds were quiet as Lilyanna made her way back to the house. The rain had let up, and no breeze challenged the muggy countenance of the day. She heard no whispers or solicitations from beings beyond the reach of humanity. Her mind was fixed on the present, the living, breathing, feeling anchor to this world. She wanted only more of him.

Lilyanna took off her shoes at the back door and tiptoed to the laundry room. She did a doubletake when she caught sight of her reflection in the mirror of the half bath. She looked like a drowned rat, with the ends of her hair wavy and damp and her eye makeup smeared under her eyes. *I can't let anybody see me like this!* In the laundry room, she quickly peeled off Tristan's clothes and put them in the dirty clothes basket. She put on the wet tank top she had worn earlier and donned a pair of Saharie's pants she found with the dirty clothes. Three sizes too big for her, they were still better than wearing her soaked white shorts from the morning.

Just as she pulled on the pants and set to straightening the hem around her ankles, Bix appeared in the doorway. She stopped dead, still hunched over, and stared at him in horror.

"Out for a swim, Mistress Rivers? I wouldn't figure you for one to dive headfirst into unknown, frosty waters, but then again . . ."

Lilyanna stood up straight with what little dignity she could muster. "I was just out for a walk, and it started raining. Now if you'll excuse me." She brushed past him and darted for the back stairs.

"Of course, we know the abruptness of the storms at Whimser, and the damage they cause." His steely gaze stalked her as she ran from her past and toward the future she now wanted.

CHAPTER THIRTEEN

Reluctant Blossoms

The mid-day sun beat down on Rich's dirty blonde hair as he leaned against a mesquite tree in the woods with his phone to his ear. He basked in the warmth radiating through his body from the sunlight above, and the display of affection Barret bestowed on him from below, as he pitched a service contract to a new Xenergy customer. "Uh-huh, a little lower. We can lower the rate if you take the full package. It's the best you can get, full service." Rich squeezed his eyes shut and stifled a moan. "So good. Sure, we can visit for a tour as soon as possible. Can't wait to come. Right, we'll finish it off. Yes, done!" Rich's face tensed as he ended his call and grabbed the top of Barret's head, a moment before Barret swallowed an indeterminable amount of time's worth of pent-up angst.

Rich clutched the tree trunk behind him for support and uttered a satisfied groan. Barret wiped his mouth with the back of his hand and pushed himself off his knees while Rich pulled his jeans up without looking at Barret. "Look, man, I know how this seems, but I'm not, you know, gay," Rich told him, buttoning his pants.

Barret paused, "What do you mean? Are you bi?"

"I mean, I'm married, to a woman. I'm just used to being physical with someone regularly."

"So you're using me for sex?"

"No! I like you. I like my wife too. When I like someone, I want to be physical with that person. I don't think that puts me into some different category."

Barret contemplated him. "I mean, I get it if you don't like labels, but if you're getting off to me like you just did, I think you're gay."

Rich rounded on him, "Well you just sucked my dick, so what does that make you?"

"Gay," Barret shrugged.

"And you're suddenly all open about it? Nah, man, don't even act like it's not an issue for you. I had no idea you were, whatever you are, until very recently. Don't get self-righteous."

"Just because I keep my sexuality private doesn't mean I'm ashamed of it. I generally keep it private because I don't think it's anyone's business. I only choose to be open about it with certain people, and I chose you because I like you, too."

Rich relaxed his stance and stared at Barret in thought.

***

Lilyanna applied moisturizer to her face at the mirror in the master bathroom before bed while Kyah sat on the edge of the tub, grilling her about her return to hookup culture. "You're in one piece, so that's a good sign," Kyah joked.

"I am, though I admit, I'm exhausted. I feel like I got hit by a bus."

"M'hmm, one of those red double-decker British buses. I'm not surprised you're a bit rundown. Pun intended."

Lilyanna narrowed her eyes in the mirror. "I just don't know. I don't know if he liked it."

"He had sex with a hot woman and got off. I promise he liked it."

"But he didn't say anything, about me or otherwise. Wouldn't he have complimented me or something if he enjoyed it?"

"Not necessarily. It's just a guy thing. You said he asked you to stay. I don't know what more you want." Kyah leaned in to look at Lilyanna more closely. "Is there something else besides your baseless worries that makes you think he didn't think you were good?"

Lilyanna sighed and examined her skin in the mirror. Her face sported a clear, youthful sheen, but the mirror quickly pointed out the fatigue lines under her eyes. "Even if he liked it enough, maybe that was all he wanted. Now that he got it, he might not want anything more to do with me."

"If so, then he's a tool, and you shouldn't have anything else to do with him."

"But, I kind of, um, want to keep him." Lilyanna shrugged and sat down next to Kyah on the edge of the tub.

"Ohhh," Kyah said knowingly. "I know what you want. You want him to look at you like you're his queen."

"That's too much to ask, isn't it?"

"I'm sorry, Lily, that's a celebrity marketing gimmick."

"So Hubs doesn't look at you that way?"

Kyah thought for a moment. "Maybe once in our honeymoon period of dating but not since, not even at our wedding. And I don't expect that of him. I'd prefer to give that up for someone I can do life with. That's what matters."

Lilyanna nodded. "I should just accept that he wants nothing more than convenient sex, then."

"I mean, normally I would say yeah, it's just a guy looking for lockdown love, but you're not exactly convenient enough for him to be using you for sex."

"That would be a poor use of me. I'm better at other things."

Kyah sighed and looped her arm around Lilyanna. "I'm sure he'll want to continue seeing you. I just want you to be able to enjoy it for what it is and not set your expectations too high. And you can relax now! The first time is out of the way, and you know you can hold your own. You can do what you want now without waiting for him to initiate. If you want to kiss him, kiss him. If you want to grab that delightfully firm ass of his, then do it. Just do what pleasures you, and hope Mother Nature doesn't send you a UTI as a welcome-back-to-the-game gift."

Lilyanna smirked, "The game, huh?"

"Uh yeah, it's a game, even when you're married. If you're ever comfortable enough to stop playing, you've lost."

***

Lilyanna sleepily poured her second cup of coffee in the kitchen Monday morning as most of the residents finished breakfast. The alarm clock had refused her the additional two hours of sleep she desperately needed for moderate functionality.

"Lily, you look tired this morning," Jillian stated matter-of-factly. No concern laced her comment, or even curiosity.

Lilyanna glared at her but kept her voice pleasant, "I suppose I slept deeply last night."

Tristan's eyes gleamed smugly at Lilyanna as he took a sip from his coffee mug at the kitchen counter. He lingered in the kitchen after the others departed for their workspaces, sauntering over to the sink where Lilyanna washed dishes. Stepping behind her, he ran his fingers over the top of her waistband and whispered, "I slept well too." Her body rested against him, her happy hormones surging in response to his touch. He gave her a chaste peck on the neck and then left to work in the library.

By the middle of the morning, Lilyanna's mind started to drift from her queue of contracts to be reviewed and emails to be answered. Casually, she excused herself from Andrew and walked to the kitchen. On her way, she saw Jillian, Joe and Alyra drinking coffee outside on the terrace. That meant Tristan would be alone in the library.

She quickly poured a cup of coffee and snuck off to the library. The door stood open a crack. Hearing no noise, she lightly tapped on the door and pushed it open. Tristan sat at the desk staring at his laptop. "Come in." He looked up in surprise when she emerged in the doorway. A cozy nook of a room, the library contained a dark cherry oak desk with matching floor-to-ceiling bookshelves behind the brown leather desk chair, and a separate wooden card table and sofa on the opposite side of the room for Jillian.

She closed the door behind her and then set the cup on the desk. "I just thought you might want some coffee," she smiled.

"Thank you, that's thoughtful," he nodded, a hint of suspicion in his eyes.

"How is your day going?" she asked, stepping behind his chair. Confidently, she took hold of his broad shoulders and set to massaging out the tension.

"Better now," he sighed, closing his eyes. She continued to rub his shoulder blades and then proceeded more softly up to his neck. He turned his head toward her and grabbed her arm, pulling her onto his lap. She smiled again and kissed him deeply. They made out for several minutes, and then he rested his forehead on her cleavage.

A knock at the door from Alyra interrupted them a minute later. "Tristan, I need your approval on some employee reports."

He rolled his eyes and sighed in frustration. "I'm just getting off, I mean, a call, I'm just getting off a call. I'll come find you in a moment," he called to Alyra.

Lilyanna snickered and climbed off his lap. "I'll let you get back to it, that call I mean." She smiled to herself as she departed the room, with him cursing under his breath and trying to flatten the front of his jeans.

***

After a tedious afternoon of work, Lilyanna sat in the kitchen enjoying a dose of caffeine with her friends when Bix abruptly stomped into the room in a tizzy. "Mistress Rivers," he panted, "there is a situation in the storage shed. Please come at once."

"'A situation in the storage shed,'" she mocked him in her best imitation of his fake pretentious accent.

"We'll come with you," Saharie assured her. The quartet trooped out behind Bix to the slate-roofed shed behind the garage. Bix pulled back the sliding door and pulled a string to cast a dim light over the concrete floor.

"Do watch your step, please," he advised.

"What is this situation, Bix?"

"Over here, madam," he gestured to the back corner of the shed where a ball of fur curled into a half spiral.

"Oh my gosh, it's a cat!" Lilyanna reported in surprise. Actually, the ball turned out to be three cats snuggled together—a white mother cat with orange stripes and two kittens, one white with grey spots and the other a calico.

"Meows!" Kyah cried. All of the women squatted on the floor and gently petted the unexpected guests.

"How old are the kittens?" Tessa asked.

Saharie held the calico on her lap. "I would guess around three weeks, but they're quite small."

"The mom looks a little fatigued. She may not be able to nurse them anymore. They need food and water. Let's get them in the house," Lilyanna directed. She sent Bix to get Sylvie and Nina to bring clean towels and sheets.

Together, they wrapped each kitten and the mother cat in a towel and carried them into the den of the house. Sylvie hurried off to order cat food and beds as the other residents began poking their heads into the den to find the source of the commotion.

"Aww, they're adorable!" Jillian and Alyra joined the others on the den floor, followed by Andrew and Tie.

Barret and Rich kept their distance. "I'm allergic to cats," Barret cringed.

"Then sleep outside," Lilyanna replied coolly, rubbing the mother cat's head.

"You plan on keeping them? In the house?" he asked incredulously.

"Yes, yes, I do. This is their home too now." Lilyanna brushed past him and went to the kitchen to get water for the cats. Barret and Rich followed her, claiming she had no authority to let the cats move into the house.

"What's all this?" Tristan asked, entering the kitchen in confusion as she filled small bowls with tap water. Lilyanna explained the situation and her decision to keep the cats.

"But people have allergies!" Barret insisted.

"*You* have allergies," Lilyanna corrected him.

"I do too!" Rich backed him.

"Then you'll have to deal with it! I'm keeping the cats. They can stay upstairs for the time being."

Barret made another appeal to Tristan, drawing increasing disdain from Lilyanna. "It is my choice, and I've said we're keeping the cats!" Lilyanna insisted, her volume rising in anger. She stood up straight and stared Tristan down.

He looked at Barret, and then at the don't-fuck-with-me stamp on Lilyanna's forehead. "The cats stay," he stated determinedly. She gave a damn-right nod and took the water bowls into the den.

"Did Daddy Tristan say we can keep the cats?" Tie jested.

"Don't call him that!" Lilyanna snapped. "And it's my decision, not his. Let's pick out names."

After a Zoom consultation with Dr. Acadi and the arrival of cat food, beds, flea medication, toys and even an unassembled cat tower, Whimser's newest furry residents settled into their proper role as the center of attention. The mother cat, Fleur, quickly regained her strength with regular meals and rest, despite the persistent pestering of the white and grey kitten, Marie, and her calico sister, Jazzmine.

The cats stole the affection of everyone in the house suffering from furry companion withdrawal. Even Barret overcame his alleged allergies for a peek at them curled up in the bed in the upstairs den, and Tristan, who initially kept his distance, citing his status as a dog person, guided Marie and Jazzmine onto the new cat condo he had assembled with Andrew and Six.

The cats' charm drew more guests upstairs, leaving the women with even less privacy. Even in the early morning before Lilyanna got out of bed, she'd hear Ms. Howard delivering plates of boiled chicken, or some of the guys petting the cats in the den before a morning run. Andrew developed a particular fondness for Jazzmine. One morning before sunrise, he crept into the master bedroom and woke Lilyanna when he couldn't find Jazzmine. Lilyanna pulled her comforter over her head and rolled onto her opposite side when he gently shook her awake. "Have you lost your mind?"

"Would I know if I had?" he quipped.

"Get out!" she whined, barely conscious.

"Okay, okay, but I just need to find Jazzmine! She's missing."

"She's right here." Lilyanna pulled back her blanket to reveal the kitten curled in a ball, eliciting a high-pitched squeak at the movement of the bed.

"There you are, my sweet," he cooed, reaching over Lilyanna and scooping Jazzmine in his arms to carry her out of the room. Lilyanna groaned in annoyance and went back to sleep.

When Lilyanna, Tessa and Kyah made their way down to the kitchen with Dylan and Waya that morning, they found Ms. Howard beaming at Tie like a proud momma beagle as he leaned over the kitchen island chatting with her. "Aww, you're such a good gentleman," she pinched his cheek.

"Oh, Ms. Howard, you're too kind," he smiled.

"What is going on in here?" Lilyanna asked suspiciously.

"Never you mind. You can count on me, Tyson," she nodded to him and went into the dining room.

Lilyanna glared wide-eyed at Tie until he explained. "I asked Saharie to go on a date with me. I mean, we can't actually go anywhere, so I just asked Ms. Howard if she would make a special dinner for the two of us Friday night."

Lilyanna paused, his plan catching her off guard.

"Wow, that's sweet, Tie. I'm impressed," Tessa approved. "We can help with the arrangements."

"Yeah, count me in," Kyah agreed.

"That would be great, thanks. I asked Ms. Howard about ordering her flowers, but she said the only florist in driving distance doesn't make deliveries."

"Could you just pick some flowers?" Dylan suggested. "That would be a cute gesture."

"Flowers don't grow at Whimser," Lilyanna reminded them. "And Ms. Howard is right—the only florist is a thirty-minute drive from the property, and it's inside the supermarket, which is likely busy."

"Oh. We'll still make it special anyway," Tessa waived her hand dismissively.

When Tie left the room, Lilyanna whispered to Tessa and Kyah, "Have they even hooked up yet?"

"I don't think so," Tessa replied.

Kyah watched Lilyanna knowingly. Lilyanna fought to keep her face void of expression and said nothing.

"Why don't we have a date?" Dylan asked Waya as they sat at the kitchen table.

"Because we're together twenty-four/seven!" Waya snapped. "If anything, I need a me-time date by myself."

"We should have a ladies' night this weekend," Tessa suggested. "Wine, beauty treatments, the works."

"Ooh, I like where your head's at," Dylan agreed. "Can Waya and I participate even though we're not ladies? I'm in desperate need of a facial."

"Of course, you're always welcome," Tessa replied.

"Right, drinks, beautification, then we do OnlyFans," Kyah added.

***

Friday night, Lilyanna and Kyah transformed the front terrace into Café de Whimser, complete with candlelight and, most importantly, privacy. Lilyanna set the iron patio table while Kyah concocted various threats against the other residents to keep them away from the date scene.

"Come near the kitchen or the terrace before ten o'clock, and I'll make sure all of your underwear gets lost in the laundry this time!" she yelled down the men's hall.

A little before eight, Tie paced in the hall in front of the staircase, fidgeting with his bowtie. He wore a sky blue button-down dress shirt tucked into navy slacks and a navy bow tie, his hair neatly combed back from his tan face.

Tessa hurried down the front stairs a few minutes later to announce Saharie's imminent arrival. "Are you nervous, Tie?" Tessa jested, elbowing his side. But he didn't hear her. His eyes fixated on the ethereal golden apparition descending the stairs. In a canary yellow strapless dress with a fitted bodice and flared skirt hitting a few inches above her knees, five-inch gold strappy stilettos and full nighttime makeup artfully applied over her sleek skin, Saharie rivaled any Miss Universe.

"I better come out of ladies' night looking like that," Waya whispered to Lilyanna and Dylan at the front of the hall.

"Wow, um, you look, so, so beautiful," Tie stammered, offering her his arm at the bottom of the stairs.

She smiled confidently, "Thanks. You're looking good yourself."

"I'll show you to your table," Dylan said and led them out the front door as Tristan walked into the house, wearing jeans, a t-shirt and black ball cap. He stopped in his tracks and stared at Saharie in surprise.

"Where on earth is she going?" he asked Lilyanna in the hall. His eyes followed Saharie as she glided to the terrace.

"What are you doing in here? Nobody is supposed to be in here right now!" She grabbed his arm with both hands and led him to the back of the hall. "Saharie and Tie are having a date, and we've been making every effort to make sure nobody disturbs them."

"A date?" he gave her a puzzled look.

"Yeah, a date. Tie asked Saharie to have dinner alone with him and arranged for Ms. Howard to make them a special dinner on the terrace. You know, it's an activity some people do to spend time together and get to know each other."

"Yes, I've got the gist of it now, thank you," he retorted. He sighed and looked at the floor. "I'm sorry I barged in at an inopportune time. I just came up to watch a game with Andrew." He turned his eyes back to her uncertainly and took her hand.

"It's fine, but I have to get back to helping in the kitchen. I think the guys are in the den." She pulled away and went back to the kitchen to oversee dinner service for the happy couple.

On the terrace, Waya filled glasses of champagne for Saharie and Tie as they chatted. "This is possibly the cutest setup ever," Saharie smiled. "Thank you for doing all this," she told Tie.

"You deserve so much more! I was a bit constrained with the available resources."

"No, no, it's perfect!" she insisted. He smiled contentedly and took a drink of champagne.

"Good evening," Dylan approached the table. "I would like to recommend the special this evening."

"And what is the special?" Tie asked.

"Whatever Ms. Howard will give me without throwing a pan at my head."

"Sounds great," Tie nodded.

"Yeah, two of those, please," Saharie agreed.

Ms. Howard's date night special turned out to be a filet, mashed potatoes and grilled vegetables, followed by key lime pie. Dylan and Tessa served the food, while Waya kept their wine glasses filled with Bordeaux. Lilyanna and Kyah remained in the kitchen cleaning up the regular dinner dishes from earlier in the evening to allow Ms. Howard to focus on the private dining experience.

While Saharie and Tie lost themselves in conversation over more wine after eating, Kyah excused herself for a private Zoom chat with Hubs upstairs, and Lilyanna and Tessa joined the guys in the den. Tessa sat on one of the sofas next to Andrew, and he opened a beer for her.

"Here, please sit," Tristan dropped his legs off the sofa and sat up to make room for Lilyanna. Notwithstanding the subconscious comparison to Tie and Saharie her mind insisted on drawing, and the resulting insecurities nagging at her, she still wanted to be near Tristan. It was in no way lost on her that he had not asked to spend time with her, or do an activity, or even eat a meal together. His lack of follow-through didn't poison her desire, but it rocked her confidence.

Lounging on the couch in his hat watching a football game, he looked the most relaxed she had seen him. She didn't want to ruin it. She pictured herself curling up against his chest and him wrapping his arms around her, like a couple would do on a casual evening watching TV. That being out of the question, she flashed him a small smile and let her foot rest against his for a second. Theirs was not normalcy, only stolen moments and discreet suggestive glances.

Lilyanna, Tessa and Kyah assumed the date went well when Tie and Saharie continued their evening in the living room to watch a movie, and Saharie didn't make it upstairs until after midnight.

CHAPTER FOURTEEN
Self-Care

Jillian spent her Saturday morning sitting at the patio table on the terrace in her sun hat reading an article from *The Economist* on her iPad. Seeing her alone, Six wandered out to the terrace to join her. "Nice day," he remarked, staring out at the lawn.

"It is. So nice I sometimes manage to forget for a moment where I am and why," she replied, without looking up from her device.

"How are you, Jill, really?" Six asked, turning to face her and leaning against the terrace railing.

"I am as you find me, Ryan." She turned off her iPad and set it on the table.

"Stunning, then?"

She smirked, "Did you really come out here to flirt with me?" She took off her reading glasses and looked up at him.

"Nah, not originally, but plans change."

"They do indeed," she partially smiled at him.

"How's your family?"

She sighed, "I worry for my son. He's working constantly treating COVID patients. He already recovered from the illness himself, but I'm concerned for his health long-term."

"I'm sorry. That sounds tough. But you must be proud of him."

"I am, yes. He's strong."

"No mystery where he got that from."

"Definitely not my ex-husband."

"How's your current husband holding up?"

"Without me, you mean? He's just fine. We're more of an absence-makes-the-heart-grow-fonder couple. Long distance actually suits us quite well. In fact, I don't think our marriage would've survived a quarantine together."

Six fell silent and stared at his feet. "Are you happy, Jill? Away from here, I mean. Are you happy?"

"How many people do you know who are generally happy with their day-to-day lives?" she replied sardonically. "Like most, I have happy times, with my son, and, yes, even my husband. Can you honestly tell me you're happy with your lifestyle?"

He thought for a moment. "I get tired. Drea gets tired. I'm happy to be part of my kids growing up, but I really don't see them that much, just nights and weekends."

"Exactly. There are times when we feel genuinely happy, but to say those moments grace us with their presence routinely would be a lie. Our society is not set up to facilitate happiness as a lifestyle. Rather, happiness is offered as a rare reward for the hustle and toil we maintain to stay afloat. It's the annual vacation we've worked all year to earn, or the living room furniture we've saved for, or a day off with our kids. In short, it's the escape from an unhappy reality that makes us happy. But now, there are no rewards, no escapes. People can't go anywhere or take their kids out or buy anything due to unemployment and supply shortages. When people can no longer find their happiness source outside of daily reality, where do you think they'll look next?

"I don't fear all change from the pandemic, Ryan. COVID is killing us quickly; our way of life is killing us slowly. We need to get control of both. Living for escapism is not really living. I would be delighted to think there could come a day in my son's lifetime when he's not living from one rare break from reality to the next in order to get through an empty existence for the majority of his life. Escapism is a dream, a vacation, not a lifestyle."

Six slowly walked over to Jillian's chair and rested his hand on her shoulder. Without hesitation, she placed her hand on top of his, and neither of them moved.

***

That night, Tessa banned all the men except Dylan and Waya from the upstairs, even for feline visitation. Saharie threw open her Pandora's box of cosmetics, turning the master bedroom into a makeshift department store makeup counter, while Lilyanna filled wine glasses with rosé.

"Saharie, my acne is flaring up. My skin is like dry and oily at the same time. What should I use?" Dylan asked, sitting on the floor reading product labels.

"Start with this rejuvenating mask." Saharie tossed him a green packet.

Tessa and Kyah, already on their second glasses of wine, slipped into bikinis for a soak in the bubble bath. "No guys better come up here once I put green goo on my face," Tessa said. "I could see a surprise invasion from any one of them, even Barret, who claims to be allergic to the cats."

"Oh, you don't have to worry about him," Saharie assured her. "He's gay." The other women gaped at her.

"Shut up! What makes you think that?" Lilyanna asked, stunned.

"I didn't pick up on it at first, but after a couple of weeks, it was obvious. I'm surprised you and Tessa didn't know."

"Did you know after spending the night with him on watch?" Tessa asked Dylan. "I'm guessing he wasn't looking at Hermione in that Harry Potter thirst quiz."

Dylan shrugged. "I'm not surprised, but it's his business, not ours."

Tessa sat down on the edge of her bed and took a sip of wine. "I swear I had no idea! All this time, and I never knew. Why would he keep it a secret? There are no gender or sexual norms anymore. He couldn't possibly think we would care."

"We would've supported him!" Lily insisted.

"I'm sure it's nothing to do with y'all," Dylan replied, sticking a mint-green collagen mask to his face. "A lot of people stay in the closet, even now, and your company is some kind of conservative construction business, right? It's not that surprising. He'll let you know in his own time, maybe."

"But he must be lonely! Shouldn't we talk to him about it?" Tessa asked.

"Noooo!" Dylan replied. "If he wants to discuss it with you, he will. Just because he doesn't share his orientation with his colleagues doesn't mean he's lonely or suffering. He just wants to keep his private life private. The best thing you can do is just keep being his friend and don't treat him any differently."

Jillian, Alyra, Sylvie and Nina arrived at the party a few minutes later. "Okay, who's doing something about my nails?" Alyra asked.

"I got you," Saharie assured her. They all went into the den to give Saharie more space to do manicures and pedicures, except Tessa and Kyah, who shared a bubble bath in the master bathroom.

Tipsy, and wine glass still in hand, Tessa propped against the opposite side of the tub from Kyah and gathered bubbles over her chest. "This feels soooo good."

"I'll take anything that makes me feel remotely good. I don't recall going this long without sex since I lost my virginity," Kyah sighed, resting her head against the wall of the tub.

"You miss Hubs, don't you?"

"Yeah, a lot. I miss his company, of course, but it's really the physical stuff that's been getting to me. He's just so good at everything. I always said, if I ever found a man who was actually good at going down on me, I'd marry him. And I did." She raised her wine glass.

Tessa laughed and looked up at the ceiling, "Ah, well, that's a feat. You know, I don't think I've ever had that done properly. The technique is always off, so much that I don't even want it attempted most of the time."

"Noooo, that's so sad! Does Alec not get the job done down there?"

"Psh, no. The few times he's tried were a disaster."

"Tess, that's like strike twelve for this guy."

"Yeah, you're right. I guess I hoped he would figure it out. I mean, it shouldn't be that difficult."

Kyah laughed, "Men are in desperate need of education on how the female body works. Have you tried guiding your guy? It can be awkward, but a little instruction can go a long way."

"No, I just make noise and pretend to like it and then move on to something else as soon as possible."

"Seriously? A guy is not going to learn if you pretend to like what he's doing wrong."

"I know, I know, it's just, to be honest, I don't necessarily like being the dominant one in bed." Tessa paused and took a deep gulp of wine. "I mean, I'm in boss mode all day. I want something different when I get home. I feel anti-feminist for admitting that."

"Don't feel that way! Look, my brand of feminism is you do what works for you regardless of whatever the gender norm fad of the month happens to be. Sure, sometimes you wear the pants, but sometimes you wear nothing."

Tessa sighed, "That doesn't help me explain to a lover how to be better at love."

"Come on, Tess. Sex has nothing to do with love."

Tessa looked down at her wine glass. "I wish it did."

"Sometimes so do I."

Tessa laughed for no reason. In her fit of laughter, she slid deeper into the tub and raised her bent leg. Kyah also pulled her leg up and put her foot flat against Tessa's as they both laughed into the bubbles splashing up to their necks.

When they rejoined the others in the den, everyone wore cosmetic face masks, and Waya sported plastic wrap stuck to his lips. Lilyanna lay on the sofa with Marie purring on her chest. "My therapy kitty," she sang to Marie.

Jillian and Alyra, at least one stop past tipsy, sat next to Sylvie and Nina, trying to give them life advice through sips from their rapidly emptying glasses. "Ladies, you've got to be strategic to get where you want to go. You don't want to be housekeepers the rest of your lives, do you?"

"Where have you two been?" Dylan asked the towel-wrapped Kyah and Tessa.

"In the bath, having an intellectual discussion on straight men's ineptitude," Tessa replied slowly.

"Oh dear, don't do that in the bath," Jillian warned. "Your skin will be pruney by the time you finish."

Alyra smirked and continued to file her nails. "I know that's right."

"Ah, you're right, now I look even older," Tessa groaned.

"Please, you're what, thirty? All of you are very young," Alyra corrected her.

Tessa refilled her glass of rosé. "People in their twenties are young. I still can't believe I'm thirty."

"Nah, the contagious social proposition that women are at their best in their twenties is fake news—as fake as the press releases coming out of DC right now. Don't fall for it. People try to feed you so much BS in your twenties, and you don't know enough of the world yet to figure out what's true and what's not."

"Like all the self-help guides for personal fulfillment?" Kyah suggested. "Those are the worst."

"Yeah, that's all garbage," Alyra agreed. "The notion those con artists market over and over in more versions than iPhones—that you have to learn to love yourself before someone else will love you— is ridiculous. Few people are actually that fond of themselves, and the ones I've seen who are don't seem very loveable to me."

Jillian nodded. "Your twenties are a pretty delusion of what you think you want your life to look like before you know better. If I hadn't been married in my late twenties, I wouldn't have been divorced in my early thirties."

"But older men are attracted to women in their twenties," Tessa pointed out.

"Yeah, for mistresses," Kyah interjected. "Take it from someone who was once a mistress and now a wife. I know what it's like to be the woman men go looking for when they get bored with their wives. In your twenties, you're in the mistress pool of shiny distractions. By the time you get into your thirties, you know what to expect from men, or not expect, and how to manage those expectations. All be damned if Hubs ever gets bored with me."

"But I'm still in my twenties, barely, and I think I'm pretty woke," Saharie added.

"I think the timing might be different for the magical age of self-assertion when you know and enforce your limits versus the existential woke," Lilyanna pointed out.

Jillian agreed, "I think that's correct. I would say I was woke by the time I graduated law school in my mid-twenties, but not confident in enforcing my limits." She leaned back in her chair, deep in thought. "I remember my first year as an associate attorney at an international firm in New York. Law firms are incestuous cesspools. One night in particular stands out from the rest. I was working late at the office, as I often did, billing an obscene number of hours.

The senior partner in my practice group and I were preparing for a merger closing the next day, a deal we'd been working on since I started at the firm.

"This senior partner, he fit the stereotype, a workaholic with a wife and kid or two in Connecticut to avoid the real estate prices in the city. He was a talented attorney, well respected in the industry, many big business clients. I looked up to him. From my first day at the firm, I set out to become his lead associate, and I did. We worked well together. I learned about all of his transactional matters and his clients. I didn't know whether I could be smarter than the other associates, but I could outwork them. He told me he noticed that, how hard I worked for him."

Jillian drank deeply from her wine glass. "Then that night happened. When we finished putting the final touches on the closing documents in the conference room, he suggested we have a drink to celebrate. A couple of glasses of Johnnie Walker later, I recall sitting on the conference table laughing at a story he told. It was then I saw his eyes change. The way he looked at me, it somehow shifted. He brushed my face with his fingers and told me how pretty I looked. I could see his wedding band out of the corner of my eye. The next bit is predictable. He was on top of me on the conference table, doing what men think they do best. But what's different here is I did nothing to try to stop him. I didn't say no or try to push him off. I did nothing at all. I froze."

Lilyanna's stomach clenched as she listened. Jillian had never shared anything personal, much less such a traumatic moment of her past.

Jillian continued, "To be clear, I had thought of him in that way before, when I touched myself at night. I found him attractive and successful. I thought I could never be someone he wanted."

"*You* thought that?" Lilyanna burst out. When everyone looked at her with a that's-what-you're-getting-from-this glare, she backtracked. "Sorry, I'm sorry. Please continue."

"Did you want to be with him that night?" Tessa asked.

"Not like that, no. I didn't want to be with a married man, and I honestly never thought I would be faced with the possibility. It wasn't naiveté—I knew that men do this kind of thing. It was my lack of self-esteem in thinking no man would ever choose me. I know now how ridiculous that sounds, as if men are only unfaithful with models.

"The strange thing is, I didn't think about his wife or my fears in those moments. I only thought about his smell. I had to wear his dress shirt out of the building because he came in mine, and I smelled of him—scotch and sweat and cologne residue. I smelled of him for two years no matter how much designer perfume I wore. I panicked in elevators and meetings because surely others could smell him, too, and then they would know I was bought, though he paid no price for what he'd taken. Only I did that."

"What happened afterwards?" Saharie asked tensely.

"Well, I told him at work the next day that I thought it best we keep things professional going forward, for the sake of our careers. Honestly, I thought he'd be relieved to know I had no intention of making trouble or demanding any type of relationship from him. But instead, he slowly cut me out of his work, and my billable hours declined. When it came time for promotions to senior associate, I was passed over. Never underestimate the fragility of a man's sexual ego."

The weight of her revelation stifled all of the voices in the room. When someone recounts an unfortunate tale, the first inclination is to say I'm sorry, but futile niceties seemed gauche here, too weak to be deemed sincere. Further, Jillian Pyke was not a figure to be pitied; she would take it as a slight.

"Should we toast to surviving the roaring twenties of womanhood?" Tessa finally broke the silence.

"I think survival is the accurate term," Kyah agreed. "Good riddance to a period of my life when survival was my goal."

Jillian laughed softly. "In your early twenties, you still think a handsome prince will show up on a white stallion to save you. In your late twenties, you're disappointed and resentful when you realize nobody is coming. By your thirties, you don't give a fuck, and actually want back all the fucks that you gave in your twenties."

"In fact, you're relieved no prince showed up on a stallion because he probably would've had no job or drive and would just make more work for you," Alyra added.

Jillian raised her glass. "M'hmm, embrace your thirties, and your forties and fifties, ladies and gents. You know what you want now, and you can no longer be conned into accepting a bill of goods for anything less."

CHAPTER FIFTEEN
Garden Party

As the weather continued to warm up over the next couple of weeks, the residents spent more time outside in the woods and at the lake in the evenings and on weekends. Six and Tessa found paddleboards and a couple of inner tubes in the garage that became hot commodities. Lilyanna eased back into evening walk/runs with the hope of managing her stress, training to outrun the bears she couldn't manage, and getting back into shape for the coming summer.

One Thursday evening, Lilyanna went out for an evening jog in the woods, while Tessa and Jillian sat in on a Zoom call with Six and his eight-year-old daughter in the kitchen. "Baby, tell me what you need for your science project?" Six spoke to the camera on his laptop.

"I have to do an experiment and put it on a board," the tiny face in the Zoom panel smiled back at him. She wore Princess Tiana pajamas, and her hair was braided back into a ponytail.

Six took notes on a legal pad. "M'hmm, okay, Daddy, Daddy will help you with that. What experiment do you have to do?"

His daughter shrugged. "I don't know. You have to think of one."

"What do you mean you have to think of one? Does your teacher not tell you what to do?"

"No, you have to pick one yourself."

He turned toward Tessa and Jillian, "You mean I pay for private school, and I have to come up with the assignments too?"

Jillian slipped on her reading glasses and opened her laptop. "Science projects are always for the parents, not the kids. Let's see if we can find some ideas online."

"Can I just order one of these on Amazon?" Six asked.

"We can find a board that's premade and just fill in the blanks for her hypothesis," Tessa surmised. "Honey, what's your hypothesis?"

"I don't know," the child shrugged.

"Don't worry, baby, Daddy will get you one of those too. Can you just find something on Amazon?" he begged Tessa and Jillian. The women nodded urgently and squinted in confusion at Jillian's search results.

When Lilyanna returned from her jog, she found the group still gathered in the kitchen. She perched on a bar stool next to Dylan and chugged a bottle of water, while Saharie, Tie, Waya and Kyah stood over the counter attempting to reassemble a few damaged cat toys. "Lily, do you have any tape?" Dylan asked.

"Sure, I'll find it." She pulled open a couple of drawers in the kitchen and then the center drawer. As she absent-mindedly scanned the contents, her eyes fell on the keys to her car, smack in the middle of the drawer. "What the . . . ?" She held up the keys in shock as all eyes turned to her.

Alyra immediately called a house meeting in the living room. "You guys are manspreading all over this couch," Dylan called out Tristan and Andrew for sitting with their legs too far apart.

"What does that mean?" Tristan exchanged confused glances with Andrew.

"It means close your legs! You're taking up too much space."

"I can't help my size," Tristan replied defensively. "Fine, I'll stand." He got up and stood at the front of the room near the doorway.

"Everyone, listen!" Alyra boomed. "I want to know who put the car keys back in the kitchen drawer. *Now!*" she enunciated. "I'm not playing around!"

When nobody responded, Joe jumped to his feet. "Look, I don't know who took the keys, or who put them back. I heard that everyone was quick to blame some combination of me and Lilyanna when I got sick, and I'm not putting up with that bullshit. I never left the property or took the keys, and neither did Lilyanna. She's been running this house, doing her regular company work and managing my work while I was out, with competence and without complaining. So, if I hear anyone tossing her name out again, I will throw you out of this house."

Lilyanna's eyes widened in surprise. Though the threat of violence seemed a bit out of proportion, she appreciated him sticking up for her.

"Okay, thanks, Joe, for clarifying your position," Alyra continued.

Joe interrupted again, "Does it even matter who took the keys at this point? The keys are back, and nobody is sick! Let's move on."

"I think everyone is a bit tense, and rightfully so," Jillian held up her hands trying to de-escalate the meeting. "I agree that we should move on and not discuss it anymore."

"We should have a party tomorrow night," Dylan suggested. When silence greeted his proposal, he continued to press, "Oh come on, you just said everyone is too tense. Let's lighten up and have some fun." The others looked at each other questioningly, but nobody objected.

***

Despite the directive to put the car key mystery to bed, most of the residents refused to accept the theft as a mere prank that went too far. They remained on their guard, suspicious that one of their own couldn't be trusted. After dinner, Lilyanna overheard Barret, Six and Tessa whispering on the terrace.

"I'm not buying into the Elsa Let-It-Go approach," Barret told them. "Something is off here."

"Yeah, I'm with you, man. I don't trust any of the commercial guys or most of the execs," Six added.

Tessa paused for a moment. "What about Andrew? He's, you know, decent."

"Nah, he's been buddy-buddy with Tristan, and that guy's shady AF. I bet it's one of them."

"What about the other commercial reps? Rich seems cool to me," Barret said nonchalantly.

Six shook his head. "Tie's okay, but not the others."

"It could be Jillian," Tessa proposed. "Nobody is quick to accuse her, so she could just be flying under the radar."

"That doesn't seem like her style to me," Six mumbled without looking at the others.

"I still think it's Lily." Barret lowered his voice even further. "She's quick to back commercial and the execs. We can't trust her anymore."

Tessa shrugged, "Maybe you're right. I admit she's changed."

Lilyanna's heart sank as she trudged upstairs. The stab in the back by Barret wounded her, but Tessa's *Et tu Brute* jab drove the knife into a fatal depth.

Lilyanna ignored Tessa as they got ready for the party upstairs. She stood in front of the bathroom mirror applying makeup until the mirror ran out of snarky remarks. She understood the evil queen's frustration. The queen just wanted the mirror to say something nice for once!

When she returned to the bedroom to dress and finish her hair, Kyah and Saharie were still making wardrobe decisions. "Does this black dress look frumpy?" Kyah asked, holding up a blouson black midi-length dress.

"I think you should wear the shorter red one," Saharie said. "I'm wearing my green and black print dress."

"Won't we look like Christmas ornaments, then?"

"Nah, it'll be fine."

Lilyanna slipped on a black V-neck dress with a slight flare into a mini length, her most cleavage-friendly dress, and turned her attention to her hair, the bane of her cosmetic existence. She pinned the sides of her hair back and set to straightening it without compromising a few waves around her face.

"You look hot, Lily!" Kyah exclaimed.

"Thanks, so do you," she beamed. Tessa also wore a black mini dress, fitted throughout, with three-quarter length lace sleeves. Lilyanna side-eyed her but held her tongue.

Dylan's party playlist blaring in the living room drew the women downstairs. Lilyanna found Tristan alone in the kitchen pouring a glass of scotch. Effortlessly sexy, he wore fitted jeans, a black t-shirt and his black ball cap again. "Hey," she smiled, stepping behind him and grabbing his waist.

"Hey to you." He pulled her in front of him and drew her into a tight hug. She hoped he would say something about her dress at the very least, but he didn't. She slid her hands up to his neck and guided his face towards hers. Before their lips could connect, they heard footsteps approaching and immediately released each other. Dismayed, she questioned her appearance and almost dashed back upstairs to change into a different dress.

Joe entered the room a second later, brushing his nostrils with his thumb and carrying a paper bag in his other hand appearing to contain a liquor bottle. "Lily, can we talk a minute?"

"Sure, yeah." She followed him toward the back stairs as panic rose in her chest. *Did he see her with Tristan?*

"Lily, I just wanted to tell you that I know what's been going on."

Her heart skipped a beat. "You do?"

"Yeah, I'm not blind. I'm sure it's been difficult for you."

"Uh, well, it was at first, but I think it's getting better."

"Good, good. I feel terrible those bastards have been blaming you for infecting me with COVID."

She exhaled in relief, "Oh, yeah, right, it's been tough, but it's not your fault."

"Well, it certainly isn't yours. I can't tell you how grateful I am for you taking care of me when I was sick. That's beyond your job description, and you also continued to hold down the fort at work. I really appreciate everything you've done, and I just wanted to give you this." He pulled a bottle of Dom Perignon out of the paper bag.

"Oh, wow, Joe, you didn't have to do that! This is way too much." Hesitantly, she took the bottle, admiring the coveted label.

"No, no, I insist. It's the least I can do. I thought I'd give it to you before the party in case you want to hide it from the drunken masses."

"Thank you so much, Joe! Seriously, this means a lot, and I love it."

"Glad you like it. I'll see you in there." He smiled awkwardly and left her standing there gaping at the bottle.

"That was nice," Andrew remarked, meandering over to Lilyanna from the direction of the laundry room. "Sorry, wasn't trying to eavesdrop."

"It's so nice! I can't believe he bought me Dom."

"You deserve it," Andrew confirmed. Delighted by Joe's grand display of gratitude, she hurried up the back stairs and tucked the bottle into her travel bag.

Lilyanna resolved not to get drunk at the party. She wanted to spend time with Tristan without being an intoxicated mess. She nursed one glass of wine most of the evening, just to relax, and avoided the drinking games that Tie, Barret, Saharie, Rich, Kyah, Sylvie and Nina played in the dining room. She opted to chat with the others in the living room and watch dance videos on Dylan's phone.

"Here's an old one of you, Lily." Dylan started a video of Lilyanna dancing a lyrical routine in front of a row of mirrors in a dance studio. "You had to be what, eighteen at the time?"

"Let me see," Tristan said with a curious grin. Dylan gave him the phone, and he watched her dance in amusement. "You were really good," he nodded in approval.

"You sound surprised," Lilyanna laughed.

"No, no, I just didn't know you danced."

"I did, for a long time."

"You've still got it! Come on, let's see it." Dylan pulled her to her feet and turned up the music blaring through the house. The volume drew the crowd from the dining room to the makeshift dance floor in the living room.

Lilyanna grabbed Tristan's hand and pulled him along with her. "If I have to dance, so do you." She spun twice on her right leg and landed against his chest, and he caught her in his arms with a laugh. Hoping everyone else was too drunk to notice, or, if not, that a mere dance would be perceived innocently, she took his hand and spun herself under his arm.

"I'm a terrible dancer," he confessed awkwardly.

"No, you're not," she insisted, grabbing his other hand and leading him into a gentle sway. "You're doing great, and you look so cute. I like the hat."

"Cute, huh?" He blushed mildly and followed her lead.

"Yes. Your hair is getting long." She reached up and stroked the course dark facial hair growing out along his jaw line. The black waves on his head were also thickening and starting to wind around his ears. "I like it. Keep it long."

"Are you sure it's not too out of control?"

"I'm sure! It suits you." In fact, all of the guys had given up on routine haircuts and shaving, opting for a rugged look. Andrew's charcoal facial hair threatened to outpace Tristan's as he reached the early stage of a full beard. Andrew danced with Tessa for a few songs, and then collapsed on the sofa, claiming to need a rest. Six had the best dance moves of the men, except for Dylan and Waya, and twirled Jillian around the living room with ease.

The group tired out earlier this time, well before midnight, with Joe, Jillian and Alyra going to bed first. Lilyanna wasn't sure how it started, but somehow she and Tessa found themselves in a towel-snapping war on the men's hall with Andrew, Tristan, Six and Tie after Sylvie and Nina distributed clean towels from a late load of laundry. Andrew and Tessa paired up against Six and Tie as partners and Tristan and Lilyanna. All were quite drunk except Tristan and Lilyanna.

Six snapped Andrew's leg with a wound towel and then ran down the hall toward Joe's bathroom. "Ow, you bastard!" Andrew cried, taking cover behind the door of his room with Tessa behind him. He then emerged to lodge a counterattack and threw one towel at Tie's face as a distraction while snapping his ankle with another towel.

Tristan then went for Andrew, who had run out of ammo. "Dude, don't do it!" Andrew warned him, backing down the hall toward his room. Tristan stalked him down the hall, tightly winding his towel on the way, a sadistic smile on his face. The second Andrew turned to run, Tristan snapped him across his calf with the towel. Andrew yelped, grabbed an empty water bottle off the floor and chucked it at Tristan.

Six took off down the hall after Tristan and whacked his back with another towel. "Ah, damn!"

Tristan flinched. Lilyanna channeled all her energy into throwing towels at Tessa, not even caring to avoid her face, that is, until Tessa and Andrew appeared with a fresh supply of towels, causing the others to retreat to the rooms at the back of the hall.

"Would you children shut up!" Rich called from his room where he sat on his bed in a deep conversation with Barret.

The others ignored him. Six and Tie bravely took on the fortified Andrew and Tessa. Tristan pulled Lilyanna in front of him and put his hand over her mouth and dragged her to the back of the hall toward Six and Barret's room.

"Shhh!" he whispered to her. He lifted her off the ground and into the bedroom slamming the door shut behind them as a mound of towels crashed against the door.

"What are you doing?" she cried when he released her.

"I just wanted to get you alone." He pulled her body against his and kissed her. She pushed back against him, massaging his tongue with hers. He slid his hands down and grabbed her ass while she kissed his neck and started to lift up his shirt.

He pulled back for a moment. "Spend the night with me," he implored.

"The whole night?"

"The whole night. Please."

"Okay," she nodded. "I'll slip out the back door and meet you at the guesthouse."

They faked a gallant surrender to end the towel battle, and Lilyanna dashed upstairs and threw a change of clothes, toothbrush and hairbrush into her travel bag with her bottle of Dom to take to the guesthouse.

As she packed, she heard Kyah and Saharie's muffled high-pitched voices coming from the master bathroom. She hurried down the hall to investigate and knocked on the bathroom door before letting herself in. Kyah knelt on the floor in front of the toilet, throwing up a night of bad decisions.

"She'll be alright. She just drank too much," Saharie said, pulling Kyah's hair back from her face.

"Is there anything I can do?" Lilyanna asked in concern.

"Nope, I'll make sure she gets to bed. Are you off for a walk in the woods, maybe with an overnight layover at the guesthouse?" she nodded at the travel bag over Lilyanna's arm.

"Oh, um, actually yeah," Lilyanna smiled sheepishly.

"Good for you! I'll cover for you. Don't worry about Kyah. She'll be asleep before you get downstairs. Have fun, enjoy it!"

"Thank you, you're the best!" Lilyanna hugged her. "Any other advice?"

Saharie grabbed her forearms and looked in her eyes. "Be confident. You made it through law school. You've been to other countries. You own and run a mansion full of shady staff and co-workers. This guy is lucky to be with you!" Lilyanna dropped her eyes and nodded furiously. "And don't get lost in the woods," Saharie added. Lilyanna stopped nodding at the last part, thinking of the bears that could get in the way of her first all-nighter with Tristan.

***

Tristan lounged on his back in bed, staring at the ceiling, waiting for his breathing to slow. Lilyanna pulled the top sheet over her naked chest and turned on her side to face him. "Is everything, like, good?" she asked, trying to keep her tone casual. Her vision swam momentarily, and then the half-empty bottle of Dom on the nightstand next to Tristan's side of the bed came into focus.

"Yeah, all good," he replied without taking his eyes off the ceiling. He gave nothing away, and Lilyanna still didn't know whether or not to interpret his silence as being underwhelmed. "Are you alright?" He flicked his eyes in her direction.

"M'hmm." Questions burned in her mind as she delicately traced her fingertips along his torso. With the pandemic came a focus on 'high touch' areas. When encountered, questions form that would never have come to mind before COVID. How many people were here before me? Who are they? To avoid the threat to peace of mind such inquires pose, self-preservation ignites an intense interest in being the one and only occupant of those areas. Lilyanna's plethora of question marks on Tristan disconcerted her. Certain things she could observe on her own, his sounds and expressions, but others required his delivery. "Tell me something about you I don't know."

His lips curved in a partial smile. "Like what?"

"Anything—something goofy or serious, doesn't matter."

"Hmmm, okay. I like science fiction novels and movies—it's my favorite genre."

She raised her eyebrows in amusement. "We're practically living in one. This pandemic is a sci-fi nerd's wet dream."

He laughed softly. "I admit the conditions are better than I anticipated."

"Tell me something else."

He thought for a moment. "Err, well, I've always disliked my teeth."

Lilyanna laughed. "What? Why? Your teeth are straight." She leaned in toward his face for a better look.

"Stop it, now you're looking!" He draped his arm over his face.

"Of course I'm looking. Stop, let me see." She tugged his arm down, but he kept his mouth firmly shut. She couldn't hide her smile at his playful stubbornness. "Fine, I don't have to look again to know there's nothing wrong with your teeth. Where does this particular self-consciousness come from?"

"I don't know, I just always thought they were weird growing up, and England is not exactly famous for its dentistry."

Lilyanna shook her head and leaned in toward his face. When his lips parted slightly, she flicked her tongue against his two front teeth and backed away. "Perfect teeth," she confirmed.

He smiled through his eyes that time and turned on his side to face her, crossing her leg over him and lightly tapping her ass. "Cheeky."

"And perfect face, and body," she mused, her dimples denting her face as their lips met in eagerness.

After a prolonged make out session, he rested his face just below her prominent clavicle. "Tell me about you now," he said.

"What about me? You know some things."

"I do. I know you like your neck kissed." He lifted his head and slowly pressed his lips against her neck. "Tell me something else. Tell me all the things about you."

Lilyanna lowered her eyes at him and massaged the inside of his thigh. "Is that really what you want?" She climbed over his legs and kissed his naval, down to his abs and beyond.

"Lily, what are you . . . I've already . . ." his voice trailed off into a deep moan, and he tilted his head back while she gave him head. She attentively covered as much length as she could, steadily progressing inch-by-inch. "Lily, oh my God!"

When she felt him shifting underneath her, she gently released him and straddled his hips before pressing him inside of her. "No man wants to know all the things about a woman," she continued to her uncomprehending audience as she rhythmically circled her hips over his. "You want to know the pretty things—the things that make this dance easy for you and tell you you're a man. But it wasn't pretty things that made me." She thrust more aggressively until he climaxed with a jaw-clenching "O."

Silks wound leisurely through the railing of the front terrace, and floor vases filled with complementary warm-tone roses led to the soiree in the lawn below. Vintage white iron garden tables and chairs loosely formed a semicircle facing the terrace, the woods a reluctant backdrop. More ceramic pots of bouquets arranged amongst the fixtures stinted the handpicked flora between its blooms and the roots to the Earth from which it could not grow.

Lilyanna perched regally on a wooden rope swing, wearing a true white corseted dress with a full hoop skirt gathered around her waist and her hair in a formal half updo. The other women wore similar-style dresses of the early 1800s English aristocracy in various pastels, the men in suits in pastel shades with matching vests. Saharie and Tie sat opposite each other at one of the tables, giggling and sharing smoldering glances. He wore a black top hat and fed Saharie a lemon macaron to preserve her white-gloved fingers. Barret, Six and Rich sat one table over, drinking scotch and engaged in a game of cards. On the other end of the lawn, Joe shared a table with Alyra and Jillian. He wore a black round-topped bowler hat and smoked a pipe with one hand while clutching a walking cane in the other. Dylan and Waya danced a waltz next to the terrace in matching bright cerulean suits.

At yet another table, Kyah sat alone in a rosy pink ruffled dress with a matching pink feathered hat, her cleavage bulging out of the top of her corset. Eagerly, she picked up a three-layer piece of pink and yellow raspberry ganache cake from the plate in front of her with her fingers and shoved it into her mouth.

Clad in a lux ivory suit, Tristan stood behind Lilyanna, gently pushing her forward in the swing, Fragonard-style. In front of her feet, Andrew lay on a picnic blanket in a pale yellow suit. He looked up at Lilyanna as she swung back and forth over him. Tessa, wearing a lilac dress and lace veil over her face, lay on the other side of the picnic blanket facing Andrew with her body between him and the swing. A basket bulging with grapes and a bottle of champagne anchored the blanket.

The lightest of spring breezes kissed Lilyanna's skin when she rose into the sky. As she soared higher, she spotted a man's figure in an upstairs window of the house. At first glance, she assumed it was Bix. The higher she swung, however, she realized the man was significantly taller, with soft grey hair. The figure moved the curtain aside and watched the scene unfolding below.

Her altitude still rising, she heard only faint sounds from the other guests on the lawn. She heard the ripping of Kyah's corset and the squish of icing between her teeth; the puff of Joe's pipe; the giggles from Saharie and Tie; the slosh of scotch; the whirl of waltzing feet. At that point, she realized she was swinging much too high. Her feet too far from the ground, she could not stop her oscillation. She wanted Tristan to slow her flight, but he continued to push her into the air toward the shadow in the upstairs window. Her voice unable to express her wish to return to the ground, up she went. *Rip, squish, puff, giggle, slosh, whirl.* Higher and higher, she rose, a billowing tangle of white silk.

Lilyanna watched the swing return to its resting position on the ground, without her in it. Standing in the upstairs window next to William, she gazed down on the lawn from which she came. What Lilyanna couldn't see from the ground were the flames engulfing the woods on every side of Whimser. Just beyond the front of the tree line of the woods and continuing in a circle around the house, a massive fire blazed, emitting clouds of smoke that blurred anything beyond the flames. William stood behind her and wrapped his arms around her waist. He rested his head on her shoulder, together the spectators of hell's garden party.

Lilyanna woke with a start, panting. The dull blue light of morning had just started to slip through the bedroom window in the guesthouse. Tristan slept next to her on his back, his face tilted slightly in her direction. She turned toward him on her side, studying his enchanting face. He looked so peaceful with his eyes closed and busy jaw muscles relaxed. He didn't snore, only inhaling deeply through his nose with the occasional "mph." She wanted to stroke his cheek, down the side of his face, but she couldn't bear to wake him. Instead, she curled against his side and drifted back to sleep to the sound of his rhythmic breathing.

CHAPTER SIXTEEN
Paper Clouds

L ilyanna began her Monday morning with a Zoom call with Jack Taylor, the attorney for William's estate, at his request to discuss 'urgent' estate business. As a courtesy, she asked Tristan if she could use the library for an hour or so for the private call, even though she didn't really have to ask to use her own library. To prepare for the call, she had Bix hunt down William's map of the adjoining lake properties. Sitting at the desk with her laptop popped open, her anxiety rose because the estate attorney would not be insisting on a call unless something went wrong. For once sharing her nerves, Bix paced the width of the library, chewing his thumbnail.

"I'll cut right to the chase, Lilyanna," Jack declared, streaming from his home office. "Like most of the country, the estate may face economic difficulties given the pandemic. The Sheldon family is a month behind on paying their rent, which allows us to charge a late fee under their lease, and they assured me they will make the payment this week but want a waiver on the late fee. I also received a call from Mr. Perry, the owner of the Lakeview Ranch Club across the lake. He claims he is not able to make his quarterly rent payment for the spring since there have been no customers. Then we have Mr. Featherbee from The Wilds of Life Preservation Society."

"Oh, yes, William used to call him Feather Brain. Don't even tell me the wildlife society ran out of money to make their easement payments."

"That's the one. Actually, Mr. Featherbee expressed interest once again in extending the society's current easement or purchasing in fee the entire tract that contains Whimser."

"That's not happening!" Bix stormed, stopping his pacing and facing the desk.

Lilyanna rolled her eyes. "That organization has been trying to buy this land for decades. They tried when William was alive and again when he died. I suppose they think we're in hardship now and hope to profit. Ummm, okay, let me think. Let's go one by one."

William's voice spoke in her memory as she studied the map of the adjoining properties. "Here's the lineup of village idiots," he had told her, pointing out each tenant and landowner to Lilyanna on the map. "Nature-worshipping cult to the north," he spouted, referring to the society's easement area. "Family of fascists to the east," he continued. "Dim-witted rancher across the lake. Oh, and the Acadis over here."

Lilyanna tore her mind from him and addressed Jack. "I've only met the Sheldons once, and they were annoying as hell, weirdly conservative. They live up here year-round. But, this is their home, and I'm not going to mess with that. Waive the late fee and offer to move their payment due dates to the end of each month instead of the first through the end of summer. Mr. Perry at the Lakeview Ranch Club is a little more complicated. How much income do we count on from him?"

Jack turned to another monitor on his desk and scrolled through a document. "This tenant is the most concerning. The majority of the estate's income from tenants comes from the Lakeview Ranch Club because the property is waterfront and the business generates considerable revenue. We collect a fixed amount each quarter and a percentage of the revenue from their business. There will be a shortfall in income for the estate's taxes and maintenance costs if we lose the rent from the ranch for more than a couple of quarters. There is liquid cash, of course, but I don't recommend making a habit of paying for routine expenses out of capital. We don't know how long the pandemic will last, and it would be best to get ahead of this while you're in town and modify the income streams to account for the economic downturn."

Bix shook his head. "Mr. Whimsergarden always made sure the estate drew enough income to cover its expenses."

"What are our options? Can we negotiate with Mr. Perry?"

"He will not speak to me, but he is willing to meet with you."

"Meet with me? You mean virtually, right?"

"Unfortunately, he insisted he does not do 'internet meetings.' He would like to speak to you in person."

"Does he realize we're in the middle of a pandemic? I can't meet with him! That would jeopardize everyone in the house."

"Oh, please, there are no COVID-19 infections up here. You can't possibly put Whimser at risk for a minor threat to some corporate employees," Bix ranted.

"I can't possibly prioritize people over property? Think again."

"I understand, Lilyanna," Jack interjected, "but these are inhabitants in Texas country. Most of them think COVID is a hoax by the Democrats. If it were any other tenant, I wouldn't press it, but the ranch's payments are critical to the estate's financial security."

"Did you explain that we can sue the Lakeview Ranch Club for breach of lease if he doesn't pay?"

"I did, and he was about as worried about that as COVID. Just think about it and get back to me. I can set it up so you would meet outside and stay six feet apart. You'll have to drive over there. Mr. Perry said they have a contractor clearing trees on the walking trail this week."

"Thanks, Jack. I'll let you know." She clicked the laptop shut to find Bix glowering at her.

***

"Absolutely not!" Tristan fumed in the dining room after hearing Lilyanna's plan to visit the ranch.

"It's not your decision. I have a responsibility to make sure this estate runs properly."

"And I have a responsibility to enforce this quarantine. No outside visits!"

"Aww, and here I thought you were concerned about my safety," she retorted.

"I am, Lily! I'm concerned about everyone's safety."

"So am I! We won't have a roof to hide under if we lose the income that pays for the house."

"Well, why can't you just call this bloke? He does own a telephone, I presume?"

"Because he's a man-Karen who thinks COVID-19 doesn't exist!"

"Being a skeptic doesn't negate his ability to pick up a phone."

"I can't force him to get on the phone."

Tristan buried his face in his hands in frustration.

"Lily, I agree it's your choice here. Do you think you can meet with this guy safely and from a reasonable distance?" Joe asked.

"Yes, I do. If I thought it was dangerous, I wouldn't consider it. There's nobody at the ranch since they've had no customers."

"Then that's it, then. On a risk scale of life in a plastic bubble to brunch in a nursing home cafeteria, I'd say the risk is fairly low," Joe decided.

"Wait, so she gets to leave the property, but nobody else does?" Rich objected. "Why should she get special treatment?"

"If that has to be explained to you, then you shouldn't be in your current position of employment," Joe snapped.

"You shouldn't go alone, though," Andrew added. "I'll go with you. We'll just wear masks and stay outside." Lilyanna thought Tristan might volunteer to go with her instead, but he didn't.

The next morning, Andrew and Lilyanna put on cloth face masks from the supply Sylvie ordered from Etsy when Joe had fallen ill. "We look like bank robbers," Andrew noted as they prepared to leave the kitchen.

"Better you than me in that ridiculous thing," Tristan remarked.

Lilyanna looked up at him in annoyance, "I agree we look like we're in a low-budget horror movie, but if masks save lives, it's a small price to pay."

"Whatever you say."

She pulled her mask down and took him aside. "You're using your grumpy voice. What's wrong? We're not going to infect the house!"

"I'm not grumpy! And I don't think you'll infect the house," he huffed.

She lowered her eyes at him. "What's wrong, then? Are you hangry?"

"No, nothing is wrong!"

"Okay, what's not wrong, then?"

"It's just a stressful day." He ran his fingers through his hair and refused to look at her.

She eyed him in concern and rubbed his arm. "Just relax. It will be alright."

With that, she made a public display of grabbing her car keys from the drawer. "We have to take the car. Normally it's walkable, but the owner said they have clearing work going on through this week. We'll have to go the long way."

"Do you want to drive, or do you want me to?" Andrew asked as they entered the garage.

"I'll drive. It feels like a lifetime since I've driven." Lilyanna stopped when she opened the driver's side door to find the seat pushed back at least half a foot from its normal distance from the pedals.

"What is it?" Andrew asked, seeing her hesitate.

"Somebody has been in the car. The driver's seat is way farther back than how I keep it." *Whoever had been gaslighting her with the disappearing and reappearing car keys had actually taken the car out.*

"Do you remember the mileage when you got here? Maybe we can figure out how far the person drove."

"I don't remember. He or she couldn't have gone too far because there's still plenty of gas."

Andrew walked over and looked at the seat. He tried to climb into the seat, but it was too close to the dash for his long legs. "It was someone shorter than me but taller than you."

"That narrows it down to everyone in the house," Lilyanna sighed.

"Except us."

"If we make that argument, people will say the culprit reset the seat position on purpose to disguise his or her height."

"Then let's not tell anyone," he insisted, going back to the passenger seat.

"Deal."

Lilyanna set her expectations low for the condition of the ranch property, and even lower for COVID precautions being taken. Apprehensively, she stepped out of the car, half expecting a sinkhole to form underneath her and suck her down into an abyss of infectious disease. Andrew walked over to her and grabbed her hand.

"You don't have to hold my hand," she told him as they walked together to the visitor's entrance.

"You relax when I do, so it's okay to let me." Her eyes flashed him a hint of a smile. He wasn't wrong. In truth, his confidence and intuition relieved a significant portion of her stress. It felt comforting to have a partner in crime taking on the unknown with her. She had to remind herself it was only temporary.

To her pleasant surprise, the Lake View Ranch Club stood poised to welcome any visitor to grace its halls. The seventy-ish-year-old Mr. Perry walked them around the property with a bandana tied around his nose and mouth. To his credit, he stayed ten feet ahead of them at all times. The grounds were neatly manicured and the lake frontage pristine.

"The property looks lovely, Mr. Perry," Lilyanna called to him.

"Thank you, ma'am. It's all ready for customers. We just don't get many now. Ya see, all the guest lodges there are empty 'cept for one couple that got stuck here when the lockdown started, and one family that rented a cabin til the end of summer." He gestured to a series of single-story wooden cabins painted red and brown overlooking the lake.

"I am very sorry to hear about your difficulties, but it's not surprising with all the craziness," Lilyanna stated the obvious, feeling like a Scrooge trying to collect money from people struggling in a global crisis. Mr. Perry and his employees were doing everything they could to keep the ranch running and bore no fault for the decline in customers.

"How are things up at Whimser, Miss Rivers?"

"Oh, please call me Lilyanna." She told him about opening the house during the lockdown and her co-workers and friends staying there.

"I'm sure old Mr. Whimsergarden would turn over in his grave at seeing the house full," he replied. "I heard he was never much for company." Lilyanna's eyes widened, and she fell silent. Mr. Perry continued his tour without realizing the impact of his words on Lilyanna. Andrew squeezed her hand and kept her moving with him.

On the back side of the property opposite the lake front, they came to a fenced pasture with an adjacent row of stables. Six horses of various size and color frolicked around the pasture, grazing and meandering in the sun. Lilyanna let go of Andrew's hand and stepped up to the wooden fence. "They're magnificent!"

"Ah, yeah, we got some good ones. We got four more on the trail through the woods. They're gettin' a lot of down time now since ain't nobody here to ride."

Lilyanna gazed at the horses. A chocolate brown mare approached the fence line and shook her mane. Slowly, she reached out and stroked the mare's snout. "Mr. Perry, I think we can come to an agreement on adjusting your rent payments."

***

"You agreed to what?" Joe growled, choking on a puff of smoke from the cigarette he held out the dining room window to technically comply with the indoor smoking ban. The other residents gathered around the dining table eager to hear the tale of the first verified venture into the outside world, or at least off the Whimser property line.

"I told the owner we would lower his rent payments through June in exchange for taking a greater percentage of profits in the late summer and fall. When the lockdown ends, people will likely be looking for easy getaways that don't require air travel, so hopefully business will improve by then. And I have a surprise for everyone." Lilyanna paused for dramatic effect. "The owner of the ranch agreed to give us free horseback riding any time we want!" Nobody responded for several seconds.

"That's the surprise?" Rich asked.

"Yes, yes, it is. Come on, you were just complaining about me leaving the property, and now you can go to the ranch, too. It's outdoors, and there are no people around. You just need to call the ranch a day in advance and let the owner know how many people want to ride and what time."

"I mean, I guess I can get into the *Legends of the Fall* thing," Dylan nodded.

"More like *Brokeback Mountain*," Joe scoffed under his breath.

Shaking off the lackluster response from the group, Lilyanna carved out time for another Zoom call with Jack Taylor in the upstairs den to inform him of the plan, hoping he would be more receptive. "I know it won't be enough to maintain the estate long-term, Jack, but it's better than nothing," Lilyanna admitted as Marie climbed on her lap with a high-pitched squeak.

"I agree, Lilyanna, you did well. In the short term, it won't be much of a loss. I'm more concerned about what will happen if the ranch's business doesn't pick up by summer, but I know that's borrowing tomorrow's troubles."

"We're lawyers, tomorrow's troubles are always on loan to us." Lilyanna rubbed Marie's head, trying to think what to do. "I suppose we only have one option—extending The Wilds of Life Preservation Society's easement. We can charge more for giving more land area and for a longer term. But I don't want to sell them any land outright. We're not that desperate."

"I understand. That should work. I'll reach out to the society and get going on the paperwork. Would you like me to draft the amendment to the lease with the Lakeview Ranch Club as well?"

"That's okay, Jack, I'll take care of that and send it to Mr. Perry. Thanks for all of your help." As soon as she ended the call, Lilyanna heard shouting downstairs.

She quickly set Marie in her cat condo and hurried down the front stairs.

In the hall, she found Tristan, Alyra, Jillian and Joe embroiled in a contentious argument while the others peeked out from various rooms, staring wide-eyed at the commotion.

"Those decisions should have gone through me!" Alyra yelled at Tristan. "I am H mother fuckin' R!"

"It was beyond my control! My job is to make numbers match, Alyra, and that is what I did."

"You think that somehow excuses you from blame? You just laid off almost a hundred employees without running the necessary HR traps!"

"That was not his choice," Jillian sighed. "None of us had a say."

"And that's the point," Joe interjected, his volume rising. "If you wanted to fire our only support staff, I should've been involved in that conversation so that I could immediately shut it down."

"They will all receive severance packages," Tristan insisted.

"Well that just fixes everything," Joe grumbled.

"What is going on?" Lilyanna asked.

"We no longer have an assistant," Joe boomed as he stomped out of the hall.

"What? You fired Carline?" The revelation knocked the wind out of her.

Tristan turned toward the front door to leave, claiming he had other work to do. "This is not over!" Alyra called out after him. "Everyone else back to work." She waved away the onlookers and went back to her workspace.

When the crowd dissipated, Lilyanna ran out the front door after Tristan. He was entering the guesthouse when she caught up with him. "I can't talk about this now," he said, trying to close the door behind him, but she squeezed into the guesthouse after him and slammed the door.

"Tristan, stop!" Finally reaching him, she grabbed his arm and spun him around to face her. "Why did you fire Carline?"

"I had no choice! Layoffs were inevitable. We've had one of the worst quarters in company history, and there's no sign of the pandemic ending any time soon."

"But why Carline? She's the only support staff for my department, and she helped with Joe's projects when he was sick. How could you do that, and without even telling me?" she stormed.

"I couldn't tell anyone!" he defended himself, his jaw muscle clenching. "And I didn't choose which employees to let go. Marks assigned certain departments a number of how many employees had to be cut, and the head of each department selected employees in their departments." He refused to look her in the eye.

That meant Justin Mercier chose Carline. "So, you were just the executioner?" she accused, turning away from him.

"It was a business decision, not personal," he insisted, her back still to him. "Lilyanna," he lowered his voice and looked at the floor, "Does this mean you don't want to see each other anymore?"

She rounded on him furiously, "So, I'm welcome to sleep with you but not important enough to even get a heads up that you're firing my only administrative help when I'm working my ass off to do my job, keep Whimser running and generate new income for the property during a pandemic? And you don't see me taking people's livelihoods in the process! I'm doing all I can to avoid evicting the tenants here or making things worse for them, and you just took the easy way out and fired people."

"Lily, please. I swear this was not easy. There were no other options." He stepped behind her and wrapped his arms around her narrow frame. "Don't be angry at me," he whispered in her ear. "I didn't want this to happen."

She relaxed her defiant stance, surrendering to his touch. She could feel his heart thumping against the back of her neck and his coarse facial hair resting against her cheek. Firmly yet calmly, she took his hands and eased his arms open to free herself. Turning to face him, she noticed for the first time the dark circles under his eyes. He had been losing sleep over this.

A defeated look in his eyes, he pulled away from her and sat on the edge of the bed. She stood in front of him, her arms crossed. "Why didn't HR at least get the chance to review the individual terminations?"

He leaned forward and rested his head in his hands. "Marks wouldn't have it. He insisted the layoffs happen immediately to boost our second quarter financial results."

Her temperature plunged at the sight of his depression, and she stepped closer to him and wrapped her arms around his neck and shoulders, pulling his head against her chest. "You should've told me."

"I'm sorry," he sighed, resting his head against her.

He's cute when he's penitent. She ruffled his hair, trying to comfort him, but in her mind she saw Marks shooting skeet at his hunting lodge, and with each trigger-pull of his rifle another employee lost his or her livelihood.

Tristan didn't respond or even move at first. A few seconds later, he reached up and put his arms around her waist, keeping his face pressed against her chest, holding onto her as a safety bar on a turbulent ride he wanted to end. Lilyanna realized he was not accustomed to receiving comfort. Functioning as a single dad and the head of a large company left no room for fulfillment of his personal needs. Any expression of resentment toward his unmet needs would surely have been greeted with eye rolls to the tune of the world's smallest violin playing for a man in his situation.

But objectivity with respect to Tristan left Lilyanna long ago. She felt his pain more than her own, and she withstood hers, but not his. She longed to chase away his guilt and stress, and any other bears threatening to drag him down from the pedestal on which she kept him shined and polished. And she was well acquainted with those bears, along with loneliness and lack of support—she knew their M.O.s. She would not let them take anything else from her. They couldn't have him.

***

Lilyanna and Tessa spent the evening collecting donations for a monetary gift for Carline, and Tessa made her an e-card to thank her for her work. Feeling calmer, Lilyanna then turned her attention back to the estate's troubles. She commandeered the library once again to draft an amendment to the Lease Agreement with the Lakeview Ranch Club.

She sat behind the desk with one foot resting on the desk and her leg extended out with her navy striped midi skirt draped over her lap, studying the Lease Agreement and William's old map of the adjoining properties. As she jotted down a few notes, Tristan tapped on the door. "Come in," she greeted him cordially. He shut the door behind him and slowly approached the desk.

"You look comfortable," he noted, humor returning to his eyes. "What are you working on?"

"I'm drafting the real estate documents for the new arrangements with the tenants."

"Ah, well, I won't disturb you. I just wanted to say thank you for your, err, support earlier. I was not myself."

She put down her pen and looked up at him. "I think you were very much yourself, and that's okay. It's a good thing, actually."

He didn't respond at first. "I see you've taken back your library," he noted, changing the subject. He put his hands on the edge of the desk and leaned toward her.

She looked down and focused on the map in front of her. "I have for the moment, but I'm good with taking turns."

Contemplating her, he rubbed his index finger over his bottom lip and then stepped behind the desk. The lease document in one hand, she swiveled her chair to face him, keeping her leg up on the desk. "I think it's your turn then," he said, dropping to his knees in front of her.

Gradually, he ran his hands from her knees up to her thighs, lifting her skirt out of the way and giving her a reasonable opportunity to object. Lilyanna lifted her eyebrows in amusement and gave him a confident like-hell-I-would-stop-you look. Fighting back a smile, she pretended to turn her attention back to the lease, never mind what might be occurring below. Taking her feigned indifference as a challenge, Tristan's face disappeared between her legs, his sumptuous lips and articulate tongue eloquently discrediting any suggestion of indifference. Lilyanna dropped her head back and gripped the arm of the chair with her free hand as she enjoyed the pleasures of working from home, #wfh.

CHAPTER SEVENTEEN
Fields of Eden

Barret woke to a melody of creaking sounds with an occasional *thud* coming from the ceiling over his room. He looked over to find Six's bed empty and assumed he had gone out for his morning run. With the room to himself, he settled on his back and listened to the overhead rhythmic creaks. He wondered if Rich was awake listening to the same song across the hall. He wondered if Rich was as hard as he was, and the thought made him harder yet. Reaching between his legs, he joined the steady beat.

Upstairs in the extra bedroom, Waya spun pirouettes in the center of the room while Dylan sat up in bed reading a paperback fiction novel. "What do you think of this turn combination for our next college routine?"

Dylan looked up from his reading to watch Waya spin fluid turns, the ball of his foot thudding the floor with each rotation. "It's beautiful. Your lines are gorgeous." Dylan snapped his book closed and strode over to Waya as he finished his turn sequence. "All of you is gorgeous." Dylan stepped toward him and pulled Waya into an embrace. "I'm so glad you're here with me, babe. I couldn't go through a lockdown with anyone else. I love you so much."

"Aww you know I love you too. I can't wait to marry you! When this is over, we're leaping down the aisle." They shared a passionate kiss. "Now give me my space," Waya shooed him away. "I need to practice." He resumed his series of turns.

A dozen *thuds* and creaking noises later, Barret came with a series of moans in the room below. Once his breathing returned to a normal pace, he climbed out of bed and went to shower, his mind refusing to switch from the singular track that he knew could only lead to disappointment.

***

Andrew knocked on the door of the guesthouse and waited for Tristan to let him in. Tristan quickly straightened his shirt and brushed his hair out of his face. It wasn't like Lilyanna to be up and about so early. He opened the door with a smile that quickly faded to confusion when he saw Andrew.

"Hey, man, sorry to bug you, I was just going to see if you have an extra charger for our company laptops. Mine stopped working, and Jillian said you might have an extra one."

"Oh, yeah, sure, come in."

"Were you expecting someone else?" Andrew asked curiously.

"No, no, I wasn't expecting anyone at all." Tristan went into the bedroom and rifled through his travel bag, his back to Andrew.

"Wow, you've got it made having this whole place to yourself," Andrew remarked, glancing around the room. His eyes stopped on an empty bottle of Dom Perignon on the bedside table. Quietly, he moved toward the table to make sure his eyes weren't deceiving him and picked up the bottle.

"Yeah, I can't complain. It's nice having the privacy," Tristan replied.

Andrew quickly set the bottle down and turned the other direction, his voice cooling. "I bet. You can do whatever you want out here."

"Here it is. I knew I had one somewhere." Tristan took the charger out of his bag and handed it to Andrew.

"Thanks," Andrew nodded, his lips pursed. "I'll let you get back to business."

***

Lilyanna struggled through the rest of the workweek without Carline to field the incoming routine work. Every time she started to work on a substantive contract project, she had to stop to answer some administrative question from her internal clients not in the house. On top of that, Andrew grew more distant, refusing to engage in their normal banter and giving her one-word answers. At first, she thought his aloofness due to family issues, but he was usually forthcoming about that with her. Eventually, she surrendered and decided it best just to give him space.

By the time the weekend arrived, she had reached her wits' end with work and Andrew's melancholy mood. She was grateful Dylan suggested a much-needed chill TV night. They took over the downstairs den to watch Hulu's new period series, *The Great*.

"This is easily the best thing that has happened to me in 2020," Dylan said halfway into the second episode. He lay on the sofa on the opposite side of Lilyanna with one blanket over their feet.

"Seriously, where has this been all my life? These hybrid drama/comedy period shows are delicious!" Tessa added from her pallet on the floor with Saharie, Kyah and Waya. Lilyanna agreed with her assessment—*The Great* lived up to its name and provided a satisfying quarantine binge in a worldwide entertainment shortage. Elle Fanning's character even had a pet bear! It wasn't chasing her; it was actually a furry companion. If only she could convince the bear she was always running from to be her friend like that. Lilyanna hoped for bear-taming tips in later episodes.

"I'm going to grab a drink. Does anyone want anything while I'm up?" Lilyanna offered.

"Yeah, bring some snacks," Dylan said. "I'm gaining the COVID-19 pounds."

While Lilyanna sifted through the pantry, Tristan entered the kitchen. "Hey, I thought you were in the guesthouse?"

"Hi, err yeah, I was, but I was actually hoping to catch you. Can I borrow you for a moment?"

"Not if you plan to return me." She closed the pantry and looked at him curiously. "Is everything okay?"

"Yes, everything is fine," he started awkwardly. He fixed his eyes on the floor.

She lowered her head, trying to get him to make eye contact with her, and reached up to rub his arm. "Okay, well, do you want to relax and watch a show or something? We can watch something British. Do you want to watch *The Crown*?"

His worry lines faded, and he broke into a soft laugh. "No, I don't want to watch the fucking Crown."

"Come on, it's a great show!" she laughed and twisted his shoulders playfully. "You need to relax."

He sighed and squeezed his eyes closed for a second. "Actually, there's something I hoped to ask you."

"What is it? You can ask me anything."

"Would you like to go ride horses with me tomorrow? You see, I called the ranch establishment you described, and they have an opening tomorrow afternoon."

Taken aback, she hesitated. She had expected bad news, not an invitation for, dare she say, a *date*? "Oh, um, yeah, sure, I'd love to. Is it just the two of us?"

He released his tensed muscles and finally met her eye. "Great, and yes, just us. I thought it might be nice to get out for a while."

"Definitely. That's really sweet of you to arrange it. I'm excited!" She grabbed his wrist above his watch and tugged his arms toward her to give him a peck on the lips. When she stepped back, he grabbed her waist and lifted her off the ground, setting her down on the kitchen countertop. Both of them smiling, their lips met in a deep kiss too justified to fear disruption from the house full of watchful eyes.

***

Lilyanna's hands shook slightly with excitement and nervous jitters as she touched up her makeup and hair that Saturday afternoon. She dressed in a powder blue V-neck blouse, slim black jeans and tall black boots. Tristan might not have used the official term, but his aversion to labels didn't change the fact that their planned outing indeed constituted a date. Her nerves reminded her how long it had been since she had been on a date—several years, in fact. Yet, despite feeling out of her league and her comfort zone, she clung to a degree of assurance of Tristan's intentions for the first time. If he were only using her for sex, he would not have asked her to go horseback riding.

Her hair styled and full makeup on, she taunted the mirror, daring it to criticize her. Before it could respond, she turned her back on the glass eye and strutted down the front stairs.

Tristan stood waiting for her on the front terrace, wearing blue jeans and his cream-colored half zip sweater with the sleeves rolled up to his elbows. Fully embracing his quarantine look, he now sported a full beard and had allowed his dark wavy hair to grow down around his ears. Though primitive compared to his traditional clean-cut office style, he still looked like a model shooting an outdoor wear campaign rather than a man living in the woods.

He turned to greet her with a smile when she stepped through the front door and out onto the terrace. A few late spring sun rays beamed through the clouds and down onto the terrace, creating the illusion that the light was radiating from Tristan. They each slid on a similar pair of Ray-Ban sunglasses to block out the glare.

"Shall we?" he asked with a boyish grin.

"We shall," she nodded. Together, they walked almost a mile to the ranch grounds making small talk, the road now traversable by pedestrians.

"Have you ridden a horse before?" he asked.

"Yeah, but only a couple of times, and it was years ago. I'm guessing you have?"

"Yes, I grew up riding horses. My grandparents lived in the countryside and had several horses."

"Okaaayyy, you are way more experienced than me," she admitted.

"Well, as I recall, you are quite proficient at picking up past pursuits after a significant hiatus," he quipped.

She stifled a laugh and shook her head. She wanted to hold his hand and hoped he would initiate the connection. When he did not, she took a deep breath and slid her fingers through his. To her relief, he didn't resist.

Two horses waited for them in the paddock when they arrived at the Lakeview Ranch Club, one the chocolate mare Lilyanna had seen on her prior visit, the other a jet black stallion. From a distance of over six feet, Mr. Perry introduced Lilyanna to the brown mare, Rainya, and Tristan to the black horse, Fynn.

"Will you two be needin' a guide? You sounded like you've done this before when you called, so I wasn't sure," he said to Tristan.

"I think I've got it in hand. We'll be fine on our own," Tristan assured him.

"Okay, the horses are all saddled up. They know the trail. Just have 'em back by five. That's when they eat dinner." With that, he waved farewell and left for the stables.

"Wait, he's just leaving us?" Lilyanna turned to Tristan in panic.

He took her arm and gently led her over to Rainya. "Don't worry, it's fine. I swear I know what I'm doing."

"I hope he doesn't do this with other guests. The tightest liability waiver in the world wouldn't release the ranch from such negligence." Lilyanna slowly reached up and stroked Rainya's coarse mane. The mare dipped her head, searching for grazeable grass.

"I'm sure they take more precautions with paying customers. Besides, I assured him of my equestrian experience, English style, of course. Now, let's get you on first." He patted the mare's snout and then walked her forward.

"Um, what do I, um, do?" Lilyanna stammered, looking up at the saddle uncertainly.

"You're going to put your foot in the stirrup, and I'll give you a lift." He stepped behind her and grabbed her waist. "Go on, then," he urged, when she still did not move. "Trust me."

Hesitantly, she lifted her foot into the stirrup and put one hand on his shoulder and one on the top of the saddle and then shifted all her weight onto that foot. "There we go, now swing your other leg over, just there," he said as he easily lifted her into the air. She did as he said and rolled her body onto the saddle with a slight groan.

"I forgot how comfortable this is," she noted awkwardly.

He grinned, "You'll get used to it, eventually. Now take the reins. You're going to choke up on the reins and hold them low at your hips. When you want to go to one side or the other, just pull back on the reins on that side and then let up. Got it?"

"Uh, sure, yeah," she nodded more vigorously than necessary. He then strode over to the stallion, gave him a pat and climbed onto his back as effortlessly as sitting on a sofa.

"Alright, now walk over to me and we'll go out the gate on the far side of the paddock."

"Okay, how do I move forward?"

"Just give her a tap on the sides with both feet and a light thrust with your hips. I know you know how to do that."

She shot him an unamused glare and then followed his instructions. "Good, now just keep your thighs tight and move with her," he instructed. Tristan and Fynn led the way out of the paddock and onto a dirt path into the woods. Tristan waited for her on the path so they could ride side by side.

"You look so natural, and I look like I'm straddling a mountain during an earthquake," she remarked as she rode up next to him, clinging to the reins and leaning back uncomfortably.

He laughed and reached over to take her hand. "You're doing great, just relax." He kissed her hand and then released it so they could each hold their reins. "Off we go."

Together, they trotted through the woods, chatting and letting their horses graze on fennel. Various species of bird chirped among the treetops, unfazed by the interlopers below. Lilyanna adapted to riding Rainya more quickly than she expected, her confidence growing with each curve of the trail. The weather generously provided a warm, partly cloudy day with enough sun dancing through the canopy to enhance the euphoric ambience without smothering them in sweltering heat. Off the top of her head, she couldn't recall feeling as elated as she did today—outdoors in the woods on a perfect late spring day, riding a horse next to the most desirable man she had ever met, and not a bear in sight.

Likewise, the ghosts of Whimser avoided the woods today, for the dead can't linger in the presence of so much life. And Lilyanna was alive. Her ears heard the tweeting of the birds and the scampering of the forest underlings on the ground. Her skin felt the moderate humidity settling from the air. Her soul absorbed every smile Tristan directed at her. Her eyes saw the gates open to a world she had believed closed to her.

"If you could live anywhere, where would it be?" she asked.

He puckered his lips and exhaled through them. "I don't know. Texas works, I guess."

She could hardly believe his words. "You're joking. You can't possibly choose Texas as your ideal home."

"Why not? It has what I need conveniently available. I've been a lot of places, and they each have their issues. Nowhere is perfect. Where would you choose?"

"Somewhere on the beach, a real beach, of an ocean or sea. I love Europe, so maybe a city on the Mediterranean."

"Ah, that's fair. But you can't tell me this isn't beautiful."

She turned to look at him with a smile. "I suppose the view isn't bad."

"Can I ask you a personal question?" he continued.

"You've seen me naked, so yeah, I think I can handle a personal question."

He grinned in reply. "Why had it been so long since you were with someone?"

She thought for a moment, self-editing each response that came to mind. "I guess I struggled in that department after William died, or maybe always, and it got worse after he died. It just didn't feel right to get back on the horse, so to speak."

"You mean you haven't been with anyone else in all these years?" he asked incredulously.

"I didn't say *that*. I had a couple of flings in law school. They just weren't serious, and I don't consider them legitimate relationships." She reminisced on her brief attempts at dating in her academic years. The guys accepted her as checking the box of a single law student and asked no other questions. At the time, she was grateful they weren't inquisitive, but a relationship can't legitimately progress when you know nothing about the other person. The connections were superficial, excessively sweet store-bought icing. Proper buttercream icing is delicious due to the kick of bitterness that makes it real. Those guys didn't know her, or her past. They didn't know the negatives, or the darkness, and she never developed any level of comfort with them. She wasn't comfortable with Tristan either, but he at least knew more about her than they did.

"What about you? Do you, like, see a lot of women?" She fought to keep her tone relaxed.

"No, not at all. I was seeing someone last year casually, but it didn't last long. There's no one else, Lilyanna." She wanted to believe him, but a guy like him being single and available . . .

After riding uphill for a time, the trail led them to a sprawling field of overgrown bright green grass on a hill overlooking the lake. "How about a break?" Tristan suggested. When Lilyanna agreed, he swiftly dismounted Fynn and left him to graze while he went to assist Lilyanna.

"I don't think I can move," she confessed, eyeing the ground longingly from Rainya's back. Her legs and thighs ached at the mere thought of climbing off her horse.

Tristan snickered, "I'll help you. Just lean forward and swing your far leg over behind you." Slowly, she did as he said, her legs so stiff they could barely bend. She ended up flat on her stomach on Rainya's back.

"This isn't working," she groaned.

"Just slide down towards me." Tristan reached up and grabbed her hips and guided her to the ground as she slid off the side of the horse.

"Ow!" she cried. Her legs immediately buckled when her feet hit the ground, and she fell onto Tristan, who easily caught her weight. She giggled at her lack of grace and failure to hide her physical discomfort.

He laughed too. "Are you alright?" He set her on her feet and tried to steady her.

"I'm good, I'm great," she assured him, taking a deep breath.

"Let's walk it off, shall we?" he suggested, and she nodded vigorously. He took her hand, and they strolled across the field to the edge of the cliff above the lake. They stopped near the precipice and admired the view of the crystal waters.

"Is this what the English countryside looks like?" she asked.

"Err, sure, I suppose it's similar. If I didn't know where I was, perhaps you would convince me I was in England, except for the weather, and the flowers. They're fond of gardens in England."

"I would like to see that."

"It might suit you," Tristan acknowledged.

"Does it suit you?" she asked.

"What suits me," he started, releasing her hand and turning to face her. He slowly backed her against a tree a few feet in front of the edge of the hill and wrapped his arms around her hips, pressing her against the tree.

"Is right here," he firmly kissed her neck. "And here," he kissed her again, on the lips this time.

Lilyanna smiled and ran her hands down his back to his voluptuous ass, pulling his body tightly against her as he assertively intertwined his tongue with hers. Nature let them be, just as they were, no questions, no judgment, no secular interference.

He paused and looked into her eyes. "Now that you've mastered walking, are you ready to run?" he asked with a sinister smile shining in his eyes.

Hesitantly, she replied, "What do you mean?"

"Take my hand," he held out his hand to her while maintaining the intensity of his eye contact. When she acquiesced, he led her over to Fynn, still grazing lazily in the field next to Rainya.

What could he possibly have in mind? she wondered, about seventy-two percent anxious, twenty-eight percent morbidly curious. He effortlessly swung his Herculean body onto Fynn's back. "Your turn." He extended his arm down to her. "Go on."

Without a second thought, she grabbed his arm and put her left foot in the stirrup, and then he pulled her up onto the horse behind him. "Hold onto me," he told her, taking the reins in each hand.

"Can do." She tightly hugged his waist and squeezed her legs against Fynn. Once secured, Tristan tapped Fynn's side with his foot and thrust his hips forward. Fynn instantly broke into a liberating gallop, with Lilyanna crying out in surprise and then giggling in delight. The breeze whipped through their hair as they soared across the field.

If not for the tingling of the wind on her skin and the warmth of Tristan's solid physique in her arms, another woman might have thought herself in a dream. But Lilyanna's dreams were never so sweet. In this reality, she never wanted to dream again. She wanted to live, to stay awake, to continue feeling this free from the darkness in her past and that lingered in her mind, always threatening to swallow her. Now she knew it possible to again feel pleasure, a garden awakening from a long winter. A garden in winter isn't dead—it's just dormant, biding its time until the return of the right conditions that allow it to bloom.

CHAPTER EIGHTEEN
Mother of Nature

The sun graciously slid behind a cloud, giving Barret and Rich a few moments of relative privacy. They had snuck off to the woods, while most of the others went for a Sunday afternoon horseback ride or for a swim in the lake, and now lay next to each other on the ground in their underwear among a cluster of trees. Rich refused to go near the lake shore out of fear of being seen by the others from the horse trail.

Barret rolled on his side toward Rich and rubbed Rich's shoulder. Rich didn't look at him, instead keeping his eyes fixed on the foliage overhead, deep in his thoughts. From a distance, it appeared just a mass of green and yellow leaves and branches, but a deep squint revealed the daily inner workings of an intricate ecosystem—insects at the bottom of the food chain scurrying to gather food while their hunters stalked them to fortify their own food supply, only to be snapped up by a rodent or snake at a higher link in the chain as the sun fueled the pigment in the leaves pluming out from the tree branches growing for decades from the forest floor. Nothing was simple, not the trees around them, the sky above or the ground below.

"Look, we can't do this anymore," Rich sighed. "I'm married to my wife. I will continue to be married when the quarantine ends."

Barret pulled his hand away. "But you clearly don't love her, or you wouldn't be with me."

Rich finally turned to look at Barret. "What does love have to do with this? If anything, I love sex." He sat up and pulled on his t-shirt.

"So, you think screwing a guy when you're married to a woman doesn't mean you love her any less?" Barret asked, struggling to his feet and gathering his clothes.

"To be honest, I don't care what it means. It satisfies my needs, and it doesn't affect my wife because she won't find out." Rich pulled on his jeans and stepped up to Barret. "If my wife ever did hear about anything, there would be hell to pay for the person who told her," Rich whispered vehemently in Barret's face. "Now, unless you want to take another stab at showing me what my marriage is missing, I'll be heading back now," Rich said as he zipped up his jeans. He brushed past Barret and stalked out of the woods.

"Deny it all you want!" Barret called after him. "Aside from your body fat percentage, you're no different from me."

***

Meanwhile, Lilyanna took the paddleboards down to the lake with Tessa, Andrew, Six, Saharie and Tie. The others went horseback riding, except for Kyah, who chose to stay in and nap. Lilyanna tried to convince Tristan to join them, but he refused, claiming he had work that couldn't wait.

Normally, she would not have worn a bikini in front of her co-workers, except Tristan, but she didn't have much choice for lake activities. Tessa didn't seem to mind at all, confidently displaying her toned physique in a black strappy bikini.

"How do we do the waterboarding?" Saharie asked as Tie and Six set the boards in the water.

"Wo, hey, no, we're not waterboarding people," Six paused and backed away from her.

"It's paddleboarding, Saharie, not waterboarding," Lilyanna corrected her.

"Better get the safe word ready for that," Tessa snickered. Andrew laughed and handed Tessa an oar. She and Six each took a board, and Saharie and Tie shared a board, leaving one board left.

"You can go first," Andrew told Lilyanna.

"That's the most you've said to me in days," she noted.

He looked taken aback. "That's not true."

"It is. You've been acting strange lately," she insisted.

He kicked a rock on the ground without looking at her. "I'm sorry," he admitted at last. "I had no right to—"

"To what?"

"To, uh, take out my stress on you," he concluded clumsily. "I've just had a tough week dealing with family stuff remotely. I'm sorry for being short with you."

She didn't buy what he was selling. "I'm here if you need someone to talk to about that stuff."

"I know. So, you want to share the last board?"

"Sure, let's give it a shot." Together they swam out from shore, each holding a side of the board before Lilyanna climbed on first and then Andrew. "Is one of us supposed to stay sitting on the board?" she asked.

"I don't know. I think we can both stand." Slowly, he rose to his feet and found his balance, holding an oar in the water. Then he extended a hand to Lilyanna.

When she shifted her weight to her feet and tried to stand up, the board rocked violently at the weight difference between her and Andrew.

"Oh, no, oh no!" he exclaimed, trying to steady the board. "Just hold still, hold—" The board pitched them over into the lake before he could finish his statement. Lilyanna plunged underwater, her hair fully immersed in the lake. Bobbing to the surface, she coughed and sputtered.

"Now I'm being waterboarded," she quipped. Andrew laughed, and she splashed him. In reply, he dove back under the water and swam over to her. Before rising to the surface, he grabbed her legs and picked her up only to toss her back into the lake. She poked her head above water, laughing at his antics and splashing him again.

Tessa side-eyed Lilyanna and Andrew from her perch on her board a few feet away. She didn't want to watch their playful flirting but couldn't look away.

Early evening arrived by the time the group returned to the house. Tie and Saharie went inside to take the first showers, and Tessa went upstairs to call Alec, leaving Lilyanna and Andrew on the terrace. Lilyanna towel-dried her hair and removed her soaked sandals. She began tying her wet hair up on her head in a messy bun when Rich appeared, stomping up to the house.

"Hey, man, where've you been?" Andrew greeted him.

"I just went for a run. Why? Do we now have to disclose where we're going every time we step out the door?"

"Um, no, I was just asking. What's with you? What happened?"

"Nothing happened. I just don't think it's anybody's business what I do."

"Well, you certainly thought it was everybody's business what I was doing when Joe allegedly had COVID, so I don't get your attitude towards us right now," Lilyanna interjected.

Rich rounded on her angrily, "That's because you act like you're above the rules, so nobody trusts you."

"What the hell is that supposed to mean?" She stood her ground as he stepped closer.

"You think you're in charge of everyone and have the right to make decisions for the group."

"I don't think that at all! I'm just trying to keep the house running and everyone alive."

Andrew held up his hand at Rich. "You need to calm down, man."

Rich ignored him and kept his eyes on Lilyanna. "The only reason you have any authority here is because you're a gold digger who got this house by fucking some old dude!"

Enraged, she thrust the palm of her hand straight into Rich's nose, sending him reeling. "You've totally lost your mind talking to me like that!" she shouted.

"Oh, shit!" Andrew grabbed her around her waist with both arms and swung her out of arm's reach of Rich.

"You don't have the first damn clue what you're talking about!" she continued to yell at Rich and struggle against Andrew's grip.

"You bitch, you broke my nose!" he shouted back, tilting his head back as a few drops of blood dripped from his nostrils and down his face.

"Both of you, calm down!" Andrew roared. He released Lilyanna, grabbed one of their lake towels and tossed it at Rich. He stepped up in Rich's face and used his extra few inches of height to intimidate him as much as possible.

"If you say anything about this to anyone, I will make sure you are out on your ass without a recommendation or a severance package. Upper management would love to cut more dead weight, and they will listen to me, not you. All I have to do is say the word. I suggest you work up a convincing story about how you ran into a tree—like the short-sighted pee-on you are—and bashed your nose." With that, he turned away from Rich, and he and Lilyanna marched into the house.

"Are you okay?" he asked her as they walked to the kitchen.

"Yeah, fine, just mad at myself. He totally deserved it, but that doesn't mean you can punch someone in the face." Besides, she could already feel her hand swelling up. Andrew glanced down at her hand and saw that she could barely move it.

"Don't worry about it. Let's get you some ice." He made her an ice pack with ice cubes from the freezer and a plastic bag. "Hold this on your hand. I'll go make sure he doesn't cause another scene."

Lilyanna leaned against the kitchen counter by the sink and iced her hand, wallowing in regret and self-loathing. She had assaulted a fellow employee, and Andrew had threatened him to defend her. Her tantrum could get them both fired, maybe even sued. While she stood there contemplating her mistakes and the worst-case scenario, Tristan stepped through the kitchen doorway.

"What did you get up to?" he asked, nodding at the ice pack on her hand.

"Oh, I just hurt my hand paddleboarding, ran into an oar."

"Ah," he nodded, slowly approaching her. "Are you sure it didn't run into Rich's face?" Her face fell in response. She didn't know what to say, so she just stared at him in horror.

"I happened to be in the dining room at the time, which has a lovely view of the terrace." His eyes lit up in amusement as he took her ice pack and gently massaged her hand. "I must say, your right hook is improving."

She winced at his touch. "You can't fire me for this."

He chortled, "Seriously? I'm not going to fire you. Even if I cared that you gave some bloke what he had coming to him, I rather like having you around. Out of curiosity, what did he say that set you off?"

"Some overly zealous comment about the quarantine hierarchy and my place in it in relation to his."

"I see. Well, as someone previously acquainted with your boxing style, I think it's safe to say he won't trouble you further. I say well done."

"I feel terrible." She rested her forehead against his chest.

Just then, they heard Rich enter the hall through the front door. "What happened to you?" Joe asked.

"Low-hanging tree branch." The sound of his footsteps drifted off toward the men's hall.

Tristan chuckled and pulled Lilyanna into a much-needed hug. All of her troubles evaporated in his arms. She wrapped her arms around his back and held him tightly against her. She wanted to remember this moment—a moment when a man gave her exactly what she needed.

***

That evening before dinner, Lilyanna and Saharie took a bottle of wine upstairs after Tessa's blowout fight with Alec. Despite Lilyanna's quarrels with Tessa, she didn't want to see her best friend hurting. Lilyanna soaked a facial towel in the upstairs master bathroom sink with cool water and handed it to Tessa, who sat on the edge of the tub crying. "I knew he was cheating on me," she sobbed, "and this morning he finally confessed. Alec's been quarantining with a woman in Fort Worth since I left!"

"Then why did you stay with that dick all this time?" Saharie asked, gently sweeping Tessa's hair away from her face.

"Why do you think? I'm an idiot and rationalize away all the selfish, egotistical shit he does so I won't be alone!"

"There are way worse things than being alone," Lilyanna told her as she perched on the edge of the bathroom counter.

"I know what it's like to be alone!" Tessa snapped. "Now, I'm alone again."

"You're not alone," Kyah insisted, sitting next to her. "You have three best friends who love you dearly and don't want to see you with a narcissistic prick who doesn't deserve you."

"Yeah, Tess, even if he hadn't cheated, you were never happy with him. He didn't treat you right," Saharie agreed.

"But that's how they all are, so what's the alternative?" Tessa continued to sob.

"You're looking at it," Lilyanna replied. Kyah and Saharie nodded in agreement.

Tessa calmed down after half a bottle of wine and a facial by Saharie to reduce the puffiness in her face. "Hold that thought, I gotta pee," she said as Saharie sat in front of her on the king bed, exfoliating Tessa's face.

The room spun slightly as Tessa sat on the toilet. Absent-mindedly, she fumbled through the closest bathroom drawer that contained only the stash of pregnancy tests Ms. Howard ordered in error. She opened one of the boxes and examined the device curiously. For kicks, she slid the testing stick between her legs and continued peeing.

"Tessa, your mom's calling," Saharie shouted from the bedroom.

"K," Tessa muttered. She set the stick on the bathroom counter next to the toilet and clumsily stood up, her head spinning. After quickly washing her hands, she stumbled back to the bedroom.

While Tessa spoke to her mom on the phone, Kyah went to use the bathroom. She checked her appearance in the mirror and fluffed her hair. When she turned toward the toilet, she saw a pregnancy test sitting on the counter and the open drawer full of more tests. Perplexed, she picked up the used test and tossed it in the trash. She then opened a new test for herself and set it on the counter when she was done.

***

At dinnertime, Lilyanna and Saharie helped Sylvie and Nina set out dishes and utensils in the kitchen. Ms. Howard stirred a pot on the stove and put the finishing touches on her signature spaghetti recipe. Lilyanna was opening a bottle of Chianti when she heard thundering feet overhead and voices shouting.

Simultaneously, Waya ran down the back stairs and into the kitchen. "Lily, you better come upstairs. Tessa locked herself in the bathroom saying she's pregnant."

Lilyanna and Saharie froze for a second before running up the stairs after him.

In the upstairs hall, Tristan, Andrew, Tie, Dylan and Waya gathered outside the locked master bathroom door. Tristan knocked on the door. "Tessa, please come out of there," he called firmly.

"Go away!"

He sighed and softened his voice, "Tessa, I really need you to come out of there. We can talk about this, just come out."

"I'm not coming out. Leave me alone!" Inside, Tessa sat on the floor curled in a fetal position in front of the bathtub.

Lilyanna and Saharie were out of breath when they reached the group. "What happened? Why are you all up here?" Lilyanna cried.

"Tessa has locked herself in the lavatory!" Tristan huffed, pounding on the door with his fists.

"The lavatory, huh? Are we on a plane?" Saharie asked facetiously.

Ignoring her, Tristan's voice deepened, "Tessa, come out of there at once!"

"Fuck off!"

Tristan grunted and ran his fingers through his hair. "If you don't come out of there, I'm going to break down the door."

"Legally, I advise against damage to property," Tessa sobbed.

"Honestly, Tessa," Tristan muttered under his breath.

"Wait, is someone in the house the father?" Tie asked in bewilderment. The men each shook their heads vigorously and looked at one another.

"She was with Alec before the quarantine, but the timing doesn't seem right," Lilyanna whispered to

Saharie. "Tessa, will you just let me in?" Lilyanna called.

"Yes, let Lilyanna come in," Tristan urged.

"No way! Lily, you're so thin, and I'm about to become a whale!" Tessa moaned.

"How about me, then? I'm not thin," Saharie offered.

"You have perfect boobs! Do you have any idea what mine will look like after having a kid?"

"You do have perfect boobs," Tie noted.

"Aww, thanks, babe."

Tristan sighed, "Tessa, your body will undergo certain, um, changes, but it's all normal."

"Are you really mansplaining what happens to a woman's body when she's pregnant?" Dylan glowered at him.

"Do you have any better ideas?"

Dylan thought for a second. "Tessa, Ms. Howard brought you some ice cream. Just open the door and come get it."

Tessa hesitated momentarily. "What flavor?"

"Uh, bacon." He shrugged as the others stared at him in confused annoyance.

"Leave the ice cream by the door and go away."

"No, no, you have to come out to get the ice cream," Tristan insisted.

"Why are you so worked up?" Saharie asked him.

"We can't have a pregnant employee locked in a room alone!" he boomed.

"So, you're concerned about the fact that she's an employee, not her personal welfare," Dylan clarified.

"Is anyone pleased with anything I do?" he asked in exasperation.

CHAPTER EIGHTEEN: Mother of Nature

"You have a really nice behind, like, the best I've ever seen," Dylan stated matter-of-factly. Tristan stared at him flatly, narrowing his eyes. Tie and Andrew curiously glanced around Tristan trying to see for themselves. Tristan banged on the door again to no avail.

"It's Ms. Howard, dear. I have your ice cream," Andrew called in a high-pitched British accent.

"Dude, Ms. Howard's not British, or a man," Tie reminded him.

"Enough of this. Tessa, what will it take for you to come out of there?" Tristan asked.

Before she could answer, Kyah made her way to the group. "What is all the noise up here?"

"Tessa's pregnant and obviously surprised," Dylan explained. "She locked herself in the bathroom and won't come out."

Kyah laughed, "Tessa's not pregnant. I am." The group looked at her and then the locked bathroom door, and then back at Kyah.

Tessa's voice steadied, "But I took a pregnancy test, and it was positive! We must both be pregnant, then."

Kyah walked up to the closed door. "I threw away your test before I took mine. Yours was negative; mine was positive. You went in the bathroom after me and saw my test on the counter, not yours. I'm so sorry for the mix-up! I thought you had already looked at your test and just forgot to throw it away."

Tessa opened the door a second later, her face blotchy and tear-streaked. As soon as she stepped through the doorway, Tristan pushed past her and opened the door all the way and blocked anyone from closing it again.

"Are you really pregnant?" Tessa asked, wiping makeup from under her eyes with her fingers.

"I am," she nodded with a smile. "I didn't even think about it until I saw your test in the bathroom, but it all makes sense. I've been so tired and hormonal and not able to keep down alcohol."

"Have neither of you had a period this whole time?" Saharie asked.

"I think that's our cue," Andrew sighed, turning to head for the stairs. Tie and Tristan agreed and followed after him.

"No, I haven't, but I didn't think anything of it because sometimes I skip a month here and there since I stopped birth control," Kyah explained. "I must have conceived right before Hubs left for Baltimore and I came here. I just missed all the signs."

"I honestly didn't even think about when I had my last period. I just thought about sleeping with Alec right before leaving the city. Too much wine!" Tessa admitted.

"Are you glad, though?" Saharie asked Kyah, still processing.

"I am! I really am, and Hubs will be happy, too. I was actually considering freezing my eggs because I didn't get pregnant right away."

"Ah, thank God! I literally saw my life flash before my eyes," Tessa leaned against the wall and exhaled deeply with her eyes closed. Realizing the implication of her words, her eyes shot open. "I mean, I'm so happy for you, though." She pulled Kyah into an aggressive hug. "Congratulations! You're going to be a mom."

CHAPTER NINETEEN
Falling Petals

Elle Woods reminded everyone that Aristotle said, "The law is reason, free from passion." However, Aristotle also said that "man is by nature a political animal." People are not meant to exist in isolation, but need society, communion with other people, to thrive. He believed the desired end of human life is to flourish. Social beings cannot be expected to flourish without passion. Thus, Aristotle may prefer to keep passion out of the law, but there's no keeping passion out of the people subject to the law. Underneath the formal façade of smartly dressed professionals treading with mechanical precision lie the needs and tendencies of humanness, demanding their due.

Tristan and Lilyanna lay on his bed, their bodies and lips intertwined. They had been in various similar positions for most of the afternoon. Tristan pulled his head back for a moment and studied her face. "Darling, I was thinking I might shave my beard. What do you think?"

Her blissful epicurean guise faded at his words. "No, you can't! I mean, I think you should keep it as it is." She took his face in her hands, ready to defend it from the threat of defilement.

"I didn't realize you were so attached. I thought you liked me either way," he jested with a smile.

"I do, I swear I do. You're gorgeous with or without it." She stroked his beard with a nostalgic smile. "I don't know, it's just so natural, my mountain man. Doesn't my opinion matter?"

"Of course it matters. But I can't look like a 'mountain man' on the investors' call next week."

"Fuck the investors! You're perfect like this."

"Uh-huh, but if we fuck the investors, there won't be a company to employ us."

"But your beard will still feel delicious against my skin." She deeply kissed him and brushed her cheek against his bearded chin.

He pursed his lips, "Then I think it should say a proper farewell." He shifted his weight on top of her and kissed her stomach down to her navel and slowly made his way to her thighs. With his eyes fixed on hers, he brushed his beard against her inner thighs, her muscles quivering in response.

When faced with the loss of a source of pleasure, people tend to remember only the good things associated with it, experiencing flashes of euphoria that make letting go that much more cathartically intense. It's not the departed they grieve for most, but a rose-colored deluge of serotonin-soaked bliss that they think they'll never experience again. Gradually, Tristan worked his way inward to the sound of Lilyanna's "ah's" and, eventually, a most welcome "O."

***

Jillian stood hunched over the front of the library desk, poring over a stack of documents, while Alyra sat behind the desk fixated on her laptop screen. "These numbers can't be right, Jill."

"It's not the numbers that lie," Jillian stated. "Do you have the report of the total layoffs with the demographic information instead of just the departmental breakdown? Let's look at the forest instead of zooming in on each tree for a moment."

Alyra turned her laptop to face Jillian. "The big picture is no prettier than its pieces."

Jillian's brow furrowed, her eyes piercing the screen. "No, it's much worse when you put all the pieces together. I'm getting Joe in here. Another storm is coming."

***

Tristan and Lilyanna walked together up to the main house before dinner, a moderate wind kicking up from the southwest. She stole as many glances at his beard as she could without being obvious, each time wondering if it would be the last time she saw him in his sexy quarantine ruggedness.

"So, what are your plans after lockdown ends?" she asked him, seeing little risk in a fishing expedition.

"I don't know, nothing special, I suppose. I'll go home, see my kids, and back to work, hopefully in person at the office."

His words struck her. "You mean, you want everything to just go back to the way it was before COVID?" *Did that mean with respect to her, too?*

"Sure, that would be ideal. Isn't that what you want?"

"Not exactly. I think the pandemic brought to light the importance of quality of life, wellness and slowing down in some ways. Despite all the negatives, I've enjoyed being outdoors more, seeing my friends and not being an office zombie every day. I would like some of the personal wellness lifestyle changes to remain, post-COVID. Obviously, I want to get rid of the illness and have society and travel reopen. Is that what you mean?"

He shrugged indifferently, "I don't travel much anymore. I've already traveled and had kids. I don't have a desire to do those things again."

Lilyanna's stomach fell to her shoes. "You don't want to do things that you've done before? Are you serious?"

"Yes, quite serious. You seem surprised."

"I'm just confused, Tristan. What do you really care about besides work? You don't want to travel or have a full-time family. What do you want?" She stopped walking and waited for him to respond.

Forced to face her, he sighed and looked at the sky. "I want to do my job, pull this company out of the financial hole the pandemic dug for our industry, and help raise my kids. I don't know why you're getting so bothered."

The disclosure of his reluctance to do things he had already done made her queasy. It seemed lost on him that his ideal future plans included no place for her. Afraid she might tear up if she met his eye, she stared at her shoes. "And just sleep with random women occasionally along the way, right? Is that your plan?"

"Ah, so that's what this is about—defining our relationship in some way," he exhaled deeply and looked away uncomfortably.

"It wasn't supposed to be, but your response made it pretty clear there's nothing to define."

"Let's not do this right now, alright? I have a stressful couple of days ahead of me."

"Fine, whatever is most convenient for you, as usual," she snapped as she stomped off back to the house, leaving him trailing behind her.

***

Lilyanna, Tessa and Saharie solemnly helped Kyah pack her things. "I know it's best for you to go, but I selfishly want you to stay," Lilyanna told her as she folded one of Kyah's t-shirts and tossed it into her bulging suitcase. Hubs finally made it back to Texas and planned to pick her up from Whimser. She would be able to return home and see her gynecologist in Dallas for essential prenatal care. Lilyanna knew that was the best-case scenario for Kyah, but the thought of one of her best friends and strongest allies in the house leaving plunged her already depressed mood into a deeper spiral.

"Same," Tessa admitted.

"Why doesn't Hubs just stay here with you?" Saharie suggested.

"The bed might get a little crowded with you in it, Saharie," Lilyanna noted.

"We can make room for Hubs," Saharie quipped.

Kyah smiled, "I'm sure he'd be more than willing."

"We could work out another room for you and Hubs. We'd have to quarantine him outside the house first, but we could figure it out," Lilyanna insisted.

"Sure, just have him pitch a tent in the yard for two weeks, and then we'll let him in," Tessa chortled.

"As thoughtful as that is, now that he's back in Texas, it's time for me to go home with him. Trust me, it's bittersweet for me too, ladies. I've enjoyed all the friend time. Life was so hectic before COVID I think I was always too tired and busy to realize what I was missing."

"Then let's not go so long without seeing each other," Tessa said. "Lily and I can come up to Dallas more when lockdown ends, especially now that we're about to be aunties."

"I can't believe we're going to be aunts, and you're going to be a mom!" Lilyanna exclaimed.

"One of us has to see what all the fuss is about," Kyah replied. "I know you're relieved it wasn't you," she said to Tessa.

"I can't lie about that," Tessa admitted. "It's just, I was so terrified when I thought Alec could be the father of my child. I think it was the nudge in the ovaries I needed to officially end things with him for good."

"I'm delighted I could contribute to that decision. Proud of you, Tessa."

"Thanks, I am too. I'll be much better in a supporting role on this one. You'll have a team of fairy god aunties by your side every step of the way," Tessa assured her.

Saharie waved them toward her, "Can we just . . ." she pulled them all into a group hug.

Kyah sighed dramatically, "I suppose I can endure a little sentimentality with no sex attached."

***

Lilyanna stopped in her tracks at the sight of a beardless Tristan in the kitchen in the morning. His clean-cut look restored to its pre-COVID state after a substantial trim from Saharie and full shave, he wore a grey suit and white dress shirt that accentuated the steeliness in his eyes.

"You look, very professional," she nodded at him cordially.

"Thanks, investors webcast this morning. I get to explain away the layoffs and show how they are in no way an indication of the declining financial health of our company." He raised his coffee mug, toasting his own funeral.

"Be sure to pick the right shade of lipstick for that pig," Lilyanna countered. He averted her eye and set his mug down on the kitchen counter. She could sense the stress coursing through him, consuming him, dragging him away from any competing sensation. Though she wanted to pull him back, back to her, back to the real him she had witnessed coming to life, she had no idea how. Cautiously, she slid her hand across the counter and rested it over his. He let it linger for a second and then pulled away and swiftly left for the library. Lilyanna watched him go, his rejection smarting.

All of the employees in the house joined the webcast from their respective workspaces to listen to Tristan and Marks do their worst to bury the layoff figures in a flurry of statistical projections and cantering about the impact of the pandemic on the future of the industry. What few anticipated was a question from an investor asking about the disproportionate percentage of women and employees of color laid off. Tristan and Marks danced around the question, pivoting back to some rose-colored view of an uptick in the industry sure to commence at any moment.

Lilyanna and Andrew exchanged stunned glances in the living room at the investor's question and management's dodgy response. *Was the investor right?* Her stomach turned at the thought of Tristan being part of the decision to lay off mostly women and employees of color. She could feel Andrew's eyes on her as her blood pressure rose and her heart pounded.

Everyone was shocked at the turn of the presentation, that is, except Jillian, Alyra and Joe. The mob stood in the main hall waiting for Tristan when he came out of the library. "Do you mind telling us what the hell happened?" Alyra confronted him. The others gradually emerged from their workspaces at the sound of the raised voices echoing from the hall.

"What do you want me to say?" Tristan sighed, placing his thumb and index finger on either side of the bridge of his nose.

"How about the truth? You haven't tried that one yet," Alyra retorted.

Jillian interjected, "We've seen the numbers, Tristan. Seventy percent of the employees laid off were women and employees of color."

The silence quickly turned accusatory. Lilyanna wanted to jump out of her skin because it felt so cringey even her own mind didn't want to be near it.

"Did you know beforehand, Tristan?" Jillian asked, her eyes daggers posed to strike.

He stared at her, his face drawn and cold eyes uncomfortably empty. "No, I didn't know until afterward."

"And you didn't think to let HR know as soon as you found out?" Alyra fumed.

Tristan glared at her. "What good would it have done? The layoffs are final."

"It might have done some good if Legal had known," Joe growled. "I wouldn't have let this shit happen."

"Legal did know. Your boss knew. All of your bosses knew," Tristan held his head up and looked at Joe, Alyra and Jillian in turn. "I can't help it if they chose not to discuss their decisions with their inferiors."

Joe advanced toward him, "Listen here, you pretentious piss ant."

"Joe, don't waste your energy," Jillian held up her hand in front of him. "This was not an oversight. Marks and your boss Justin Mercier deliberately chose to keep this from the three of us who would have fought for a different outcome." She stepped away from Joe and closer to Tristan, her movements graceful, yet assertive.

There was a sensuality to the way she spoke and moved. For a target of her tongue-lashing who didn't know her, it would be reasonable to view it as a toss-up as to whether she intended to kiss you or slit your throat, or maybe both, in that order. "Your *superiors* made damn sure the people who have their heads out of their asses in this company were not in a position to interfere with their masterful plan to save a buck." Now within a foot of him, she physically stood several inches below him even in her three-inch heels, but somehow she still managed to shrink him. For the first time in the confrontation, doubt and discomfort shrouded his demeanor.

"Your superiors chose the one inferior they knew they could trust to carry out their idiotic plans, and you did not disappoint." Her voice dropped to a whisper, "How fucking stupid are you?"

He didn't take the bait. As usual, there was no viewing window to his inner turmoil. His already icy glare just grew frigid. "Apparently stupid enough to make sure all of you made the cut." If his words caught her off guard, Jillian didn't show it. She continued to stare in his arctic blue eyes, but they had no effect on her the way they did Lilyanna.

"Who says we would want that?" Alyra asked. "Whether I stay here is my decision!"

Tristan shook his head, "Please, we have you! You work at an infrastructure company during a pandemic. There's nowhere for you to go."

Alyra put her hand on her hip, "Oh you have me, do you?" she howled in exasperated laughter. "I'll tell you what you have, or more accurately, what you don't. You have me, in my capacity as an employee, only to the extent you remain the highest bidder. Everyone here is for sale, all day every day. We can all be bought. That's what you counted on when you orchestrated this sequestration."

"So you're going to sell yourself to some competitor?" he raised his voice.

"No, I'm going to sell your ass to the press if you keep pushing me," she warned.

"Hold up, can we just pause for a sec?" Andrew cut in. "If you didn't know in advance that the majority of the layoffs affected women and BIPOC, then how did this happen? Someone must have known. Are you saying it was Marks?"

"I don't know for sure. He didn't choose the individual employees laid off, nor did I. Certain departments were assigned a number of employees to cut, and the highest-ranking manager in each department made the call."

"And you rubber-stamped their choices without following our internal termination policy or even notifying Alyra," Joe concluded.

"I did what I had to do to keep this company afloat."

Jillian shook her head, "You did what you had to do to keep yourself off your knees in the boardroom. I don't hate to break it to you how disappointed you're going to be in the fruits of that labor." She turned her back on him and left the room, refusing to be an audience for his rationalizations.

Tristan's actions were despicable, but it was his lack of remorse that shook Lilyanna as she stared in the mirror of the upstairs master bathroom. Forcing herself to make eye contact with her reflection, the image disgusted her. She wasn't Alice through the looking glass; the glass was looking at her, and it saw too little and wanted too much. It saw that she had given herself to a man who didn't care about her or any other human. She was unsure of whether he told the truth about his lack of prior knowledge and thus negligently participated in the discrimination instead of doing so willfully, but, either way, he did so unapologetically and without regret. Even if she could forgive him at some point, not that he would ever ask, she couldn't forgive her own ignorance.

Kyah shouting at Hubs on the phone reminded Lilyanna of the other impending loss on her calendar. "What's taking you so long? You should've been here by now! It's not like there's traffic during a state-wide lockdown. This stress is not good for the baby! Do you want it to come out with an anxiety disorder? I don't know why you have an opinion either. Do you have a fetus forming on top of your bladder? Whatever, just take all the time you need, selfish prick!" She hung up on him and tossed her phone across the bedroom. The tears started flowing as she sank onto the edge of her bed. A moment later, she dialed Hubs' number. "Hi, I'm sorry, babe. No, no, it was my bad. Thanks, I love you too," she sobbed. "Okay, just get here whenever you can, but in five minutes, okay?"

Lilyanna, Tessa, Tie and Saharie carried Kyah's luggage downstairs to a black Ford truck in the side drive. "Hubs quarantined before driving out here, but I told him he has to wait in the car, just in case," Kyah explained. She hugged Six, Barret, Dylan and Waya and waved to the others before turning her attention to her best friends. "Well, one more hug for the road, ladies?"

"Promise you'll let us know when you make it home and keep us updated on all baby developments!" Tessa instructed. "We'll come visit when it's safe."

Lilyanna felt her eyes welling up with tears as she watched Tessa and Saharie each hug Kyah. "I'm an emotional wreck." She looked up and dabbed under her eyes.

"Me too, and I'm not even on my period," Saharie groaned.

"Aww, don't be sad, loves. Just think Saharie, you get the whole bed to yourself, or better yet, share it with someone else," Kyah told her with a scandalous wink.

"And you, my hot little hostess," she pulled Lilyanna into a tight hug.

"Oh my gosh, I'll miss you," Lilyanna told her. "Thank you for being here."

"Thank you for having me." Kyah took Lilyanna aside. "Listen, your terms, nobody else's."

Lilyanna nodded at her.

"Good. Love you, ladies! Don't do anything I wouldn't do!" The group stood in the drive watching until the truck disappeared into the woods.

Lilyanna tossed and turned in her bed that night, emotionally exhausted yet too disconcerted to sleep peacefully. She turned on her side to find William lying next to her on the dunes. "I've been waiting for you. I was hoping you'd visit me tonight." He brushed a strand of hair from her face.

"I've been busy." She gazed at him in remorse.

"Do you miss me sometimes?" She didn't reply but took his hand in hers and closed her eyes. "I love seeing you at Whimser," he remarked softly.

His words chilled her. "You can see me?"

"Of course, My Flower. I'm never far away."

Her eyes popped open.

CHAPTER TWENTY
Poppy Fever

Morale among the Xenergy employees living at Whimser hit rock bottom and continued digging. "Did upper management seriously think we would be so grateful that we weren't the ones who got fired that we would overlook the fact they're racist pigs?" Six ranted as the younger residents downed their first serving of morning coffee in the kitchen.

"I don't think they thought at all, and that's just as inexcusable," Tessa said.

"Damn, Lily, I thought your company was more woke," Waya added.

"Why would you think that?" Lilyanna sat staring foggily into her teacup, partly wishing she could drown in it. In her reflection in the glass table, she studied the dark circles under her eyes that she hadn't bothered to try to cover with concealer.

"What should we do? Are you prepared to quit?" Tessa asked Six and Barret.

"Maybe we should," Barret sighed. "We can't just do nothing."

"Man, I have a wife and kids. There's no guarantee I could find another decent job right now in the midst of the pandemic." Six shook his head and looked at the floor. "That's exactly what they're counting on. You heard Tristan—'we have you.' The way things are right now, they do have us."

"They don't pay me that much. I could walk," Tie shrugged.

"But then you'd have to quit sucking Rich's and Andrew's dicks, and we know how fond you are of that," Tessa smirked.

"Whoa, shots fired!" Waya remarked, sipping his coffee casually.

"Really, Tessa?" Tie scowled defensively. "I respect my supervisors. What's wrong with that? You can't think those two are the problem."

"True, they're members of marginalized groups," Barret added. "They can't be pleased about the layoffs."

"Uh, Rich is a White dude," Six corrected him. "Isn't Andrew from South Africa or something?"

"Right, I meant just Andrew," Barret murmured under his breath.

"Andrew is biracial," Tessa clarified. "His dad is from South Africa, and his mom is American." She stood up and paced around the kitchen. "Maybe you have a point, Tie. It's not every manager. It's a couple at the very top pulling the strings while morally drunk. I think it even goes above Tristan."

"There's only one person above Tristan, President Marks," Barret replied.

"I would argue Justin Mercier is as high up as Tristan. Legal is kind of its own unit apart from the traditional corporate ladder, but he's up there and clearly in cahoots with Marks."

"Yeah, it's definitely them. How does that help us?" Barret asked.

"I don't know. I'm just identifying the issue. That's usually the first step in legal analysis, isn't it? I didn't say I had a solution. I'm just saying it's not the whole company that should go down, just them."

"Isn't that usually what *should* happen with poor leadership, but it's always the opposite?" Tie said.

"It's not happening to us. We gave up too much for this company. I'll talk to Alyra. She might actually know something that matters," Six proposed.

"What about Jillian?" Tessa asked.

"I don't know where she stands," Barret admitted. "Whose camp is she in?"

"I'm not sure either," Tessa admitted. "She seems tight with Alyra and Joe, but she works closely with Tristan. What do you think, Lily?"

Lilyanna's eyes remained fixated on the hazy image of her drawn face in the glass table, her mind blank. "Lily!" Tessa snapped her out of her brain fog.

"What?" Lilyanna groaned in annoyance.

"Where do you think Jillian's loyalties lie?"

"With Jillian," she stated flatly. Barret and Tie snickered.

"I mean, is she on upper-middle management's side or top-upper management's?"

"I don't know," she sighed. "I'm sure she swings both ways."

"I'm sure she does. I don't trust her," Barret decided.

"You don't trust me either," Lilyanna retorted.

"I trust you more than her."

Lilyanna's face remained blank. "Thanks for that."

"Are you with us, Lily?" Six pressed.

She turned her I'm-so-over-it-all gaze on him. "Of course, I am. I can't believe you'd even ask."

Lilyanna grudgingly forced herself to the living room to start her workday, though she had no mental energy or motivation. On the way, she ran into Bix. "There you are," he stopped her. "Mr. Taylor sent over the original signed documents from the wildlife society and the Lakeview Ranch Club." He handed her an unsealed manila envelope.

"Oh, right, good." She removed the documents and scanned over them to make sure they were signed. "These look fine."

"Well done," he nodded approvingly.

She gaped at him, too brain foggy to show any enthusiasm for the first, and likely the last, compliment he'd ever granted her. "Glad something worked out," she managed to utter. "Um, please put them in the desk drawer in the library." She handed the envelope back to him.

"I believe Mr. Anderson is occupying the library this morning."

"Then if the interruption bothers him, he can work elsewhere. You have more of a right to the library than he does."

Bix regarded her cautiously for a moment and then nodded. "As you say, madam."

***

Before dinner, Tie called Lilyanna, Tessa, Dylan and Waya into the dining room for a private chat. "Look,

I know everyone is pissed right now, but we have to get ready for Saharie's thirtieth birthday this weekend."

Lilyanna could've kicked herself for not taking the lead on her best friend's birthday. It slipped her mind with Kyah leaving, her fight with Tristan and all the workplace drama. "Oh, you're right. I'm sorry I didn't bring it up sooner. We need to get it together."

"Uh, did I miss something? Did the whole corporate discrimination elephant in the room suddenly get resolved?" Waya asked.

Tessa shook her head. "No, you didn't miss anything. I overheard Jillian, Alyra and Six strategizing in Jillian and Alyra's room earlier, but none of them have made any announcements. We're not going to solve that issue by letting Saharie feel unimportant. Life doesn't stop to give us time to tackle one task at a time."

"Right, and I want it to be a special day for her," Tie insisted. "I ordered her this necklace. It should be here in the next day or so. Do you think she'll like it?" Tie held up his phone to show a picture of a sterling silver circular pendant necklace with a small emerald stone in the center.

Lilyanna, Tessa and Dylan aww'd in unison. "She'll love it, Tie," Lilyanna confirmed.

"Yeah, I'm obviously not in the mood for a party, but we can't let our employers ruin our friend's thirtieth birthday," Tessa agreed.

"All the more reason to have a party," Dylan added. "Tell your racist employers you're not working on Friday so you can have a party for a Black woman." The others exchanged glances.

"I'll ask Ms. Howard to make a cake," Tie grinned.

CHAPTER TWENTY: Poppy Fever

"I'll handle the decorations," Tessa volunteered. "That just leaves the task of telling management we're taking the day off." They all turned to Lilyanna.

***

Several deep breaths and an explicit internal monologue later, Lilyanna knocked on the door to Jillian and Alyra's bedroom. Jillian cracked the door open. "Hi Jillian, I'm so sorry for the interruption. Can I have a minute of your time?"

Without answering, Jillian held the door open for Lilyanna and then closed it behind her. Lilyanna stood awkwardly by the side of Jillian's bed, hearing Alyra running the shower in the en-suite bathroom. "Have a seat, it's your bed," Jillian said. "Sorry for the mess." Lilyanna looked around in confusion, as the room looked like nobody lived in it. In contrast to the upstairs master bedroom, Jillian and Alyra's room remained neat with no clothes on the floor and the dresser and vanity uncluttered except for a few cosmetics.

"Uh, no, there's no mess at all. This room is pristine!"

"It's not that I personally care about everything being clean and organized like you would expect from your stereotypical inherent control freak," Jillian mused as she walked over to the dresser and pulled a black sports bra and matching yoga pants from the top drawer. "Truth is, and I didn't know this when I was your age, too much perfection is a turn-off. People act like they want someone who has it all together, but nobody actually gets wet for that." Without warning, she slipped out of her blouse, down to a neutral silk bra. Lilyanna looked away, trying to hide her blushing face.

"Think about it," Jillian continued, staring at her reflection in the vanity mirror. "When people are getting intimate, they don't fold their clothes and put them in a drawer. They throw them on the floor. It's a signature of physical passion." She tossed her blouse on the floor next to her feet. She then unhooked her bra and threw it on the floor as well before pulling on her sports bra and changing into her yoga pants. "But then, over the years, you get so used to cleaning up other people's messes that it becomes a habit. You know if you don't do it, nobody else will." Sighing, she picked up her blouse and bra, folded them, and set them on the vanity. "Now, what did you want to chat about?"

Lilyanna continued to look away from her. "Oh, um, well," Lilyanna struggled to gather her thoughts. In her head, she heard Jillian repeating Miranda Priestly's words from *The Devil Wears Prada*, "By all means, move at a glacial pace."

Lilyanna took a deep breath and looked up at Jillian. "I suppose I'm hoping we can schedule a break from cleaning up other people's messes for a day."

***

"You did what?" Tristan fumed at Jillian in the kitchen.

"You heard me. I gave the employees in the house the day off tomorrow. Morale is low, and everyone is burned out."

"Since when did burnout become an excuse to stop working? If that were the case, none of us would have jobs."

"For us, no, it's not an excuse—for the employees we have to retain in order to keep this company operating, it's a concern. I agree, up until this year I wouldn't have given it a thought, but up until this year we would never have sequestered employees away from their families, either."

Tristan ran his hand through his hair and rested his hand over his mouth, his wheels spinning in overdrive frustration. "You should've discussed this with me first. Let me choose my fate."

"Is that how fate works?" she smirked. "Like the way you discussed the layoffs with me first?"

"It was better for you that I didn't. I did you a favor," he insisted.

"That's for me to decide," she snapped. "But if that's how you see it, allow me to return the favor. I put your name on the day-off gift label next to mine. I know you don't care about making amends because you don't think you did anything wrong, but you do care about a full-scale mutiny in this house."

He sighed and gazed at her in defeat. "Jilly."

She stepped closer to him and relaxed her stern expression.

"I didn't mean for this to happen," he said softly.

"I know." She swept his wavy hair out of his eye. "But that doesn't matter. You're not accused of a crime, so lack of malicious intent does not absolve you. You're not innocent until proven guilty in the court of public opinion. People look at us, and they see the old guard. They never liked us. They just grit their teeth and bear us. The tolerance for the fuckery of the status quo has run out. People aren't just hoping for progress, they are demanding it. If we don't adapt, we won't survive."

***

On Friday evening, Tie escorted Saharie on a walk to give her the necklace, while Lilyanna, Tessa, Dylan and Waya decorated the living room and dining room. Lilyanna set out several bottles of champagne and flutes on the dining table, and Tessa and Dylan hung a happy birthday banner over the dining room window.

"Where does the 'Dirty 30' sign go?" Waya asked, holding up a gold aluminum sign.

"Hang it from the chandelier," Dylan told him.

Lilyanna and Tessa then took a bottle of champagne, a bucket of ice and two glasses upstairs to prepare a special honeymoon suite for Saharie and Tie at the end of the night. They cleaned up the room and made the bed with clean sheets and then sprinkled rose petals Tessa had ordered in the shape of a heart on the center of the bed.

"I'll sleep downstairs," Tessa said as she tossed more rose petals on the floor next to the bed.

"I'll sleep up here in the den," Lilyanna replied.

When Tessa finished sprinkling more rose petals in the hall leading to the room, they surveyed their work. "Well, it's not the Four Seasons, but it'll do," Tessa approved. They quickly got dressed and freshened up in time for Saharie's arrival back at the house. Lilyanna opted for charcoal jeans and a short-sleeve low-cut sweater, complete with a fake smile. She and Tristan hadn't spoken in days, and all she wanted to do was lie around and wallow in self-pity alone. However, she would feel even more guilty if her miserable mood ruined Saharie's birthday, so she did the minimum to make herself presentable and joined the others downstairs.

Everyone waited in the dining room for Saharie, except for Tristan who remained locked in the guesthouse. Saharie returned proudly wearing the necklace from Tie over her black mini dress.

"Happy Birthday!" Everyone shouted. Ms. Howard emerged from the kitchen carrying a chocolate sheet cake.

"Oh my gosh, you guys are so sweet!" Saharie cried. "I really didn't expect all this."

"No candles, I'm afraid. Can't have someone blowing on a shared cake these days," Ms. Howard noted.

"I'll make a wish in my head anyway," Saharie said as Six and Andrew popped bottles of champagne. Tessa made a toast to Saharie turning thirty, and the group clinked glasses. Lilyanna continued to smile until the others started to disperse into the living room and den. She remained behind, staring out the window at the light shining in the windows of the guesthouse and chugging down her champagne. She wondered what he was doing in there. He probably wasn't sulking or feeling guilty. He was too self-righteous for that. Maybe he was talking to another woman on the phone, or getting off, or both at the same time.

For a second, she thought she might rush out the door to find him. Ashamed of her weakness, she popped another bottle of champagne instead, just for herself, and drank from the bottle. Going straight to drunk without passing tipsy, she stumbled into the hall. The raucous laughter echoing from the den deflected her from that side of the house. She had no desire to be around the others.

The last time she had spent quality time at Whimser, William had just died, and she only stayed in the house one night thereafter. Initially, she thought Whimser might be magical. All she had to do was open the right door. Open a wardrobe, and it might lead to Narnia. Open another door, and maybe her parents would be standing there, or William. *If that happened, would that mean they were alive, or she was dead?*

Hazily, she wandered the hall, stopping in front of the portrait of her lying in a non-existent garden of flowers that never grew. She chugged down more champagne. The more she drank, the more the colors in the portrait bled into each other, the white dress a swirl of green and pink and sky blue. It really didn't even look like her in the portrait. Maybe William had been picturing one of his other whores in a white dress.

Later into the night, Tie and Saharie eagerly left the party for their makeshift love nest. "This is cute," she smiled, sitting against the head of the bed and running her hand over the rose petals. "Thank you for tonight," she told him sincerely as she pulled off her heels and put her feet up on the bed.

"Oh, the night is just beginning." He opened the bottle of champagne on the nightstand and handed her a full glass. Leaving his glass on the nightstand, he sat down on the bed at her feet and draped her legs over his lap, stroking her smooth skin. "I want tonight to be special for you." He turned to face her and slid his body up between her legs. "You're so beautiful." He went down on her as she lounged against the head of the bed, sipping her champagne.

Downstairs, Lilyanna took another deep drink from her half-empty bottle and continued meandering through the hall, her mind on a summer night when she and William danced in the hall to jazz music. "You look lovely tonight," he whispered to her while he twirled her around the hall. She rolled her eyes at his hopeless romanticism but couldn't hide her giddy schoolgirl smile. Holding one hand and wrapping the other around her waist, he guided her in loose spirals on the marble floor.

Tonight, she danced alone through the hall, the music and William's voice only in her head. Yet, she felt eyes on her. William must be watching her dance. She pirouetted in the center of the room, the art on the walls blurring into one impressionistic vision with her spinning on one foot in the middle.

"What are you doing?" a concerned voice called from the doorway of the living room. Lilyanna spun out of her turn and looked around her, expecting to see William watching her, but she saw no one except Andrew walking toward her, looking worried.

"What do you care what I'm doing?" she turned away from him and chugged more champagne.

"Okayyy, I think you've had enough. Come on, let me help you upstairs." He held out his arm to her.

"I'm just fine, thank you." She pushed past him and stumbled into the empty living room.

He followed behind her. "I think you should call it a night. Just give me the bottle."

She pulled the bottle out of his reach and took another drink. "You should stay away from me. People die on my watch here when I'm drunk."

"Lily, don't say that. William Whimsergarden didn't die because you were drinking."

"You're right," she pointed at him, "that's not why he died. In fact, I'm not sure he died at all. I think he's here. He's been here all along, watching everything we do."

"Stop it, Lily. Just give me the bottle and go to bed!"

"You want the bottle? Fine, here ya go." She smashed the bottle against the edge of the fireplace behind him, sending pieces of glass flying into the carpet.

Andrew ducked out of the way. "What the fuck? You're going to wake up the whole house!"

The noise jolting her from her fog, she nearly burst into tears. "I'm sorry! I don't know why I did that." She covered her face and started to fall over, unable to balance herself.

Andrew caught her and quickly pulled her out of the living room and up the back stairs before anyone came to investigate the noise. "Because you're wasted."

"Just get off me," she groaned, trying to push him away when they reached the upstairs hall.

"No, you're self-destructive."

"You don't get to decide what I am!" she elbowed him in the ribs and tried to kick him.

"Ow, damn it!" He pulled her into a hold and they both fell to the ground, Andrew keeping her arms pinned. "Stop trying to make me hurt you," he whispered into her ear. "I'm not going to." Her body went limp, and she tried to control her sobs. "Come on." He stood up and lifted her onto her feet, guiding her into the upstairs den. He led her over to the couch and then closed the door behind them. "Hi, Jazzmine," he cooed at the calico cat sprawled out on the top of the cat tower. Fleur and Marie slept in their bed on the floor.

Lilyanna was already lying on the sofa, drifting into an intoxicated sleep. Andrew climbed over her and lay down behind her on the sofa. He wrapped his arm around her, and she scooted against him. She shifted slightly against his body, settling next to him.

He tightened his lips and pressed down on her hip to stop her from grinding on him. "Just go to sleep," he said.

Lilyanna felt the warmth of Andrew's body against hers as she dozed fretfully. Pressing into him, his lips brushed her neck, her body tingling in response. Gracefully, he rolled on top of her, and they kissed passionately. Her breathing quickening, she pulled his shirt over his head and embraced him. They continued making out, more aggressively still. Suddenly, she opened her eyes to find William on top of her, looking down at her with a sultry grin. When he sat up, Lilyanna saw blood dripping from an open wound on his neck. Startled, she reached up and dabbed the wound, her hand shaking. Casually, he took her hand and licked the blood off her index finger. "Mmmm, tastes like raspberry."

She woke from her dream and bolted upright, panting. Next to her, Andrew was sound asleep in the same position, clothes on, undisturbed. The room spinning from the sudden disruption of her equilibrium, she rolled off the sofa clumsily to go to the bathroom. She stumbled down the hall, following the trail of rose petals, her vision blurry. The rose petals sticking to her feet resembled blood in the natural light streaming in from the upstairs windows. Panicking, she reached down and grabbed a handful of petals that immediately melted into blood. She stared in horror at her open palms dripping red. Her heart pounded in her ears as she ran to the bathroom and switched on the light. Once her eyes adjusted to the light, the blood instantly disappeared from her hands. She turned her palms over and examined them and then checked her feet. Nothing.

Dizzy and terrified, she looked in the mirror to find eye makeup smeared under her eyes and her hair tangled and disorderly. Her surroundings still spinning, her stomach churned, and she ran to the toilet, falling on her knees in front of it just in time to throw up seven years' worth of regrets.

CHAPTER TWENTY-ONE
Beyond the Bluff

Lilyanna woke up alone on the sofa the next morning with a raging headache. Her vision grew fuzzy when she hoisted herself to her feet and staggered to the master bedroom, where she found the remnants of Tie and Saharie's romantic night in Whimser's *Bachelor* fantasy suite. The room smelled like a brothel dipped in champagne. It wasn't the tangled sheets waded in a pile on the king bed or the empty bottle of champagne on the carpet next to an elliptical stain that caught her attention, however. It was the keys to her car on her pillow.

Shakily, she snatched up the keys and examined them like a murder weapon. If there were anything left in her stomach, she would have hurled again. *Who put the keys on her bed?* Tie and Saharie were the only people she knew for sure had been in the room, and they wouldn't have done this. It was too passive-aggressive for Tessa. It had to be someone else. She stared at the keys and paced the room, her head pounding. Andrew was upstairs last night. It would have been easy for him to put the keys in her room while she slept, but she had no idea as to his motive.

Adrenaline chasing away her hangover, she quickly threw on a hoodie and stuffed the keys in her pocket. She had to discreetly return them to the kitchen drawer before someone found them. She tiptoed down the back stairs and listened outside the kitchen to determine if it was occupied. Relieved to hear no noise, she hurried inside and stopped upon seeing Jillian pouring a cup of coffee.

"Morning," Jillian stated coolly. "What's with the deer-in-the-headlights look?"

"Oh, sorry, I just, uh, slept later than I meant to."

"I can see that. I'm already on my second cup of coffee. Can I get you one?"

"Sure, thanks." Hesitantly, Lilyanna stepped over to the kitchen bar, moving as carefully as she could out of fear the keys would jingle in her pocket. "So, you were the first one up this morning?" Lilyanna tried to keep her tone casual.

"I think so. I usually am." Jillian poured a mug full of black coffee and pushed it across the counter.

Lilyanna kept her eyes locked on Jillian, studying her face for clues. *Did she know about the keys? Maybe it was her all along.*

"Everything alright with the coffee?"

"Oh, yeah, thanks." Lilyanna nodded.

Jillian frowned at her. "You should consume something without any alcohol content, whole food perhaps. You look a bit drawn."

"Right, yeah, I'll take that under advisement, thanks."

Jillian took her coffee cup and left the kitchen, glancing over her shoulder at Lilyanna. As soon as Lilyanna confirmed Jillian's exit, she darted to the kitchen drawer and quietly replaced the keys with a sigh of relief.

Hearing glass clinking in the dining room, she went to investigate. Andrew plodded around the dining table, toting a trash bag and filling it with empty beer and champagne bottles. "Hey," she said awkwardly.

"Hey, feeling alright?" he asked.

"Fantastic. You?"

"Same," he nodded curtly.

"Are you, um, okay with last night? Are we good?" she asked, trying to take his temperature.

He continued cleaning the table without looking at her. "Yeah, I mean, nothing to worry about. I won't tell your lover, Tristan, if that's your concern."

She froze. *How long had he known?* Trying to recover her composure, she spat back, "I won't tell your wife."

He dropped the trash back and strode over to her and lowered his voice. "What the hell is that supposed to mean? Nothing happened last night! I was just trying to help you, to be a good friend!"

"If that's how you see it, then why the snarky comment about Tristan?"

He massaged his temples. "I don't know. I'm sorry, I shouldn't have said that. It's just, we had an agreement that you're off-limits."

Taken aback, she paused. "Wait, what? Who made the agreement?"

Andrew sighed, "There was no official agreement or anything. It was just something the guys said offhandedly during a private conversation when we first got here. We wanted all of the women to feel comfortable, out of respect."

"Oh, I'm sure the purpose of your private conversation was to show respect for the women." She started to storm out of the room and then turned on him. "If it were, you wouldn't have posited that you had any right to make choices for any of us. My choices were mine alone. Right or wrong, wise or absurd, they were made by me, not a room full of men with their unspoken rules." In her head, she gave Tristan kudos for knowing his own mind and acting on it. She felt relieved to know that was possible.

Lilyanna left Andrew standing there gaping as she sought to put as much distance as possible between herself and another heterogametic disappointment and the smoking gun in the kitchen drawer. Any number of eyes could be watching in this house full of voyeuristic ghosts and volatile guests.

***

Rich knocked on Barret's bedroom door. "Hey, man, you want to go for a swim?"

Barret blinked at him, perplexed by the invitation. "You mean with you?"

"Yeah." Rich studied his feet. "Look, I know things have been messed up, and that's my fault. I'm sorry. Can we just hang out for a bit, maybe clear the air?"

Barret thought for a second. "Um, okay, yeah, sure. I'll just throw on my trunks."

At the edge of the lake, Rich and Barret pulled off their t-shirts and waded in up to their waists. "You ready to put your new swimming skills to the test?" Rich asked playfully.

Barret faked a smile. "How so?"

Rich pointed to a buoy about a quarter of a mile out from shore. "Let's swim to that buoy and back."

Barret put his hand up to his forehead and squinted into the distance. "I think that's a little out of my reach," he laughed nervously. "I'm not that great a swimmer yet."

"Ah come on, you're better than you think. Just follow my lead." Rich dove beneath the surface and began slow but steady breast strokes. Reluctantly, Barret took a deep breath and plunged in after him.

**

Lilyanna trudged upstairs to convert the master bedroom from the honeymoon suite back to a shared bedroom. Saharie sauntered into the room a minute later, wearing sunglasses and carrying a cup of coffee. "Hey, morning, birthday girl," Lily greeted her. "How was last night?"

Saharie grinned sleepily, "Surprisingly fantastic. I didn't expect turning thirty to feel so . . . invigorating."

Lilyanna laughed, "I'm guessing Tie rose to the occasion?"

"That he did, over and over." She collapsed on her bed, her smile unfading. "I have to say, he continues to impress, in every way. I've never been with a guy who makes me feel as important as he does."

Lilyanna smiled and sat on the edge of Saharie's bed. "I'm happy for you," she told Saharie earnestly. "I'm glad you met someone who keeps you smiling like that." Lilyanna poked Saharie's cheek playfully.

Saharie giggled. "It's exciting to see that it's possible."

Suddenly, Tessa stormed into the room looking for Lilyanna. "What were you and Andrew arguing about downstairs?" she asked in an accusatory tone.

Saharie groaned, "Tessa, please, volume down."

Lilyanna gaped at Tessa and didn't respond.

"What, you thought I didn't know about you two?" Tessa continued.

"Tessa, I don't need this right now," Lilyanna sighed, getting up from Saharie's bed and resuming her cleaning efforts.

"Uh, then you should've thought about that before you slept with a married client."

"What are you talking about? I'm not sleeping with Andrew! I can't believe you would think that for a second."

"How could I not? I see you two always whispering and smiling at each other. I see the way he looks at you."

"Whatever you think you're seeing is in your head. It's true that Andrew and I get along well, and we're friends, but that's it. Why are you so upset, anyway?" Lilyanna scooped a pile of clothes off the floor, tossed them on her unmade bed, and then faced Tessa. "Wait, do *you* have feelings for Andrew?"

"This isn't about me!" Tessa snapped.

"Oh, it absolutely is," Lilyanna insisted. "It's you who has a thing for Andrew, and you think I'm in your way. Psh, you have a way bigger obstacle in your path than me—his wife."

Saharie chortled, "Seriously, Tess? It took a mental overhaul for her to have sex with one guy after years trapped in the celibacy desert. I don't think she started sleeping with two guys at the same time. Tristan's more than enough to keep her occupied."

"What? You've been with Tristan all this time?" Tessa cried in bewilderment.

Lilyanna and Saharie exchanged confused glances. "Um, yeah. I thought you knew. I thought everyone knew by now."

Tessa looked like she might leap out of her skin. "No, I didn't know! I thought you just had a little crush. How would I know when you didn't tell me? You apparently told everyone but me. How could you do that, Lily?"

"Tessa, I swear I thought you knew. You know everything about everyone at our company. I thought you just chose not to bring it up so you could claim plausible deniability if need be at some point."

"Well, now you know I didn't know, and that's your fault for assuming, Lily. I tell you everything, about Alec and everything else!"

"Bullshit! You didn't bother to tell me about your feelings for Andrew. So don't blame this all on me! You keep things from me too."

"Maybe because the guys are right—you can't be trusted. They were right about your loyalty to Tristan. Maybe they're right about the rest too."

"Whoa, Tessa, chill, that's not true. Lilyanna's thing with Tristan was separate from work, and I support her in that. You should too."

"I didn't have a chance to be supportive because I didn't know! Why would you exclude me of all people? I helped you pee in a trailer at Glastonbury two years ago when I had just taken molly for the first time because you were even more faded than I was! Do you know how hard that is? That's how much I bend over backwards to help you!"

"I do the same for you! I held your hair when you threw up your night of molly in the woods the next day while I could barely stand up because I also took molly!" Lilyanna shouted.

"Then do me the honor of cluing me in now. How's your fling working out for you now that you've seen the direction upper management is going?"

"You'll be glad to know it's going as well as everything else in 2020, right on par with Clorox injections to cure COVID and the idiocracy that is our government. Thanks for asking." Lilyanna scooped up Fleur off her bed and left the room for Dylan and Waya's room. Without a word, she climbed into bed between them, holding Fleur, and pulled the comforter over her head. Dylan put his arm around her and dozed off again.

***

Barret kicked his feet with all his might and stretched his stubby arms to the extent of their reach, urging them toward the buoy. The current, however, carried him sideways away from his destination. No matter how hard he kicked, he couldn't close the distance between himself and Rich, nearly fifty feet ahead of him. Panic seized him, as his legs and arms began to tire.

"Rich!" he called in desperation. "Rich, it's too far! I can't make it any farther. Rich! I can't, I can't," he called again before slipping under the surface.

The cries echoed in Rich's ear as he continued swimming. He slammed his arms harder against the surface of the water, trying to drown out Barret's plea for help. He tried to convince himself that it could just be the sound of a bird and that he couldn't hear clearly from such a distance with his head partially submerged.

Barret kicked to the surface and turned his body in the water in a clumsy attempt to swim back to shore, but the current maintained its unrelenting grip. His chest constricting and beginning to throb, Barret gasped for air, kicking harder to stay afloat. The sunlight beat down on him as he floundered, fighting the current and the depths threatening to drag him under. With one last anxious splash, his head bobbed above the water for another two seconds before the lake filled his nose and mouth and darkness swallowed the sunlight.

Hearing the splash behind him, Rich turned his head in time to see Barret slip beneath the surface of the lake. He turned back to look at the buoy off in the horizon and then again at the spot where Barret disappeared. "Damn it!" he yelled and swam furiously in Barret's direction.

Barret was unconscious by the time Rich towed him to shore. Rich struggled under Barret's weight as he hauled him onto the beach. He slammed him on his side and punched his back a few times until Barret coughed up a pint or two of lake water, then sat up, still coughing and sputtering.

Rich caught his breath and sat down on the beach next to him. "You okay, man? You okay?" Rich asked, handing him a towel.

Barret gasped for air and looked at him in shock. "What was that? Were you trying to kill me?"

"What? No, I saved you!"

"No, you were going to let me drown! Is that why you asked me to go for a swim, so you could get rid of me?"

"No, no I . . ." Rich stammered.

"You knew I couldn't swim that far. You wanted me to drown!"

"If I wanted you to drown, you would have," Rich snarled.

"This was supposed to be a warning, then?" Barret spat incredulously. With all the strength he could muster, he pushed himself off the ground and staggered to his feet, his jelly legs swaying beneath him. "To what, stay away from you? No problem there, buddy! Did you really think I would be pining after you or something, or, like, blackmail you to be with me? Dude, you're a hypocrite about sexuality, you don't get along with my best friend Six, and you just tried to kill me. Why the hell would I want to be with you? Just because you're better looking and more fit than me doesn't mean I want you at all costs. Here's a warning to you: keep your crazy ass away from me!" Barret grabbed his shirt and stumbled off the beach and into the woods, leaving Rich behind shaking.

CHAPTER TWENTY-TWO
Tangled Vines

The next weekend marked Memorial Day, 2020, with no cause to celebrate. Lilyanna sat on her bed talking to Luke on the phone. "I miss you, brother. I feel like I'm going crazy in this place."

"You should just come here! I have a guest room ready for you whenever you want. You can quarantine with me and bring your new meows." A series of low whooshing sounds drowned out the rest of his proposal.

"Wait, are you in an airport?" she asked.

"No, I'm on my balcony. The orange monstrosity in the White House released a squadron of World War II planes to fly over DC to salute his delusions of grandeur again. I can hear it now—the authoritarian hand jobs spouting White supremacy and international embarrassment all over the city and telling everyone to swallow the patriotism, all for him."

"Yeahhh, I still I think I'd rather suck corporate dick than the government's."

"We have some decent hybrid options here in DC. You're welcome here whenever you change your mind. You could be happy here, Lily."

"I don't want to be a grass is greener person."

"How about just go for grass period instead of the social desert you live in? Plus, grass is actually legal here."

He always knew how to make her smile no matter the circumstances. "I'll keep that in mind."

It wasn't the ego-stroking aerial ode to political depravity that people would remember, however . . .

Everyone in the house gathered around the TV in the den to watch the coverage of the death of George Floyd. In silence they stood, watching the atrocities played over and over, the man who couldn't breathe, killed by a broken, racist 'law enforcement' system. Nobody spoke. Nobody moved. Tie became the first person to show any sign of life when he grabbed Saharie's hand.

"Well, maybe this one will be enough," Six stated. All eyes turned to him. "A Black man going for a run, a Black woman sleeping in her own home— none of them were enough for anybody to do anything. Maybe George Floyd will finally tip the scale weighted against Black people. If not, then how many bodies is it going to take? Who's next? Is it me? Is it Alyra? Is it Saharie over here? Where's the turning point? I'm going to call my family." He stormed out of the room.

Lilyanna studied the sea of faces around her, most conveying a different phase of grief: Andrew, dejected sadness; Alyra, anger; Waya, outrage; Saharie, battle fatigue. Jillian looked disgusted, and Tessa, livid. She swallowed the bile rising in her throat.

When the group quietly disbanded, Lilyanna followed Andrew and pulled him aside near the back staircase. "I'm sorry," she said pathetically.

"What exactly are you sorry for?"

She couldn't meet his eye. "I don't know. I'm just sorry for everything that's happening."

"Why? This has to happen. Nobody with authority has acknowledged any wrongdoing, no matter how many people get killed. Six was right, maybe this is where that starts. So, I'll ask you again, what are you sorry for?"

She did her best to fight back tears, but her deepening voice betrayed her emotions. She didn't know how to answer him. "I'm sorry I went off on you earlier. I'm sorry for everything, and this lame-ass apology," she desperately tried to convince him. "I, um, I care about you, as a person."

He sighed, "You were right about what you said earlier, but that's a separate issue. I don't know how to begin sorting through all that right now. All I know is I care about you, too. Can we just agree that you and I are good on a personal level, please?"

"Yes, for sure!" she nodded eagerly. She was losing relationships in the house left and right, and she couldn't stand to lose him.

***

Lilyanna thought moods could deteriorate no further when President Marks held an unsolicited live webcast for the employees quarantined at Whimser. Out of curiosity and sheer boredom, Saharie, Dylan and Waya joined the group in the den to watch Marks' address on the TV connected to Jillian's laptop. "I see President Snow is streaming live from the Capitol," Dylan remarked.

"I will not be volunteering as tribute," Lilyanna retorted, taking a seat on the sofa between Dylan and Andrew.

Standing at the front of the room next to Tristan, Jillian switched on the TV broadcasting President Marks sitting at a desk with a stag head mounted on the wall in the background. He not-so-discreetly slid a half-empty glass of scotch out of the frame before beginning his speech. "Good afternoon, this is your Xenergy president, Harlyn Marks." His white hair neatly combed and his navy Brioni tie knotted at his neck, his appearance remained untouched by the pandemic. "I'm addressing you during this difficult time in light of the recent devastating events in our country.

"First, I want to thank you all for leaving your homes to prioritize the survival of this company. Your sacrifice is not in vain. Despite the pandemic and resulting downturn in the industry, our company is holding strong. In addition to our outstanding performance in the face of so many obstacles, one of our most significant achievements has been our sustained focus on diversity."

Lilyanna couldn't even hear anyone breathing in the room. Silence is not usually awkward to an introvert, but the silence in response to Marks' diversity comment could have embarrassed even the most reclusive hermit who waited his or her whole life for a state-mandated lockdown.

"Our dedication to diversity is represented by all of you quarantined at one of our female attorney's houses here in Texas. We are currently in talks with several national news stations regarding a press release on our groundbreaking quarantine of select employees. There will be more information to follow on this matter. Again, thank you all." Jillian grabbed the remote and turned off the TV.

"What the actual fuck was that?" Joe scoffed, pulling a cigarette and lighter from his pocket.

Six jumped to his feet, "Hold up, is he saying upper management, which just laid off a bunch of women and employees of color, is using us to promote an alleged focus on diversity?" He directed his question to Jillian, but she quickly took a seat on the end of the sofa.

"I know no more than you. Marks sent an email to Tristan and me saying he wanted to address the employees here in the house," Jillian explained. "I had no idea what he planned to say, and I don't endorse it."

"Does anyone here endorse it?" Six stepped closer to Tristan and glared at him, bewildered stares following him.

Tristan looked at him defensively. "This is not my doing, if that's what you're insinuating. I also did not know the subject of the message."

"But you knew about this shit with the press, didn't you? You know the real reason we're all here."

"What do you mean, the 'real reason'?" Tie asked. "We're here to stay away from COVID exposure to make sure business keeps going."

"But Six has a point—why us, specifically?" Tessa asked suspiciously. "Marks made a point of specifying the quarantine was at a female attorney's house, and the only three female attorneys at Xenergy are here . . ."

"Are you saying upper management picked us based on gender and ethnicity?" Alyra cried. "I know HR didn't approve that!"

"Who did approve it, then?" Barret asked.

Tristan sighed and raised his head to face the room, bracing for an uprising. "Marks and Justin Mercier made the final decisions."

"Why did they exclude me?" Jillian stormed. "My rank is as high as Justin's, and my brain is free of numbskull sycophant placations!"

Before Tristan could respond, Tessa cut him off. "That's why you weren't included, Jillian, and the fact that you have a vagina, and it's off-limits. What exactly did they decide?"

Tristan took a deep breath. "Marks worried the public would find out about our quarantine, and if that happened, he wanted to make sure it would be viewed favorably in terms of demographics."

"Why did they choose me, then?" Barret asked. "I bring no diversity to the table."

Lilyanna and Tessa inadvertently met eyes with the same thought: Big Brother Xenergy probably knew about Barret's membership in the LGBTQ community from the day of his hiring.

"Yeah, I'm the same as Barret," Rich added quietly. He looked at Barret and lowered his voice further. "I'm just like you."

"There are no other members of marginalized groups in management positions," Alyra clarified. "Short version, they chose the only women, Black and Brown people in the company in at least mid-level positions and sent us out here and then fired the others who didn't make the cut." Lilyanna glanced around the room as bulbs lit in realization among the employees, each handpicked for the bouquet in the front window.

Tristan shook his head, "Nobody planned the layoffs at the beginning of the lockdown, and, to my knowledge, the layoffs were not determined by gender or ethnicity."

Enraged, Six jumped to his feet. "How are we supposed to believe that? You lied to us from the beginning!" Six didn't yell, but assertively made his point with the eloquence and sharpness of years of experience commanding a courtroom. "Now you expect us to smile when you put us on display to the public like zoo animals? You can forget that. You don't get to paint us White and then wash it off when our Blackness is the only thing that stands between you and cancellation!"

Andrew looked at Tristan in desperation. "Man, tell me you weren't on board with this. Tell me you don't support Marks' plan."

Tristan replied, "I don't think there was a plan to make us a spectacle, until—"

"Until George Floyd!" Six boomed, stepping within a couple of inches of Tristan's face. "Say his name!"

Tristan's jaw muscles clenched as he grunted and put his hands up to Six's chest to block him. "Get out of my face!"

"Whoa, hey, stop!" Andrew leaped off the couch and stepped between the two men. Rich and Tie got up too, to back up Andrew, and Barret scurried over to Six. Jillian also rushed over, placing her hand on Six's shoulder. Joe stood next to Jillian, poised in wait to yank her out of the way.

"You're out of line, man," Rich told Six.

"Shut up, Rich, nobody rang your bell," Jillian cut in.

"Let's just all take it down a notch," Andrew urged.

"I'm not going to sit by and let Marks and his cronies discriminate against Black people and then turn around and use my color to their advantage!"

"I am not racist!" Tristan shouted, enunciating his words.

Six closed the remaining distance between them and dropped his voice, his lips curling in disdain with each word he hissed at Tristan. "That's not good enough."

Tristan pushed him out of his personal space again, and Andrew raised his arm in front of Tristan in caution. "You should be grateful to me," Tristan raised his voice, "all of you. It's because of me you're all here and still have jobs!"

Six's eyes widened, "Grateful to you? You're crazy, man!"

"You should be on your fucking knees for me!" Tristan continued, his deep voice slicing through the tension.

"Well, we all know Lily's already there," Barret smirked, "so just give an extra swirl of the tongue on our behalf, Lil."

"Excuse me!" Lilyanna jumped up and rushed at him. Joe held his cigarette between his lips and stepped away from Six and Tristan to block Lilyanna.

"What the hell are you talkin' about?" Joe asked Barret.

"It sounds like you're jealous," Saharie called out Barret.

"Don't bring her into this, man," Andrew bellowed. "That's uncalled for."

Lilyanna shouted around Joe and Andrew at Barret. "So according to you guys, I'm sneaking out, spreading COVID and sleeping around. Please continue to tell me more about my personal business."

Dylan raised his hand, "Actually, I think I started at least two of those rumors because I was bored." Saharie and Tessa snickered under their breath.

"I don't know about all that, Lily," Six admitted, lowering his voice an octave, "but I see you making this about you right now. It's always about the White folks. That's called pri-vil-ege."

"He brought me into this!" Lilyanna yelled defensively, pointing at Barret and failing to fight back the angry tears forming in her eyes.

"We're all in this! Nobody gets a free pass," Alyra interjected.

Lilyanna sank back onto the sofa. Six had a point— she was privileged. She recognized how it must look from the outside—a White lawyer with a mansion left at her feet. But they didn't know the price of inheriting Whimser. They didn't know William.

"I feel dirty," Dylan cringed, wringing his hands. "We need to scrub the White male supremacy out of this house."

"Hand sanitizer can't kill White male supremacy," Waya reminded him.

Shaking his head, Six stepped away from Tristan and plopped down on the sofa, his eyes on the floor. Jillian followed him and rested her hand on his back.

Nobody spoke for a minute or two. Then Jillian broke the blaring silence. "We need to first figure out where we go from here. Obviously, we're not doing any press interviews unless it's to pull back the curtain on this scandal, in which case that's the end of the company."

"We would lose all of our government contracts at the very least. They can all be terminated if we violate federal civil rights laws," Tessa noted.

"I say let it fold, then," Barret shrugged. "The company showed its ass too many times this year."

"Then we've done all this for nothing, and we'll be unemployed during a pandemic," Tessa pointed out.

"She's right," Joe agreed, taking a puff from a cigarette. "The employees will get fucked even harder while Marks enjoys a cushy early retirement. If the press shows up, send 'em over to Marks' place. They'll find a clusterfuck of rich old White geezers at his summer house."

Lilyanna nodded in agreement. Unlike the Whimser quarantine, arranged to tout diversity, the exclusive club of White male executives quarantined at Marks' hunting lodge would be the all-white flowers at the company's funeral.

"If we want this company to survive and do an immediate policy one-eighty, I think there's enough brainpower in this room to make that happen," Jillian said.

"Yeah, I vote for saving the company, ya know, and fixing it," Tie stated.

"There's your brain trust, Jill," Joe quipped.

"There's no quick fix for systemic racism or else we would not be where we are," Alyra snapped. "It's going to take actual work, by everyone, and I have yet to be convinced this company is worth saving."

"We have to start somewhere," Jillian pressed. "We should notify the Board of Directors of what we discovered about Marks' plan. Then, I think we give them a list of our demands. If they don't meet them, nothing is to stop any one of us from running to the press with the real story."

"Demand number one: Marks leaves the company. His removal is non-negotiable," Six stated.

Alyra nodded, "That has to happen for me to even consider staying at Xenergy. I'll make that demand to the Board myself."

"What about the composition of the Board?" Andrew asked. "I don't know who all of the directors are, but I'd bet my net worth there's little to no diversity. I'd like a seat on the Board."

"Yes!" Lilyanna and Tessa agreed in unison.

"You deserve it, man," Tie approved.

Lilyanna made notes in her phone. "I'll type up a list of our demands, and I think everyone in the house should sign it. Not all of our opinions will carry as much weight as others, but, like you said, any one of us could run to the press if these demands are not met."

"What about you?" Jillian turned to Tristan. "You have a decision to make. Do you want to run back to Marks, or work with us?"

"You shouldn't even have to think about it," Alyra chided him. "Your fellow execs are sitting in a cigar room in Marks' mansion, drinking five-hundred-dollar scotch and reinforcing each other's elitist White male supremacist schemes, and they didn't invite you! They left you here to blindly do their bidding and deal with the fallout. Why would you care about protecting them?"

"I don't care about protecting Marks," he stated flatly. "I care about the success of this company."

"Then you no longer work for Marks," Jillian confirmed.

"I'll still have more demands," Alyra added. "Rooting out a few bad weeds at the top isn't enough to put this company on track to legitimate progress, and I'm not throwing my support behind anything less."

"Could you ask for some sort of commitment to a long-term plan that would promote women and people of color?" Tessa asked. "There needs to be a substantive plan or else we're just going to get left behind again."

Alyra nodded, "Let me think on it. I'll raise this to the Board, and then, depending on the Board's response, we can discuss options."

Suddenly, Sylvie and Nina rushed into the den. "Lily, you need to come out to the cottage, now! Bix is sick, and this time I'm sure it's COVID-19."

***

Lilyanna slid two bottles of water and a thermometer through the window above Bix's bed in his cottage. When Bix sat up in his bed to accept the delivery, Lilyanna secured the cloth mask over her nose and mouth and then stood back and waited for Bix to take his temperature for the third time that day. She and Sylvie took turns monitoring

Bix's condition, delivering food and water and administering temperature checks throughout the day. For two days, his temperature averaged 102, and he remained bedridden with chills, aches and a body-shaking cough erupting from his chest.

"It's 101.5," he told her in a raspy voice.

"Down slightly, that's good. Take two more Tylenol in the next hour, and we'll check it again this evening. Bix, I really need to know how you think you caught COVID."

Bix retreated from the window and lay back down in his bed. "Another time, Mistress Rivers. I need to rest." It was the same response he'd given each time she pressed for information, and it drew the same rebuke from the guests that afternoon when she returned to the house.

She paused upon entering the living room to find all the guests except Tristan and Joe wearing face masks. "What happened? Did someone else get sick?"

"No, we were hoping you'd tell us Bix is fine, and we're overreacting," Barret replied.

"Oh, no, he's super sick, and he still won't talk." *Cue sighs and groans.*

"Do you think these masks cover or induce resting bitch face?" Dylan asked.

Jillian threw up her hands in frustration. "He does realize the health of a house full of people is on the line, right? How can we figure out whether the rest of us have been infected if he won't tell us anything?"

Lilyanna sighed, "Nobody could accuse Bix of being selfless." *If he were well, he'd probably be getting off to the thought of causing chaos and unrest.*

"Well, I have to say this is terrible timing," Jillian lamented, pacing the room. "As if we don't have enough to deal with right now. The state is opening up, and, now that our group quarantine has been potentially compromised, we're running out of time."

"Are you concerned that Marks could force us to go back to the office right away?" Barret asked. "That would be insane."

"Uh, we've been away from our families for months and would like to spend some time with them," Andrew added miserably.

"I hear the people that have been quarantined with their families just want to get away from them," Barret quipped.

"What are employees with kids supposed to do with schools doing the distance learning thing?" Six asked.

Jillian massaged her temple with no possibility of relieving her pounding headache. "I will figure all of this out. Lily, please keep working on the Bix situation, and, when I say working, I mean succeeding in learning what secrets he's hiding."

CHAPTER TWENTY-THREE
Song of Swans

Jillian paced the library, with Alyra, Tristan, Six, Joe and Andrew scattered around the room. "When is the Board supposed to respond?" Joe asked, gazing out the window.

"The directors should be calling any minute," Jillian replied stiffly.

Andrew tapped his foot absent-mindedly on the wood floor. "How much did you and Alyra tell the Board?"

"Enough to call for Marks' termination. We told them of the motivations behind our group quarantine and the results of the layoffs. Those debacles combined with Marks' handling of everything of substance since the Stay-At-Home Order paints a bleak picture of the direction of this company."

"I made it clear that if the Board stays the course and keeps Marks as president, I'll make sure that picture is broadcast to any news station and social media platform that will listen," Alyra added. "We also gave them the list of demands signed by everyone in the house."

Jillian stopped pacing and perched on the edge of the desk facing the group. "Even if Marks hadn't directly orchestrated the quarantine selection, we can't have him speaking for the company on social issues anymore. If you alternate between being the punch line and the punching bag of a story, you're not the right person to tell it."

"Is it safe to say congratulations, then?" Andrew said to Tristan. "You're next in line for the corner office."

Tristan shuffled his feet awkwardly and forced a partial smile. "I'll support whatever the Board decides."

"Does that mean you'll actually be different from Marks?" Joe asked in his low, scratchy voice.

Tristan narrowed his gaze at him, the natural light from the window highlighting the fatigue in his eyes. "I will do my best to make better decisions for this company and its employees than my predecessor."

"Good, but you might want to throw in a little more enthusiasm when you recite the scripts Jill gives you," Joe retorted.

Before anyone could speak, Jillian's cell phone vibrated on the desk.

* * *

Bix's symptoms worsened in the evening with his temperature rising to 102.5 and his breathing forced. "What did the hospital say when you called?" Lilyanna asked Sylvie as they slid a tray of soup and crackers through the cottage window.

"Which one? The main hospital an hour away has no beds available, and the closest clinic has beds but no staff to service them. Both told me not to bring him in unless it's an absolute emergency. There's a high risk he'll just get sicker being exposed to other patients or infect someone else."

Lilyanna pondered, watching Bix reject the food and pull his comforter up under his chin. "Let's check on him again tonight. If he gets any worse, we won't have any choice but to take him to a hospital."

Back at the house, Lilyanna was the last to join the group gathered in the den. "There you are," Andrew inclined his head to the side and led her to a corner in the back of the room.

"What now?" she asked.

"Jillian called a house meeting. Two directors on the Board are about to send a video message."

"About what?"

"You'll see." They rejoined the group just as Jillian clicked on the TV. Two heavyset balding men appeared in separate Zoom boxes on the screen.

The heaviest and baldest spoke first. He didn't give his name or even an introduction. "Good evening. We are addressing you this evening on behalf of the Xenergy Board of Directors. Given the, unique, difficulties our company is facing this year, we have deemed key staffing changes to be in the best interest of the company." Everyone held their breath, the room as silent as the grave of the employees about to be terminated.

"Effective immediately," the second man in the frame announced, "Harlyn Marks is stepping down as president of Xenergy. He will be replaced with our new president . . . Jillian Pyke. We have every confidence she will lead us forward into a brighter future. Also, effective immediately, Alyra Cole will serve as senior vice president while remaining in charge of HR. The new chain of corporate succession will be Jillian Pyke, followed by Alyra Cole and then Tristan Anderson. Furthermore, a special meeting of the Board is being held to replace several of our director seats. We are pleased to announce that Andrew Heatherton will be joining the Board."

Lilyanna's eyes widened in surprise. She didn't hear the rest of the directors' address among the gasps echoing throughout the room as eyes shifted among Tristan, Jillian, Alyra and Andrew. Lilyanna looked at Tristan. His countenance remained expressionless, but she could see the tightness in his jawline. He didn't look at anyone; he just stared blankly at the TV even after Jillian clicked it off.

"I know this, um . . ." Jillian had an uncharacteristic loss of her usual smooth articulation, "comes as a shock," she recovered. "But we did achieve our goal—Marks is gone, and, though it wasn't announced, so is Justin Mercier. Six has been offered the role of general counsel, and Joe will remain associate general counsel."

"Best to switch out the lawyers behind the scenes," Joe noted.

"So that's it?" Six spoke up with potent disdain. "They didn't say anything about the racially-motivated quarantine or the layoffs. No apology, no admission!"

Jillian sighed, "No, the apology will not come from them. They claim they had no knowledge of any of it. As the new president, I will issue an apology on behalf of the company to all of the employees."

Six shook his head. "I'm happy for you, Jill, and I agree it's best for the company that you replace Marks. But I don't see how we're all just supposed to move on like nothing happened."

"Six is right," Barret chimed in. "I don't see the future being so bright without acknowledging what went wrong in the past."

"I think it's a crock. The Board doesn't care about discrimination in our company or anything else except the bottom line. None of that has changed. This is all ass-covering," Lilyanna stated flatly.

"Yeah, it's, like, don't look over there at our discriminatory employment practices, look over here at how progressive we are to name a woman as president," Tessa added. "I'm glad it's you, Jillian, and it's past time for a woman to be in charge. Countries with female leaders are faring better with COVID, like Germany, Denmark and New Zealand. On the other hand, it doesn't feel sincere coming from directors with their backs against the wall, and it reeks of White saviorism."

Alyra chortled, "Psh, we talked about this—no white stallions, no White saviors, and no White saviors on white stallions!" She then burst into exasperated laughter. "It's hilarious to think any of you could possibly save anyone or anything! I've seen how you all live. Even at your best when you're semi-functional, which has become exceedingly rare over the last few weeks, you can barely take care of yourselves. I've never seen so many grown-ass adults who failed to develop any skills other than the one job they get paid to do. I'm talking hot messes in this house!"

The room fell awkwardly silent again as the others exchanged glances, their faces contorting in various degrees of resentment, but nobody denied her charge. Barret scratched his head and looked at the floor.

Andrew looked at Lilyanna, who looked at Tessa, who scrunched up her face and shrugged.

"None of you are wrong," Jillian confessed. "We, as women, deserve more, our employees of color deserve more. The Board's response was far from ideal, but they did meet our demands, and thus gave us the authority and opportunity to make the changes we want to see. I know that I'm not the right person to speak for our employees of color or determine what policies would benefit them."

"No one person should presume to know what is best for our whole employee base," Tessa explained.

"And you shouldn't presume to know a person's interests just based on their skin tone or gender," Alyra added.

"That's why I want to put together the best upper management team of people with different perspectives on how to address these complex social issues and the skills to make good policies for the company," Jillian continued, "and that requires the two of you," she looked at Alyra and Six. "Please, this company needs your expertise. The only way we have a chance of success is if you two are on board."

"Do you really think you'll find a workplace with fewer degenerates?" Joe asked.

Alyra thought for a moment. "Nah, turns out I have a soft spot for the ones in this room. I wouldn't want to work with anyone else."

Tie smiled, "I knew it! You like us, Alyra."

"You're entertaining, I'll give you that, and you're not phonies. That's worth saving. But to be clear, I will not stay at Xenergy for more of the same BS policies. If I stay, it is to build something worth having."

"I want to build that with you," Jillian assured her. "This goes beyond staying employed to make a living. We have a chance here to overhaul the corporate environment and be a positive example in our industry—a place where people actually want to work. We've had the ideas and the motivation, and now we have the power."

"Then we're going to do this my way," Alyra insisted. "Going forward, nothing happens without HR approval, and nobody will override my HR decisions. We're going to form a new Diversity and Inclusion Committee under my watchful eye to evaluate and adjust our hiring practices. We need to make sure we hire and retain a diverse workforce going forward. There will also be a focus on the advancement of women and employees who are members of marginalized groups."

"Your way, my word," Jillian agreed.

"I'll be on the committee," Six stated. "And we're all going to be paid appropriately for our new positions."

"I'm sure the senior vice president in charge of finance can make those numbers match," Alrya said, turning to Tristan. He nodded coolly and remained silent. "Good," she turned back to Jillian, "then you have my skills, so long as you remain the highest bidder."

Jillian's lips curved in a partial smile, "I always will."

"You'll have our new employment contracts with our new roles and compensation information in your inbox tomorrow," Six stated.

Jillian nodded, "Let's get to work."

***

At sunset, Lilyanna found Tristan sitting on a fallen tree trunk just inside the tree line of the woods. She said nothing as she sat down, leaving a couple of feet of space between them. In silence, they sat watching and listening to the wildlife beyond, the nocturnal creatures awakening for their dalliances in the dark.

"I suppose you're pleased with Jillian's promotion," he began without looking at her.

She hesitated for a moment, eyeing his flawless profile. "It's a start. But I didn't come to talk politics. I just wanted to see if you're alright." Part of her wanted to hug and kiss him and massage his shoulders, to make him smile and relax like she had before. She still felt protective of him but couldn't protect him from his own short-sightedness.

He smirked, "You think I'm upset I wasn't chosen for the big chair? No, I don't care about being president. I've said from the beginning my only desire is that the company stay afloat, and appointing Jillian is the best way to make that happen. Appointing a woman as president during these times is a wise move—the only move, really."

Lilyanna turned to face him, her eyes flashing accusations. "Are you saying you support her appointment because it looks good for the company to have a woman in that position, and not because you think she deserves it?"

He dipped his head. "I didn't say that. Jill's talented. She knows how to do the job and do it well."

"Then it was a long time coming, and she should've been promoted regardless of the events of this year." Lilyanna internally begged him to agree.

"Perhaps, but it wouldn't have happened so soon if 2020 hadn't forced the Board's hand."

"So soon? It sounds like it's happening years too late to me," she contradicted him. "But of course, there must be some existential circumstance for a woman to get promoted over you. It can't just be that she's best for the job and earned her spot."

"Don't put words in my mouth, Lily."

"Then say something that doesn't sound abhorrent!" She slid over to him and took his face in her hands, forcing him to look her in the eye. His eyes glinted like icicles in the last glimmer of sunlight. "Say something that shows me you're the man I fell for and haven't stopped wanting! I've seen how amazing you are. You're better than this. You realize I'm a woman, right, and your actions have harmed professional women? Do you really care so little for me?"

"I do care for you, Lily, and I swear I had no intention of harming anyone, especially not you." They closed their eyes and pressed their foreheads against each other. Softly, he raised his head and rested his lips against her forehead, looking beyond her into the darkening woods.

He pulled away a minute later and looked at her. "I think you saw what you wanted to see in me, and I'm grateful for that. I never would've thought I could enjoy this experience, but you made it so. I can't thank you enough for what you've done for me, and I hope you enjoyed our time as well. I hope you got something out of it, too."

She leaned back from him. "I was never trying to get anything from you."

"Well, no man had touched you for some time before me."

She rolled her eyes, "Sure, your touch fixed everything." He pursed his lips and looked away from her. "And now you want everything to go back to how it was before the quarantine," she spoke for him, trying to keep her voice steady.

"I want the company to be successful, which, yes, requires things going back to how they were in many ways. I want employees back to work in-person full time. I want a Republican to remain in the White House. I want to continue supporting my kids. I want my kids back in school. Anything that threatens those interests, and, honestly, anything beyond them, I don't welcome."

"Then you've learned nothing from all of this, about people in general or yourself. We have very different goals, Tristan. Yours is to survive. Mine is to live. I know that now. I have no doubt you'll achieve yours." She stood up to leave and walked slowly around the side of the trunk where he sat, hoping he would come to his senses and stop her. Her heartbeat quickened when he reached up and grabbed her arm. She stopped and looked at him, her eyes pleading for him to pull her back, to give her a reason to stay.

All he said was, "I'm sorry."

"I wish that were enough." She turned and strode out of the woods. She wiped the tears from her eyes as she left Tristan behind. She stopped by a mature oak and clung to it for support while she sobbed. For a moment, she thought she might run back to him and throw her arms around him and insist they could work out their differences. But even if she could overcome her scruples, which was out of the question given the significance of said scruples, he made it clear he didn't deem their relationship worth continuing. He did not care about her the way she did him. The thought of never kissing him again or holding his hand threatened to break her right there in the woods. Her heart still longed for him, her body still craved his, and her mind had no control over either.

Lilyanna didn't want Tristan to be happy; she wanted to be the one to make him happy. Any happiness she gave him proved to be as fleeting as the spring rains at Whimser, as fleeting as the contentment she and William had shared. She thought of the scripture from First Corinthians many people turn to either at the beginning or end of a relationship—that love is patient and kind, and never jealous. They tell themselves the relationship is or isn't worth continuing based on whether it meets the foregoing criteria for love.

To Lilyanna, however, love was neither patient nor kind, and it was definitely jealous. It's not natural to patiently wait for a loved one to come around or be kind when they constantly fuck up and disappoint you. It is, on the other hand, natural to be jealous at the thought of a loved one preferring someone else. She and Tristan had no patience for each other's values, and Tristan never offered kind words. Not to mention, she felt jealous of his potential interest in other women from the beginning. Maybe it was love after all.

When Lilyanna emerged from the woods, she saw Sylvie sprinting toward her. "Lily," she paused when she saw Lilyanna's tear-streaked face. "What's wrong? What happened?"

"Nothing," Lilyanna choked. "What were you going to tell me?"

"I'm sorry to upset you more, but Bix is a lot worse. Lily, I think he may not make it. He's asking to see you."

"Then his mind must really be going. I'll go see him. You call the hospital again."

Bix lay in his bed, sweating, his face ghostly white. Three antique oil lamps flickered on his bedside table. He struggled to breathe while trying to speak to Lilyanna through the window. "Hold on, Bix. Sylvie is calling the hospital. We'll get you an ambulance."

"Don't want a hospital," he uttered between coughing spells. "Need to tell you the truth."

"I don't think you should talk."

"No, listen," he wheezed. "I'll tell you where I was going when I got COVID. I went out for the same reason Mr. Whimsergarden left the night he died."

Lilyanna froze, trying to absorb his words. "It was you leaving the house. But how? You can't drive."

"I can. Learned after you left Whimser years ago. I went to buy flowers for the late Mrs. Whimsergarden's grave, like I do every spring."

"The closest florist is in the supermarket. That's where you got COVID," she deduced.

Bix continued without confirmation one way or another. "Mr. Whimsergarden was on his way to her gravesite as well, the night he drove off the ravine."

"Why would he suddenly visit her grave?"

"Because I told him someone from the cemetery called and said her headstone would be torn down if he didn't go there immediately."

Lilyanna stared at him in confusion. "How is that possible?"

"It's not, I lied to him, but he was too drunk to realize it. You see, I knew Mr. Whimsergarden had changed his will when he brought you here, and that at the end of the summer he planned to sell Whimser and move to the city year-round to be with you while you attended law school. I couldn't bear to lose Whimser. It's all that is left of Mrs. Whimsergarden. I promised her I would take care of it. I promised . . ." Bix erupted into another coughing fit. "It was Mrs. Whimsergarden's money that built this place. Everyone gave all the credit to Mr. Whimsergarden. All of you harlots worshipped him, for his money and his fame. But Whimser exists because of her, so refined, so elegant. Whimser *is* her; it's not him."

Lilyanna paused, deep in thought. "So, you planned for William to die so you could keep living in the house? I assume that means you thought I'd be with him and die too, but I ruined your plans."

"No, I didn't want to kill you. I chose you!" Bix spoke slowly, his breath making a wheezing sound, but the determination to speak was clear in his watery eyes. "I knew that if you inherited Whimser, you would keep it because you would think that's what Mr. Whimsergarden wanted. I chose you over him because you would be loyal, and he wouldn't.

I thought it might not work in the end, though, because Mr. Whimsergarden always said he left instructions for you, but he mumbled about them being behind the garden one night when he'd been drinking. I thought him mad, or drunk. There are no gardens at Whimser."

Lilyanna looked away from the window, processing. "Behind the garden?"

"Yes," Bix coughed again and forced more air into his failing lungs.

Lilyanna shook her head. "This is crazy. Why didn't you just convince him to change his will to name someone else in one of his drunken episodes?"

"Because the person he named before you would've certainly sold Whimser out from under me."

"Who did he name before me?"

"Sylvie Thompson."

She gasped, "Sylvie? Why?"

"Because she was his whore before you, of course. I thought you knew."

Lilyanna's chest tightened. "Uh, no, I had no idea they were intimate! You think I would've hired her back if I had known she'd been with William?" Lilyanna gaped at him. Accepting his story would mean Sylvie worked at Whimser and treated her as a guest when the whole time Lilyanna had replaced her in William's affections. Lilyanna's stomach turned at the thought. "Why are you telling me all this now? It can't be just to clear your conscience."

"I always knew you were the smartest of the bunch, Mistress Rivers. I'm telling you the truth in hopes you'll extend me the same courtesy. There's one major blank I haven't officially filled in from the night Mr. Whimsergarden died. I informed Mr. Whimsergarden of the fake phone call from the cemetery, but I didn't leave his car keys out where he could find them. I always kept them hidden in the kitchen drawer so he wouldn't drive drunk. When I went into the kitchen that evening to set out the keys, they were already on the counter. For a while, I thought Sylvie had done it, but she could never stand up to him. There was only one person it could be. I thought placing the keys on your pillow might elicit a confession."

Chill bumps formed on Lilyanna's arms as her mind flashed to the night Bix had revealed to her William's propensity for collecting and promptly disposing of young mistresses—the unmasking of a devil in a knight-in-shining-armor disguise. With each photograph and letter Bix showed her, her affections for William shed away like petals from a wilting rose. She then recalled the following night, the night he died, and the wine on the terrace . . .

Lilyanna faked an endearing smile as she poured glass after glass for William, all the while visualizing his lineup of mistresses. "It's a nice evening for a drive, don't you think? I'm sure the rain will stop soon," she noted sweetly. Lilyanna left William on the terrace to finish the bottle. Instead of going straight upstairs to nap, she detoured to the kitchen. *William often fancied an evening drive.* If William wanted to drive, she could hardly stop him. Why come between a fool and his errand? She took the keys out of the kitchen drawer and tossed them in the middle of the counter.

"Is that why you took it upon yourself to tell me about all of the other women?" she confronted Bix. "You wanted to turn me against William? Was any of it actually true?"

"Yes, all of it. I swear to that. You played the grieving lover well, Mistress Rivers."

She narrowed her eyes and shot him a glare so cold it could freeze Lake Whimser in summer. "I did grieve for William. I still do."

"That's why I knew you'd keep Whimser going, and you did. I must say, you've done well. All these years I suspected we played on the same side, but I could never be sure. Now, the game is at an end, and so am I."

"I am not on your side! You poisoned my relationship with William, and this house, and who knows what you've told Sylvie over the years."

"All of that was poisoned the day Mrs. Whimsergarden died. I stayed here because I made a promise to Mrs. Whimsergarden, and I have fulfilled that oath." Bix began coughing uncontrollably. He turned on his side as he spat up blood and reached for a tissue next to his bed. His hands shaking, he wiped the blood from his mouth with the tissue and tossed it into a pile of used tissues on the floor.

"Bix?" Lilyanna stepped back from the window just as Sylvie came running down from the house.

"Lily, they say it could be four hours before an ambulance gets here," she panted, holding her cell phone to her ear.

"Then we need to take him in the car. Bix, I need you to get in my car. Can you walk?" Lilyanna called through the window.

"No more," he wheezed. Expending the last bit of energy in his body, he reached over to his bedside table and swatted surprisingly energetically at the oil lamps until, one by one, they crashed, almost exploding on the wooden floor. Lilyanna stared in shock as the piles of wadded tissue on the floor added fuel to the flames, spurring them on in every direction. The floor, the curtains, the bedspread, all burst into flame at once, while Lilyanna and Sylvie screamed.

"What do we do?" Sylvie cried.

Lilyanna pulled her back from the window. The flames crawled quickly up the walls. "Bix! Bix, climb through the window!" Lilyanna shouted. Sylvie screamed again as the exterior caught fire and smoke diffused through the open window. Guests ran from the main house at the sight of smoke, and Lilyanna continued pulling Sylvie away from the cottage.

"We have to do something!" Sylvie cried.

"We can't. We can't go inside."

"What happened?" Andrew roared, the first to arrive on the scene, with Six, Tristan, Tie and Tessa on his heels.

"Bix couldn't breathe, and he set the cottage on fire," Sylvie cried, tears streaming down her face.

"Take her inside," Lilyanna ordered, passing Sylvie's weight off to Tie and Tessa.

Lilyanna stood between Tristan and Andrew, watching the roof of the cottage cave in. Andrew and Tristan each looked at Lilyanna in concern. "What can we do?" Andrew asked.

"Let it burn." She turned away and walked determinedly back to her house.

A team of two funeral home employees arrived the next day in hazmat suits to remove the remains from Bix's cottage. When Lilyanna signed the funeral home director's paperwork, he made the comment that it would've been best to burn down the cottage anyway after Bix died since it would be too risky to enter such a confined, infected space. Bix's ashes were to be placed near the late Mrs. Whimser's grave as he would've wanted.

Lilyanna remembered William's private funeral at his gravesite at the cemetery on the hill overlooking Lake Whimser. She stood, a pale statue, next to a bouquet of white roses, while the minister read the well-known passage from Ecclesiastes 3:1 beginning with, "For everything there is a season," so often used to remind people that seasons, cycles of life, are natural, but a final end is not. Death is not final because after death will come life.

Lilyanna stood on the terrace, lost in her memories and reliving the defining events of her recent past. "For everything there is a season. A time to be born, and a time to die; a time to plant, and a time to pluck up that which is planted; a time to kill, and a time to heal . . ." Lilyanna saw herself walking arm and arm with William on the dunes and laughing with him over manuscripts in the parlor. Then, his Range Rover on its side over the ravine. She fell to her knees and screamed at the last sight of his body on the stretcher being taken away.

"A time to break down, and a time to build up; a time to weep, and a time to laugh; a time to mourn, and a time to dance . . ." She looked at Tristan's blue eyes as he held her in the freezing lake water, and she danced with him and her friends at the house parties. "A time to embrace, and a time to refrain from embracing . . ." Andrew smiled at her in their makeshift office and lay next to her on the upstairs sofa. "A time to keep silent, and a time to speak." Six berated Tristan for his political and social views. The Board appointed Jillian as president. "A time to love, and a time to hate; a time for war, and a time for peace." Lilyanna kissed Tristan, the two wrapped up together in his bed sheets, and their one perfect day riding horses. And then their fight over layoffs, and farewell in the woods. Bix's confession, and his cottage burning. The end of an era; the beginning of what follows degeneration.

CHAPTER TWENTY-FOUR
Full Bloom

"Good afternoon, this is your Xenergy president, Jillian Pyke." Jillian recorded her first live webcast from the library to be viewed by all employees of the company. "I am honored to serve as your new president, but I'm not here to talk about me. I'm here to talk about the future of our company. As you know, we have faced unprecedented challenges this year, and I recognize those challenges are not just with respect to business, but also with personal lives. I want to thank you all for your endurance and commitment to this company as we continue to navigate the pandemic.

"Many of you may have heard of layoffs primarily affecting women and employees of color earlier this year. On behalf of Xenergy, I apologize for these misguided employment mistakes. Going forward, I can say with confidence we are not anticipating any additional layoffs, and all future employment decisions will be made following our revised internal policies and managed by our Human Resources department.

"For over a month now, the state of Texas has been on a trajectory of reopening. We will continue to monitor the state's progress, while keeping our focus on the safety of our employees. All decisions will be made in accordance with CDC guidelines. We will give employees at least one month's notice prior to any return to office initiatives, and any return to in-person work will be on a staggered schedule. Our Human Resources department is also working on a new employee support program to ensure anyone who needs mental health and wellbeing support can get it free of cost and evaluating more flexible schedule policies. We will also make accommodations for employees with childcare needs due to the closure of schools and daycares. I will follow up soon with more information. Thank you all for your time and hard work. Stay safe."

***

Lilyanna sat alone at the dining room table drinking straight vodka after everyone else had gone to bed. A dense fog filled her head by the time Sylvie hesitantly stepped into the dining room.

"Sylvie," Lilyanna stated flatly. "Take a seat, please." Sylvie rubbed her red and swollen eyes as she sat down opposite of Lilyanna at the table. Lilyanna poured a glass of vodka for her. "Sylvie, why didn't you tell me about you and William?"

Sylvie's eyes widened slightly, but she didn't seem totally surprised by the question. "What difference would it have made?"

"Well, first of all, I wouldn't have hired you to work here! It's cringeworthy to think you felt you had to work for me after having a relationship with William."

"Exactly, Lily, I would've lost my job, and, unlike you, I had no way out. I needed the work. I don't have a career yet or any other way to provide for myself and my sister."

Lilyanna's stomach dropped. "Just tell me one thing. Did you want to be with William, or did you think you had to in order to stay employed?"

Sylvie remained silent and took a deep sip from her glass without flinching at the bitterness of the liquor. "I, I did feel a connection to him. You know him. William was a beautiful man, but a man nonetheless. At first, he seemed so keen to help me because he cared for me, and that made me want him more. I thought he was different, but I was wrong. He soon forgot about me when the next shiny thing came along."

"Me."

Sylvie nodded and drank from her glass. Lilyanna grabbed her purse sitting on the table and took out a checkbook for the Whimser account and pen. "I'm going to write a number on this that should allow you and your sister to have a fresh start." Lilyanna signed the check and slid it across the table to Sylvie. "You have a way out now."

***

All the residents except Lilyanna spent the next day packing their belongings. With the safety of the house compromised, Jillian ended the group quarantine and arranged for the employees to return home. Lilyanna left the house and walked alone to the dunes above Lake Whimser. She didn't want to hear all the scuffling in the house, knowing that it would seem that much emptier once everyone left. Her friends and co-workers would go back to their real lives with their families, and she would go back to a vacant apartment alone.

Lilyanna removed her shoes and strolled through the dunes barefoot, the soft breeze blowing sand up around her ankles. One had to be trying not to find peace on the dunes. The chaos brewing elsewhere in the world didn't dare pass the hills of sand standing guard over the tranquility of the beach below. They kept faith this afternoon as well, allowing Lilyanna entry while blocking the bears and shadows of regrets that stalked her wherever she went.

Lost in thought, she danced around the vines weaving through the silted ground, kicking up sediment as she went. The dunes admitted another visitor a few minutes later. Andrew cautiously approached her, sinking into the sand with each heavy step. "I thought you might be out here."

"Shouldn't you be packing?" Lilyanna asked without looking at him.

"I'm a guy, doesn't take me long," he replied, closing the distance between them.

"I'm sure it doesn't," she murmured under her breath.

"I won't even ask if you're okay. I can tell you're not, as you shouldn't be."

"Don't worry about me. You're going home to your family, and none of this will be your problem."

"Lily, don't shut me out. I understand you feel like you're being abandoned, but please know that I don't care for you any less just because I'm going home."

"A man in your position can't legitimately care for me." She drew random figures in the sand with her toes.

"Sure I can. I can love my wife and still care about you, Lily. I think the best way I can show you that is to go home to her. You're used to seeing men cheat, or use, or both, but we're not all that way."

"You must think I'm a hopeless cynic."

"I think you believe a man can't love a woman."

Lilyanna paused and finally turned to look at him, her eyes wide and cold.

"My wife thought the same when we first got together, and I've spent the rest of our marriage trying to convince her otherwise."

"Do you think leaving her during a pandemic and being here with me right now is very convincing?"

Andrew pushed the sides of his lips together with his hand. "No, I'm sure I've forfeited some of the ground I gained, but I won't give up. I don't want you to give up either. You're a fantastic woman, and you deserve the best of everything, of life, of men, if that's what you want. I'm not surprised that you think it doesn't exist, given your lifestyle. You're in a small pond of people who marry young or are just too closed-minded to relate to your generation."

Andrew paced in William's footsteps in the sand. The breeze carried his voice as it had carried William's. Lilyanna was no longer certain who was speaking to her. "Plant a flower in the desert, and it might survive but won't thrive. You can't blame the flower for failing to grow; it couldn't foresee its doom. Plant it in a garden, though, and watch it bloom."

The breeze settled, and the quiet peace returned. Andrew gently took Lilyanna's hand. "I'm here whenever you need a friend, Lily." He solemnly followed the blowing sand away from the beach. When he departed, Lilyanna turned and looked around her, finding herself alone on the dunes.

***

Lilyanna saw Tessa sitting on the front steps of the terrace when she returned to the house. "Hey," Tessa greeted her hopefully with a partial smile. "I was waiting for you."

"I see that." Lilyanna sat down next to her.

"I feel terrible, Lily. I'm sorry you're dealing with another death in your life. I'm sorry you thought you couldn't trust me."

"I do trust you, Tessa! I trust you more than anyone. You know, you're the person I always put down as my emergency contact on paperwork of any kind because you're the only person in Austin who I thought would show up in an emergency." She teared up again for the countless time in the past twenty-four hours.

Tessa put her arm around Lilyanna's back and pulled Lilyanna against her side. Lilyanna failed to hold back the waterworks and sobbed onto Tessa's shoulder. "I'll always be your emergency contact. I'm not leaving tomorrow with the others. I'm staying with you," Tessa told her.

"I don't want to stay here," Lilyanna admitted in her crying jag.

"Then let's go somewhere else. I don't want to go back to Xenergy either. You and I can leave. We can start over, just the two of us. That's all we need."

Lilyanna lifted her head and looked at Tessa, nodding.

***

Jillian knocked on Joe's bedroom door and entered without an invitation. "Do come in," Joe greeted her sarcastically. She locked her eyes on him and walked over to his half-packed suitcase and rifled through it.

"Uh, can I help you find something in my private things?"

"It's your private things I'm after." She pulled out two pairs of socks and pushed her hand inside each one until she found a mini rectangular aluminum box inside one. She opened the box to find Joe's coke stash. "You're going to quit this shit." She snapped the box closed. "And this!" She snatched his cigarettes from the top of the dresser. "I need you alive and functional to help us run this company. You're going to pull your weight. Do you understand?"

He glared at her, considering her directives, and then shrugged. "You're the boss."

***

The concept that death pays for life is universal—it's literary, theatrical, Biblical. It occupied Lilyanna's thoughts in the parlor as she tagged William's belongings that would soon be removed. Who had William's life paid for? What about her parents' lives? And Bix's? And all those dying of COVID-19? How do you value one soul against another? Surely the market rate for a soul was less than it used to be. And the darkest thought of them all—what if one of their deaths had paid for her life? Whether or not that was true, she was ready to start living that life to the fullest.

"Lily, the cars are starting to arrive," Tessa called to her from the front door. Dylan, Waya, Saharie and Tie left first in a rideshare back to Dallas, with Tie planning to stay with Saharie and work remotely. Lilyanna hugged them all and graciously accepted their thanks for the hospitality with the promise she would visit them soon. She also ordered a car for Sylvie, Nina and Ms. Howard to depart. She had no plans to see them again.

The other employees loaded their luggage onto the smaller stepchild of a Greyhound bus, an upgrade from the white van in which they arrived. Lilyanna and Tessa helped their co-workers carry their bags out of the house.

"Damn right they didn't think to put me in a rundown white van again," Alyra asserted. "I am H mother fuckin' R."

Lilyanna paused to say goodbye to Joe on the terrace, but Tristan interrupted them. "I'll need you both to sign this insurance waiver before we go. Lily, you'll be compensated for any damage to the house, except the cottage."

"That's what you have to say to me right now?" she scoffed.

Joe grabbed the document, wadded it into a ball and tossed it over the terrace railing. "We'll talk soon, Lily," Joe told her, ignoring Tristan. "Take care of yourself out here."

When Joe left the terrace, Tristan turned to her apologetically. "I'm sorry, Lily. I'm truly sorry if I hurt you. Things just wouldn't have worked out between us."

"For once we completely agree."

Tristan clenched his jaw before placing his hand on her back. "I'll see you back in the city."

She penetrated his alluring blue eyes with hers. "No, you won't."

Dejected, he dropped his arm and turned away from her, sorrowful yet resigned. She watched him walk away without regret, only disappointment knowing his affection was only for a mechanistic illusion of an artificial entity, not the people behind it. It was easy to say a silent goodbye to that person, less so to the side of him she'd seen during their relationship at Whimser. Those goodbyes would take time, and tears, and likely booze. She draped her forearms over the terrace railing and stared at the woods, not wanting to see her colleagues preparing to depart.

Tristan loaded his luggage onto the bus and then turned toward the terrace and studied Lilyanna's profile as if hoping to memorize it. He visually traced her expressive blue eyes and narrow face, her statuesque neck, and down to her long legs, carving each feature into his mind. He could find her there any time, waiting for him in their private paradise.

Lilyanna went to the kitchen and found Jillian doing last-minute cleaning. "Oh, please, don't worry about any cleaning. I'll take care of that," Lilyanna told her.

"It's the least I can do," Jillian replied. "You've done very well, Lily, and I thank you. There will always be a place for you at Xenergy if you want it."

Lilyanna stood next to her behind the kitchen counter. "I think I just need to go in a different direction for now."

Jillian turned to face her and lowered her voice, "I understand. Let me know if you change your mind. Permit me to give you one piece of advice before I go. Sometimes, the things we want most are not in the most obvious of places. The cravings of our hearts and bodies and minds can be satisfied in different ways. You'll only be forced to live unfulfilled if you continue to look to the wrong sources for fulfillment. Does that make sense?"

Lilyanna nodded thoughtfully.

"Good. I wish you all the best." Jillian said earnestly. Then she took Lilyanna's face in her hands, slowly guiding her face closer to her own, and gave her a solid kiss on the lips. She smiled, nodded and strutted out of the kitchen.

Stunned, Lilyanna slouched against the counter in reflection. Her face broke into a smile, and she laughed softly.

***

Lilyanna and Tessa spent the rest of the day packing and tagging furniture and household items that would be moved to storage, and Lilyanna e-signed documents from Jack Taylor to sell the property. The leased property would be gifted to the tenants, and the house and underlying fee property would be sold to the wildlife society, which would certainly knock down the house to build a wildlife sanctuary.

While taking down the paintings in the main hall, she stopped when she reached William's portrait of herself in a fictional garden. Bix said William left instructions for her behind the garden, and there were no gardens at Whimser, except this one. Hastily, she took the painting off the wall to find a sealed envelope taped to the back. She opened the envelope and found a letter on William's stationery.

***

Lilyanna and Tessa loaded the last of their luggage in the trunk of Lilyanna's car, along with the portrait of Lilyanna in the backseat. "That just leaves the Aristocats," Lilyanna said. "I'm worried they will miss their upstairs sitting room."

"They'll adjust to a new one with us," Tessa assured her. As expected, the cats were not thrilled about the relocation and hissed in their carriers in the backseat of Lilyanna's car.

Lilyanna walked back to the front terrace to take one last look at the house. *Farewell, Whimser. You are beautiful and strong, but this is not your garden.* Swallowing a lump in her throat, she returned to the car and drove away from the lot, Whimser appearing in the rear-view mirror. As Lilyanna adjusted the mirror, she glimpsed the portrait of her in the backseat and heard William's final words from the letter he left for her behind the painting.

"My Flower, if you're reading this, it's because I'm not there to speak to you in person. Once again, I must rely on my writing to speak for me. I did not tell you about my will because I knew you would object. Surely you know by now I would give anything I have to spend one last day with you. You have given me peace, joy and hope, and my greatest wish is that I can reciprocate in some capacity.

Thus, I leave you my life's work and most beloved possession, as they are second to you in my affections and dedication. The property belongs to you now to do with what you will. Please do not hesitate to sell Whimser or anything else I have left to you because you think it is what I want. My sole desire is that you have yours, and I have no doubt you will achieve it. I cannot wait to watch. Through this painting, you are immortal, you cannot die. You will live on forever, and so will I. All of my love to you, Lily. Flourish."

Made in the USA
Columbia, SC
10 December 2021

50920252R00238